LANCE
BEARER

Other novels by Alfred Dennis

Chiricahua
Lone Eagle
Elkhorn Divide
Brant's Fort
Catamount
The Mustangers
Rover
Sandigras Canyon
Yellowstone Brigade
Shawnee Trail
Fort Reno
Yuma
Ride the Rough String
Trail to Medicine Mound
Arapaho Lance - Book 1

To see more books by Alfred Dennis visit
www.alfreddennis.com

LANCE BEARER

Crow Killer Series - Book 2

by

Alfred Dennis

wСp

Walnut Creek Publishing
Tuskahoma, Oklahoma

Lance Bearer: Crow Killer Series - Book 2

>>> ➤ ⤍

ISBN: 978-1-942869-26-9
First Edition, Paperback
Published 2018 by Walnut Creek Publishing
Front cover painting: Alfred Jacob Miller/Storm: Waiting for the Caravan/
Wikimedia Commons/Public Domain
Library of Congress Control Number: 2018940905

Books may be purchased in quantity and/or special sales by contacting
the publisher;
Walnut Creek Publishing
PO Box 820
Talihina, OK 74571
www.wc-books.com

This book is dedicated to
Gerald Dennis, highly decorated Vietnam Veteran,
Oklahoma State Senator, County Judge,
Trial Lawyer and a man I proudly call Cousin.

CHAPTER 1

The radiant beauty and dazzling colors of the summer flowers were purely awesome to Jed as he sat the piebald while watching the lone horse and rider disappear from the remote valley on the north pass. Jed had brought the old scout, Lige Hatcher, to the high mountain valley, to show him the paradise he had found and where he would make his new home. The valley was a place of serene beauty with majestic mountain peaks standing guard over the high meadows, keeping the valley safe from outsiders. A place so quiet and peaceful, only the cool mountain breeze blowing its breath across the land made any sound at all. Occasionally, the bugling of an elk or the spine-tingling sound of a howling wolf broke the eerie silence; otherwise a man had only his thoughts to listen to. The wide, flat valley lay blanketed in tall grass, rolling on for miles, making it the perfect feeding ground for the many grazing animals inhabiting the land. Again, Jed drew in a deep breath because in this place of quiet tranquility, he finally found a home. He found peace, not only from trouble, but peace of mind and for once he was completely happy.

A cold, clear stream coming down from the mountains meandered through the length of the valley floor, snaking through the flat ground, and supplying water to the animals grazing on the green meadows. Trees of every size and of many species grew abundantly along the mountain slopes. The timber from the trees was sorely needed for logs, shakes, and lumber. Jed would use the timber to build a cabin to ward off the hard, cold winters he knew would be severe in the high lonesome.

Jed looked down at the double-bladed axe in his hand, a parting gift from the trapper. Lige Hatcher turned north, leaving him with a nod and a farewell wave. Hatcher hadn't wished him good luck because the old scout knew Jedidiah Bracket well. Jed was also known as Crow Killer, the Arapaho Lance Bearer, and didn't need luck, he made his own and he would be fine. Jed waved one last time as the old scout disappeared over a small rise, then vanished into the tall mountains.

The tall, dark-skinned young man turned to survey the huge valley, his valley, the valley where he had seen the bright beacon of flashing light that had lured him to this very spot. The beacon White Swan had prophesied from a vision he had seen in the bones and smoke that foretold of things to come. Jed remembered the old one's words; he would see what was not to be seen, and it would be a sign for Jed to follow. So far, White Swan had spoken true as Jed had not been able to locate the spot where he had seen the bright light or whatever it was that beckoned to him on that first day. Still, in his heart, he knew it existed. He remembered the old Medicine Man's prophecy that a bright light would call to him, beckoning him back to this valley. Whatever his future was, it would begin here in this remote but wondrous place.

Feeling the razor-sharp edge of the axe blade and the file Hatcher had left him, he nodded, not much to build with; an axe, a piebald paint horse, his bare hands, and memories of his friends, the Arapaho people. One day, he would return to the south, but for now, winter was coming and he had to work hard to build a cabin. Firewood had to be gathered, meat killed and brought in, and furs readied for the cold times that would soon come to his valley. Letting his eyes work their way along the bank of the small stream, he mounted the paint horse and rode down to a lower sandy bar of the creek and splashed across. The stream was a thing of beauty, flowing over small rocks and pebbles, and its rippling water so clear, he could see fish swimming lazily on the bottom. The stream's flat gravel bank led gradually down to the water's edge. Across the water a high embankment stood back in a heavy stand of timber, a natural shelter with a barrier for his cabin and corrals against the north winds. There was also plenty of room for a lean-to and other outbuildings for the horses. His dark eyes took in the beauty of the place as he listened to the soft moaning of the wind blowing softly through the trees. The place was picturesque; here he would make his home, build his cabin, and here he would stay.

"Well, old son, there ain't no better time than right now to put you to work." Jed spoke absently to the oak-handled axe. Hobbling the paint, he turned him loose on a patch of tall grass, and then started pacing off a place to build his cabin. First, he had to build a corral to keep the horse safe at night so he wouldn't wander or run off with a wild band of mustangs. Tomorrow or the next day, he would hunt for food. He still had some jerky left that Red Hawk had sent with him. Smiling, he thought of the Crow, he was as good a friend as Walking Horse was, no matter his tribe.

For three weeks, the ringing axe could be heard in the valley as it bit time and again, deep into the virgin trees. The heavy groaning and crashing of the green trees shook the ground as the blade did its work, felling them to the ground. Next, Jed turned the blade to lopping and smoothing the limbs, getting the logs ready for the cabin walls. Around his small campfire at night, Jed's mind thought back to the ropes and harness he had left at the two trapper's camp back on the Snake River. Right now, the tack sure would come in handy. He wasn't a carpenter and hadn't figured out yet how he was going to drag the heavy logs to his cabin site without some rope. Biting into a lean piece of back-strap deer meat, he pondered his dilemma and there was no way around it; he needed a rope and harness to do the heavy lifting. The big river would be at least a four-day ride and even then he wasn't sure the camp hadn't been robbed. Shaking his head, the thought disgusted him as he looked into the fire. There was no way he would take from men he had killed, even if they deserved it.

The straight logs for the cabin walls were down on the creek's bank, ready to be dragged to the cabin site. Afterward, he would need tools to make shakes, shave the logs flat, and bore holes into the heavy green timbers for his doors and windows. Flat rocks for his fireplace and floor were in abundance in the valley, ready to be brought in. Everything he needed was close at hand. Now, all he needed was a harness and rope to do the heavy lifting.

Jed looked up at the clear sky, and for now, the weather was holding. The mornings were colder this high, but so far no snow had threatened.

He had built a corral to keep the piebald at night and let him out to graze during the day. The horse was safe out on the tall grass, hobbled and in his sight at all times. Resting against a downed log, Jed fed the small fire just enough wood to keep it burning, then stared into the flames and relaxed, pondering his future. Living alone in the high meadow, the days were lonely and a fire gave him something to stare into. At night, the fire was something to share the darkness with until sleep came. Breathing in the smoke, Jed smiled as he was a mite lonely, but he had what he wanted, this beautiful valley was his, all his. Tomorrow, he would decide whether to ride into Baxter Springs to somehow get what he needed to work on the cabin. The trip would stop work and slow him down for a few days, but he had no choice, he had to complete the cabin before the first heavy snows arrived. A snug cabin wasn't a luxury, it was needed to keep him warm and give him a place to store the pelts he would trap during the cold times.

As the new day brought the brightness of the sun, Jed pondered his decision to head north to Baxter Springs. Suddenly, the horse drew his attention as he snorted and pointed his ears toward the far end of the valley. Quickly grabbing his bow, Jed led the piebald into the shadows of the heavier timber, holding his hand across the animal's nose.

"Easy, old son, we may have visitors for dinner." Jed spoke quietly to the horse. "We wouldn't want to invite them too quick."

The dark eyes of the tall young man surveyed the open valley floor and along the tree line that ran the entire length of the grassland. He searched closely for whatever caused the horse to react. As Jed watched from his place of concealment, nothing moved out on the valley floor, only the tall grass swayed as the wind blew softly against it. Again, the horse pricked its small ears forward, and there was no mistake, something or someone had his attention. So far, Jed could see nothing, but the valley was more than ten miles long with rolling swells in the grass, hiding anyone approaching from the naked eye.

Jed patted the horse's neck softly as the piebald started to fret. "Easy, old son, we'll see them pretty quick now."

Jed followed the horse's eyes, there was definitely something out there. He knew the piebald's senses were far keener than his own. He remembered one of Walking Horse's first lessons about watching and paying attention to his pony. Finally, after almost an hour, Jed caught movement far down the valley. Riders, small as ants in the distance, were coming out of the trees to the north. Four animals, in a line, slowly worked their way out onto the flat ground of the valley floor and they were coming straight toward him. Closer now and visibly in sight, Jed could see only one horse had a rider and the rest of the animals were led.

"Lige Hatcher." Jed swung upon the piebald and rode down the valley at a high lope to meet the old scout.

Reining in, Hatcher smiled as the piebald drew up in front of him. "Well, Jedidiah, you're still here I see."

"Still here." Jed looked over the heavy-laden pack mules. "Question is, what are you doing back here so soon?"

"A little bird told me a young feller I know would need a few things to build a cabin."

Jed could only shake his head. "That little bird wasn't lying to you, Lige. I was thinking on riding into Baxter Springs this very day."

"Well, you won't have to ride anywhere now." Hatcher grinned. "Unless, that is, you might be a wanting to see someone special."

"No, not until the cabin is ready."

"You know, you had company before I scared them off?"

"I figured." Jed nodded. "The piebald sensed something, but I didn't know it was you."

"Weren't me, Jed. You had company spying on you when I come down the trail." Hatcher shook his head. "They pulled out the south trail in a hurry when they spotted me on the ridge."

"Who?"

The old scout shrugged. "Maybe Blackfoot or Nez Perce. They were too far so I couldn't see them well enough."

"Well, I knew I couldn't stay here forever without being discovered." Jed shrugged and looked down the valley. "I was hoping it would take longer to spy me out though."

Jed turned the piebald, leading Hatcher and his pack string back to his campsite. He couldn't believe his good luck. The old trapper and his supplies were a blessing because without them the cabin couldn't be built. Hatcher saved him at least two weeks of lost time plus the long ride into Baxter Springs.

The old scout looked about the staked outbuilding site as he crossed the small stream and dismounted. "You've picked you a fine place here, Jed. There's plenty of water, good high ground, and that ridge behind you to hold off the driving snowdrifts."

"I think it'll do."

"Far enough back so you can't get flooded out, and the wind can't get to you very hard." Hatcher nodded. "Yep, she'll do."

"We'll unload, and then I'll fix up some hot deer steaks."

"I'm starved. You cook while I unload." Hatcher laughed. "I'm so hungry I can't even hold my belt on."

"All right, Lige, I'll get some steaks on the fire." Jed studied the valley.

"They're gone for now, but I figure they'll be back." Hatcher followed Jed's gaze up the valley.

"How many were there?"

Hatcher shrugged his thin shoulders. "Only counted five, but there could have been more."

"Reckon I'll have to keep a sharp eye out from here on."

"Good idea, if'n you want to keep your hair." Hatcher nodded. "It's a good idea anytime. Never, ever let down your guard in this country."

Hatcher went to work on the deer meat as if he hadn't eaten in months. Smacking his lips in satisfaction, he smiled over at Jed. "Hoss, there ain't never been anything tastier when a man is hungry."

Nodding, Jed checked the pan fried biscuits in his new Dutch oven, and pulled them back from the hot ashes of the fire. A light wind picked up, making the tall sycamores sway slightly in the failing light. Leaning back against a stump, Jed studied Hatcher as he ate hungrily. Tossing Hatcher a brown biscuit, he smiled as the older man caught it in midair. Only a mighty hungry man and one that had ridden many a mile could truly understand the pleasure another man got out of a good meal. Up in the high meadows, mostly everything was hardship, few pleasures and enjoyment were found, but eating heartily of the bountiful mountain critters was one pleasure a man could enjoy.

"How's everything in Baxter Springs?"

The grey eyes of the old scout looked over the brim of his coffee cup quietly. "I relayed your message to Miss Sally Ann."

"And?"

"She's waiting and willing." Hatcher dropped his eyes.

"Is something wrong?"

"Yep, her pa."

"What?"

"I forgot to tell you, boy." Hatcher put down his cup. "Her pappy is the magistrate of Baxter Springs."

"The law?" Jed blinked. "Sally Ann never mentioned it."

"Anyway, he's what they call law out here."

"I surely didn't figure on this." Jed frowned. "I reckon he's in a boil over them trappers I did for?"

"Well, now that depends on you, Jed." Hatcher pulled at a pouch.

"Tell me, Lige."

Pulling a pipe from his shot pouch, Hatcher tamped it full of tobacco. "He ain't real high on you bringing her up here to the mountains to live. No siree, not high on it at all."

"Why? I'll take care of her."

"He ain't having it, said so." Hatcher blew smoke in the air. "Said you could marry up with Sally Ann, providing you promise to live near the settlement."

"And if I don't?"

"You come in to take her away, and he'll charge you for them murders." Hatcher puffed slowly. "I watched his eyes, Jed. I believe him."

"You tell him how it came about?" Jed frowned. "You tell him they tried to ambush me?"

"I did, told him exactly that, the way I seen it. They tried to put you under." Hatcher nodded. "But, he's the law, judge and jury, the only law, and his word is final. Boy, if he says so, they'll hang you. Those boys in the settlement don't want to see the gal go either."

"What does Sally Ann say?"

"She don't know anything about the killings." Hatcher smiled. "Pretty little filly, she's in a whirl for you to come for her."

"You got any suggestions?"

"Stay here and stay alone, or go back and live in Baxter Springs, where you ain't gonna be a bit happy, or steal her away like an Injun would."

"That's it?"

"Don't see you got any other choices, Jed, none at all." Hatcher relit his pipe. "You try to do this all Christian like and that old man of hers will hang you. I know him."

"He didn't seem like a bad sort."

"He ain't, except when it comes to his girl." Hatcher leaned back and studied Jed. "He sure ain't gonna let you bring her into the wilderness if he has his way, says it ain't civilized."

"I'll finish the cabin first, then I'll decide what to do." Jed walked across the clearing. "She's got to have a place to live."

"Bad weather's coming, and soon." Hatcher looked up at the sky and nodded. "I've got to be traveling, but I'll stick around and help you with the heavy work before I pull out."

"That would surely be appreciated, Lige." Jed smiled. "You're a good friend and I ain't much of a carpenter."

"I'm sorry about Sally Ann."

"Don't be, Lige. You tried your best and it ain't over yet."

"No, I expect it ain't over." Hatcher looked deeply into the fire. "Bad trouble out here is never over with."

"Did you see my step-pa?" Jed stared hard at the man. "Does he know about Abe and Vern?"

"No, I was in a hurry to get back up here." Hatcher shook his head. "I reported their deaths to Duncan, then started back. I doubt he told Wilson, but someone probably has by now."

A solid month of hard work had passed, then both men stood back to admire their handy work. The cabin was finished, the green logs all chinked and a plume of smoke drifted from the rock chimney. A small barn, lean-to, and corrals for Jed's livestock stood attached to the south wall. Jed smiled, knowing the cabin would be snug and warm in the coming months of cold and snow. Even the Blue Northers and blizzards that could blow for days would not penetrate the thick walls. Less than fifty paces from the cabin, a clear creek rushed rapidly past the structure, providing Jed and his animals all the fresh water they would need.

"It's strong, and to me, it is beautiful." Jed stared at the cabin proudly.

"It should be, you pert near worked me to death a building it." Hatcher laughed. "Yes, it is a strong cabin. You'll be cozy as a hibernating bear all winter."

Jed looked up as snow flurries started to fall from the graying skies. "Looks like just in time."

Hatcher eyed the dark clouds. "Snow's coming for sure. I've got to be traveling."

"You could winter here, Lige." Jed smiled. "You're welcome."

"I know Jed, but I've given my word to be at Bridger's Fort to help with the immigrants come spring."

"That's a long ride in this weather."

Hatcher shrugged. "I'll make it, den up with the bears if'n I have to for a spell."

"When will you be back this way?"

"Late summer, I figure. After the thaw, I'll hook up with Chalk Briggs and head up another train back this way."

"Well, I wish you the best. I'll pay you back for these supplies next time we meet."

"No rush, your pap put up most of the money and I signed a note in Baxter Springs for the rest."

Jed was shocked. "My step-dad paid for these goods?"

"He did, and told old Elmer Woods the store man, he owed your mother." Lige nodded. "This was her share."

"I'll be dogged."

"Ain't figured how he knew you'd need this stuff, but he did leave money with Elmer for you." Hatcher shrugged. "I figure he was just guessing."

"I'll bet old Seth was happy about that."

"Woods said he was none too happy about you, but not for the reasons you might think."

Jed stared at Hatcher. "What do you mean?"

"Elmer said he watched the young man's face when the girl and the mountains were mentioned." Hatcher tapped on his pipe. "He said Seth's face turned into a mask of pure hate and jealousy, if'n he ever seen hate."

"He never let on like he cared for Sally Ann."

"I would watch out for that one if'n I were you." Lige stood up. "He's got a way of looking at a man. I don't like or trust him."

"Like his brother Billy?"

"Worse." Hatcher shook his head. "Billy was mean, but you knew what you were getting with that one. Seth is sneaky and he'll go at your back."

Jed nodded. "I may not go after her at all."

"Now, don't go playing old Lige for the fool." The scout grinned. "All my talking ain't done any good. I know you'll be going for her come break up and the big thaw. All I meant was that old Seth may just be waiting and scheming your demise."

Jed laughed as he hadn't fooled Hatcher, one bit. "A cabin is lonely and needs a woman's hand."

"You be careful, Jed. They'll hang you for sure, if'n they catch you down there after her."

"Yeah, funny ain't it?"

"What?"

"People back in Baxter Springs knew how no-account Abe and Vern were." Jed shook his head. "Yet they still hold for them."

"But, they were white."

"I'm white."

"Not to them folks, Jed. They've heard the talk." Hatcher started toward the cabin. "Even in the settlements, mountain talk gets out, and they've heard of Crow Killer the Arapaho. Around the trading posts, the Nez Perce swear you're a demon."

Shaking hands, Hatcher pulled himself up onto the dun horse and looked down at Jed. "I've reintroduced you to the rifle and you are a tolerable good shot, and you know how to set the traps and snares. Now, all you've got to do is hunt, trap, and live the free spirit of these grand mountains."

"I'm grateful for all your help." Jed's shoulder was sore from the heavy recoil of the Hawkins slamming into his shoulder.

"Your step-dad told Woods it shot a mite high at a distance." Hatcher looked over at the rifle. "One other thing I want to tell you now, beaver plews ain't gonna bring near what they did in their heyday, even prime ones."

"How much?"

"It's kinda hard to say. Every year since the shining times left us, the price of a prime plew has gone down." Hatcher shrugged. "They'll feed you maybe, but they sure ain't gonna make you rich."

"Well, I'll give it a go this winter." Jed nodded. "There's always other critters to catch."

"The rifle, your pa left with old Elmer, keep it close, always loaded, and ready." Hatcher's grey eyes flashed across the broad valley.

"It was considerate of him to send it." Jed looked to where the rifle rested against the cabin. Actually, he had forgotten about leaving the Hawkins behind. "I still like the bow better."

"If it comes to a fight, your friends out there will respect that rifle a lot more than the bow."

"I know, I remember Walking Horse telling me that also."

Hatcher looked across the creek and into the valley. "You stay alert, Jed. Until the heavy snows come, raiders looking for scalps could be riding these mountains."

"Nez Perce or Blackfoot?"

"Doesn't matter, either can kill you." Hatcher shrugged. "And boy, you are outnumbered in these old mountains, maybe even cornered."

"I'll be fine, Lige." Jed reached out his hand. "Good-bye, old friend. You watch your back trail."

Hatcher turned his head as he shook hands with Jed. He knew the youngster didn't know the meaning of fear. "You watch your'n. Be seeing you come late summer or early fall."

Jed watched as Hatcher slowly made his way out of the valley, leading only one of the mules. The other two mules along with the piebald stood hobbled out on the valley floor, grazing on the browning grass across the creek. Hatcher left the mules behind, saying something about Jed needing them to carry trade goods or some nonsense. He knew the scout was referring to Sally Ann.

Picking up a brand-new sickle blade, Jed walked to where the dead grass started to wilt and turn brown. It was that time of year, the time of cold and dying. The sharp blade made a swishing sound as it cut easily through the tall meadow grass. With two mules and a horse to feed all winter, he would need plenty of hay stored in the small barn behind the lean-to.

For two solid weeks, he worked at cutting the dying grass. Using one of the mules and a travois he had designed for a transport, he hauled the dried out grass and stacked it in the barn. Looking at the blisters he had worked up from the hickory handle, he studied the barn full of hay and nodded. "That should be enough to feed you boys and girls till spring."

His luck held and his timing was perfect, as the hay was barely put up when the temperature dropped and the first snow of the year started to fall. Looking about the cabin, he tried to remember everything Hatcher had told him and what he had learned from the Arapaho about surviving the cold winters. Several cords of wood were cut and neatly stacked against the cabin wall, and candles were dipped and readied. Fresh deer meat hung outside the cabin, out of reach of any passing bear or varmint. Many a day, Jed and Bow Legs would lie around the Arapaho Village, watching the women cure and jerk meat for the winter. Until now, he never had to cure hides or pound dry meat, but thanks to the squaws, he knew how and how hard the women's work had been. Warriors were proud, too proud to do menial squaw's work, and now Jed knew why; raiding and stealing horses was much easier, maybe more dangerous, but a whole lot less work.

Pulling on his lighter hide parka, Jed stepped out into the falling snow. Already the ground was covered with the powdery white stuff and the flakes were getting heavier. Walking to where the horse and mules stood grazing, Jed removed their hobbles and led them back to the corral. Winter was here and already the animal's hair started to thicken as their coats became heavier, giving them the protection they would need when the temperature dropped below freezing.

Before he left the valley, Hatcher had predicted a hard, cold winter and already his words were proven true. Signs of the coming winter were everywhere. Jed watched as squirrels carried acorns from underneath the large oaks up into their nests and red ants were banking their anthills against the south side of trees. The fat bears he saw ignored him, completely intent on searching out their last morsels of plants and berries that hung dead on the vines. Jed knew Hatcher was right; winter was close and was probably going to be a long, cold one. Watching the busy squirrels, he had to laugh at their antics. No sooner would they bury an acorn in the ground, when a crow would try to steal it and the battle would be on. Usually, the crow would fly on a limb and wait for the squirrel to busy himself with another nut, and then they would quickly dig it up and be off. Funny, Jed thought to himself, someone or something was always trying to steal what wasn't theirs.

In the high elevation, the darkness came early, and with it the cold intensified. Jed took a final look across the dimming valley, then closed the cabin door and moved to the split oak table where he had been working on a pair of snowshoes. Pushing the coffeepot closer to the fire to heat, he looked around the snug cabin. It was all a trapper could want, but what about Sally Ann, was her father right? Would this way of life be too much of a hardship on a girl like her? He knew there would be many times when he would have to leave her alone while he ran his trap lines. Was she tough enough to handle being by herself, cooped up in the cabin? Perhaps, Hatcher's unspoken words were true, and maybe this was no place for a white girl. Jed didn't know but he did know the final decision would be hers. He said he'd come for her in the spring and he would. It was her choice, she could refuse to come back with him to the high meadows, but he had a feeling he would return with her in the spring. As White Swan had spoken, this valley had beckoned him. The light or whatever he had seen never reappeared, but still the valley called to him and it was home. Now, all he needed was someone to share it with.

By midnight, the snow stopped falling and morning found the ground covered in fresh snow. With the coming of the new day, the sun brought a clean, bright, pleasant warmness to the valley. Jed hobbled the horse and mules on the valley grass, then shouldering several traps and his rifle, he started across the valley. In his travels, he had discovered the valley was alive with game. His long stride was brisk as he headed to the closest of the beaver ponds where he found fresh signs. Hoof prints of deer, elk, antelope, and smaller animals showed plainly in the fresh snow. As Hatcher had taught him, Jed searched out the pond banks looking for the best places to set his steel traps. He wanted good sets close to the gnawed trees and branches of small saplings. Now, being in debt for the supplies Hatcher had brought, he needed to catch all the beaver he could to repay what he owed the store. Wading knee deep into the backwater of the small beaver ponds, Jed was surprised the water wasn't all that cold and was warmer than he figured it would be. The sun was not yet high in the sky as Jed set the last of his twenty traps, then retraced his steps back to the cabin. Later, after drying his feet, warming himself, and having something to eat, he would set another twenty traps. Hatcher had brought at least sixty traps with him, and with a little luck they would enable Jed to pay back his stepfather and the store in Baxter Springs. Returning late in the afternoon, almost at sundown after setting another twenty traps, Jed removed his soaked leggings and moccasins, replacing them with warm dry clothing. Sitting at the table sipping on coffee, he looked about the cabin and nodded, the day had been a good start. Tomorrow, if his luck held, he would be skinning beaver. If the Great Spirit smiled down on him by spring, he would have pelts that would bring him money for supplies, more traps, and hopefully Sally Ann. Hatcher's words of warning about Sally Ann's pa didn't scare Jed. If she wanted to come, he would bring her back to the valley.

Leading the animals in at dark, Jed stopped on the bank of the stream to let them drink. The still waters of the stream were starting to ice over at the edges, but the fast moving water would be some time before freezing solid. To some the valley would be a lonely place, but to Jed it was home. Looking across the small creek, he breathed in deeply, taking in the fresh air, the beautiful valley, and the majestic mountains looming over it. So far, the heavier snows held back, and most of the snow already on the ground melted when the bright sun came out during the day. Shutting the gate on the horse and mules, confining them in the corrals, Jed sat down outside the cabin and enjoyed the coming night. Staring up at the tall, dark mountains, he smiled, feeling content and completely at home in his valley. He thought of the sweet aroma of Hatcher's pipe, and maybe he would buy one of his own in Baxter Springs and take up smoking. Relaxing against the cabin wall, Jed looked up at the gentle swaying of the lofty trees and listened to the creek's gurgling water as it passed over the rocks. His mother had talked about heaven, and as earthly as possible, he knew this valley was close to what she spoke of.

Jed looked over at the red mule, hanging from the packsaddle were seven beaver out of his first twenty traps. The other traps were empty so Jed left them untouched. He grinned as seven out of twenty wasn't bad for a beginner, especially someone who has never set a trap in his life. Hopefully, the other traps on the north end of the valley would produce more. Halfway back to the cabin, the old mule threw up her ears and focused on a far tree line. Jed knew if anyone was in the trees, he had already been spotted and there was no need to try to conceal himself. Reaching the cabin, Jed unloaded the beaver and led the mule into the corral. After removing the packsaddle from the mule, he walked to where the piebald was grazing, and quickly bridled him. Retrieving the Hawken and his bow and quiver of arrows, he swung up on the horse and started across the valley, riding directly to where the mule had focused on.

Letting the horse stretch out in a hard run, Jed reined in and slowed down as he approached the tree line. Circling the trees, Jed studied the ground closely for any sign before moving closer. Nothing showed, the piebald didn't alert on anything as Jed rode him into the dense trees. Several times, over the past few days, the animals had pricked their ears and watched the valley. They were keeping Jed jumpy and today he was determined to find out what was there. Casting back and forth through the trees, Jed kept the Hawken ready for any surprises, man or animal, but nothing showed itself. Finally, as Jed was about to give up and turn back, before him on the ground, bear tracks showed plainly in what was left of the snow beneath a large spruce tree. A bear, Jed shook his head in relief, then turned the piebald back toward the cabin. A slight cold chill went up his back as he remembered the grizzly that had done for Billy Wilson. However, this bear's tracks were much smaller, but he was still a grizzly roaming close, not far from the cabin and his stock. Any hungry grizzly was a dangerous foe to be watched. The piebald never sensed the intruder, but three sets of bloodshot eyes were watching from a nearby stand of cedars as the man and horse retreated down the ridge.

By candlelight, Jed finished skinning out and pegging the last of the eighteen beaver and two silver foxes. Tired and bloody, he washed off in the cold creek water before returning to the cabin to eat a hearty meal. He was content, even proud of himself for taking so many skins his first day. With his good fortune, his confidence swelled. He was tired, but ready, even eager, for the coming day. Relaxing in a chair, he made from oak and covered in soft elk hides, Jed sipped his coffee and stared into the warm fire. His thoughts drifted back to Little Antelope, Walking Horse, and the Arapaho people. Hopefully, he could return to see them in the coming summer.

For three solid weeks, Jed had been busy skinning, scraping, and pegging beaver hides along with scouting the valley. His luck with the trapping had been phenomenal. He had all sixty of his traps set, plus many deadfalls and snares, and almost a hundred pelts lay stacked in the smaller barn behind the cabin. The huge valley had never been trapped, but it turned out to be a trapper's paradise with beaver abounding in every pond. On dry land, silver fox, otter, bobcat, lynx, and coon were fighting one another to get into his traps. His only problem was he had no skinner, leaving him with all the work. The constant coldness of the pond water and the skinning of the wet pelts kept his hands blistered and sore. Winter just arrived and spring was far away. Jed studied his catch of furs, smiling contentedly because he had trapped less than half the ponds in the valley. By spring, if his luck held, he would have a small fortune in skins ready to take to Baxter Springs. Sally Ann would have whatever she wanted for the cabin.

A week later, a Norther hit unexpectedly with vengeance and fury. Seeing the boiling clouds coming, Jed raced the piebald across the valley to each pond, taking up his traps so they wouldn't freeze solid beneath the deep ice. Quickly putting the piebald back in his corral, Jed concentrated on bringing in enough meat and wood to last him several days. Piling hay into the troughs, made from rough lumber, Jed fastened the gate and forged his way through the blinding snow and wind back to the cabin. Tomorrow, if the blizzard subsided, he would have to water the animals, but for tonight the hay would have to suffice. Now, returning inside the snug cabin, hot biscuits, coffee, and a tasty deer steak sounded good.

The heavy winds and blinding snow roared and blew for three solid days, holding Jed a prisoner inside the cabin. A fire blazing in the fireplace kept the cabin cozy warm as he passed back and forth trying to water the animals. With the blinding snow it was far too dangerous to try for the frozen creek. The best he could do was fill buckets with snow and set them near the fire to melt. A slow process, but the animals had to have water. A tight rope tied to the outside of the door and stretched to the corral gate, helped Jed find his way to the horses in the blinding storm. Another rope tied around his waist, tethered him to the lead line, keeping him from becoming disoriented and lost in the storm. Getting turned around and losing his way could result in freezing to death in minutes. The piebald and mules were huddled together back in the small barn, chewing on the life-giving grass Jed had put up before the snow started.

The morning of the fourth day, Jed woke up to complete silence, the blizzard was over. The roaring wind and snow had subsided, leaving a quiet void in the cabin, making him shake his head in dismay. To his ears, the cabin was eerily silent, making him think perhaps he had lost his hearing. Pushing on the heavy oak door, he finally managed to open it enough to slip outside into the blinding brightness of the sparkling snow. He was amazed as snowdrifts were piled high on the cabin's north wall and against the lean-to with two feet of snow resting atop the roof. Everything was covered in snow, making the valley a winter wonderland. Stomping a trail from the cabin door to the corral, Jed examined the animals, finding they had weathered the storm well. Tossing the hungry animals several armfuls of hay, he patted the piebald and turned back to the gate. Closing the corral gate, he trudged and plowed his way through the deep snow to the frozen creek. Standing by the bank, he studied the snow filled landscape of the wide valley with no bare ground showing. There was a flat layer of snow, dotted with taller shoots of grass protruding up above the crust, and deep windblown drifts piled up against the trees. The valley was barren and nothing living moved out on the flats, nary a rabbit feeding or grey fox hunting. Turning back to the cabin, Jed noticed the warming sun already started the eaves to drip. The storm had come early, and he remembered the Arapaho people called an early storm as this, a storm with no power. They meant it was a bad storm but wouldn't stay for long on the ground.

A week passed, the Blue Norther had come and gone. The sun melted most of the snowdrifts and only remnants of snow lay under the cedars, out of the sun's heavy rays. Mounting the piebald before daylight, Jed turned the horse to the far southern end of the valley. Tomorrow, he would reset his traps but now, he wanted to search the large valley to be sure he was still alone. Almost four months, Jed knew he must have been discovered by now so he had to look for interlopers. He had remained near the cabin working on his pelts, but something he couldn't put his finger on had been nagging at him for two days so today, he would find out. The ground was soft from the melting snow of the past week and tracks would be hard to conceal. He had discovered grizzly tracks before the storm hit, but Jed wasn't convinced the bear was what held the attention of the mules and piebald the last two days. The bear should be in its den, and he knew it was well past time for the animal to hibernate. Several times in the last two days, after he had hobbled them out to pasture, he watched as their ears pricked up as they looked to the south. It had been more than a week since the storm, and the trails would have cleared in the passes. There was plenty of time for an enemy to ride into his valley and search him out, if they knew he was there.

Jed checked the priming on the Hawkins and started the horse up the slopes on the south end of the valley. After staying in the corral for several days, the piebald was full of energy and frisky, wringing his tail, and trying to crow hop under Jed as he worked his way over the switchback bordering the ridge. Jed studied the higher trail above, then glanced down and checked the game trail he was following. He knew if interlopers were above him, he would be easy to spot, out in the open, on the trails. For two hours, the piebald climbed steadily until he was almost halfway up the mountain and so far Jed had neither seen nor spotted anything suspicious. Reining the horse in, he looked across the lower valley toward the far tree line where smoke from his cabin curled into the air. The smoke was like a beacon, pinpointing his cabin's location if anyone was watching from the higher peaks. Exposing his location couldn't be helped, he had to heat the cabin because the cold at this high elevation was too extreme at night. Also, if the fire died out in the hearth and he returned to the cabin with cold or half frozen fingers, it would be almost impossible to use the flint and steel to start a fire.

A smile crossed his cold face as the valley, from this high up, was even more picturesque and pristine. Several groups of deer and elk moved out from the cover of the timber and were grazing peacefully out on the valley floor. Everything in the valley was quiet, and nothing suspicious showed. Maybe his mind was playing tricks on him and nobody was watching from the higher elevation. The paint horse didn't twitch an ear or sense anything out of the way. Looking up at the sun, Jed figured it was almost noon by its position overhead. Nudging the horse, he decided he was wrong and no enemy lurked anywhere in the valley. Following a well-used animal path, Jed knew it meandered slowly back down to the valley floor. The trail would bring him out on the flats, almost halfway to his cabin.

Casting his eyes to the ground, where two trails intersected, Jed reined the horse in hard. Tracks plainly showed in the soft trail, two riders with unshod horses had passed down the switchback ahead of him. How long ago, he couldn't be sure, but muddy water still pooled in the fresh tracks. Jed knew he had come in above and behind his visitors and with the two riders focused on the valley below, apparently they weren't aware of his presence. Sliding from the horse's back, Jed led the piebald cautiously down the trail, his eyes alert for any movement. He didn't know who was ahead, but he knew they were Indian, not white.

Two Blackfoot warriors sat their horses, looking out across the valley as they studied the smoke from the cabin. Concealed, sitting far back under the trees and across the creek, the cabin was invisible from where they were waiting on the ridge. The two mules Jed had hobbled out on the valley floor grazed contentedly, but sensing the warriors were there, they would occasionally look up at the high ridge. The bigger warrior's eyes were focused on the mules, and unaware of Jed closing in on them from above.

"It is smoke from a white man's cabin."

"Frog Belly and his warriors reported there was one lone Indian living in this valley when they passed through."

"They didn't kill this one?"

"They wanted to, but they spotted a white man coming into the valley from the north, leading several mules." The smaller warrior shrugged. "The long shooting thunder guns of the whites are dangerous, so they departed."

"I will not be so afraid, Blue Darter. We will watch and wait longer to see how many are here."

"We have been here two days and have only seen one Indian." The smaller warrior shook his head in disgust. "This one stays close to his lodge."

"Maybe the white has left."

"There are only two of us. Frog Belly had four warriors with him and they did not dare attack this one lone warrior."

"This one leaves his animals unprotected and easy for us to take." The bigger warrior argued. "I do not see the spotted black horse that has been with the mules."

"Two mules?" The other warrior scoffed. "Would Small Mountain waste his time and maybe get us killed for such a trophy as two mules?"

"Do not forget the horse." The other shrugged. "This has been a long trail. Now, we ride to our village, but we must take something back with us."

"I say this is foolish and dangerous. I tell you, Small Mountain, if a white is here, he will carry the far shooting rifle and they shoot very well."

"Is Blue Darter afraid of one man, Indian or white?"

"We do not know if he is alone, and I am not afraid." Blue Darter straightened on his horse. "Only a fool would risk his life for two mules and maybe a horse."

"Not only two mules, his lodge will hold many trophies for us if we kill him, and the rifle." Small Mountain argued. "He is in our hunting grounds and he is the enemy."

"Our lands are far away. This is not our hunting grounds." The smaller warrior shook his head. "You know this."

"Wherever a Blackfoot walks, is his land. I Small Mountain choose to walk here."

"I think this is a very foolish thing to do, my friend." Blue Darter shook his head again. "But, as usual, I will ride with you."

"It would be very foolish, my friends." Jed's voice sounded behind them causing the two Blackfoot to whirl their horses. "If you raise your weapons, you will die here, far from your lodges."

"You are Arapaho." Small Mountain took in Jed's clothing and his long hair. "You are far from your lands."

"I am Arapaho."

"This white man lodge, back in the tall timber, is it yours or does another live there?" Blue Darter motioned down the valley.

"It is my lodge."

"Why do you live here? Were you banished from your people?" Blue Darter was curious why the Arapaho was so far from his own land.

"I found this valley and no tribe lived here or hunted here. Now I, Crow Killer of the Arapaho, claim this valley and everything in it to be my hunting grounds." Jed watched their faces. "If the Blackfoot or any others come here in peace, they will be welcome."

"And if they come as enemies?"

"This I do not wish, but if you come as an enemy, you will die."

Small Mountain stared hard at the piebald standing behind Jed. "That paint horse looks like the same horse as Black Robe the Nez Perce rode. Is it the horse of Black Robe?"

"It is the same horse."

"We have heard a demon killed the Nez Perce."

"I am Crow Killer, the Arapaho, I killed Black Robe. Do not make me kill you." The Hawken rifle rested across Jed's arm.

"Black Robe was a great warrior." Blue Darter studied the warrior before them. "Tell us Arapaho, why have you come here to this place so far from Arapaho lands?"

"I have told you already, this valley is my hunting grounds now. I would like to live here in peace." Jed studied the two warriors. "No other claimed it, so now it is mine."

Small Mountain yelled at Jed. "No, this is Blackfoot land!"

"No." Jed nodded at Blue Darter. "Your friend there said it never was and it sure ain't now."

Blue Darter held up his hand. "Much talk is on the winds, it is said by the Nez Perce only two of their warriors came back to their villages after Black Robe was killed by an Arapaho Lance Bearer. They told of a demon spirit attacking them, killing many Nez Perce warriors."

Jed knew most Indians were superstitious of anything they couldn't understand. With Sally Ann coming into the valley it wouldn't hurt to let them think he could be a demon. "To my enemies I am a demon; to my friends I come in peace."

"Do you wish this Arapaho for a friend or enemy, Small Mountain?" Blue Darter looked across at his friend.

"Come to my lodge and we will eat and get warm." Jed looked at the bigger warrior. "Then Small Mountain can decide if we will fight or be friends?"

"No Blackfoot is the friend of an Arapaho." Small Mountain swiped his hand. "This could never be."

"The Crow said the same thing." Jed smiled. "Now, the great Red Hawk of the Crows is my friend."

"This could never be. We have heard of this warrior. He is mighty in battle." Blue Darter shook his head. "He rode this trail alone and stole the great spotted horse from the Nez Perce."

"Yes, he is a great warrior and he is my friend." Jed swung up on the piebald.

"We will come to your lodge, Crow Killer."

CHAPTER 2

J ed stood back as he watched the two warriors studying the cabin nervously, both hesitating to enter the log lodge of the whites. He was curious because on the trail he had heard the larger warrior talk of stealing whatever was in the cabin, but now they were afraid to enter.

"Come, the Blackfoot are welcome in my lodge."

"It is the lodge of a white man." Small Mountain shook his head. "Perhaps, the den of a demon."

"It is my lodge, the lodge of Crow Killer the Arapaho." Jed smiled. "My friends will always be safe here."

Shaking his head, Blue Darter stepped into the warm cabin. "We have been in a white man's lodge many times when we traded our skins at Fort Reed."

"You did not trade your plews with the two white traders, Abe and Vern?"

"No, only the foolish ones like the Nez Perce traded with them." Small Mountain shook his head. "Now, these whites are dead by your hand."

Jed was shocked when he heard the words. "Who told you this?"

The warrior seemed to laugh. "It is told in every campfire how the demon killed two white trappers near the great river, days after he killed the Nez Perce Black Robe and took his horse."

"Sit and we will eat." Jed wanted to change the subject. "You are welcome here as friends."

"You live as a white man would." Small Mountain refused the chair Jed offered and sat down beside the fireplace. "How can this be?"

Jed set cups out for the two warriors and filled them with coffee. "I plan to stay here for a long time. I do not have a woman to help build a hide lodge of the People."

Tasting the coffee, both men seemed to like its taste. "The Nez Perce will learn you are here, as we have, and they will come here to kill."

"I am sad to hear this. There has been enough killing." Jed studied the warriors before him. "The Blackfoot, will they come here to kill?"

"I do not know this." Blue Darter sipped the hot coffee. "We are not fools, Arapaho. You could have killed us earlier, and we know that."

"I just wish to live here in peace." Jed walked to the table and picked up the newly made moccasins and a butcher knife. "These are for my friends, the Blackfoot."

"We have nothing to give you in return." Small Mountain refused the knife.

"Your friendship is all I want in return and to live in peace." Jed offered the knife again.

"You wish to buy this land for a knife and moccasins?"

"Not buy; they are a gift for friends. This land does not belong to the Blackfoot; it belongs to the strongest and the one who can hold it." Jed's voice hardened. "Do not be fooled Blackfoot, I will kill to keep this place."

"You, Arapaho, you think you are stronger?" Small Mountain leaped to his feet and disappeared through the door racing to his horse.

"I am sorry, Crow Killer. I would have liked you for a friend." Blue Darter laid the moccasins on the table. "He tries to make strong medicine for himself and someday it will get him killed."

"I am sorry too, Blue Darter. Tell your people, the Blackfoot, are always welcome in this lodge, if they come in peace."

Jed watched as the two warriors raced their horses across the broad valley, heading southwest to the only south pass leading out of the valley. He would have liked to have them for friends, but now he knew it wasn't meant to be. The warrior, Small Mountain, had insulted his lodge by not accepting his gifts and refusing his friendship, which meant they would be enemies. The other warrior, Blue Darter, was different, but he was Blackfoot and could not go against one of his own people. Suddenly, the two Blackfoot stopped and appeared to be arguing far out on the valley floor. Jed looked over to where the Hawkins stood against the doorsill.

"You insulted Crow Killer in his lodge." Blue Darter shook his head at Small Mountain. "Why do we stop here?"

"No, the Arapaho insults us by coming into our country."

"You know we have never hunted these mountains so far from our villages." Blue Darter shook his head. "We would never have seen his lodge in this place if our chief hadn't sent us to the east to speak with Chief Lone Bull, or if we hadn't talked with Frog Belly."

"I say these are Blackfoot lands."

"The land of the Nez Perce lies between this valley and our hunting grounds."

"Then they are weak to let one lone Arapaho keep this land."

"What will Small Mountain do?"

"I will challenge this demon Arapaho, and kill him."

"You are foolish, my friend. If he is Crow Killer and a demon as the Nez Perce have said, we should leave him alone." Blue Darter looked toward the cabin where he could see Jed watching them. "Why do you do this thing? Does the demon fill your head with foolishness?"

"He challenged me."

"No, my friend, he did not. He said he wanted to live in peace."

"If we kill him, we get the horse of Black Robe and the white man's rifle." Small Mountain grinned viciously. "Our medicine would be strong, and people would sing our praises."

Blue Darter shook his head. "He treated us with respect. I want no part of this."

"Then I will do this thing alone. You can have the mules." Small Mountain kicked his horse into a lope toward the cabin. "Did you not see the fear in his eyes? That is why he wants peace with us."

"I found nothing in his eyes that showed fear." Blue Darter shook his head at his friend's foolishness. "Only strength."

Jed didn't take his eyes from the two warriors, and now the bigger of the two was riding back toward the cabin. Jed watched as Small Mountain tossed his bow and arrows along with his sleeping blanket to the ground, then screamed at him. Larger than Jed, the warrior figured he was stronger and without the white man's gun, the Arapaho would be easy to defeat. Mounting the piebald, armed only with his war axe and shield, Jed rode out to confront the challenge of the Blackfoot warrior.

Neither of the two said a word as they sat their horses, only yards apart. The confrontation was almost the same way the fight started with the young Crow. Jed had heard, pride goes before the fall, and one of them was fixing to learn the hard way that the old saying sometimes comes true.

"We do not have to fight." Jed swept his hand. "Go in peace, Blackfoot."

"You say this is your valley, but I say it belongs to the Blackfoot." Small Mountain pulled his war axe from the hide belt and raised it. "Now, we find out who the Spirit People want to have this land."

Jed looked back at the cabin, he didn't want to fight or kill the warrior, but he had worked too hard and wouldn't give up this valley to anyone. White Swan had foretold of a beacon of light and a beautiful valley. Jed had seen the light and the valley was his. He found this place and wasn't letting a lone warrior run him out. The Blackfoot were a warlike tribe. Hatcher told him, they were the bloodiest of the northern tribes, and to kill one of them could bring the whole tribe down on him. Alone in these mountains, against so many, he would have to be always on guard.

"I do not want this Blackfoot."

"I do! Now, you die, Arapaho! I will take your scalp and decorate my lodge with it."

Blue Darter watched as the two horses clashed together, and he could hear the ringing of the war axes across the valley. He knew Small Mountain had been wrong about the Arapaho being afraid.

Now, the Blackfoot was fighting for his life. Small Mountain was still young and inexperienced, and never fought against an enemy with Jed's strength and speed. The Arapaho seemed to be everywhere, striking powerful blows against his hide shield, causing his arm holding the shield to ache with every blow. The paint horse was pushing his smaller horse across the valley floor with little effort, making Small Mountain's heart beat with fear. Was the Nez Perce right about this warrior being a demon dressed as a man?

Only pride kept the Blackfoot fighting, refusing to yield to the demon screaming before him who was crushing his war shield with every blow. Blue Darter watched in dismay as the body of Small Mountain slumped and slid sideways from his tired horse. Kicking his horse, Blue Darter rode to where Jed sat the piebald, looking down on the fallen warrior.

"Is he dead?" Blue Darter raised his hands as Jed whirled ready to fight. "I have not come to fight."

"No, he still breathes." Jed lowered his war axe. "It was a glancing blow, but I reckon he might have a sore head for several days."

"You do not kill him?"

"No, I told you, I would like to be friends with the Blackfoot."

"My friend, Small Mountain, is a hothead. He is also the son of our Chief Deep Water." Blue Darter knelt beside his friend. "You have shamed him. He will never be friends with Crow Killer."

"Tell me, Blackfoot, why does every warrior wish to fight me?" Jed looked down at the unconscious warrior. "I only want to live here in peace."

Blue Darter shrugged his shoulders sadly. "It is the way of some to fight. Your people, the Arapaho Lance Bearers, are the same. I have heard of their ferocity in battle, even here."

"Then we will be enemies!" Jed's face grew hard. "You tell your Chief Deep Water, if any Blackfoot comes here to raid, I will raid the Blackfoot Villages and take revenge."

"One against so many?" Blue Darter studied the angry face. "Are you truly a demon?"

"Go, I can kill both of you now, if I want to." Jed raised his axe. "There is nothing here for the Blackfoot that they don't already have in other hunting grounds."

Helping the groggy Small Mountain to his horse, Blue Darter mounted his horse and looked over at Jed. "I watched you fight this one. I know you are a great warrior and speak the truth. I will tell our chief of your wish for peace. We go."

"This land belongs to me."

"Stay alert, Crow Killer." Blue Darter nodded. "This one has an uncle that is touched in his eyes by the evil ones. Some say he is crazy, but he is a great warrior, and he will come against you."

"What is this warrior's name?"

"Standing Bull!"

Shaking off the excitement of the fight, Jed led the piebald back to where the mules stood watching and hobbled him. He turned to where the two warriors were slowly passing from his sight, heading for the far end of the valley. He spared Small Mountain's life and had no idea if they would return with more warriors. Still, he wondered if he should have killed them both. No, he wasn't a murderer, even though the warrior wanted to kill him. Now, there would be no more time for relaxing. After this day, he would have to be always alert.

The weather had held for almost two weeks. Jed kept busy running his traps and snares during the day, and skinning out his catch at night. The small barn was starting to fill up with plews. Already, he figured there were enough hides to pay his debts and supply him and Sally Ann with everything they would need to bring back to the cabin to set up a home. For him, living alone in the valley, the mountains supplied almost everything he needed, but Sally Ann was a woman and she would need more. Curtains, spinning wheels for yarn, and the niceties of civilization had to be bought and brought back on their return.

The temperature had fallen, and now the beaver ponds were frozen solid, much too thick to break the ice to set his traps. Now, his attention turned to the land animals, wandering the landscape of the valley in their quest for food. His trapping had been good, but Jed wanted buffalo hides to make into warm robes and coats to sell in the settlement. When the cold snows and icy winds blew in from the north, the hides would give him something to pass his time working on. He was also getting tired of deer and elk meat, and a good tasty buffalo tongue or steak sounded mighty fine to him.

Jed knew the buffalo he had spotted on his way from the Snake River would now be grazing in the lower valleys. The grass would still be abundant beneath the snow, even though it already turned brown from the cold. After putting the animals inside the corrals, Jed studied the sky. The weather was cold and crisp, and nary a cloud floated above.

He wondered if he had time to ride to the lower valleys, kill buffalo, skin them, and get back to the cabin before a heavy snowstorm blocked the trails leading into his valley. He knew the ride would be risky, but Jed wanted buffalo hides and there were no buffalo in his valley. Nodding, he looked over to where the piebald chewed on the rough forage Jed had tossed them. Tomorrow, he would go after the shaggies.

Sally Ann sat on a three-legged stool, milking the jersey cow that gave them plenty of milk and butter. The milk also fattened the pen full of young shoats that supplied them with bacon, sausage, and ham through the winter. She had her hands full as she tried to milk the cow. She had to keep the cow's greedy calf back by tapping his ankles with a stick as he tried to push his way in to get more than his share of the milk. Several times, she had to slow her strong hands as she daydreamed about Jed and their life together. She was squeezing the cow's teats fast and hard, causing the foam to rise in the bucket and spill over, and the cow wasn't half milked yet. She knew her father would scold her soundly if he saw the foam lying on the ground. She couldn't help herself, ever since Lige Hatcher had brought Jed's words, her thoughts wandered mindlessly to the mountains to what he was doing.

"You sure are squeezing old Jers hard there, Sally Ann."

"Seth Wilson, what are you doing here this time of day?" Sally Ann was shocked out of her daydreaming.

"We're out of sugar, and Pa was wondering if you have any extra we could buy?"

"I reckon Pa could fix you up with some." Finished with her milking and leaving a back quarter for the calf, Sally Ann stood up from the stool. "Why did you come here instead of riding into town?"

"I figured the store would be closed by the time I got there."

"Uh huh, last I heard the store didn't close until eight at night."

Seth's face turned slightly red. "I didn't know that."

"Come on, we'll go to the house." She knew he was lying. Seth Wilson had become a regular at the lone saloon in Baxter Springs that is after his pa had turned in for the night.

Wilson grabbed her by the arm as she started around him, causing milk to slosh from the bucket. "What's the hurry, Sally Ann?"

"Turn my arm loose, Seth Wilson."

"I heard what old Hatcher said about my stepbrother coming in after you in the spring." Seth sneered wickedly. "I thought maybe I'd get my bride's kiss early."

"You thought wrong. Now, turn me loose." Sally Ann winced as his grip became brutal.

"You know your pa ain't about to let you marry that killer."

"Killer, what are you talking about?"

"Reckon you'll have to ask your pa." Seth pulled her to him. "Right now, I've got other things on my mind."

"Turn me loose, Seth." Milk spilled as he pushed her against the barn wall. "I mean now."

"Sally Ann is that you in there?" The barn door screeched open, causing Seth to quickly turn her loose. "Oh Seth, I didn't realize you were here."

"He was just leaving, Pa."

"He could come in and visit awhile. Maybe have supper." The old man looked down and spotted the spilled milk.

"He's leaving now. His pa wants him home."

Backing from the barn, Seth walked to where his horse was tied. "I'll see you later, Sally Ann."

"What went on out here?"

"Nothing!" Her face was red from anger. "Absolutely nothing."

"Come, let me carry the bucket, child."

Fire glowed red in the wood stove as supper heated in the iron skillets. Her temper still raged as she slammed and rattled the skillets atop the stove.

The old man sat sipping his coffee and watched her as she cooked. "Tell me what's wrong girl?"

"Seth Wilson, he's what's wrong."

"What did he do?"

Pointing a flat fork at the table, she shook visibly. "He said Jed was a killer."

"He said that?"

"Don't play innocent with me, Pa." Sally Ann frowned. "Tell me what he meant."

Rubbing his forehead, the old man slumped. "Young Mister Bracket killed two trappers after he left here last summer. The story's all over Baxter Springs."

"Who says so?"

"Lige Hatcher found the bodies and said Jed killed the men." Duncan didn't add the part where Hatcher said it was self-defense. "Said Jed admitted to the killings."

"That's it?" Sally Ann shook her head. "Lige Hatcher says Jed killed two men, and that's gospel, even with no witnesses?"

"I believe Lige. I've never known him to lie." Duncan would not meet her eyes. "I believe him and that's it."

"What is it, Pa?" She walked to the table and looked down at him. "What are you not saying?"

"Nothing gal, nothing." Duncan lied. "Let's eat."

"There's more, Pa. I feel it." She went back to the stove, then turned and glared at him. "I'm marrying Jedidiah Bracket, and you better not interfere."

"Fine, marry him, but you'll live here in Baxter Springs, not way back in those mountains of his."

"He'll be my husband and we'll live where he says." Sally Ann slid the plate of ham and beans across the table. "You try to use your authority to stop us and you'll never see me again."

"I never knew you could be so hard, girl."

"Hard?" Sally Ann turned toward the stove. "I love him, Pa. Have you forgotten how to love?"

"I just want you safe, daughter, that's all." Duncan picked up his fork.

Shaking her head, she smiled slightly. "Don't you realize I'll be safe anywhere with Jed?"

Pushing his plate away, Duncan stood up. "No, I don't know any such thing. Jed Bracket is a killer. He's become wild as any heathen Indian."

"How can you say that, and be so cruel?"

"I'm not cruel, girl. I'm the appointed constable of Baxter Springs and all those folks in the settlement are my responsibility."

Throwing her apron on the table, Sally Ann looked him straight in the eye without flinching. "You hear me Pa, hear me good. Jed Bracket is my man, we will marry, and if you use this as an excuse to try to stop us, I'll curse you till my dying day."

"Sally Ann!"

Jerking open the door, she started out into the cold. "Don't Sally Ann me, Amos Duncan!"

Six buffalo hides plus several pounds of buffalo meat, enough to last Jed until the spring thaw, was lashed across the packsaddles of the two mules. Jed broke camp and had the mules packed early in the far-off valley where he had found the buffalo. Now, he wanted to get an early start on the three-day ride back to his cabin. Snow clouds were gathering and the sky overhead was darkening, threatening another storm. The temperature was already dropping as he climbed higher up the rough trail. He could smell the storm that was brewing over the mountains. With luck, he would reach his valley before the bad weather hit; if not, the journey over the steep trails could be cold and dangerous.

Late on the second afternoon, the wind shifted out of the north, whipping through the tall trees that lined the steep trail. The wind seemed to gust stronger as the sun disappeared in the west, dropping the temperature. Jed studied the sky and trail as the piebald climbed steadily. Should he make night camp now or push on to try to reach the mountain summit before making camp? The piebald eagerly climbed as the narrow path led up, over the mountain, then dipped down into the valley where the cabin was located. Looking back at the mules, he noticed the older red mule was struggling with her load of hides and needed rest. Not wanting to break the mules wind or cripple her in any way, Jed turned the piebald into a stand of cedars and slipped to the ground.

"It'll be a cold and hungry camp, old man, but we'll be home tomorrow with any luck." Jed absently spoke to the horse. "Then you'll have a warm barn and plenty of grass."

The animals had been on good graze while he hunted and skinned out the buffalo. They were full, but tonight they would have to suffer a dry camp. The green hides were heavy, weighing at least five times heavier than dried, cured hides. Jed had packed each mule with only three hides and a portion of the meat. Nevertheless, the load was too heavy for the red mule. She was an old and good honest mule, and he didn't want to cripple her. Jed had to pull his blankets from the piebald and remove the packsaddles with their load of furs from the mules, before he could roll up beside a downed log and work his way deep into the leaves carpeting the ground.

Early morning found a heavy downfall of snow as Jed loaded the mules and continued back up the trail. The night's rest had helped the old mule regain her strength and she followed easily along the steep trail. The wind stopped blowing, but now large flakes of snow fell, covering the animals and Jed's shoulders. The trail and mountains turned into a winter wonderland as everything was covered in snow; the ground, the limbs on trees, the white stuff blanketed everything along the trail. Jed could see the trail where it topped out the mountain, another few hundred yards and it would be all downhill to the cabin. Jed's hands were cold and the chill penetrated his hide parka, chilling him to the bone. His mind was almost numb from the cold, and only the thought of the warm cabin kept him moving forward.

It was late afternoon, almost dusky dark as Jed reined in at the corrals and slipped stiffly to the ground. Holding onto the piebald's mane, he needed several steps before his legs and feet loosened up enough to walk. The weather remained constant as the snow was still falling, floating lazily to the ground, covering everything. Jed unloaded the meat and frozen hides, then uncinched the packsaddles, freeing the tired mules. All three animals hurried to where Jed had pitched their hay and started eating. Turning from the corral, with his body numb to the bone, he made his way slowly to the cabin to start a fire. Several minutes later, after getting the cabin door open and blowing on his cold fingers to warm them, he finally got the flint and steel working well enough to spark a blaze in the cold hearth of the fireplace.

The hides and meat had to be moved to a safe place or the varmints and hunters of the night would ruin them before morning. Finally thawing out, Jed dreaded the thought of having to face the cold and snow outside the warming cabin, but he had no other choice. Riding to the cabin earlier, he had spotted many wolf tracks around the corrals and cabin, and to leave the meat where it lay would only cause it to be lost. He had only been away from the cabin for six days and already several wolves had moved closer, leaving tracks everywhere in the fresh snow.

Pulling on his parka, he opened the door and jumped back as a figure fell toward him. Pulling his knife, Jed automatically moved away from the staggering figure that leaned heavily against the door.

"Who are you?" Jed questioned the figure standing before him.

Slowly the warrior slipped to the floor unconscious. Quickly looking outside for others, Jed closed the door and pulled the unconscious man closer to the fire. Removing his frozen leather shirt, Jed placed a hot cup of coffee to the warrior's mouth. Only coughing and a low gurgle came from the cracked lips. Dragging the almost frozen body, he placed the young warrior on his bed and covered the shivering body with several warm hides. Checking his body for any other injuries, Jed shook his head, as this one only missed freezing to death by a hair. Luckily, he found the cabin before any of his fingers or toes had frost bite badly enough to lose them. Seeing the youngster had passed into a deep sleep, Jed turned to the door to put the hides away, out of reach of any wolves.

During the night, Jed placed hot rocks at the young warrior's feet to keep him warm, trying to knock the cold from his body. At sunup after a long night's restless sleep, the youngster finally woke up and opened his eyes. Motioning to the half frozen youngster, Jed pushed him back onto the warm bed as he tried to rise.

"What tribe are you?" Jed tried to communicate, but to no avail, the young Indian was unable to speak.

Only a shake of the head came from the young man. Jed finally resorted to hand signs he had learned from the Arapaho and Lige Hatcher. Watching Jed's fast moving hands, the young man's hands tried to form the signs to answer. Jed was curious why the youngster could not speak as he tried communicating with him. Did the cold affect his vocal cords and throat? Walking behind the bed, Jed moved closer to the fireplace and looked back where the youngster lay with his back to him. Picking up a tin plate, Jed deliberately dropped it on the rock hearth. Nothing, the lad had no reaction to the loud noise as any normal person would. Moving in front of the bed, Jed motioned at his ears and mouth, and then at the youngster. It was as he feared; the young Indian was apparently deaf and mute.

After several minutes of hand signals, Jed finally figured out his name was Silent One and he was of the Assiniboine Tribe. Long into the morning, after Jed had finished his feeding, the two talked as best they could without speaking. Silent One had been banished from his people, who thought the evil spirits had cursed the youngster, making him unable to speak or hear. Jed wasn't surprised, the Indian people led a hard life and they were very superstitious, afraid of anything they couldn't understand. Older people, cripples, or ones like Silent One were put out from the village and left to fend for themselves or starve. In the high mountains, only the strong survived the ordeal of the elements, and this was the way of the northern people. Luckily for the youngster, somehow he found his way to the cabin in the storm.

Using hand signals, Jed communicated with the young warrior. "Your people cast you out, why?"

"My people say I am cursed by the evil ones."

"Do you believe this?"

"It is no matter what I believe. My people no longer know me."

"I am sorry."

"Could I stay here one more sleep to regain my strength?" Silent One signaled. "I will leave with the coming sun."

Jed walked to the table and brought the youngster a hot cup of coffee. "The storm is bad and will get worse. If you leave, you could freeze to death out there."

"What am I to do, tall one?" The brown hands seemed to hesitate sadly with his question. "Where am I to go?"

"Stay here with me."

"I am a cripple. Why would you want me to stay here?"

"You are deaf, not a cripple."

"You do not wish me to leave this place?"

"No, stay here and help me with the skinning and hunting." Jed shook his head. "I need help with so many animals to skin."

Silent One looked quietly at Jed. "You would let me do this?"

"I would welcome the company."

"You wouldn't think me a cripple?"

"No, Silent One, I would not think you a cripple." Jed shook his head. "A man doesn't have to speak or hear to be a great warrior."

"I believe you, Tall One. I will stay here." Silent One smiled silently. "How are you called Arapaho?"

"You know I am Arapaho?" Jed blinked.

"I cannot hear or speak, but I am not blind, Tall One."

"I am sorry."

"Don't be, I have grown used to being different." The youngster nodded. "I have learned to use other senses that I possess."

"I am Crow Killer of the Northern Arapaho People."

"A good name for a warrior." Silent One nodded, then stood up slowly and moved to the table. "I thank Crow Killer for saving my life and letting me stay in his lodge."

"You are welcome." Jed studied the dark eyes of the youngster and the muscular body. Silent One wasn't tall, but he was powerfully built for his age. Jed figured him to be young, perhaps fifteen or sixteen.

For a solid week, the snow and howling winds had kept Jed and Silent One confined to the cabin, only venturing outside to feed and water the horse and mules. The Assiniboine was quick to learn and eager to work with the animals. Rising as soon as he saw Jed move on his bed, the youngster would have the coffee boiling and steaks sizzling on the hearth, and then he would move outside to feed the waiting stock. Jed was amazed as the youth was more adept at working the green buffalo hides than he was. Silent One even gave Jed tips on using the awls and hide scrapers needed to flesh out the heavy hides.

"You are good at this." Jed finally stopped forgetting the youngster couldn't hear him and would always get his attention before signaling.

"Yes, I should know, I was given to the women of my village to work." Silent One jerked the heavy hide. "They worked me as they would a captured slave."

"Your father and mother said nothing?"

"My father was killed in a raid on the Sioux." Silent One shrugged. "My mother could do nothing. She was given to my uncle Grey Badger and he too thought I was a cripple."

"And so you left?"

Again, the hands signaled. "I am a man, not a squaw to do woman's work."

Jed laughed as he signaled. "You are doing the same thing now."

"Here it is different, I work for myself and you." Silent One frowned.

Finally, the storm passed and Jed was quick to teach the youth the use of the white man's steel traps. While cooped up inside, Jed wove another pair of snowshoes for the young Assiniboine. Now, they were both striding along the valley's timbered area looking for places to set traps and snares.

"Remember where we set our traps." Jed looked at the youngster. "Tomorrow, you will run this end of the line and I will take the other end."

Nodding, Silent One signed. "I will remember, Tall One."

With the heavy storms, the fur bearers had been compelled to remain in their lair. Now, with the sun shining brightly across the snow covered landscape, fox, lynx, wolves, and every meat eater were out looking for food. The traps Jed had baited weren't always full, but they caught enough hungry varmints to keep Silent One busy skinning and stretching hides. The young Assiniboine conquered the younger black mule after she had dumped him unceremoniously a dozen times before she gave up and quit bucking. The molly mule was broke to carry a heavily laden packsaddle, but being a mule and naturally spooky and suspicious, live cargo was not to her liking. Jed was impressed with the youngster's grit and fortitude as he landed time and again head first, tail first, and on his back atop the snow covered ground. Finally, as quickly as she had started bucking, she quit cold and was docile as he swung up on her.

Laughing, Jed waved as Silent One rode the mule down the valley to the first of the trap lines. Mounting the piebald, Jed turned toward the north end of the valley. The weather was cold, below freezing, but the sun was warm as its bright rays peeked overhead from the east. Both men had traps and snares set at different ends of the valley, remote from the cabin and set back in the heavy forested areas of the huge valley. As the sun reached its zenith, Jed was high on the ridge. He was halfway through running his trap line, when he looked down at the valley floor to see the Assiniboine racing the black mule as fast as he could induce her to run toward him. Quickly mounting the piebald, Jed forgot the trap line and pushed the horse out onto the valley floor. Whatever was troubling the youngster had to be serious since there would be no other reason to run the mule across the deep snow.

Sliding his horse to a stop in front of the blowing mule, Jed quickly read the hands of the excited youth. "Enemy!"

"Enemy?" Jed looked down the valley. "Where?"

"There."

Jed watched as Silent One pointed to the southern end of the valley, then nodded. "You have done well, my friend. Could you tell what tribe they are?"

"They were too far to see clearly. It will take them time to work their way down the snowy trails." Silent One shook his head as he signed. "I think they are Blackfoot."

Jed was shocked. Why would raiders ride to these mountains in this kind of weather? The passes must be heavy with snow as the storm had just passed. What tribe could this be? Small Mountain, the name formed on Jed's lips as he thought of the warrior and his hate of the Arapaho. Never would he have thought the Blackfoot would ride here in the middle of winter with snow so deep in the passes. Jed had spared the warrior's life, so why did he ride to this valley in the cold times of winter? Perhaps it was other hunters, but if it was indeed Small Mountain, he knew there would be a fight today.

"We will ride to the cabin after the rifle. We'll find out who these warriors are and why they come to this valley." Jed turned the piebald back toward the cabin.

"That is easy Crow Killer." Silent One signaled before Jed turned away. "If they are Blackfoot, they want our scalps, horses, and anything they can steal."

Four Blackfoot warriors made their way slowly down the steep trail, pushing through the deeper snow where the drifts had formed at the edge of the tree line. Plowing through the drifts, the four riders rode out onto the flatter ground of the valley and started toward the cabin. Jed and Silent One watched from their place of concealment as the warriors followed in single file across the valley, breaking trail for one another. All were heavily armed carrying heavy bows, quivers full of arrows, heavy bull hide shields made from the thick neck hide of a bull buffalo hung from their backs, and war axes hung from their sides. As Jed watched the riders, there was no doubt, he knew they were coming here to raid and attack him. He tried to search the faces, but most were covered in animal hides to protect their faces from the cold. He could not detect if the Blackfoot Blue Darter rode with the warriors and for this he was thankful. Today in this valley, men would probably die, and he hoped Blue Darter was not among the raiding warriors.

"What will we do, Crow Killer?"

Jed shook his head as he watched the hands move. "I will ride out to meet them. You will wait here."

"Give me your bow and I will fight with you, my friend." Silent One moved his hands. "Even the great Crow Killer cannot fight four Blackfoot alone."

"You are young yet, Silent One. Wait here." Jed kicked the piebald forward from the trees to intersect the approaching riders. Stopping the horse, he turned back and handed his bow and quiver of arrows to the Assiniboine. "Stay here. If I am killed, use this bow and hopefully it will protect you."

"I will heed your words."

"Do you know the bow?"

Only a frown came from the youngster. "I am not a squaw."

Less than fifty feet separated Jed and the Blackfoot warriors as he rode from the cedars and stopped in the middle of the valley floor. The four warriors spread out in the knee-deep snow and sat their horses silently studying the lone warrior before them. Small Mountain grinned wickedly at Jed. Outnumbered four to one, he knew the advantage was with him, unlike the last time he had challenged the Arapaho. Today, he would have his revenge and wipe out the shame he felt of being beaten so easily.

"You have not left this valley, Arapaho."

"Nope, and I ain't fixing to either, Small Mountain." Jed turned the piebald, angling him sideways to the warriors. "Your hate must be great for you to ride so far from your lodges and women in the cold times?"

"It is below a Blackfoot to hate a lowly Arapaho." The big warrior raised his huge arm and screamed. "We talk no more! Now, you die Arapaho dog!"

The rifle belched fire and lead, knocking a warrior back off his horse into the snow. The warrior, in his eagerness to reach Jed first, had ridden in front of Small Mountain. Dropping the rifle to the ground and waving his war axe, Jed kicked the piebald and charged at the oncoming warriors. Only the tremendous power of the big paint and the swiftness of his legs saved Jed as he closed with the three warriors. Clinging to the side of the plunging horse, Jed smashed the heavy war axe into the head of the leading warrior. In their haste to kill the hated Arapaho, both of the remaining young Blackfoot had fired arrows hastily at the charging warrior, missing their target. Whirling their horses in the deep snow, the three opponents closed in, hand to hand fighting with their knives and war axes, slashing and cutting at one another. Their horses pushed and shoved, straining with all their might, as they surged forward through the snow. The piebald was a strong war horse, powerful and easy to handle, taller by two hands than the smaller Blackfoot ponies. The horse was well trained and seemed to enjoy the deadly combat as he pushed forward, biting and pawing at the other horses.

Whirling and slashing, Jed felt the bite of the Blackfoot blades as he fought off both remaining warriors. He tried to keep both of them on his left side and not let them get on both sides of his horse. The deep crusted snow was tiring the Blackfoot horses as their riders pushed them hard, trying to get in a killing position near the Arapaho. Blood seeped from several wounds as Jed warded off knife thrusts and axe blades from the two warriors.

Small Mountain charged forward yelling out in his eagerness to kill the Arapaho. "Now, Arapaho, I Small Mountain will have your scalp."

Jed felt the burning heat of the knife slashing into his shoulder as he was drug from the piebald by the other warrior, landing him in the snow under the Blackfoot. Rolling and struggling as the warrior stabbed him repeatedly, Jed finally rolled to his feet and slashed down hard with his war axe, killing the third warrior. Whirling to where Small Mountain was astride his horse, taking aim with his bow, Jed blinked in amazement as the big Blackfoot suddenly stiffened in pain and slid slowly to the ground. Amazed as he saw the arrow sticking from the warrior's back, Jed turned to where Silent One stood beside the black mule, holding his bow.

"I am sorry, Crow Killer. I know he was your kill, but I got excited and my arrow accidentally killed him."

Jed motioned his hands. "Thank you, my friend. You saved my life."

"No, you would have won if I had not spoiled your fight." Silent One nodded.

"Thank you, Silent One. Now, we are even."

"What will we do with the bodies?"

"Gather their horses and weapons, and tomorrow we will care for the bodies." Jed mounted the piebald slowly. "I go to the cabin."

"You do not want the scalps?"

"No, and you don't either."

"They come here for ours. I would scalp them." Silent One shook his head. "They were stupid and earned the right to lose their hair."

"No."

"Are you hurt badly?" The Assiniboine studied Jed's bloody shirt. "Your hunting shirt is bloody."

"Nothing serious, but I have lost blood." Jed looked down at his ripped and bloody hunting shirt. "Reckon I'll need another hunting shirt."

Jed sat before the fireplace as Silent One smeared bear grease on his many knife cuts. None were deep or serious, but all would leave scars on his body. Pulling a deer hide across his shoulders, Jed slipped slowly into his chair and accepted the cup of coffee he was offered.

"More will come here when these warriors do not return to their village." Silent One signaled. "Their people must know they have come here to this place to raid."

"I did not wish their deaths."

"No, but they are dead. Now, there will be no peace in this place." The youngster shrugged. "The Blackfoot will want revenge when they find out their people have been killed, and does not matter why they died."

"What do you think we should do?"

"Run." Silent One dropped his head. "I am no coward, but I think you have too many enemies here."

"And?"

"I think we should leave this place, find another."

"This I will not do, my young friend." Jed shook his head. "There are not enough enemies to drive me from this valley."

"I knew this would be your answer." Silent One shook his head sadly. "Then perhaps we will die here together."

Winter was long gone and the ice started to thaw, opening the running creeks. The deep snow started to disappear across the valley floor and along the high ridges. The sun could not reach the southern slopes, letting the snow up high, hold on longer. Jed remembered Hatcher's words of warning about the price of beaver hides so he had focused his traps on catching the land animals which would bring more. On the cold winter nights, as the wind howled and the snow beat against the cabin walls, both warriors worked on the buffalo robes the white traders prized so much. Now, four robes and two warm winter coats lay neatly folded in the corner of the cabin.

Sipping on his coffee, while Silent One was outside feeding the animals, Jed's thoughts turned to Sally Ann and his promise to come for her in the spring. He nodded slowly as spring was almost here and he would have to decide when to ride into Baxter Springs. Little Antelope and Walking Horse were also in his thoughts, as he wondered how they and the Arapaho people were doing. Looking at the warm fire burning in the rock fireplace and around his snug cabin, Jed nodded. He loved the valley and this cabin was his home. The trapping was almost over for the season, and soon the weather would be warm enough for him to ride west after her. Only the raging rivers, flooded from the winter snow thaw, had prevented him from riding north already. His thoughts turned to Hatcher, who said he would return in late summer. Maybe the trapper would have news of the Arapaho and how they fared.

The door squeaked open slowly as Silent One entered and removed his heavy trade coat, compliments of the dead Blackfoot. "The animals are fine, but we run short of grass to feed all of them."

Jed nodded. "I know, I only put up enough for three animals, but now we have seven to feed."

The youngster grinned. "There will be enough, besides I got me a fine Blackfoot horse to ride, not that mean little mule."

Jed laughed and looked at the youngster's arm where the mule had bitten him. "Well, she's a mule that's for sure."

"She is the reason I would never have a wife."

"What?"

"A woman will treat you good many years, then one day when you turn your back, she will bite you like the mule bit me."

"So now you know all about women?" Jed knew Silent One was against him going after Sally Ann.

"Not all, but I have watched the women in my village." Silent One signaled. "They can be mean like the mule. I have seen enough to keep far away from a squaw, any squaw."

Jed laughed out loud, making the youngster's face turn red. "One day you will think different, my young friend."

"I do not believe this, never."

The weather had remained above freezing, and only small amounts of snow had fallen in several days. Jed built a frame press to pack his furs into hundred pound bales. Working with flat pieces of strong oak, Jed fashioned another packsaddle for one of the Blackfoot horses. Using left-over buffalo hide striping, he lined the swells underneath to protect the horse's withers.

"You will need four packhorses?" Silent One was busy folding pelts, getting them ready for the press. Still, he watched Jed with curiosity.

"The red mule is too old to carry two bundles over the mountain." Jed nodded. "She will stay here with you."

"Ugh." Silent One frowned. "That will leave me the black devil to ride while you are away."

"Sorry."

"How will you cross the mighty river to the north?"

"The Snake." Jed didn't know the Assiniboine had been that far north. "I'll take my axe with me and make a raft to float the furs across."

"The water will be cold this time of year." Silent One signed. "I am a good swimmer."

"No, someone must stay here and watch over the stock and cabin." Jed knew what he was asking.

"What if the Blackfoot come here into this valley while you are gone?" The youngster pouted. "They could have me for dinner."

Jed knew the youngster wasn't worried about the Blackfoot, he just wanted to go. "Then you better be able to fight or run."

"I hear they eat young Assiniboine boys." Silent One insisted.

"You would be bitter." Jed shook his head. "Stay here and tend the stock. When I return, I'll bring you a rifle just like mine."

Smiling, Silent One nodded, then signaled his okay. "I will stay."

"You know, I figured you would at that." Jed nodded. "You stay alert, young man, and keep watch. If the Blackfoot come here, you hide and do not try to fight them."

"I am deaf, Crow Killer, not stupid."

"You remember that."

The pack animals were lined out and tied in line from their pack-saddles. Jed knew Hatcher had tied the mules tail to tail, but he also knew the Blackfoot ponies weren't about to go for that. He sure didn't want the horses to buck themselves bare at the first jerk of the rope on their tails. Walking from the cabin to where Silent One held the piebald, Jed checked each animal over and nodded at the youngster.

"Will you be alright while I'm away?"

"I will be okay." The hands fairly flew in their response. "How long will you be gone?"

"Maybe a whole moon, maybe less, but no more."

"That is good." Silent One nodded as his hands worked. "Is there anything you want me to do while you are gone?"

Jed swung upon the piebald and looked down at the youngster, who he had grown fond of and one he had come to care for as family. "Just stay safe and always be watchful."

"I will watch like a hawk, slip around like a panther, and run like a coyote if I see something." Silent One grinned.

"They will come from the south if they come so watch over there real close."

"I will be fine, Crow Killer, but you are the one that better watch carefully."

"What for?"

"The white squaw you go after might bite you as the mule did me."

Jed thought of the fiery Sally Ann. "You might be right about that, little friend."

CHAPTER 3

The trails were clear of most of the snow, but Jed found them muddy and slick as the barefoot horses slipped and slid down the steeper parts of the mountains. He knew a good set of the white man's heel caulks would sure be nice to stop most of the sliding. On the rougher places, he slowed the pack animals and let them pick their way cautiously down the muddy trails. For two days, he followed the animal trail to the north and west, the same trail he had followed east after killing Abe and Vern. The mighty Snake River should come into view just over the next rise. Baxter Springs and Sally Ann were only a couple days away, depending on how long it would take him to build a raft heavy enough to ferry his furs across.

Riding onto the gravel bank of the Snake, Jed looked across the great river. From the higher ridges, he figured the river was up some, but it wasn't as high as he feared it would be. Now, he would build a raft, lash it together, and load his pelts. Next, he would have to get the burden-laden craft steered safely across, without getting the pelts wet. He had watched Lige Hatcher and Chalk Briggs build one to ferry a wagon load of immigrants across the mighty Missouri many years ago. The rudder would be the hard part. The raft would be too clumsy and heavy to steer with just a homemade paddle, and the river was far too deep to use a pole. Unloading the animals, he hobbled them on the new sweet grass alongside the river. The piebald finally bonded with him and usually came when beckoned with just a whistle, but today Jed wasn't taking any chances with the big paint so he hobbled him with the others.

The ringing of the axe sent chopping sounds up and down the river as Jed felled trees. Finally, after a day of backbreaking work, Jed stood back and surveyed his handy work. The raft was finished, lashed together with rawhide strips Jed had brought along. The cedar logs he used were lighter and would ride higher on the water, keeping his valuable load dry. He decided to cross the raft loaded with furs first, at least he would be dry on the first trip across, and he hoped there would be no unforeseen problems. He tested the raft by tying a rope to a stout elm tree by the riverbank, then he let the craft with him aboard, drift into water deep enough to float. Satisfied the raft would carry his heavy bundles of furs, high above the current, Jed pulled the float back to shore to start loading. He knew the river current would carry him downstream, but with the rough-made rudder, he hoped to guide it a little.

After loading the raft, Jed was a little nervous at the thought of losing his hard winter's work so he studied the river current carefully. Finally satisfied, he quickly checked on the animals. Finding the hobbles tight, he turned with a shrug, then untied the raft and poled out into the current. His fears subsided as the double layered raft floated high in the water, keeping his furs well above the river water. Jed was surprised and thankful the rudder was working better than he had hoped. As the current caught the raft it bobbed and twisted, but the rudder accomplished its job, pointing the craft toward the far shore. Jed grinned as the raft drifted downstream, safely making the crossing as it touched the gravel bar, grounding itself long enough for him to jump ashore and secure the craft to the nearest tree. Nodding thankfully as he tied off the raft with its valuable cargo, Jed looked back across the river where the horses stood grazing.

"Now, for the cold part." Jed knew the swim across and back with the animals would be cold and tiring, but he wasn't about to leave his winter catch, rifle, and possibles bag unprotected on the riverbank.

Slipping his leather hunting shirt and leggings off as he walked back up the shore, directly across from the horses, Jed waded naked into the cold water. Shivers ran up his shoulders as he moved out into the deep river and studied both banks. Seeing nothing, he pushed off with his strong legs kicking hard. The current was fast and strong as it pulled him downstream, but since childhood Jed had always been a strong swimmer. Stroking hard, he crossed the river and trotted back upstream to the horses. He knew he was alone on the river, but the idea of being buck naked and someone riding up on him was embarrassing to think about, so Jed lost no time trying to warm himself.

Removing the hobbles, Jed led all four animals to the riverbank and mounted the piebald. He knew his horse was a powerful swimmer, but the rest he wasn't sure of. The Blackfoot brought them to his cabin from the west, so they had to cross deep water at least once. Kicking the piebald into the river, Jed slid from his back and held onto the horse's mane to help paddle across as they hit swimming water. As the raft drifted downstream, so did the horses, splashing ashore just yards from the moored raft and bundles of furs. Quickly dressing, Jed looked up at the sky, dark was only two hours away, not long enough to make it worthwhile to reload the pack animals and make any miles before sundown.

Tethering the animals along the shore, Jed quickly unloaded the raft and packed the heavy bundles back into the trees, away from the river. Using the piebald, Jed towed the raft into a backwater cove and pulled the heavy raft far onto the bank, up on dry land, to keep it safe. Quickly piling loose brush and limbs across the raft, he tied the craft securely to an elm tree. Finally, he was satisfied the raft would be safe until he returned from Baxter Springs with Sally Ann. Jed led the piebald back to where the other horses stood tied and then kicked together a small fire. Checking his rifle, he walked to where the remnants of Abe and Vern's camp had been. Surveying the deserted camp, he strolled about the desolate campsite. Only two grave markers and an old circle of fire-blackened rocks remained of their campsite, everything else had been removed. Jed wondered if Lige Hatcher took the furs and supplies back to Baxter Springs or maybe someone pilfered the camp.

Late evening of his second day from the river found Jed passing the farmhouse where he had first asked about his stepfather many months ago. The owner waved as the pack train passed, but Jed didn't stop to talk to the farmer. Riding into Baxter Springs at sundown, he reined in at the tie rack in front of the sign that read, "Fur Buyer." Jed looked up and down the street as people stood in every doorway, craning their necks to see him. Slipping to the ground, he tied the tired horses and pushed open the store's front door. The putrid smell of green hides, a smell he was well accustomed to, accosted his nose. The rotund form of Bate Baker, a man Jed remembered from the wagon train, looked up from his ledger book and squinted at the newcomer.

"Come in, young man, can I help you?" Baker looked Jed up and down closely, but the buckskins, long hair, and dark skin made him take a second look.

"I've got furs outside to sell."

"You Injun, boy?" Baker studied the long scar running down Jed's face.

"Does it matter, the furs ain't."

"You talk good American for an Injun."

"Cut the talk, you know me, Mister Baker. You buying or not?"

"Now, take it easy, young feller." The fat man removed his eyeglasses. "Oh yes, now I remember. You're Jed Bracket; stepson of Ed Wilson ain't you?"

"I am."

"You've changed a lot, boy." Baker looked through the open doorway. "You say your furs are outside?"

"Yes, sir." Jed thumbed over his shoulder. "My horses are tied to your hitching rail."

"I'm buying. Fetch them in here so I can grade their quality."

Jed stacked the bundles side by side on the long counter, and then cut the rawhide strips binding the bales. Replacing his knife, he watched as Baker smelled, blew, and felt the well-tanned hides as a mother would pet a newborn. Nodding his head greedily as he counted and separated the pelts, Baker made several pencil marks on a paper, then looked over his glasses at Jed.

"Well, young man, seems you had a good year." Baker patted the pelts almost lovingly. "I make the count at one hundred seven beaver, thirty-two silver fox, eighteen wolves, twelve otter, four buffalo robes, and fifty-five assorted badger, bobcat, cougar, and skunk hides."

"You count good." Jed could see the greed flashing from the buyer's eyes every time he stroked the pelts.

"That's a powerful lot of money, boy."

"Sounds good to me."

"I can use all except the beaver, they ain't bringing nothing nowadays." Baker looked across at Jed. "They're worthless to me so you'll have to sell them somewhere else."

"Nope." Jed placed the buffalo coats, he and Silent Owl had worked on so many hours over the winter, on the counter, and then started repacking the bales of hides. "All or none."

"I'm the only buyer in Baxter Springs, young man." Baker eyed the coats hungrily. "Take my price or leave it."

"I'll be leaving it, Mister Baker. There's other towns to the east."

As Jed started to heft his first bundle of furs, Baker picked up one of the coats. "Now, don't be hasty, young man. How much you figuring on wanting for these coats."

"They ain't for sale if the beaver don't go with the deal."

"Alright, alright." Baker was almost foaming at the mouth. He was so eager to get his hands on the coats, they were beautiful. In the North Country, warm coats were hard to find and in great demand. "If the coats are priced right, I'll take them all."

"You're doing the pricing, Mister Baker." Jed smiled. "If your price is right, you've got 'em."

After recounting the pelts along with the coats and figuring on a piece of brown paper, Baker pulled out a box of coins. "You're a hard dealer, Jed."

"You remembered my name after all." Jed read the numbers Baker handed him. "This will do fine."

"Ain't my fault, in those hides you look and smell Injun." Baker counted the gold coins out to Jed, and placed them in a leather bag. "Here's your money. If I was you, I'd put some of that gold to good use and get out of those Injun duds."

"You ain't me, Mister Baker." Jed shook the heavy bag of coins and walked from the store. "And sir, you are right, I can be mighty headstrong sometimes."

"You know Constable Duncan is looking for you, don't you?"

"I figure he'll be seeing me soon enough."

"One other thing, boy." Baker pointed at the beaver pelts. "Don't expect me to let you hold me up next year on these."

Jed grinned. "Why Mister Baker, I'm just a poor old Injun trapper. How could I hold up a smart trader like you?"

Seth hesitated, then looked up from where he was at the chopping block, splitting wood. Seeing Jed riding up to the house, leading three horses, he hollered to where Ed Wilson sat in the barn milking. Sinking the double-bladed axe deep into the chopping block, Seth waved and walked to where Jed dismounted.

"Well, I see you're back."

"I'm back for a day or two."

"Pa sent you supplies. Now what are you needing, stepbrother?"

"Jedidiah." Ed Wilson's booming voice called out as he exited the barn with a bucket of warm milk. "You're back, boy."

Jed smiled as he was truly fond of his stepfather. "I believe I owe you some money."

"Them supplies were a gift from your mother and me, boy." Wilson shook hands with Jed. "You owe me nothing."

"I owe you, Pa."

"Far as I'm concerned, you don't." Wilson smiled. "But, if'n you're determined to pay, I figure I've got ten dollars coming."

"Ten dollars!" Seth almost choked when he heard the amount. "That's all?"

"Mite short, wouldn't you say, Seth?" Jed grinned at his red-faced stepbrother.

"Ten dollars." Wilson repeated. "Not a penny more."

"All right then." Jed knew Ed Wilson. He knew the man was set in his ways. "Ten dollars it is. I'm thanking you, Pa. Those supplies came in mighty handy, that was kind of you."

"You're welcome." Wilson nodded. "Now, come along with you and let's put some vittles in that lean stomach of yours."

Seth followed Jed and Wilson to the house with an armload of wood. "You come after Sally Ann? Rumor has it you're fixing to marry up with her."

"Figuring on it."

"That ain't gonna sit well with old man Duncan." Seth dumped the wood in the wood box beside the stove. "No, sir. Said he'd peg your hide to his smokehouse if'n you try to take her away from Baxter Springs."

Wilson shoved sticks of wood into the stove and opened the damper. "That ain't none of your business. You best stay out of it."

"Just warning my stepbrother. Wouldn't want his hide stretched on an old smokehouse wall would we?" Seth shrugged. "I'll toss your horses some corn and hay."

"That'll be enough, Seth Wilson."

"Yes, sir."

"Seth talks too much, Jed, but he speaks the truth." Wilson replaced the stove lid as the fire flared up. "Duncan has spoken against you and Sally Ann right along."

"How old do you figure Sally Ann is now?"

"She's twenty." Seth spoke up.

"Then she's old enough to make up her own mind."

"Maybe she is, but Duncan is the he hog around here." Wilson placed side meat in the iron skillet. "What he says normally goes in these parts."

"I've seen his eyes, Jed." Seth grinned. "They light up like fire when your name is mentioned."

"What about Sally Ann?" Jed looked at Seth. "What does she say, or does it matter none?"

"Don't matter a spoonful to old man Duncan what she thinks." Seth snickered. "No, sir, not one little bit."

Wilson nodded. "Seth's right for once, you watch that one."

"He's an old man."

"Yep, he is, but that old man has plenty of help in Baxter Springs." Seth nodded in agreement.

"Who?"

"I done told you, brother. Every man in the settlement is in love with your girl. They sure ain't about to let you waltz in here and take her off somewhere to live like no red Injun."

"They fixing to die over her?"

"You are, ain't you?" Seth grinned. "Sides, there's still the matter of poor old Abe and Vern getting themselves ambushed."

"I told you, Seth, shut your mouth." Wilson turned from the stove. "Not another word."

Seth shrugged. "I just want to let Jed know what he's in for is all."

"Thank you, Seth. You've given me a pretty good idea." Jed watched Seth's eyes. "I reckon I'll ride over in the morning and speak with Mister Amos Duncan."

With supper over, the three men sat on the front porch stoop. Wilson told of their trip west after Jed had been lost and how they had homesteaded the land they were farming. In turn, Jed told of his exploits with the Arapaho after falling from the wagon.

"I'm telling you Jed, in the storm and excitement, me and Billy didn't even know you had fallen from the wagon for several minutes." Seth whittled on a small stick. "Then it was too late to help you."

"Lige and the boys searched the river for you for two days."

"Yeah, he told me."

"You've spoken with Lige then, since Billy was killed?" Seth cocked his head.

Jed nodded. "He knows Billy is dead, if that is what you're asking."

"Yeah, we know that, brother." Seth frowned. "He reported his death to Mister Duncan, also the killing of Abe and Vern."

"It wasn't a killing; it was a case of self-defense."

Wilson looked across the table at Jed. "You want to tell of it, Jed?"

"Nope, ain't nothing worth telling."

"Killing a man is something to talk about, least for me it is." Seth spoke up. "I ain't never killed me a man yet."

"We won't speak of it anymore." Wilson lit his pipe, and looked hard at Seth. "No more, not one word."

"Yes, sir." Seth knew when he had pushed the older Wilson too far. "What about Sally Ann?"

Jed looked sideways at the redhead. "What about her?"

"After all I told you." Seth cut a long sliver of wood from his stick. "You still aiming to sashay out of here with her?"

"If she's willing, I am."

Wilson smiled. "I reckon the young lady is willing."

"This could be quite a show, if I know Mister Duncan." Seth laughed. "You'll have a fight on your hands, I bet."

Wilson nodded slowly. "We'll be here if you need us."

"No, Pa. This is your home and you have to live here with these people." Jed shook his head. "I'll fight my own battles."

"You'll be outnumbered, Brother."

Jed thought about the troubles of the past. "Won't be nothing new."

"Well, just the same, if you need us, we'll be here."

"Thank you, I know you will be."

Seth stood up and stretched. "When you going after her?"

"Come daylight, like I said. Ain't no sense putting it off and waiting for trouble to catch up to me here."

"If'n it were me, I'd sneak her out after dark." Seth leaned back against a porch pole. "Lot safer that way."

"No, I ain't sneaking around. We'll be coming and going, and doing our trading in Baxter Springs for many years to come. 'Sides, we got to go into the settlement to get married."

Seth shook his head. "Brother, you're just asking to be shot or hanged if you ride into town in broad daylight with marrying up on your mind."

"That's the Christian way, Seth." Wilson spoke up. "Wouldn't hurt you none to read the Bible."

"Not me, no sir, that's the dead man's way."

"Pay him no attention, Jed." Wilson glared at Seth. "I told you, we'll back you in this."

"Does she even know you're in these parts?"

"No, I stopped here first. Like I said, I'll be riding to Duncan's come sunup."

"Well, we'll be here when you ride back this way." Wilson stood up. "We're family, Jed, and blood sticks by blood."

"Thank you, Pa."

"If you make it back this way…" Seth had to get the last word in before heading for bed. "I'll be seeing you."

Daylight was just breaking in the eastern sky when Jed started the piebald to the west, toward the Duncan farm. Before leaving, he fed the horses a large helping of Wilson's corn, then went in the house for coffee and breakfast before riding out. He knew his stepfather was worrying far more than he was letting on. Jed knew Seth's warnings were probably true; the younger men in the settlement could be dangerous when they find out he's coming for Sally Ann. He knew men in the west never interfered with a woman's choice in a husband, as it could be dangerous, even deadly. No, someone was putting the young men in Baxter Springs up to stopping Jed and keeping her from leaving the settlement. It had to be Duncan; no one else would dare interfere without some prompting. Only small talk came from the table as their breakfast was quickly eaten. Standing, Jed said his goodbyes, walked to the barn, and led the horses from the corral. Swinging up on the piebald, he hit a short lope to the west as a slight pang of loneliness swept over him as he remembered his stepdad and mother. Looking back once, he could barely make out Ed Wilson standing in front of the barn waving.

Less than a mile from the Wilson farm, Jed watched as two riders emerged from a stand of trees alongside the trail. Both riders were young men, carrying a hard look on their faces as they sat their horses, blocking the sandy road leading to the Duncan farm. Jed said nothing as he reined in his horse, less than twenty feet from the two strangers.

The bigger of the two pointed his rifle in Jed's direction. "You gotta be Jed Bracket, ain't you, pilgrim?"

"Looks like a red Injun to me, Luke." The other rider grinned. "I can smell him from here."

"Tell me, Willie, what would a looker like Sally Ann see in something like him?"

"Beats me, he's about the sorriest looking critter I've seen around these parts."

Jed pushed the piebald closer to the two riders. "You boys gonna talk me to death, or are you gonna tell me what you want?"

"Well, what do you know, this Injun talks, Luke."

"Sounds to me like talk, Willie, smart talk." The one called Luke nodded. "No, Mister Bracket, we're not here to start a fight yet, just to pass on a little warning to you."

"Warn me, about what?"

"You ain't taking Sally Ann from here." The face of the rider turned cold, no longer attempting to hide his thoughts. "You hear me good, Injun. Don't try to take Sally Ann from Baxter Springs. This is your first and last warning."

"Well now, I appreciate a good warning like that, Luke." Jed fingered his war axe. "That is your name isn't it, Luke?"

"It's my name."

"I've been warned. Now, get out of my way." Jed kicked the piebald forward, shouldering the powerful horse into the smaller horses blocking the road.

Jed watched the two men's faces as he pushed between them, knocking them sideways. They were primed, and he knew they wanted to fight, but something held them back. They were well armed with rifles and pistols protruding from their coats and belts. The two weren't scared in the least as Jed could see in their faces, arrogance and self-confidence issued from both young men. Still, they made no move as they watched him ride away, only staring after him before turning their horses toward Baxter Springs. Jed knew the trouble wasn't over. Whoever they were speaking for didn't want him dead yet, but if he insisted on taking Sally Ann from the settlement that could quickly change. Again, kicking the piebald into a short lope, the horses being led, kicked up a dust cloud as he neared the Duncan Farm.

A white rooster crowed defiantly from his perch on a fencepost as Jed reined in at the house and disturbed him. Slipping easily to the ground, Jed looked at the farmhouse as the screen door screeched open. Sally Ann emerged from the porch as Amos Duncan was carrying a bucket of milk from the barn. Stopping quickly when he saw the horses and their rider, Duncan almost sloshed his milk on the ground.

Jumping from the porch, Sally Ann rushed to his side and hugged him tightly, then looked to where Duncan was striding toward them. "I told you, Pa, he'd come."

"I was hoping you wouldn't come back here, Jed Bracket." Duncan passed them without stopping. "Bring the young man in, Sally. We've got words to speak. At least we'll act civilized."

Winking up at Jed, she took the reins of the piebald and led him to the corral. "We'll be in, soon as I feed his horses, Pa."

"Don't you get any ideas about riding out without our talk, girl."

"We ain't running, Mister Duncan. You best get that in your mind." Jed's voice grew hard. "I already told your men earlier this morning."

"My men?" Turning, Duncan looked the buckskin-clad young man up and down. "What men? No one works for me."

"A rough looking pair stopped me earlier on the road." Jed stared hard at Duncan. "I ain't looking for trouble, sir, but I'll not turn from it either."

"Hatcher said you were a hard case."

"I am."

Entering the barn, out of sight of the house, Sally Ann threw herself into his arms, kissing him hard. "Oh Jed, you did come. I couldn't hardly stand it all winter. I almost got the ailments with the waiting and all."

"Your dad is going to cause trouble, ain't he?"

"We'll go in and talk with him." Sally Ann assured him as she reached for several ears of corn. "He'll come around okay."

"No corn, they've had plenty. Hay will do." Jed stopped her. "Tell me straight, are you still wanting to marry me and go back to the mountains to live?"

Jed could see the color come into her face as she stepped back. "Are you taking me for a loose woman, Jedidiah Bracket? I don't go around kissing men like I just kissed you."

"I wasn't calling you a loose woman." Jed smiled slightly. "I just want you to know, if we try to get married and leave here, there could be bad trouble."

"Trouble be hanged. I'm a full-grown woman, white and free." She moved closer to him. "I'll marry who I please, and mister, that happens to be you. I love you, Jedidiah, and don't you be forgetting it."

"'If you're sure." Jed smiled down at her. "Today, we will ride into Baxter Springs to be married, and then we'll return to our valley."

"Is it really as beautiful as Lige Hatcher says?" She smiled widely. "Is it really, Jed?"

"No, young lady it isn't, it is more beautiful."

Sally Ann whirled and laughed with glee. "But, you don't even know what he said about the valley."

"Don't have to know, mere words cannot express its beauty."

"Oh Jed, is it really that beautiful?" She laughed. "He said your valley was magical."

"Our valley and it is." Jed smiled as she threw back her head with joy. "It's spectacular, majestic beyond words."

"I can't wait to see it, and the cabin." Sally Ann laughed out loud, making the horses shy sideways. "I just can't wait to see it all."

"It's just a small log cabin, Sally Ann, nothing like your house here."

"There's where you're wrong, Jed." She whirled again, her face turned to him in rapture. "It'll be ours and I'll have you, and that makes a home."

"Then the sooner we get your pa satisfied we're leaving, the sooner we can return to your new home."

"Hurry, Jed, I can't wait. I just know I'll explode from excitement." Sally Ann pushed him toward the house.

Even with the heat, coming from the wood cookstove, the small kitchen was cool like a snowy mountain slope as Jed and Sally Ann stepped into the room. Tension was as thick as a heavy fog on a cold damp morning as they took seats around the wooden table.

"You hungry, Mister Bracket?" Duncan flipped fried side meat in the iron skillet.

"No sir, thank you." Jed accepted the cup of coffee placed before him. "I ate before riding over this morning."

"There's plenty." Duncan looked down at the skillet. "You best eat before you ride back to your mountains."

"No, thank you."

"I guess you two need to say your good-byes so you can get on the road." Duncan turned from the stove. "Wouldn't want to hold you up."

"When I ride out, Mister Duncan." Jed pushed the cup back, looking over at the older man. "Sally Ann will be going with me to Baxter Springs, where we intend to be married."

"You try that and I'll have you hung for the killing of Vern Grey and Abe Stone." Duncan slammed the skillet down hard. "I'm warning you."

"I've been warned already twice this morning." Jed stood up. "I would like to have your blessings, sir, but we'll be married without them, if need be."

"Listen to sense, boy. Stay here in civilization and you will have my blessings." Duncan blustered. "Sally Ann is a lady, raised in comfort. She's not fit to stand the harshness of them mountains like your Indian women."

"No, Pa, you're wrong." Sally Ann stood up. "I'm as strong as any woman, red or white. We're going to live at Jed's cabin. Lige told you about it."

"You best listen to reason, girl." Duncan looked over to where his rifle rested. "You're aiming to get him killed, if you ride with him into Baxter Springs."

"I'm leaving, Pa. That rifle and your authority aren't stopping us from getting married." Sally Ann looked at the rifle. "If Jed's killed, I'll be beside him and you'll have to kill me too, one way or another."

"Then leave, get out and don't come back." Duncan pointed at the door.

"You can't mean that, Mister Duncan. She is your daughter."

"Try me, if she leaves with you." Duncan raised his hands. "I don't ever want to see her face again. I've had my say."

"I asked you to let me go with your blessing but you couldn't do that, could you?"

"I'll not give my blessing to you, going into those mountains to be killed by wild Indians or worse."

"If I am killed, I'll die happy with Jed." Sally Ann started for her bedroom. "You just don't understand."

Sally Ann rode one of the Blackfoot horses taken from Small Mountain and his warriors. The packsaddle she sat on was heavily padded with soft robes to make it more comfortable for her, as she wasn't used to riding horseback. Jed had left the old red mule back in the valley, not wanting to bring her over the rough mountain trails. He didn't trust the black mule, Silent One had been riding, so he left her behind for the youngster. That left only one of the half-wild horses of the Blackfoot for her to ride. Sally Ann didn't care what she rode, she was elated that Jed finally came for her, and she was going home. Now, all they had to do was stop in Baxter Springs, get married, pick up supplies, and then they would head to their magical valley.

"Oh Jed, I can't believe we're actually on our way." Sally Ann smiled widely over at Jed. "We're going home, our home."

Her enthusiasm and happiness was invigorating, spreading to where Jed led the other horses. "Yes, we are, but first we have to worry about Baxter Springs."

Bringing herself back to reality, she rode closer to the piebald. "Do you think there could be trouble in the settlement?"

"There could be." Jed thought of the two young riders. "Yes, there probably will be some sort of trouble."

Sally Ann remembered Seth's visit to her farm earlier in the week and the threats he had made. She didn't mention Seth's actions to Jed.

She didn't like or trust Ed Wilson's oldest son, and in his own way he was as mean as or meaner than Billy Wilson. She's known him for several years, and the redhead was sneaky, cruel, and worse than a loafer wolf.

"Couldn't we just bypass Baxter Springs?"

"Where would we get married or get the supplies we need?" Jed shook his head. "No, Sally Ann, we have to go in."

"We don't have to get married." She winked. "We could live in sin, or maybe one of your Indians could marry us."

Jed laughed, knowing she was joking. "We'll be married in the settlement."

Sally Ann looked at the Hawken rifle that rested across the withers of the piebald, and the bow and quiver of arrows strapped across his back. She knew he would not waver and hoped that her father would give in and stop the young men in town from causing trouble. Wilson's farm came into view almost at noon, where two horses stood tied in front of the house. Jed didn't stop, just rode on by the farm, not even looking over at the house. If he could help it, he didn't want his stepfather involved in whatever was fixing to take place ahead in the settlement. Ed Wilson had to live here with these people, while he and Sally Ann could move back into the deepest reaches of the mountains, far away from the problems of Baxter Springs. No, he didn't want his stepfather bringing trouble down on himself.

Twenty minutes later, the hard drumming of a lone horse brought Jed up short, reining in the piebald. Ed Wilson pulled his blowing horse in beside the group of horses.

"You didn't stop to pay your respects when you passed."

"I told you, Pa, you need not get mixed up in this." Jed shook his head. "Go back home."

"You're my son, Jed. Whatever happens, I aim to stand by you in town." Wilson grinned. "Besides, you'll have to have someone stand up for you to give this beautiful young lady away."

"You're a hardheaded man, but I'm thanking you." Jed nodded and looked up at the near ridge. "Someone's up there, Pa."

Wilson followed his gaze and watched as a lone rider crossed over a small ridge off to the south. "I fear that is Seth taking a shortcut over the ridge, trying to get to Baxter Springs ahead of us."

"Why would he do that, Mister Wilson?" Sally Ann watched as the rider disappeared.

"If trouble starts, I'm afraid Seth may side in with the young men in town." Wilson dropped his head. "I'm sorry, Jed."

Sally Ann stared hard at the big man. "He would side against you?"

"Seth has feelings for you, Sally Ann." Wilson's face turned red. "I'm afraid he's behind most of these problems, even more than your dad."

"That's even more reason for you to stay clear of this, Pa."

"I've seen his face, son. He's crazy jealous of you and Sally Ann."

"He's never showed that to me, but once, Mister Wilson." Sally Ann remembered the night in the barn.

"I don't think he cares for you, me, or anybody, missy. He's just like his brother Billy, he has to win at everything, and that's you."

"Maybe that's more reason for you to stay clear of these doings." Jed was worried for his stepdad.

"No, Jed, that's exactly why I should take a hand." Wilson shook his head. "I've let my boys get away with causing trouble for far too long."

The town of Baxter Springs was completely silent except for an occasional dog barking as the three riders, leading the pack animals, plodded down the dusty main street, reining in at the General Store. No one milled about on the porches, but every window was occupied with curious people watching as they dismounted and entered the store. Several customers inside the store recognized them and quickly stopped what they were doing. They made a rush for the door, pushing past them in their hurry to vacate the store. The store clerk glanced briefly at the exiting people with a frown, then turned his attention to Wilson and Sally Ann as they walked toward the long counter. Visibly shaken, the clerk's eyes kept returning to the empty doorway and back to them.

"Ed Wilson." The voice was strained. "What can I do for you today?"

Wilson looked at the door as the people disappeared. "They act like we got the plague or something."

"Could be worse than that, Ed."

"These young folks want to be married, Elmer." Wilson nodded at Jed and Sally Ann. "And they'll be needing supplies."

"Uh huh."

"Now, you remember my stepson, Jedidiah Bracket, don't you?" Wilson smiled easily. "Jed, you remember, Mister Woods?"

"Yes, sir. I remember him." Jed stared over at the store man.

"I've got the supplies sure enough, providing they've got the money to pay, but I ain't no preacher." The one called Elmer regained his courage.

"I've got money for supplies and for supplies Lige Hatcher put on credit last year."

"Yes, yes." The store man mumbled nervously under his breath. "I had forgotten about them."

"Now, we know that you ain't no preacher, Elmer, but you could fetch Reverend Miller, couldn't you?"

"I s'pect I could do that."

Wilson smiled. "Good, first let's get Jed's supplies and get them loaded."

"You must be in a hurry." Woods was noticeably scared.

"They are for sure." Wilson agreed. "Now, let's shake a leg, okay?"

Jed stood by the window, watching the street as bags of supplies were piled on the long counter. Motioning for Sally Ann to pick out what she needed, he turned his attention to the Fur Trading Post directly across the street where several men were gathering. Two young men stood in front of the others, the same two that had given him a warning earlier when he was riding from the Wilson farm. Seth Wilson or Duncan was not in the group, or at least they didn't put in an appearance.

"You know they'll never let you leave town with her, don't you?" The store clerk looked through the window.

"Do tell." Jed slipped a hardtack cracker in his mouth. "She'll be my wife. How are they gonna stop me?"

"Duncan has posted you for killing those two trappers." Elmer pushed flour sacks in the hand-sewn skin bags, Jed had made over the winter. "That's the excuse they'll use."

"But, it's really Sally Ann, huh?"

"That's about the size of it, young feller." Elmer nodded. "Most of them are in love with her."

"What kind of men or law y'all got in this town?"

"Duncan's law, that's what." Woods swallowed hard, wanting out of the situation he found himself in. "He's dead set against you taking her away from here, married or not."

"Tell you what, Elmer." Wilson looked across the street at the gathered men. "We'll load the pack animals while you go round up the good reverend."

"And if he won't come, Ed?"

"Now, he wouldn't want this young couple living in sin, would he?"

"I'll go find him." Relieved to get away, the small clerk ducked hastily through the door.

Following the store owner as he hurried from the store, Wilson moved to the front door. Several men, armed with rifles, stood in front of the trading post, staring across the dusty street. No one made a move. They all seemed to be waiting for the trouble they knew was coming.

"You two wait here for the minister." Wilson studied the group of gathering men uneasily. "I'll go out and load your animals."

"No, Pa, stay in here with Sally Ann. I'll pack the horses." Jed stepped in front of Wilson. "If they start trouble, I want you two in here, out of danger."

"Alright, son, I'll cover you from the store."

Grabbing two leather bags full of flour, sugar, and other needed supplies, Jed stepped from the store into the bright sunshine. His dark eyes took in the surly group of young men, but so far nothing was said, nor did the men move. Strapping both leather bags on the first horse, Jed turned his attention to where the group stood glaring, talking, and shaking their heads. Jed recognized the store man, Elmer Woods and another man dressed in black broadcloth, the attire of a minister as they appeared on the boardwalk, walking toward the store.

Two of the men, the same ones that had warned him earlier in the day, stepped out from the group and raised their hands. "You turn around now, Preacher. You ain't doing any marrying today."

Both men stopped, studying the rifles pointed at them. "You are interfering with God's work, Luke Grisham."

"No, Preacher. I'm stopping you from marrying Sally Ann to a heathen red Injun and killer."

"I'm going into the store, Luke." Reverend Miller stepped forward. "Now, you put that rifle down before someone gets hurt."

The rifle rose slightly. "You take one more step and you're a dead man, Preacher."

Willie stepped forward and grinned, pointing his rifle. "I think I'll take a piece of your ear right now, Elmer."

Turning abruptly, the store owner quickly disappeared down a side alley. Standing alone, the preacher straightened his coat and started forward as Jed raised his hand. "Stay back, getting married today ain't worth you getting hurt over."

"You ain't marrying Sally Ann today or any day, and you sure ain't leaving town with her, Injun." Luke turned to Jed. "Willie, you watch the preacher, if he moves, take off one of his legs."

Several of the men watching, shook their heads and moved back from the confrontation. Stopping what they thought was an Indian from taking a white woman into the mountains was one thing, but threatening to shoot the town's preacher, a man of the cloth, was entirely another. In seconds, only a few of the men were left and Jed could see the rest were wavering with uncertainty. They didn't figure on a real shooting to stop the wedding as they were told only a small bluff would be needed. Moving away from the packhorse, Jed smiled across at Luke.

"Your friends quit so why don't we settle this, just you and me, Luke?" Jed stood his rifle against the porch post and touched his knife. "If you're man enough, that is. Tell you what, you can have Willie there help you."

"Alright, Injun. Put your rifle down, Willie, let's see how tough this red heathen is." Luke grinned widely and started to stand his rifle against a tie rail. "A knife is as good as a rifle ball."

Suddenly, from the alleyway beside the trading post, two rifles roared. One bullet missed Jed by inches and the other cut a flesh wound in his side. Both of the heavy caliber bullets thudded into the storefront, punching their way through the thin board walls.

Throwing his hands in the air in shock as he saw Jed lunge for his rifle, Luke backed away from the confrontation, hollering at Jed. "It weren't us that fired, Injun." Luke backed away from the street. "It weren't us."

"You set me up, Luke." Jed raised the rifle. "You low life polecat."

"No, we were just trying to bluff you into leaving." The man was scared. "We didn't aim to shoot anyone."

"Well, you bluffed me, sure enough." Jed's finger tightened on the set trigger just as a running horse came racing down the street, taking his attention away from Luke.

"Jed!" The strangled cry came from the front of the store where Wilson held the limp body of Sally Ann in his arms. "She's hit bad, Jed."

Whirling, Jed lunged onto the porch where Wilson was holding the bloody girl in his arms. Looking into the pain-wracked eyes, Jed took Sally Ann into his arms and brought her to a long bench. Laying her down softly on the bench, Jed knelt beside the moaning girl and held her hand.

"Get the doctor, hurry." Wilson shook his head sadly.

"Sally Ann." Duncan dropped from his horse and raced to the porch after realizing his daughter had been shot. "Daughter."

Jed ignored the distraught man, his attention fixed on the blue eyes staring up at him. "Tell me of our valley, Jed, our beautiful valley."

"It's beautiful, Sally Ann. You're gonna love it there." Tears rolled down his dark cheeks.

"I can see it already, the flowers, streams and all the wild things." Gasping, she squeezed his hands. "It's so beautiful, so beautiful."

"Hang on, little one." Jed glanced at the gathered men and back at Sally Ann. "The doctor is on his way."

"Oh, Jed, I can see the beckoning light you told me about."

"Sally Ann." Duncan knelt beside Jed.

"Papa, we'll be so happy in our valley." Sally Ann looked at her father.

"I know you will, Daughter."

"Then we have your blessing?"

"Yes, Sally Ann, you have my blessing." Duncan sobbed as the blue eyes tried to focus. "Oh, my God, what have I done?"

"You heard him, Jed. I knew he would..." The words trailed off as the beautiful face relaxed and turned sideways with her two last words. "Our valley..."

Wilson turned on the gathered men and raised his rifle. "You men get out of here, right now."

"We didn't want this." Luke tried to speak. "We didn't."

"Get away now, Luke Grisham, before I shoot you myself." Wilson looked back at Jed. "If you're still here when he stands up, he'll kill you, and with my blessing."

"We didn't want this." Luke repeated as he pushed Willie away from the storefront as if he was in a trance.

"You better run and hide, Luke. Run as far and as fast as you can." Wilson screamed. He could see the pain and wildness in Jed's eyes as he stood up.

Rising with Sally Ann in his arms, Jed started toward the church at the far end of the street. "Let me help carry her." Duncan reached out his hand.

"Touch her and I'll kill you right here." The words came out hard and cold, almost inaudible. "If I see any man on the street when I return, I'll kill him."

Motioning for the preacher to follow, Jed carried the limp body into the quiet church and placed her on one of the front pews. Looking about wildly as Wilson, along with the preacher and Amos Duncan were following him in the church, Jed looked to where the preacher stood.

"Now, Preacher, I want you to marry Sally Ann and me." Jed glared at the stricken minister. "If anyone dare speak one word against it, he's a dead man; you have my word on it."

Nodding, the preacher took up his Bible and spoke the solemn words. Kneeling beside the pew, Jed held her hand and repeated the vows of wedlock. Not a word was spoken as Duncan and Wilson removed their hats and stood quietly.

"I'll get a man to build a casket, Jed." Wilson started away.

"Bring some men back with you to dig a grave."

"I'll try, but they're scared of you."

"Bring 'em or I'll give them something to be scared about." Jed turned, his eyes as wild as a cornered lobo wolf.

Jed stood holding Sally Ann's hand as a casket was produced and several men took turns digging a grave in the small cemetery plot behind the church. No one said a word as the casket was lowered, the grave was filled, and the final prayer was given.

"Get out, all of you." Wilson followed the men out of the churchyard, leaving Jed alone beside the grave. "Any of you men see the shooters?"

"No, sir, Ed." A tall farmer spoke up. "We heard the shots but we didn't see who did the shooting."

"He's gonna want blood for his loss." Wilson looked at the men, shaking his head. "He is white by birth, but he thinks Indian now."

"What's that mean, Ed?" Another man spoke up. "We didn't do any shooting."

"I don't know myself, but I figure he's gonna want blood for blood." Wilson spoke quietly. "We both seen you all in front of Baker's place."

"No one wanted Sally Ann shot, it was an accident."

"She's dead, Lars. We can't bring her back." Wilson swore. "Maybe it was an accident but I don't figure he sees it that way."

"Whoever done it was shooting at your boy." The man called Lars spoke up. "They weren't aiming to hit her."

"Maybe not, but the girl is dead." Wilson nodded for the men to leave.

Leaving the churchyard, Jed walked to the alley where the shots came from and examined the tracks in the soft dirt. Old hides, tin cans, bottles, and all kinds of trash littered the small alley along with several sets of tracks. One set in particular took his attention, tracks that led down the alley and turned to where a horse had been tied. Studying the horse tracks, Jed turned and started back to where his horses stood. Wilson and Duncan watched Jed as he finished loading the horses.

After swinging up on the piebald, Jed turned the horse toward the two men and looked down at the lowered head of Duncan. "I should kill you, Duncan, you caused this. You didn't pull the trigger but you might as well have." Jed touched his war axe.

"There's no need, I've killed myself." Dropping his head, Duncan couldn't look up at Jed. "I wish you would kill me, boy."

"No, you'll carry this day to your grave, old man."

"To my grave?" Duncan's shoulders shook. "I'm already there, you just can't see it."

Wilson watched as Jed kicked the piebald and turned east, away from Baxter Springs. "Will we see you again, Jed?"

Reining the horse in, Jed looked down at his stepfather. "The ones that do will see for the last time."

"Revenge is no good, Jed." Wilson looked into the hard face. "She's dead, let it go."

"You tell her that, Pa." Jed stared over at the churchyard. "She was innocent and never harmed anyone."

"Your side, boy." Wilson noticed for the first time the bloody hunting shirt. "You're hurt."

Nodding, Jed blinked away his feelings. "Today, I've been hurt far worse than this."

CHAPTER 4

Wilson watched as Jed rode out of sight, and then walked into the alley where Jed had examined the ground earlier. The tracks before him were plain for any blind man to read. He read the signs and knew the horse that had been tied there. Mounting his horse, Wilson kicked the heavy plow horse into a slow rough lope toward home. Not slowing as the blowing animal splashed across the Pennybrook, the big man ran him all the way to the barn. Dismounting, Wilson walked to the corral where three horses stood. One animal was wet with sweat like his own horse after the four-mile run from town. Pulling a bullwhip from a wooden peg, Wilson started for the small house, his face flushed with anger. Inside the house, he picked up Seth's rifle that stood by the door and smelled the barrel.

Kicking open the door to Seth's bedroom, he came face to face with the young man as Seth rose from his bunk. "You came here to pretend sleep after the black deed you had done?"

Seth looked at the bullwhip, then at the redness of his father's face as he backed away. "I've been out hunting. What am I supposed to have done this time?"

Only the hard slap of Wilson's hand against Seth's face was heard as the younger man fell backward into the wall. "Don't you lie to me, boy. I can read sign."

"What sign, Pa? I told you, I've been out hunting."

"You are a liar." Wilson's boot caught the quivering Seth in the side. "I followed your horse tracks from town and your rifle had been fired."

"Honest, Pa. I was in town but I came home after hunting."

"Get outside, Seth."

"What do you aim to do to me?"

The hard handle of the whip slapped Seth across the back as he staggered to the front door. Turning as they made their way into the open yard, Seth turned white as Wilson unlimbered the black snake. He knew what the man was capable of with the whip as he had seen him cut the head off a coiled rattler many a time. He could cut a man clean to the bone with every flick of the dangerous weapon.

"Why, boy? Why did you shoot her?" Wilson flicked the whip behind him ready to strike. "Why?"

"Who? I didn't shoot anybody." Seth knew he had missed Jed before he raced from the fur store. He had no way of knowing Sally Ann had taken a stray shot. "I swear, we didn't shoot anybody."

Only the hiss of the striking leather made a sound as the whip wrapped around Seth's middle, making the shaking man yell out in pain. "You tell me, boy, or I'll cut you to ribbons. Why?"

Holding his hands up to protect his face, Seth shook his head. "Who did we shoot, Pa?"

Again the whip struck, cutting a long slash in Seth's shirt bringing blood. "This is your last chance, boy."

"Who?" Seth pleaded.

"Sally Ann Duncan is dead, and you shot her."

"Sally Ann, dead?" Seth was shocked. "We didn't even see her in town."

"I'm gonna skin you alive, boy."

"I'm your son."

"No longer." The whip lay ready, strung out behind Wilson. "No longer."

"Alright." Seth's eyes showed terror as the strong arm of his father started forward. "No more, I'll tell you."

"The truth." Wilson acted as if he had gone completely mad. "You lie to me again and I'll lay you bare."

Nodding his shaggy red head, Seth dropped his eyes. "We didn't mean to hit anybody. We were shooting at Jed, just to scare him. The shots must have hit her through the wall if she was in the store."

"Who's we?"

"Adam Beale was with me."

"But why, boy?" Wilson shook his head. "Jed is your brother."

"He was never my brother." Seth regained some courage. "He was taking my woman away from me, making me the laughingstock of the settlement."

"Your woman?" Wilson was shocked when he heard the words. "Sally Ann was never your woman."

"Jed's an Injun, Pa. He has no right to be with a white woman."

"He ain't no Injun."

"Yes, he is. His ma was an Injun."

Only the cracking of the whip sounded as Wilson turned on the redhead with a fury, lashing him as he rolled into a ball on the ground. The sound of the racing horse was not even heard as Seth screamed out in pain, begging for Wilson to stop.

"Stop it, Ed." Duncan grabbed Wilson's huge arm "You'll kill him."

"He needs to be killed." Wilson flung the smaller man from him and lashed out with the whip cutting a deep streak across Seth's back. "He killed your girl, Duncan."

"No more than I did." The smaller man stood to his feet. "Whip me if you have to whip someone."

"Don't tempt me, Duncan."

"If your boy killed my Sally Ann, it was by accident." Duncan fell to his knees. "I killed her on purpose."

Looking down at the man, Wilson dropped his arm and stepped back. "How did you kill her, Duncan?"

"I told the young men of the town no charges would be filed against them if they stopped Jed from taking my Sally Ann with him into the mountains." Duncan dropped his eyes. "I didn't mean for them to shoot."

"You aimed to kill him for loving your girl?"

"No, not kill; just rough him up a bit."

"Get off my place, Duncan. As long as you breathe, don't show your face around here again."

"I deserve worse, Ed." Duncan mounted his horse slowly. "I've resigned as Constable of Baxter Springs, I ain't fit."

"No, you're not. Now, you git."

Wilson didn't bother to watch as Duncan turned his horse west toward his place. Looking down at Seth, he shook the fog and madness from his eyes. He had lost one son, now the other one was lost too.

"No more, Pa. You've beat me enough." Seth stood shakily to his feet.

"I'm no longer your Pa." Wilson glared at the redhead as if it was the first time he had seen him. "Get your things together, take one horse and get out of my sight."

"Pa?"

"Don't come back, ever."

"But, this is my home."

"This ain't your home. The next time I see you, I promise, I'll kill you." Wilson pointed his long finger. "And you take that no-account Adam Beale with you, same goes for him."

"You can't just cast me aside like I was nothing."

"To me, that's exactly what you are, nothing," Wilson raised the whip. "I figure Jed will be back for you, so you better head east in a hurry. Now, get and don't stop running, you yeller cur."

Jed didn't remember the long ride back to his cabin as his mind was numb, thinking over the events of the last days. Her last words haunted him. Why hadn't he taken the threats more seriously? She would still be alive, laughing and dancing around if he had. His hands tightened on the Hawkins as he thought of the tracks he had seen behind the alley. He knew the tracks and who the horse belonged to. There had been two shots fired, and at least one of the shooters was known to him. Before he died, he would get the name of the other man involved.

Early morning found Jed passing over the last ridge, crossing the same trails he had first followed into his valley. Pausing halfway down the steep trail, Jed took in the valley, making his eyes fog over. Today, in his grief, the valley didn't hold the beauty it once held for him. If she could have only seen her beautiful valley, the one thought that brought joy to her heart and a smile on her face as she lay in his arms dying.

"They will pay, Sally Ann." Jed mumbled. "I promise you, they will pay." Suddenly, Jed reined the piebald in hard, making the led horses bump into him. He couldn't believe his eyes, across the narrowest part of the valley, the blinding ray of light showed itself again. Jed blinked, as he thought he could see the outline of Sally Ann's face, smiling through the beam of light. He knew her image could be his imagination, but once again the light revealed itself, reflecting the early morning sun. Riding the piebald toward the light, Jed reined in again. The beam disappeared, the same way as the first time it had appeared to him. Sitting the piebald for several minutes, Jed finally turned back to the trail. One day, the secret of the beckoning beam would be revealed, but today, he needed to ride on. He knew Sally Ann was on his mind and her image was likely his own mind playing tricks on him. The thought of leaving the valley and riding back to the Arapaho entered his grief-stricken mind.

Nearing the cabin, Jed detected the hard running black mule with Silent One clinging to her back, waving his arm as he raced down the valley. The little mule had her ears laid back and was giving everything she had, with her neck fully extended, the black mule was running as fast as she could toward him.

Silent One grinned broadly as he see-sawed the mule to a jolting stop and started signing. "You are back, Crow Killer."

"Yes, I am back, my friend."

Noticing the sad looks, the youngster looked back up the trail. "Where is your squaw, the white woman, who was to come back with you?"

"She will not be coming. We will talk later."

Nodding solemnly, Silent One watched Jed's hands and followed him to the cabin where Jed led the tired horses into the corral. "You fix something to eat, and I'll unload the packs and feed the animals."

With supper finished, Jed sat in front of the fireplace and stared hard into the small fire for over an hour. Silent One could sense something was very wrong, but he knew if Jed wanted him to know, he would speak of it in time. Setting his coffee cup on the rock hearth, Jed unwrapped one of the last bundles and handed the youngster a thirty caliber Hawken rifle.

"It's not as large as my fifty, but it'll bring down most anything with a well-placed shot." Jed signed to the youngster. "Tomorrow, I will teach you how to shoot and care for it."

"It is beautiful, my friend, but have I earned such an expensive weapon?"

"You have worked hard, young one." Jed looked over at the sack of coins lying on the table, all he had left after paying for the new supplies and the supplies Hatcher had put on credit at the store. "You deserve it."

"Silent One thanks you."

"I wanted a larger caliber, but the thirty was all the storekeeper had that was worth bringing back."

"It looks new." Silent One studied the stock and bluing on the rifle.

"It's been shot only a few times." Jed didn't tell the youngster, he had bought the rifle for Sally Ann. There were four other rifles in the bundles of wrapping, but young as he was, the thirty would do him nicely for now. Jed had bought the extra rifles fearing one day he might need them to protect the valley.

"I do not deserve such a weapon."

Jed nodded. "I think you'll take a liking to these."

"What is it?" Silent One studied the tin full of peaches, not knowing what to do with it.

"You eat what's inside the tin."

"How do you get into its body?"

Jed nodded, even in his time of mourning it was better to be home. Maybe, in time, the sadness of Sally Ann's death could be eased. Never forgotten but maybe eased. "Let me show you."

The youth's eyes lit up with delight as he tasted the canned peaches. In the wild, he had eaten berries and some wild apples, but he had never tasted anything with the sweetness the peaches held.

"I think I would trade the thunder gun for these." The youngster held up the half-empty can. "Well, maybe."

"Peaches are good, but they won't keep you from wanting meat." Jed felt cooped up inside the cabin. "Tomorrow, we will ride the valley and find new places to set our traps this winter."

Jed sat back in his hide chair, drinking coffee, and fingering the fine material Sally Ann had picked out for curtains to decorate the windows. Silent One watched as Jed folded the material carefully and wrapped it back in the brown paper. He sensed something bad had happened, but now wasn't the time to ask. One day, Crow Killer would tell him what had become of the white squaw he had spoken of so often.

Blue Darter was summoned to his chief's lodge where the elders of the tribe sat around the perimeter of the lodge. Normally, this time of year they would have sat outside, but Chief Deep Water summoned him into the lodge where no one could hear their words.

"My Chief has summoned me?" Blue Darter stood, as he had not been asked to sit.

Motioning to a place in the circle, the tall chief nodded. "Four warriors left this place many sleeps ago on a hunt, they have not returned to their village or women."

"Yes, my Chief."

The cold black eyes penetrated Blue Darter's own. "Small Mountain is your friend, yet you did not follow him on this trail."

"No, my Chief."

"Tell the elders why all young warriors look for glory and scalps." Deep Water looked across the fire. "Were you not invited on this hunt?"

"No, Small Mountain did not wish me to ride with him." Blue Darter knew he could not lie to the gathered elders, even if he wanted to. "Small Mountain rode to his death, I felt it. He knew I would not follow."

"Speak! Tell us of this death you talk of."

"Many moons ago, coming from the east, after you sent us to speak with Lone Bull, we found a lone warrior living in a white man's lodge as a white man. Frog Belly had first seen this valley and told us of seeing two warriors." Blue Darter spoke. "Out of curiosity, we sought out this hidden valley when we were returning from the trail our chief had sent us on."

"I remember sending you to the east to speak with Lone Bull and his people. Go on."

"This warrior fed us, treated us good, and invited us into his lodge, but Small Mountain challenged him, ordering him to leave the valley or die."

"Why would Small Mountain do this, if the warrior had treated you as you say? What happened then?"

"Small Mountain would not leave in peace and challenged the warrior to fight." Blue Darter shrugged. "They fought and your son was easily defeated."

"This warrior did not kill him?"

"No, he let Small Mountain live and still he wanted to be our friends."

"Why did Small Mountain challenge this warrior?"

"He said the valley belonged to the Blackfoot." Blue Darter thought back to the hidden valley. "He ordered the warrior to leave or die."

"This valley you speak of, is it our hunting grounds?"

"No, my Chief, the Nez Perce live between the valley and our lands."

"So, it is theirs?"

"I am but a Blackfoot warrior, my Chief. I do not know who the valley belongs to."

Deep Water nodded slowly as he looked around the circle. "What tribe is this warrior from?"

"He is Arapaho, a Lance bearer." Blue Darter answered. "His name is Crow Killer."

The Chief stiffened. "Even in this land, we have heard that name."

"He is a mighty warrior, my Chief." Blue Darter nodded. "I have seen this one's greatness."

"He killed many Nez Perce and maybe two Blackfoot warriors many moons ago." Deep Water spoke to the elders. "The Nez Perce, who returned from seeking a spotted horse taken from them, say he is a demon who can change himself into a bear."

"I do not believe this." Blue Darter shook his head. "He is just a man who fed us, treating us as friends."

Another elder spoke up. "Did Blue Darter say this warrior defeated the mighty Small Mountain easily?"

Blue Darter remembered the fight. "Easily, my Uncle, but he did not kill."

"What do you think happened to Small Mountain and his warriors?"

"If they returned to the valley, they are dead." Blue Darter dropped his eyes. "He warned us never to come against him to fight."

"Then he is a demon, as the Nez Perce said?"

"No, my Chief, but he is a great warrior as I said, a Lance Bearer of the Arapaho Tribe."

"You're saying one Arapaho can defeat four Blackfoot in battle?"

"Yes, my Chief, I Blue Darter say this." The warrior shrugged. "I do not know if this warrior is a demon or man, but I do know he is a mighty warrior. Our people do not need to make an enemy of one such as him."

Deep Water's face hardened. "Do you fear this Crow Killer?"

"No, not for myself, but yes for our people. We do not need him for an enemy." The warrior looked at the elders. "He desires peace and to be left alone, not war."

"I am Deep Water, Chief of the Piegan Blackfoot Tribe." The chief glared around the lodge. "I will say who we make war on, who will be our enemy, not you, Blue Darter."

"I know who is chief here, Uncle. I only wish to protect our people."

Another wise elder spoke. "Are we to believe a village with hundreds of warriors should fear one lone warrior, whether he be man or demon?"

"Yes, I say this."

"You would do nothing to this Arapaho, even if Small Mountain and his warriors have been killed?"

"If my chief says fight, I will fight." Blue Darter studied the circle of elders. "But, I would urge caution, my Chief."

"Tell me." The chief glared across at Blue Darter. "Will you search for Small Mountain?"

"What do you want of me?"

"You know this valley and the Arapaho." Deep Water looked into the fire. "You will lead a small party of warriors to this valley and seek out Small Mountain and his warriors."

"And if they are dead?"

"Bring me proof, then we will talk more of this."

Blue Darter nodded. "If this is your wish, my Chief."

"Go now, bring me proof if my son and his warriors live, or if they are dead." Deep Water dropped his eyes.

"Yes, my Chief." Turning, Blue Darter started from the lodge.

"Take Standing Bull with you."

"Standing Bull?"

"Go."

Blue Darter took in a long breath as he exited the lodge. Deep Water was worried for his son, Small Mountain, and his warriors. The elders had heard of the Arapaho warrior, Crow Killer, whom the Nez Perce believed to be a demon. Now, they had persuaded Deep Water to send a party of warriors on the trail in search of the missing Blackfoot. Deep Water had ordered him to take a few warriors and search for Small Mountain to the east. Worst of all, he was to take Standing Bull, the only warrior in the tribes that was equal to the Nez Perce, Black Robe, in battle. Standing Bull was Deep Water's younger brother; a nephew of the mighty Chief Lone Bull to the east, a bloodthirsty warrior, mighty in battle, and a warrior some people thought was strange. He never took a woman, never joined in tribal dances, never smiled, and only lived to make war and kill. Blue Darter feared the warrior as his pale eyes were empty when they focused on him. If there was such a thing as a demon, Blue Darter knew Standing Bull was it.

Three warriors sat in his lodge, waiting as he entered and took a seat. Standing Bull, Crowfoot, and a warrior named Little Horse greeted him. With a nod, he looked across the fire at them.

"Already you have been summoned for this trail?"

"We have been asked to ride with you."

Deep Water already knew he was sending them out before he called me to his lodge. Blue Darter thought these things, but did not speak of them in front of Standing Bull. Little Horse was his lifelong friend who had ridden many a war trail with Blue Darter. Crowfoot was of a different branch of the Blackfoot Nation, his village was Lone Bull's people. He had taken a woman of Deep Water's Village, as custom dictated, left Lone Bull and now has his lodge with Deep Water. The third warrior was Standing Bull, the brother of Chief Deep Water, the strange one with the pale eyes. The warrior was like no other Blue Darter had ever met, his eyes were pale, almost albino color, giving the warrior a repulsive look. It was said no person could look him in the eye without looking away. It was widely known, Standing Bull obeyed nobody while on the warpath or in the village, with the exception of his chief and brother. Blue Darter did not like the warrior riding this trail with him, but he had no choice, no warrior dared disobey their chief's commands. Standing Bull was dedicated to his brother, but he craved greatness, to be known as the mightiest warrior of any tribe.

"You were told to lead us, Blue Darter, because you know where the valley lies." The voice was low, raspy, and cold as ice. "You will lead us to this place."

"I will lead you." Even though he tried not to show it, Blue Darter was afraid of Standing Bull, the warrior was pure evil. "We will leave at first light."

"How far away is this place?"

Blue Darter ignored the question from Standing Bull. "Be prepared for a long ride and carry much dried meat."

"There is no game in this country?"

"Our chief wants to know what happened to his son, Small Mountain." Blue Darter looked at Little Horse. "We must hurry, there is no time to hunt."

"We will be ready."

Little Horse stayed behind as the other two warriors left the lodge. "Why has our chief sent Standing Bull with us on this trail?"

"He worries for Small Mountain."

"No, Blue Darter, I think he has sent his brother to kill this Arapaho Lance Bearer and prove how great the Blackfoot are."

"Black Robe did not kill him." Blue Darter looked into the fire. "Why does our chief think Standing Bull will defeat him? I believe Standing Bull will fail."

"Standing Bull is indeed a strange one, but maybe even greater in battle than the Nez Perce, Black Robe." Little Horse shook his head. "Everyone knows he is crazy, but none will say it to his face."

Blue Darter remembered his last words with Jed. "Perhaps, soon we will see how great Standing Bull really is."

Deep Water watched as the four warriors came from their lodges and took the horses the younger boys of the village brought to them. Motioning at Blue Darter, the chief waited as the young warrior led his clay bank horse over to where he stood.

"This is your trail, Blue Darter." The Blackfoot Chief stared stonily. "You will lead the warriors, but you will let Standing Bull do the fighting, if he is needed."

"Yes, my Chief." Blue Darter looked to where the strange one sat his horse. "Do you believe we will have to fight?"

"I have sent a runner to the Nez Perce." Deep Water ignored the question. "I have asked that a warrior named Squirrel Tooth meet you at the split forks of our hunting grounds near the Snake River."

"Why would you do this, my Chief?"

"I wish for him to tell you of this Arapaho Warrior, Crow Killer. How he fights, and maybe convince you this warrior is a demon." Deep Water nodded. "The Nez Perce has seen this warrior kill. He swears the Arapaho is a demon who has been sent from the evil ones."

"We will talk with this warrior."

"Go then, and bring my son home."

Silent One watched as Jed moved about the cabin and worked outside, making stretching boards and willow holders for the many skins that would have to be stretched with the coming of the cold times. He could sense the sorrow in the Arapaho, but not a word had been spoken of why the white woman had not come back with him to the valley. Several times, they had ridden the valley and searched out the hidden beaver dams and game trails. He wanted to ask and his curiosity wanted him to ask, but it would not be polite. A man's sorrow was his alone to endure and no other could question him, if he wanted to speak of it, then he would.

Silent One kept his questions to himself as he followed Jed through the valley, riding one of the Blackfoot horses. The long days of summer were care free for the young one. Hides were no good during the warm days, so there was no trapping. Soon, when the deep grass was high enough, they would begin to gather hay for the winter, and wood would have to be drug in and stacked for the cold times ahead. For now, the warm days were lazy days for the two young warriors. A little hunting to fill their cooking pots, but mostly swimming in the clear creek or fishing for the trout and bass that filled the streams.

Jed taught the young Silent One how to use the Hawken and keep it clean. With the sharp eyes and steady hands of youth, the youngster became a good shot with only a few practice shots. Unable to talk or hear, his other senses seemed to be even sharper. Several times, the deaf youngster had sensed the presence of elk and deer before they came into view. He also had the ability to feel the slap of a beaver's tail, sending out its warning across the ponds in the valley, as they approached. As they explored the beautiful valley and its many hidden resources, the young warrior had become great company. With the coming of the cold times, he would be a great help skinning what they trapped.

Jed had been back from the north several weeks before he finally felt like signing to Silent One what had happened to Sally Ann. Sitting outside the cabin in the warm summer evening, Jed signaled, trying to make the youngster understand what had happened in the white settlement. The grief he had felt could not be expressed fully with hand signing. However, Jed watched Silent One's face as he nodded with respect. Perhaps, Jed was wrong and maybe the youngster could feel Jed's sadness.

"This is a sad thing for you, my friend."

Jed nodded. "Yes, young one, it is sad."

"Will you return to this place to seek vengeance for her death?"

"The men responsible will die a slow death."

"I will help you do this thing."

"No, Silent One." Jed shook his head. "This is for me to do alone."

"After you kill these men, will you go back to this place to trade your furs?" Silent One looked closely at Jed.

"We have to sell, and it is the closest trading post and fur buyer."

Silent One shook his head and signed. "There is a place further north and east, with far less trouble."

"What place?"

"Fort Bridger." The hands replied. "My people take their furs and horses there to trade."

"Is it far?"

"Yes, it is far, but not much further than where your woman was killed."

"Maybe, we will seek out this place in the spring when the cold times pass."

"Maybe I will see my people again." Silent One smiled, he knew he would make quite an impression on the people who had cast him out from his village. "Now, I am a warrior."

"Yes, my friend, you are a warrior." Jed nodded. "There is none that I would rather have beside me in battle."

Blue Darter and his warriors arrived on the bank of the Snake River where Blackfoot and Nez Perce lands separated, and found Squirrel Tooth and his men waiting at the appointed crossing. Hesitating for several minutes before crossing the river, Blue Darter studied the far bank carefully, searching for any hiding warriors. Earlier, Deep Water had sent runners to the Nez Perce. Upon returning to the village, they reported a party of Nez Perce warriors had agreed to meet them at the river to sit in council, about the Arapaho they thought was a demon. Squirrel Tooth's talk of a demon dressed as an Arapaho warrior and grizzly bear had spread throughout the northern tribes, making the name Crow Killer known and feared.

Dismounting, Blue Darter again studied the nearby trees closely before turning his attention fully on the Nez Perce warriors. The Nez Perce and Blackfoot hunted the same hunting grounds and were not hereditary enemies, but they were not allies. Since the battle caused by the redheaded white trapper in the far valley that killed many of their warriors, the tribes stayed far apart, neither trusting the other. The tribes never learned that Crow Killer, not Billy Wilson, had killed the two Blackfoot warriors, which started the big fight, causing so many warriors to be lost.

"My chief ordered me here to speak of the one in the far valley. I am Squirrel Tooth of the Nez Perce." Looking about the clearing, the warrior was nervous and hadn't shaken his fears. The mere thought of the demon spirit and the killing of the redhead by the crazed grizzly made him shake. He worried the demon would learn of the council and come to their meeting place.

"I am Blue Darter of the Blackfoot people." The warrior looked around. "I have met the Arapaho you are to tell me of."

"You have seen this demon in his valley?" Squirrel Tooth was shocked. "He did not kill you?"

"No, I still walk the land." Blue Darter nodded. "Tell me, how do you know of this valley?"

"The valley is near our hunting grounds." The warrior spoke. "We do not claim this land. The mountain passes are high, a long hard climb for hunters, and no shaggies live there."

"Now, with a demon living there, I think you are afraid to hunt there."

"Our warriors have reported an Arapaho living to the east." Squirrel Tooth nodded. "If this one is Crow Killer, yes, I would be afraid to hunt there."

"He seems like a normal man to me." Blue Darter nodded.

"What does Chief Deep Water want to know of this Arapaho warrior, who can turn himself into a bear at will?" Squirrel Tooth ignored Blue Darter's words. "You say you met this demon and know where his valley sits. What do you need of me?"

Blue Darter studied the warrior and he could smell fear in his voice, the way it quavered when he spoke the name, Crow Killer. "Tell me, Squirrel Tooth, do you truly believe this warrior can turn himself into a demon bear?"

Turning to the slender warrior standing beside him, Squirrel Tooth nodded at Many Feathers. "We have both seen this demon change as he killed the redhead and our leader, Black Robe. Tell him, Many Feathers, what was seen."

"I watched as he easily killed our greatest warrior." Many Feathers waved his hands. "I myself watched as he changed into a bear and killed the redheaded one."

Blue Darter could also see the fear in the Nez Perce warrior's face. "You actually watched as this Arapaho changed into a grizzly bear?"

"His words are true, Blue Darter. We both watched as he killed Black Robe and another at the great river." Squirrel Tooth seemed to pale. "The Arapaho demon killed Black Robe and the other as if they were children."

"Bah, your greatest warrior, he was nothing." Standing Bull stepped forward. "Tell us of this demon, speak."

"Let us sit in council." Squirrel Tooth motioned to the small fire. "We have food."

Standing Bull growled. "We did not come here to eat. Tell us of this warrior."

Blue Darter raised his hand as Standing Bull stepped forward. "We will eat and sit in council with you."

Standing Bull would not be silenced. "Will Squirrel Tooth ride with us?"

"I have seen with my own eyes the power of this demon." Squirrel

Tooth shook his head. "No, when I ride, I ride west to my village. I want nothing more to do with this evil one."

"Are the Nez Perce cowards?"

"I tell you this; your people do not want this demon spirit to make war on your village." Squirrel Tooth touched his knife as he looked into the pale eyes. "I say this; I fear this demon, but I do not fear the Blackfoot."

"This demon must be terrible." Blue Darter tried to placate the warriors. "Speak more of this warrior."

Squirrel Tooth's head nodded slowly. "Before our eyes; first he was a man, then he changed into a bear with huge claws and blood dripping from his mouth. I do not wish this evil one to follow us to our village."

Blue Darter could feel the fear in the warrior's voice. This one truly believed the Arapaho was a demon from evil spirits that could turn on villages with a vengeance. Many tribes had suffered from mysterious sicknesses and unforeseen misfortunes when the tribe had done something to provoke the spirits. Blue Darter believed Squirrel Tooth. He wished Deep Water had listened to him by not sending them on the trail to search out something that was perhaps not mortal and possibly could not be killed.

For two hours, the two different bands of warriors sat in council, speaking of Crow Killer and how they would kill him, if indeed he was a demon. Standing Bull only frowned as he was a warrior who feared nothing and did not believe in spirits. He was bored as he sat talking to Squirrel Tooth and could feel the fear emitting from the warrior whenever the demon was mentioned. Disgusted, he leaped to his feet and shouted the council was finished. Not wanting to camp near the Nez Perce, Blue Darter with his warriors following, turned to the east, toward the far-off valley where he had last seen the Arapaho warrior. Standing Bull rode behind the warriors, his face a mask of hate and disgust.

As the Blackfoot warriors departed, Squirrel Tooth looked over at Many Feathers. "They are as dead men already."

The warrior agreed. "They are foolish not to listen to our words, for with our own eyes we have seen the demon."

Jed enlarged the small barn and lean-to, making room for the enormous amount of dried hay he would have to store to feed the horses and mules through winter. The small amount of hay he had put up the previous fall had barely fed his three animals until spring thaw. Now, he has four extra horses of the Blackfoot to feed. He remembered his two winters with the Arapaho when their horses had to fend for themselves all winter. They ate what dead grass they could paw down through the deep snow and chewed the rough bark off the trees by the village. By spring, their war ponies had grown gaunt, just skin and bones. A few of the older animals had died of starvation and the elements. With their horses weakened from hunger, the hunters had to wait until the new growth of grass strengthened the horses enough to ride out on a hunt or raid. Jed did not want his animals to suffer from hunger. He wanted the horses strong in case they were needed, so he had to store more hay.

The days were long and tiring, swinging the sickle hour after hour, but Jed and Silent One kept cutting with the sharp blades. Slowly, as the cut grass cured and dried in the warm summer days, the barn started filling up as load after load of hay was piled in.

Silent One looked to where the black molly mule stood hobbled out on the valley floor. "She will eat better than we do this winter."

"You know she is your favorite animal."

"I am reminded every time she throws me onto the hard ground." The youngster looked at the barn full of hay and frowned. "The Assiniboine make their horses fend for themselves or go hungry during the cold times."

Jed laughed. "I want our horses strong when the snow comes, just in case we need them, and that takes work, my young friend."

"Maybe, squaw's work." Silent One swung the sickle easily, laying the tall grass in a row so it could be gathered easily. "A warrior would not do this kind of work."

Two more weeks of backbreaking work found the barn stacked to the rafters, full of dried grass. Finished with the hay, Jed turned their attention to bringing in enough firewood to see them through the long winter ahead. The sound of the ringing axes sounded across the valley as they chopped into the dead trees lying along the tree line. From time to time, Jed would look out, near the tree line where the mules grazed, to see if they had spotted anything, animal or man. Jed trusted the mules more than he did the horses because mules are naturally suspicious of everything, especially strangers.

"I thought you would ride back to the west before the cold times and kill the ones that killed your woman?" Silent One signed, looking up from where he was sharpening an axe. "Soon, it will be time to trap again."

Jed nodded. "I'll let them forget what they have done and think they are safe, then I will strike."

"That will be good." The youngster nodded. "I would like to see their faces when Crow Killer springs on them."

"Tomorrow, my young friend, we will ride the valley and cross the mountain to the west." Jed studied the low fire that was heating their coffee. "We have worked too much and become lax in our vigilance of the valley."

"Do you think an enemy is on his way here?"

"This I do not know, but by now the Blackfoot have started to wonder where Small Mountain and his warriors are." Jed walked to the open front door and studied the valley floor. "If they do come, we must not get caught by surprise in our lodge."

"Then we will ride." Silent One handed Jed the axe. "How is that blade?"

Jed thumbed the blade and nodded. "You have done well, my young friend. I will make a white man out of you yet."

"I would be a funny looking white." Silent One signed.

Morning found Jed and Silent One already far across the valley. Jed wanted to reach the timberline before full daylight in case sharp eyes were spying on them from the far hills. Both warriors carried their rifles and a small bag of food. Water wasn't needed because the valley had an abundant supply of cold drinking water flowing down from the high mountains. In the cool of the morning, the piebald was full of energy and wanting to run, causing Jed to jerk his war bridle to rein him in. Busy watching both the ground for sign and searching out the tree line along the valley, he didn't have the time or inclination to put up with the fractious horse. Nothing aroused his suspicions, but he remembered the teachings of Walking Horse; always be alert and expect the unexpected.

Reining in the piebald at the base of the trail, leading up out of the valley on the south end before turning west, Jed sat the horse and studied the trail. They had spotted nothing out of the ordinary, only tracks of the animals inhabiting the valley. Still, Jed was uneasy, something he couldn't put his finger on gnawed at him. He tried to shake off the feeling, but he was uneasy even though the piebald never showed any signs that other horses or enemies were near.

"Are we going over the pass, Crow Killer?" Silent One felt concerned in the way Jed was acting so uneasy.

Nodding, Jed kicked the piebald and started the climb up and out of the valley. The trail was a game trail made by the many animals, crossing from one valley to the next in their habitual travels, looking for better grazing. The aroma of the mountain spruce and flowers sweetened the air as they were carried on the wind. Jed thought of Sally Ann as the piebald climbed steadily upward. If only she could have seen the valley, he knew her blue eyes and pretty smile would have glowed radiantly. Why did she have to die? Jed knew the Arapaho people believed in the afterlife, so now she was looking down from the stars where she could see the whole valley and its beauty, he hoped it was so.

"If we travel this trail further, we will not get back to the lodge before it is late." Silent One signed to Jed as they sat on the peak of the trail that gave them a good view of the next valley and its broad plain. Nothing moved down in the valley except for the elk, deer, and a few head of wild horses.

"We will camp here tonight." Jed kicked the piebald forward. "We will ride down and water the horses, then return here and camp."

"Do you sense an enemy is near?"

"Maybe, we will stay here and watch."

Silent One shook his head sadly. "The ground will be hard."

"Has my young friend grown soft?"

The youngster laughed. "If I have, the white man's lodge has made me that way."

CHAPTER 5

Crossing the far mountain ranges, the Blackfoot warriors trekked steadily east as they made their way along the game trails following Blue Darter. None of the warriors spoke as the tired horses plodded on, covering mile after mile. The animals were exhausted from several days of unbroken travel, harsh trails, and deep rivers. From time to time, the warriors would slip to the ground and lead their horses to let them rest.

As the trail widened, Standing Bull rode up next to Blue Darter. "How many more sleeps is it to this hidden valley you speak of?"

"One." Blue Darter never looked over at the pale-eyed warrior.

"Then, we will be there tomorrow?"

"Two sleeps, then we will rest our horses and let them graze before we ride into the big valley to look for Small Mountain and the others."

"First, we will kill this Arapaho." Standing Bull argued. "Then, we will look for my nephew."

"There have been no signs of our warriors. Perhaps they did not come to this valley."

"No matter, we will kill this Arapaho." Standing Bull grunted. "Then, we will search for Small Mountain and the others, or look further to the east."

"Why do you wish to kill one you have never seen?"

"Is he not the one that killed Black Robe?" The pale eyes squinted, trying to block the sun's rays. "I should have been the one to kill the Nez Perce. Now, I will kill this Arapaho and take Black Robe's paint horse."

"From what I have heard and seen, many have tried to kill him." Blue Darter shook his head. "Do not challenge this Arapaho."

"I am Standing Bull, and no warrior can stand before me." The warrior frowned. "His scalp will be a great coup."

"Do as you will, Standing Bull. If we find him, I will speak with him first so I can ask him about my friend, Small Mountain."

"Do you think he would tell you, if he killed Small Mountain?"

Blue Darter nodded, remembering the tall, proud Arapaho. "He will speak the truth, this one will not lie."

"Not even to save his life?"

"You have not killed him yet, Standing Bull." Blue Darter looked over at the large warrior. "Listen to me and do not try to do this thing."

"I will kill him." The pale eyes focused on Blue Darter. "You and the others are not to interfere, and this kill will be mine alone."

"Have you forgotten Squirrel Tooth's words?" Blue Darter shook his head. "Black Robe spoke the same words just before the Arapaho killed him."

Seth dismounted behind the corrals and flipped his reins over a small limb before walking around the barn. Near the woodpile, Adam Beale was preoccupied with splitting wood, unaware of anyone near. Finally, noticing the redhead approaching, his axe wavered in midair before the young man sunk it deep into the hickory chopping block. Looking at the back door of the house, Beale quickly motioned Seth inside the barn.

"What are you doing here, Seth?" The voice was almost shrill. "We agreed not to be seen together for a while, a long while."

"The jigs up, Adam." Seth frowned at Beale. "My pa knows we shot Sally Ann."

"What?" Beale's jaw dropped. "How?"

"He knows." Seth repeated himself, showing Beale the scars on his back. "He drove me from our place with his whip."

"When?"

"Three weeks back." Seth cussed, remembering the whipping.

"The talk is all over the settlement about Sally Ann, but no one knows it was us that fired the shots." Beale looked at the house. "Where you been? I ain't seen you around town."

"Hiding out, letting my back heal, and trying to figure out how we're gonna get ourselves out of this mess."

"Does Constable Duncan know?" Beale was visibly shaken. "Is the old man after us?"

"He knows alright, but he blames himself more than us. Last I seen of him, he was riding to his place like a dead man." Seth shook his head. "I think he may have slipped off his rocker."

"Who else knows?" Beale looked around like a spooked deer.

"I don't know." Seth shook his head. "I sure ain't waiting around for anyone to learn about it and start wanting to stretch our necks."

"What are you saying?"

"Wake up, Adam. When your pa finds out we killed Sally Ann, he'll boot you out too, or worse."

Beale nodded, deep in thought. "Probably worse, but it was an accident."

"I know we didn't mean to kill her, but we did." Seth shook his head. "My pa said he'd kill me the next time he lays eyes on me."

"You believe him?"

"I believe him. You should have seen him, he was crazy."

Wide eyed and scared, Beale studied Seth's face. "What are we gonna do?"

"We have worse problems than either of our pa's or Duncan."

"What else, for crying out loud?"

"Jedidiah Bracket, my stepbrother." Seth looked about the barn. "My pa says Jed knows. He found my horse's tracks behind the trading post."

"They call him Crow Killer around the trading post, from the Nez Perce, they think he is a demon." Adam seemed to shake.

"That's him and believe me, to us, he will be a demon." Seth nodded.

"What are we gonna do, Seth?" Adam was scared. "He'll kill us for sure."

"I spoke with Jake Carter two weeks ago, before coming here." Seth nodded. "He says Jed passed his place, after the burying, and he was leading packhorses, heading for the mountains."

"Then he ain't after us?"

"Not now, but he'll be back for us the minute we get careless."

"If he comes back?" Beale seemed to wilt. "We're dead men."

"Not if we get him first."

"Are you serious? Abe and Vern tried to get him and they were a lot better mountain men than we'll ever be." Beale was shaking like a leaf. "What's your plan?"

"I've spent the last three weeks locating a tracker." Seth nodded. "I finally found out where he stays."

"A tracker?"

"Lem Roden."

"That drunk? He couldn't track nothing unless it was a jug of whiskey." Beale shook his head. "Shucks, last time I seen him, he couldn't even find the saloon door."

"Does your pa know what happened?" Seth looked at the pale face. "I mean about Sally Ann."

"He hasn't been to town since the shooting." Beale swallowed hard. "No, my pa doesn't know anything."

"Good, meet me at Carter's at dawn." Seth looked to where the older Beale had walked from the house. "We're going hunting."

"Are you crazy, Seth?" Beale was scared. "We ain't hunters and we don't even know the mountains."

"Don't forget who my brother was." Seth started for his horse. "Billy Wilson taught me a lot when he was home. We'll be okay, but we've got to kill Jed before he comes for us."

"I reckon you're right, we have no choice." Beale slumped. "If my pa finds out about this, I'm dead. If your brother catches up to me, I'm dead. I'll be there, I have no choice."

"Bring supplies, or stay here and let the town's people hang you when they find out." Seth swung up on his horse and turned to Baxter Springs.

"Why can't we just ride east and disappear?"

"Because stupid, Jed is from back east and he probably knows that country a lot better than we do." Seth was frustrated with Beale's scared looks and questions. "I know how hardheaded he is, and believe me, he will come for us sooner or later. We've got no choice in this, Adam. It's either him or us, so we have to kill him."

The trail where Jed and Silent One waited was narrow, only wide enough to let two horses pass, side by side. Jed picked the place well, if the enemy did come, only two warriors at a time could get to him and the young one. With the deadly Hawken rifles and higher ground, they could defend themselves, even against a large raiding party. Most tribes didn't like a stand up deadly fight or to lose any of their warriors.

"You have chosen the place to fight well, Crow Killer." Silent One signed. "How long will we wait here?"

"If we don't see anyone by morning, we will ride back tomorrow."

"You think someone is there?" The youngster looked into the darkness.

"I don't know, I just feel someone is coming here."

"I will take the first watch."

"Okay, but I don't think they'll come in the dark." Jed hobbled the horses and found himself a soft place on the ground. "The trail west is too rough to travel at night."

Jed shivered slightly as he studied the steep trail leading down into the next valley. The wool trade blanket he had brought from Baxter Springs was not heavy enough to hold out the cold air of the high mountains. He should have brought a warmer elk hide, but elk hide was bulkier and heavier to carry. While chewing on dried meat, Jed let his eyes rove the darkness of the valley below. Finally, with the coming morning, after a chilly night standing guard and shivering, the air was beginning to warm the mountain pass as the sun showed itself in the east. Below, elk and deer rose from their beds, and started out onto the grassy flats, unaware of the human's presence. Jed nodded in satisfaction as he watched the animals, if any warriors were below, the wild ones would sense their presence and run into the timber.

"No one comes, Crow Killer." Silent One awakened and stood stiffly. "It is cold up here on the ground, not like the cabin."

"Perhaps, I was wrong." Jed shrugged. "We will head back."

Mounting their horses, the two warriors turned back down the steep trail in the early morning dawn. Neither of the men looked behind them as Blue Darter and his warriors rode into view in the lower valley, spooking a large herd of deer.

In his haste, after a night's rest, Standing Bull kept his horse in a hard trot. They started across the valley and up the last trail where they would top out above the valley where Jed had built his cabin. The warrior with the pale eyes was in a hurry, as he thirsted for battle and blood of the Arapaho who many thought a demon. The words of the cowardly Nez Perce as they talked about the powers of the Arapaho did not scare him in the least, and he wanted to meet this enemy in battle. The Blackfoot warrior did not believe in demons, believing only in his own strength as a warrior, and now he would prove his prowess and invincibility. Standing Bull was a cold-hearted warrior, but none could deny his bravery.

Jed reined in the piebald and surveyed the valley from the prominence of a high flat before making his final descent to the flat ground and his cabin. His lungs filled with the cool fresh air as he surveyed his valley. "It is beautiful, Silent One." Jed spoke absently, forgetting the youngster couldn't hear him. Motioning forward, Jed started the piebald down the trail that flattened out on the valley floor a short distance ahead.

Jed and the young Assiniboine had ridden only a few yards onto the valley floor when the piebald pricked his ears and turned his head slightly back up the trail. Alerted to the danger, Jed whirled the horse and focused his eyes on the trail, hoping to see what the horse was sensing.

"Someone comes, Crow Killer." Silent One signaled as the horse he rode pricked its ears, sensing something behind them on the trail as well.

Jed read the signal and nodded. Kneeing the piebald hard, Jed with Silent One right on his heels raced into a large stand of mountain cedar and dismounted.

"We left our lookout too quickly." Jed cursed his actions.

"What will we do?" The young warrior signaled. "Our horses do not lie, horses and maybe riders come."

"We will wait and see how many come against us." Jed checked the priming on his Hawken. "Are you afraid, young one?"

"Not afraid, Crow Killer, but maybe slightly worried."

"Only a fool is unafraid of the unknown."

Silent One grinned. "I'm deaf, but not a fool."

Blue Darter reined in on the same flat outcropping as Jed had earlier, overlooking the valley. He studied the far end of the flat land where the Arapaho's lodge was located. Fresh tracks showed on the muddy trail they stood on, but nothing moved in the valley as far as he could see. Blue Darter studied the tracks and knew these horses had riders because the tracks were close together on the rise.

"His lodge is there." The dark arm raised and pointed down the valley. "In the tall trees, but something is wrong, there is no smoke."

Without speaking, Standing Bull kicked his horse hard and took the lead. Today, he would kill this demon so all the northern tribes would know of his prowess, and know he and he alone was the greatest of warriors. His coup stick would carry the scalp of this Arapaho and he would ride the black piebald horse of Black Robe the Nez Perce, smiling to himself as his chest swelled. After today, all tribes would know and fear the name of Standing Bull.

"I will speak with him of Small Mountain before you fight." Blue Darter rode up alongside the pale-eyed warrior.

"You have led us here. Now, I will lead this trail."

"You gave your word, Standing Bull."

Reining in hard, the large warrior glared at the younger Blue Darter. "Speak with him, but do not interfere again in a true warrior's path."

Nodding, Blue Darter pushed his horse down the steep trail before riding out onto the flats. He remembered how Crow Killer had surprised them their first time into this valley, and how the Arapaho seemed friendly. Blue Darter had listened to Squirrel Tooth's words of warning that were full of fear, but still he did not believe Crow Killer to be a demon. The warrior had been friendly by inviting them into his lodge and offering them food and presents. It had been Small Mountain who had challenged the warrior to fight over the land he said the Blackfoot Tribe claimed. Even then the Arapaho hadn't killed. No, Blue Darter did not feel the warrior was a killer or a demon. Still, he remembered how the warrior had ridden up on them, unheard and unseen, as they studied the valley. Reining in his horse, he gave the others a final warning before moving down the valley. Thinking on the tracks he had seen, he felt Crow Killer was near, even watching them now.

"There are four Blackfoot." Silent One signed. "Let us kill them before they move closer to the lodge."

Jed already recognized the warrior, Blue Darter, leading the warriors as they moved closer to the tree line where they sat watching. He knew the Blackfoot were here to look for the warriors he had killed earlier in the winter. If the warriors rode closer to the cabin, they would see the loose horses and would recognize them as Blackfoot.

"I do not wish to kill unless they provoke a fight." Jed shook his head. "I will talk with the warrior leading them."

"They have no rifles." Silent One signed and raised his Hawken. "We can kill them easily."

"There is no honor in killing from a distance."

"No, my friend, no honor but safer." Silent One frowned as he signed.

"Wait here. If they attack, use your weapon and don't miss." Jed kicked the piebald.

"I won't." Silent One stroked the smooth barrel of the rifle. His finger itched, wanting to fire on the warriors riding down the valley to find out how the rifle killed. Still, he would obey Crow Killer's words.

Clearing the tree line, Blue Darter sensed the Arapaho would be there, and wasn't surprised as Jed rode out ahead of him onto the valley floor. He shook his head, perhaps this warrior was indeed a demon. How else did he know exactly when an enemy rode into his valley? He remembered Squirrel Tooth's words and the fear in his voice, and now his own confidence waned. Watching as Jed stopped his horse facing them, Blue Darter questioned himself. He had heard of the evil ones all his life and the Blackfoot people were superstitious, so he wondered if this warrior was truly a demon.

"Wait here, I will speak with the Arapaho." Blue Darter did not ask, he ordered the others. Deep Water had appointed him the leader on this trail and no one dared to question his word.

"When you are finished, stand aside and let a real warrior decide what is best." Standing Bull nodded over at Blue Darter.

"When I am finished talking, do as you wish."

Jed watched Blue Darter on his horse walking toward him. The other three warriors remained where they were, not moving.

"Welcome to my valley, Blue Darter." Jed signed his greeting. "Have you come this time in peace?"

Blue Darter studied the tall warrior before him. "Our Chief Deep Water has sent us here to look for his son, Small Mountain, and the ones who rode with him."

Jed wasn't going to deny killing the warriors, there was no need as the horses in the valley would tell the story. "They came here to kill and gave me no choice."

"Small Mountain has gone to meet his ancestors and the three that were with him?" Blue Darter asked hoarsely.

"Yes, it was the same as last time." Jed nodded. "He came to kill. He came for my scalp and this horse. I hope Blue Darter doesn't make the same mistake."

"Where is his body?"

"He was placed on a burial scaffold, the same as your people would have done for him." Jed pointed up at the rim of the valley. "He was not scalped, nor his body mutilated in any way."

Nodding, Blue Darter looked the way Jed pointed and knew this one did not lie. "I thank you for this."

"I am sorry, Blue Darter, but your friend came here to kill. He brought death on himself and the others."

"Tell me, Crow Killer, are you a demon as the Nez Perce say?"

"I am just a man; a warrior of the Arapaho people, nothing more."

"I believe you."

"What will happen now?"

"I will ride back to tell my chief his son is dead." Blue Darter looked back where his warriors sat their horses. "Will he be permitted to come here in peace and bring his son home?"

"He will, if he comes in peace."

"There are many Blackfoot warriors in our villages."

"I told you once, this is my valley." Jed's face grew hard. "If you come in peace, you are welcome. If you come to fight, I will bury you with Small Mountain.'

"You are only one man, Crow Killer. Only a demon could stand against so many."

"I have told you, I am no demon, but I will fight for my home." Jed shrugged. "The same as Blue Darter would fight for his people."

"I will return to tell my chief his son is dead."

"Go in peace, Blue Darter."

"I wish I could." Blue Darter pointed behind him. "The big warrior behind me will challenge you to fight when our talks are finished."

Jed's eyes took in the large warrior. "Why does he wish to fight?"

"You killed the Nez Perce, Black Robe. He wants your scalp and the black horse you ride to bring back to our village."

"What has that to do with the Blackfoot or is it just to build his ego?" Jed shook his head.

"I do not know this word, but your scalp will give him much pride and respect in the Blackfoot Villages." Blue Darter shrugged. "This warrior is crazy."

"Bragging rights are what the whites call it." Jed looked across at the warrior. "Tell him if he comes out to fight, I will kill him."

"I told him that already.'

"Good-bye, Blue Darter. If you come back to this place, come in peace."

"Good luck, Crow Killer." Blue Darter nodded. "The warrior is Standing Bull, the greatest of Blackfoot warriors, do not underestimate him."

"Tell him to go home, alive."

"He will not listen."

"Do not join him, Blue Darter." Jed warned. "I do not wish your blood on my hands."

"I speak for myself, Crow Killer. I wish to be your friend." The warrior looked behind him. "Standing Bull will fight. I cannot speak for the others."

"Tell them if they fight, I will bury them alongside Small Mountain." Jed's face turned hard, as he slashed his hand downward. "I have spoken."

Jed watched as Blue Darter rode his horse back to his warriors and spoke several minutes telling them of the deaths of their friends. The large warrior waved his war axe and yelled over at Blue Darter, then started toward Jed. The warrior carried only his war axe and hide shield as he closed in on the waiting Arapaho. Easing his rifle and bow to the ground, Jed pulled his axe and positioned his heavy war shield on his arm, before nudging the piebald forward. Black Robe had trained the animal well, as he sensed there was going to be a fight.

The Blackfoot was a formidable looking foe, tall, heavily muscled, and in his prime. Jed could tell the warrior was proud, almost arrogant, believing in himself and his strength. Remembering the warrior, Black Robe, Jed felt this was even more of a dangerous opponent. Riding the powerful piebald forward, Jed remembered the old Medicine Man White Swan's words when they had talked of Jed becoming a lance bearer. "It will be a hard and dangerous life, but you will be honored above all, as a great warrior."

The pale eyes were the first thing Jed noticed as the two warriors faced each other with less than twenty feet separating them. Even among the whites, Jed had never seen eyes as lightly colored as this warrior's watery eyes. Seemingly blank as they stared across at Jed, the eyes did not betray what they were looking at. Only the small pin-like pupils pinpointed their target in an almost totally blank whitish eye. The warrior's hair, what there was of it, was completely white and half of his scalp was missing, leaving only a wrinkled scar atop one side of the warrior's head. This one was a mighty foe, but even more, he was hideous in appearance.

No words were spoken as the two warriors sized each other up carefully, then repositioned their shields and axes. In the dense trees, Silent One slipped from his horse and held the Hawken cocked, resting across a small limb. If the three warriors holding back out of the fight made a move forward, the youngster would fire, and at this distance he could hardly miss.

As Standing Bull screamed his war cry and charged forward, Blue Darter held his arm out, preventing the other warriors from joining the fight. Both Crowfoot and Little Horse were friends of Blue Darter and both respected the young warrior. On this trail, he was their leader, and they would obey his commands.

"We will not help him?" Little Horse questioned as the two warriors raced toward each other, throwing up clods of dirt under their charging horses.

"Standing Bull wanted this fight. Now, we will let him fight." Blue Darter watched as the two combatants closed in on each other. "No, we will not interfere."

"What if the Arapaho kills Standing Bull?" Little Horse was worried, as he had listened to Squirrel Tooth as he told of the demon. He knew the fear in the warrior was real. "What will we do then?"

"We will not have to help him. Standing Bull will kill the Arapaho." Crowfoot studied the two combatants. "He is the greatest of our warriors."

Little Horse shook his head. "We will soon see who is the greatest."

"I will wager my best buffalo runner against yours, Little Horse." Crowfoot nodded.

"You have a wager, my friend." The warrior agreed. "But, you will lose."

Little Horse looked at Blue Darter. "Do you wish for the Arapaho to kill Standing Bull?"

"Standing Bull challenged the Arapaho, and would not listen." Blue Darter shrugged. "If he is killed, it is of his own choosing, not ours."

"Our chief will be enraged if his son and brother are both killed by this Arapaho." Crowfoot watched as the combatants charged forward. "He will blame us, call us cowards."

"Go, if you want to help." Blue Darter pointed. "Go, but Standing Bull will not thank you."

"They fight." Little Horse yelled.

Plunging forward, both fighters swung their war axes with all their might as the racing horses clashed together. Both men were unhorsed unexpectedly as their war axes locked together, pulling both riders from their lunging horses. Rolling apart as they landed on the ground, the warriors faced each other across the grassy flat.

"The Arapaho limps; he is hurt." Crowfoot grinned. "Your horse is mine."

"He is no demon, he is only a man." Little Horse laughed in relief. He had many horses, but only one life.

Both warriors slashed and swung their war axes as they fought, moving back and forth across the grassland. First one and then the other gained the advantage in this battle for life. Neither man would give an inch as they strained and pushed against each other, feinting and dodging the deadly weapons. Blood showed on each man's arms as the flicking knives found their mark. Jed knew he was in the battle of his life. Black Robe had been a great warrior, but this pale-eyed warrior was far superior in strength and speed. He fought with pure hatred and his physical strength was that of a crazed man.

Using his feet, Jed was able to trip the Blackfoot, but each time the warrior, with blinding speed and unerring agility, regained his footing, darting away from the deadly range of the war club Jed wielded. Never had Jed fought a fighter with this one's speed. His kicks missed their mark, time and again, and the warrior managed to step back out of harm's way with each pass of the club. Both men were bloody, but neither managed to gain the advantage as they struggled. Falling from the horse had numbed Jed's leg temporarily, but now it was fine.

The three watching warriors shook their heads in disbelief as the fight waged on. Never had they seen two warriors struggle and fight on as these two were doing. Most knife fights were over in minutes, but these two were so equally matched that one would have to make a mistake or slip for the other to be victorious.

"The Arapaho is a courageous fighter."

"As Standing Bull is." Crowfoot watched as the men strained in each other's grasp. "They are like two enraged buffalo bulls, maddened with blood lust, crazy to gore each other."

"Ugh!" Little Horse yelled. "Standing Bull has taken a bad wound!"

The warrior had seen Jed break the grasp of Standing Bull and slip under the arm of the warrior, swiping his blade along the rib cage with the razor sharp knife, cutting him clean to the bone. Blood ran down the bare torso of the Blackfoot warrior, spilling across both men's hands, making their grip on each other slippery. Jed pulled away from the hard-breathing Standing Bull and took in a deep breath. His quarry was badly injured, blood gushed from the deep wound. Jed knew now, to take his time and press the weakening man, being careful not to get in reach of Standing Bull's blade. As a wounded animal fought with the instinct for survival, Standing Bull, knowing he was hurt bad, desperately rushed forward, trying to reach the retreating Arapaho.

Blue Darter watched as Standing Bull started to stagger. "He is weakening, the Arapaho will finish him."

"Then we must kill the Arapaho." Crowfoot touched his bow. "We must save Standing Bull."

"Would that be honorable?" Little Horse looked at the warrior. "Standing Bull wanted this fight. Now, he has lost."

"I tell you if we do not, our chief will call us cowards."

"Do as you wish." Blue Darter shrugged. "I will not kill a helpless warrior who has fought as courageously as this one."

Watching, as the two combatants fought with all their might, they knew Standing Bull was almost finished, as his great strength was sapped. Suddenly, they saw the Arapaho wrap his leg around the warrior and trip Standing Bull backward. Landing on top of the exhausted and weak warrior, Jed plunged his knife deep into the stomach of the Blackfoot and ripped upward, completely gutting the warrior. Staggering to his feet, they watched as Jed sliced with his knife and ripped the grey scalp from the dying man's head.

"Perhaps this one is a demon." Little Horse stared in shock. "Standing Bull was still alive when he scalped him."

Holding the scalp up for the warriors to see, Jed flung the long white hair onto the quivering body of the dying man. Blood completely covered Jed's ripped buckskins as he staggered back to where the Hawken lay in the grass. Never taking his eyes from the watching Blackfoot, Jed picked up the rifle and checked its priming. Blue Darter held up his hand as he rode forward slowly, cautiously approaching the bloody warrior.

"You have won, Crow Killer. We will not dishonor the Blackfoot people by attacking a wounded enemy who has fought with honor." Blue Darter looked over at the now dead Standing Bull. "He wanted this fight, to win glory. Now, he may rest in peace. He has his glory."

"Glory is always fleeting." Jed breathed hard.

"For this one, it was." Blue Darter looked down at Standing Bull's limp body. "He will be forgotten in time, but I will always remember him for a fool, but a brave fool."

"I am curious, Blue Darter, what happened to this one's hair?"

"Many, many moons ago, when he was but a youth, he fought with our warriors, and a mighty warrior of the Mandan people took half his scalp but let him live." Blue Darter shrugged. "His hair turned white. I think that is what made him so vicious, cruel, and crazed the remainder of his life."

"I could understand that alright."

"I am sorry for this day, Crow Killer."

"Two times now the Blackfoot have come to this valley to kill me." Jed looked hard at Blue Darter. "Leave this place and do not return."

"I have not fought against you, Crow Killer."

"You have led warriors here that came to fight me." Jed shook his head, trying to clear it. "Leave here now, before you die."

"My friend, Small Mountain, can we return for him?"

"Their bodies lay there." Jed pointed up on the ridge. "Take them now and leave this valley. If you return to this place, you and all who come here will die."

Blue Darter looked to where Crowfoot and Little Horse sat their horses, just out of hearing, as he considered turning them loose on the Arapaho. What would he tell Deep Water when they returned to their village?

"I need horses to drag the travois."

"You have horses."

"It would be a long walk home if we use these to drag the travois."

"If you're thinking about killing me, Blue Darter, you will wind up with your friend Small Mountain." Jed warned. "I have tried to be the friend of the Blackfoot. It is finished."

"I have already said we would not dishonor the Blackfoot by attacking you." Blue Darter spoke quietly. "We will build the travois to take our people to their home."

"Go then, and never return to this place, if you come to kill."

Nodding, Blue Darter turned his horse and rode back to where Crowfoot and Little Horse waited. "We will take our dead and leave this place."

"I say we kill him." Crowfoot studied Jed.

"No, my friend, he will kill us." Blue Darter shook his head sadly. "Squirrel Tooth the Nez Perce was right, this one is a demon."

"Bah!" Crowfoot whirled his horse. "He is just a man, you see how he bleeds."

"Do not be a fool, Crowfoot. He waits to kill you." Blue Darter warned. "Come, we will take our dead and leave this place."

"Deep Water will think us cowards." Crowfoot was enraged. "I am a warrior, not a squaw."

"Then go after him. You will share a travois with Standing Bull."

Little Horse shook his head. "Standing Bull was the greatest fighter in our nation. Blue Darter is right, none of us would stand a chance against this warrior."

"We go."

Jed watched as the three Blackfoot turned and started the steep climb back up the mountain, disappearing as they passed over the high ridge where the scaffolds holding Small Mountain and his warriors stood.

Seeing the warriors ride out of sight, Silent One raced from the tree line to Jed's side. Weaving as a mask of darkness enfolded him, Jed crumpled falling forward in exhaustion. Flying from his horse as it slid to a stop, Silent One knelt beside the prone form.

The young warrior signed as he studied the many wounds covering Jed. "The Blackfoot fought well. He has left you with many wounds."

"Take me home." Jed was weak from loss of blood, his wounds, and bitter struggle, but he could still read the young one's signs.

Catching the piebald, Silent One tied their weapons onto his horse, then strained as he lifted the limp form onto the horse. The piebald stood still as the smell of blood filled his nose as the half conscious man was slowly pushed across him. Leaping up behind Jed, the young warrior held him tight, supporting and keeping him astride the horse. Turning the piebald, he rode slowly north to the cabin.

High on the ridge as Blue Darter and his warriors loaded the bones of the dead ones on the travois, they watched below as the two horses made their way across the flat valley.

"Someone helps him." Crowfoot pointed.

"Yes, another was watching from hiding as the Arapaho fought." Blue Darter nodded. "We were lucky today, my friends."

"How were we lucky?" Little Horse questioned.

"If we attacked the Arapaho, the other one would have used his thunder gun."

"We do not know if he had a white man's rifle." Crowfoot frowned.

"The Arapaho held one as we spoke." Blue Darter pointed toward the valley. "The other warrior probably had one too."

"You are just guessing this."

"Look at the horse being led, my friends. Those could be rifles hanging from the horse's mane." The horses were too far away for the Blackfoot to see plainly.

"It is too far to see." Little Horse held his hands over his eye, blocking the sun. "They could be rifles."

"Blue Darter speaks true." Crowfoot finished lashing hides over the travois. "We were lucky this day."

"Come, we will pick up Standing Bull's body and return to our lands."

CHAPTER 6

Returning to the cabin, Silent One placed Jed on the bed and removed the bloody, shredded doeskin shirt, shaking his head in amazement. Cuts, small and large, some shallow wounds and others deeper, completely covered Jed's body. Blood seeped from the wounds as the young one softly wiped the cuts clean, and placed soft linen over the them, trying to thwart the bleeding. He didn't know the cotton linen he was using was to be used for curtains Sally Ann had picked out for the cabin before she was shot. Slipping outside, he pulled several long pieces of hair from one of the horse's tails and returned to the cabin. Retrieving a sewing awl from the fireplace mantel, Silent One brought a bowl of hot water from the hearth, and took a seat alongside the bed.

Scalding the awl, he threaded a piece of horsehair and looked into Jed's dark face, and signed. "This is gonna hurt, my friend, but it must be done."

Only the slow nodding of the wounded man showed he understood. Several moans came from Jed as Silent One pushed the bone needle through the tough skin bordering the deeper cuts. Again and again, Silent One bound the open cuts together as Jed gritted his teeth against the torturous pain. The black tail hairs of the piebald made the stitches stand out profoundly against Jed's lighter skin. Finally, the youngster smeared the wounds with bear grease, then stood up.

The tight stitches stopped the bleeding. Now, only rest and hope that no infection from the evil ones would set in, was all that could be done. Only a nod came from Jed's sweaty face as Silent One signed he was finished.

"Rest now, Crow Killer, while I feed the horses and bring the others into the corral."

"Thank you, my friend." The hands slowly signed. "Watch closely for the Blackfoot."

"I will watch closely." The Assiniboine picked up his rifle. "You do not need to thank me. You would do the same for me."

Ed Wilson wasn't surprised when Joseph Beale rode into his yard, almost three weeks to the day, after he had told Seth to leave his land. He hadn't seen the farmer for months, as the Beale farm was located several miles south of his. Watching as Beale approached, Wilson already knew why the man was there. Seth had admitted to him weeks ago that Adam Beale had been the other shooter in the killing of Sally Ann Duncan.

"I'm surprised to see you, Joseph." Wilson shook hands with the farmer. "Light and rest your backside."

"I know I am long overdue for a visit, Ed."

"What brings you here today?"

Beale removed his battered hat. "Adam and Seth are friends, and I hoped Adam would be here."

"He's not home then?"

"No, he rode out two days ago at sunup; said he had something to take care of." Beale ran his hands through his hair. "I ain't seen him since he pulled out."

"Is that unusual?"

"No, not normally. He likes to hunt but this time is different." The farmer shook his head.

"How's that?"

"He took his rifle, food, blankets, and our best horse when he pulled out." Beale looked over at Wilson. "He didn't mention a word about leaving, just rode out. It looks like he's planning on being gone awhile."

"Come in for coffee, Joseph." Without waiting, Wilson started for the house. "I have things to tell you that may not come easy for you to swallow."

Beale never touched his coffee as Wilson told of the shooting and that he ran Seth from the farm. Shock crossed the wind weathered face as he listened, holding on to every word.

"You're saying my Adam shot and killed Sally Ann Duncan weeks ago?"

"Along with Seth, that's what I'm saying."

"It can't be." The man swallowed hard. "I ain't heard nary a thing about it."

"I take it you haven't been to Baxter Springs?"

"No, I have a lot of work around my place." Beale shook his head. "I only ride in if'n I'm really needing something bad. Normally, I send Adam."

"I'm sorry to have to tell you this." Wilson sipped his coffee. "Our sons are both guilty of killing an innocent girl, and there's no denying it."

"Where have they gone?"

Wilson thought of Jedidiah. "I figure they're heading east."

"Why would they go east?"

"Seth knows his brother Jed will come for him, seeking revenge, sooner or later." Wilson sipped on his coffee. "They're on the run."

"Would Jedidiah kill them?"

"Wouldn't you, if they killed your wife?"

"His wife? He married Sally Ann?" Beale wiped his face. "My boy, Adam, is just a kid."

"So was Sally Ann."

"Just kids, how could this happen?"

"No, Joseph, they're grown men." Wilson set down his coffee. "Jed and Sally Ann were married, and both of our sons should be hanged."

"You would hang, Seth?" Beale shuddered. "You said it was an accident. They were just trying to scare your Injun boy."

"No more of that, Joseph." Wilson's face turned red. "He's also my son."

"If it were an accident, none of the men here would hang them."

"That's probably true." Wilson knew Beale was probably right. "I s'pect hanging would be easier than what Jed's got in store for them."

"What can we do?"

"Wait, we can't go running all over the mountains when our crops are in need of harvesting." Wilson shook his head. "Plus, we have no idea where they've run off to."

Wilson watched the farmer ride slowly back down the road to his farm, then turned toward the corral.

After an hour's hard ride, Wilson tied his blowing horse to the tie rail in front of the fur trader's store. Pushing through the door, he found Bate Baker busy sorting out traps behind the counter.

"Ed Wilson." The trader reached out his chubby hand. "Man, it's been a month of Sundays since we spoke last."

"Yeah, I've been pretty busy on the farm."

Embarrassed, the storekeeper looked across the counter. "I'm sorry about Sally Ann and your stepson, Ed."

"Yeah, that's why I'm here."

"Speak up; if I can help, I will."

Wilson looked around the interior of the post, not being a trapper he had never visited the trading post much. "I need Lige Hatcher. You know his whereabouts?"

"This is midsummer, and last I heard him say his plans were to meet up with Chalk at Bridger's and bring a train over the mountains." The storekeeper rubbed his chin thoughtfully. "Figure they're about at the breaks by now, if'n they're on schedule."

"You reckon they'll be here next month?"

"I reckon they will."

"You know any other scouts that know the mountains east of here?"

"Maybe. You planning on hunting up Jedidiah?"

"If I knew where to look, I just might."

"I figure he's headed back to the Arapaho."

Wilson shook his head. "No, he spoke of a valley, his valley."

"Man, there's a million acres of valleys in those mountains." Baker shook his head. "I doubt any man would know where to look for him."

"Lige would." Wilson turned. "If any trappers pass through, get word to him to look me up."

"I'll do it, Ed." Baker nodded. "I saw you with the boy the day of the shooting. I'm sorry about the girl."

Hesitating, Wilson turned slightly. "I am too. Tell me, Bate, did you try to stop it?"

"That ain't fair, Ed." Baker seemed to puff up. "I had no part in it."

"Funny, that's what everybody claims." Wilson studied the red-faced trader. "Except Amos Duncan, that is."

"Her pa? What part did he play in her killing?"

Wilson turned without answering. "Just get word to Lige, if you can."

For several days, Jed had experienced fevers and chills, at times burning up, and then freezing. He could remember the youngster's face staring down at him as he had worked tirelessly for two days without rest, trying to bring down the high fever. The morning of the third day, the fever broke, leaving him weak and clammy from sweat. Finally, with Silent One's help, he managed to move from the bed to the chair and finally out into the warm sunshine.

Two weeks had passed, and Silent One removed the stitches from Jed's body, leaving pink scabs all over his torso. Sitting in the shade outside the cabin, Jed looked out across the valley.

"How are your wounds today, Crow Killer?"

"I'm sore." Jed nodded. "Feels like I'm being stretched in every way."

Silent One laughed to himself and signed as he applied bear grease to the scars. "This will loosen your skin up in a few days."

"I hope so. We need to do some work."

"You sit and rest, I do not want your wounds to reopen." Silent One warned his patient. "The evil ones could come back."

"I will rest a few more days."

"Good, I do not want to use the needle on you again if the evil ones raise their heads again."

Jed knew the youngster was referring to the high fevers that had set in after the wounds had been stitched. "You saved my life, young one."

"No more than you have done for me."

"I'm indebted to you."

Signing, Silent One turned to the cabin. "I will bring you some food."

"I hope not that watery stew you've been shoveling down me."

Laughing, the young warrior walked away.

The sunshine felt good on Jed's sore body as he pushed his way under the shade tree beside the cabin. The fight with Standing Bull could have gone either way as the Blackfoot had been fearless and strong. Jed looked down at his bare chest and shook his head. He was beginning to look like some of the old bulls that ruled the herds. He carried scars all across his body, scars that would remain with him for a lifetime. He could see White Swan's nodding head and hear his words, "You are a Lance Bearer, Grandson, and your scars are a badge of honor among the Arapaho."

Two more weeks of convalescence found Jed on his feet, regaining his strength and agility. The scabs were beginning to fall away, but he knew the scars underneath would remain forever. Climbing slowly on his horse from a tree stump, Jed crossed the small stream and rode across the valley. Kicking the piebald into a short lope, Jed filled his lungs in elation. Nothing made him feel more carefree than a good horse and miles of grasslands to ride on. The piebald was fresh from being penned up and now he was ready to run for miles, but Jed reined him in. He knew Silent One would be angry if he broke open one of his scars.

Turning the horse, Jed returned to the cabin and slipped slowly to the ground, putting the piebald back in the corral. Entering the cabin, Jed found Silent One cooking deer steaks over the open hearth.

"Tomorrow, we will search out the valley for signs of raiders." Jed sat weakly into his hide chair.

"You move like an old woman with the creeps." Silent One signed. "Perhaps you should wait another week."

Accepting a plate of wild onions, greens, and deer steak, Jed nodded his thanks. "We ride tomorrow."

Since the young Assiniboine was a deaf-mute, their conversations were signed with a series of nods and waves. The two young men had grown close, both knowing mostly what the other was thinking.

True to his word, at daylight, Jed and Silent One moved out across the valley, heading back to where the fight with the Blackfoot had taken place. Each man carried his Hawken across the withers of his horse. Riding slowly, they searched out every place of concealment and every tree line before pushing forward through the valley. Jed knew this was very dangerous, as he was in no shape to fight, but he could still aim and fire the Hawken. He had to know if any enemy had entered the valley.

"There is nothing, Crow Killer." Silent One signed. "You are in pain. We should return to the lodge."

Nodding, Jed turned the piebald north, toward the cabin. Today, they had ridden far, but the youngster was right, his wounds were starting to ache. Tomorrow, he would rest, and they would ride out again to scout the valley. He hadn't intended to kill, but by defending his valley, he had been forced to fight, forced to kill many Blackfoot warriors, and one day they would return to avenge their losses. He did not fear his closest neighbors, the Nez Perce. After the battle with Standing Bull and thinking him a demon, they would not dare come to his valley. Blue Darter had spoken of how scared they were of him, thinking he was one of the evil ones. Jed shook his head, if he had been there watching as the grizzly mauled and killed Billy Wilson, he would have thought the same.

Daylight, the next morning, the sudden banging of a bucket against the door grabbed Jed's attention, causing him to hurry to the cabin door.

"Enemy!" Silent One signaled and pointed across the creek.

Six figures were barely discernable as they sat their horses, staring at the cabin. So far, none of the warriors made any movement forward to cross the small creek. Jed motioned Silent One back into the cabin, and signaled for him to bring the rifles. Standing beside the open door for several minutes, Jed studied the silent warriors through the thick fog covering the creek. As the fog slowly lifted, he let out with a bloodcurdling yell and limped slowly forward.

"Your rifle, Crow Killer." Silent One stopped as Jed waved him back.

Jed walked toward the creek, when a chorus of bloodthirsty screams went up and the unknown warriors charged forward, laughing as they splashed across the creek. Jed looked behind him to reassure Silent One all was okay, before the youngster fired at the oncoming riders. Reaching Jed, the warriors dismounted and gathered around him, slapping him on the back.

Bow Legs held onto Jed's arm as he flinched from the happy reunion. "The great Crow Killer looks like he has been held captive by the Crow women."

Jed was bare-chested which allowed the warriors to see the many fresh scars running across his upper body. Apart from the pain of his body being slapped, Jed was in shock, almost speechless, as his friends Bow Legs, Big Owl, and White Bird were standing before him along with others.

"What are you doing here, my friends?"

"We are hungry. We come to eat."

"Hungry?" Jed looked about him at the smiling faces. He didn't realize how much he missed them until now. "How did you find me?"

"The old one, White Swan told us where you were."

"How?"

"Something about a valley and a light."

"Feed us and we will tell you." White Bird grinned. "Have you been away so long, you have forgotten your manners?"

"I apologize for my bad manners." Jed pulled a new deerskin shirt across his shoulders and bare torso. "Come."

Jed, with the warriors in tow, stopped in their tracks as they turned and found the barrel of Silent One's Hawken staring at them. Throwing up his hand, Jed smiled, signing to the youngster.

Bow Legs looked at the rifle and frowned. "Is he as mean as he looks?"

"He cannot speak or hear, but he is my friend and this young warrior saved my life."

"An Assiniboine?" Big Owl studied the rifle. "He is an enemy."

Laughing, Jed led the warriors past the frowning youngster and into the cabin. Signaling for Silent One to prepare the warriors something to eat, he introduced the youngster to the Arapaho.

Silent One only nodded as he looked at the fearsome, warlike Arapaho. He couldn't help but study them closely as he heated coffee and started frying deer steaks.

"Why are my friends here, so far from your hunting grounds?"

Bow Legs looked over at Silent One. "First, tell us how one as young as this one saved your life."

Jed raised his shirt, pointing at his torso, revealing the many scars Standing Bull had given him. "The young one brought me home, sewed me up, and took care of my wounds after the fight."

"We have heard of this fight." White Bird smelled the coffee that Silent One handed him.

"It is good; drink it."

"You have made many enemies, my friend." Bow Legs took his coffee. "This warrior Standing Bull was widely known. He is the brother of the Blackfoot Chief, Deep Water and another, Chief Lone Bull."

"You have become famous. They speak the name, Crow Killer the demon, in every village, but very quietly." Big Owl grinned.

"That is not why you ride so far from your lands, to tell me of my fame." Jed looked at Bow Legs. "Tell me why you are here, and how did you hear of the fight?"

Bow Legs shrugged. "White Swan sees everything in the fires."

"Our Chief Slow Wolf wishes for you to return to the people." White Bird added, trying to be serious.

Silent One interrupted the talk as he handed tin plates full of food to the hungry warriors.

Bow Legs laughed as he bit into the tender steaks. Signaling to the distrustful Silent One, giving a compliment to the youngster. "You are a good cook."

"He is a better cook than my squaw." White Bird laughed.

Seeing the youngster's face grow red, Jed quickly signaled that the warriors were just paying him a compliment. "They are my friends, young one, as you are."

"Yours, not mine, Crow Killer." The youngster signaled. "They are rude."

Bow Legs looked over at the young warrior and nodded. "He is a brave, young man."

"That he is." Jed agreed. "Now, tell me why Slow Wolf has sent for me?"

Bow Legs set his plate aside and looked hard at Jed. "We need all our Lance Bearers, and he asks that you come."

"Where is Walking Horse?"

"Walking Horse protects our village until you return." Big Owl spoke. "He is still very weak from his wounds, but he rides with the warriors."

Jed studied the faces before him. "Why has he not regained his strength, it has been many moons since he was hurt."

"The evil ones stay in his body. White Swan cannot cure him." Big

Owl belched loudly and rubbed his stomach. "Slow Wolf fears for his life. One place, where the arrow of the Crow bit him, will not heal and allows the evil ones to enter his body."

"That is why he wishes you to return quickly." White Bird looked at the others. "We need a strong leader."

"There is more, tell me; speak." Jed could sense something had been left unsaid.

"Yes, there is more." Bow Legs nodded. "Many suns ago, there was a big fight with the Pawnee, we killed many of them in battle."

"Now, they will come against us for revenge." White Bird added.

"Did we lose many Lance Bearers?"

"In battle, my friend, we always lose warriors, but we won a great victory." Bow Legs shook his head.

"How weak is my friend, Walking Horse?"

No one spoke, as none wanted to be the bearer of bad news. Finally, Bow Legs shook his head. "If he still lives when we return..." The sentence was not finished.

"You will rest your horses tonight." Jed stood up. "We leave with the coming sun."

Big Owl shook his head. "We don't need rest, Crow Killer. We must get back."

"Maybe you don't, but your horses do."

Reading their signs and guessing the rest, Silent One stepped forward. "Crow Killer is still too weak from his wounds and cannot travel far."

As the sun was rising in the east, Jed motioned for Silent One to follow him outside. Opening the heavy door, the new morning greeted them with birds calling and the fresh smell of the valley. Jed didn't want to leave his valley, but Slow Wolf had summoned him and he could not refuse. Perhaps, if he hurried, he would be back in time for the winter trapping.

"These are the famous Lance Bearers of the Arapaho?" Silent One signaled.

Jed nodded. "They are as you, my friends."

"Then, I will not kill them." The youngster looked back at the cabin.

"You are still too weak to travel on this long trail. Wait until you are stronger."

"I must return to the south to my people." Jed looked into the dark eyes as he signaled. "You stay here and take care of our valley and the stock."

"You are in no shape to ride."

"I must ride, my people need me."

"Then, I will ride with Crow Killer to fight his enemies."

"Then, my friend, who will take care of our lodge and horses." Jed smiled. "If I am not back in time to set the traps, you will have to do that for me."

Signing, Silent One gathered the rawhide leads and walked to where the Arapaho had left their horses hobbled. "I will catch the horses."

Jed didn't try to signal his thanks as the youngster already turned his back. He didn't want to leave the young Assiniboine there alone, as there could be great danger in this valley, should the Blackfoot or even the Nez Perce come to raid. He knew in the south there would be fighting and the young Assiniboine was still too young to fight against experienced warriors. No, he would be safer at the cabin.

Bow Legs passed Jed as he limped back inside the cabin. Walking to the horses, he helped Silent One place the rawhide bridles on each horse. Studying the straight powerful back of the youngster, he smiled; someday this one would make a formidable enemy. "I know Crow Killer has been in many fights, the scars on his body speak for themselves." Bow Legs signed. "Has something else happened?"

"Yes."

"Tell me, Assiniboine." The Arapaho looked toward the cabin. "He is not the same. He is hard now and his voice holds no laughter as it once did."

"Yes, something terrible has happened but he will have to tell you." Silent One signed and turned toward the cabin, stopping at the gate. "It is not my place to speak of it."

"I respect you for this, young one."

It was still early morning when the warriors had biscuits, deer steaks and coffee. Now, they gathered their weapons and horses, ready to ride south to their own hunting grounds.

Jed studied the sad face of Silent One and smiled. "Remember, young one, the coyote runs and hides when a stronger enemy appears, but he is smarter and will survive many battles for doing this."

"I know of the coyote."

"I will bring you a young Arapaho woman when I return."

"Bah, I would rather have the peaches in the metal hide."

Jed laughed lightly. He hated to leave the youngster behind. "When I return, we will ride to the settlement and fill you up on them."

"I do not think you will return, Crow Killer."

"This is my home." Jed studied the youngster. "Nothing could keep me from this place."

"Ride hard, my friend, and return to your valley." Silent One signed. "I will protect it for you, and I will set the metal traps."

Three days of hard riding brought the dust covered, tired riders to the edge of the Yellowstone where Jed called a halt for the night. Figuring he would be sore and weak from the long ride from the valley, he actually worked-out the soreness from his body, regaining most of his strength. Before leaving the cabin, he had given the four rifles, he had brought back from the settlement, to the warriors with powder and shot. Silent One had his new rifle for protection. Jed didn't want the rifles falling into enemy hands if they did raid the valley and knew they would be needed against the Pawnee.

During the few stops they had made on their way south, he went over the handling of the rifles many times. Not exactly crack shots as Silent One had become, nonetheless the warriors were making progress in the short time they had the rifles and the few times each had fired one.

Sitting around the crackling fire, Jed watched the red embers pop causing hot embers to rise into the night air. Normally jovial, the warriors were quiet, saying little as they ate the dried meat Jed had brought from the cabin. Several times, Jed had caught Bow Legs looking across at him, studying him, but saying nothing.

"Two more days and we will be home." White Bird ventured, tossing a small stick into the fire.

"Tell me of the Pawnee." Jed eased himself against a log. "Are they strong?"

"They are many in numbers, but they are not ferocious fighters as the Arapaho, Sioux, or Cheyenne."

"What caused the fight you spoke of?"

"It was an accident." Bow Legs shook his head. "We came upon them unexpectantly."

"Tell me, how can Arapaho Lance Bearers come upon an enemy unexpected?"

"We rode around a sharp place in the trail and ran right into the Pawnee."

"And?"

"The Pawnee would not give ground and let us pass."

Jed nodded, he knew what happened before he asked. "The Arapaho wouldn't give ground either?"

"What, and lose face to a Pawnee dog eater?"

"So, now we have a bigger problem than who gives ground?"

Bow Legs nodded. "Yes, we were foolish."

"No, we were not foolish." Big Owl shook his big head. "Well, maybe a little."

"Tell me, White Bird, how many Pawnee were there?"

The warrior looked at the others before answering. "Maybe, thirty."

"And Lance Bearers?"

"Ten."

"Now, that was a pretty even fight." Jed shook his head.

"We thought it was." Big Owl smiled.

"I bet you did." Jed nodded. "Was Walking Horse there?"

"No."

"It wouldn't have happened if he had been there to lead us, Crow Killer." Bow Legs chimed in. "We were talking and not watching the trail."

"I'll bet about women."

"What else does Bow Legs talk about?" White Bird laughed.

Bow Legs and the others looked into the fire, ignoring the question. These warriors were the elite of the Arapaho Nation, and now, they had inadvertently managed to start a war against another tribe. Now, the Arapaho People would have to endure the result of this battle.

The village dogs first alerted the village to the warriors riding in as they swarmed around the horses, barking and snapping until Big Owl reached down and whipped a couple of them back. People raced from their lodges in fear until they recognized the riders as Arapaho. A sudden shout went up as they recognized Crow Killer among the riders. Reining up in front of the large lodge of Slow Wolf, the tired warriors dismounted as the chief exited the lodge.

"My sons, it is good to see you back safely." The chief's eyes went to Jed.

"My Chief, we have brought the great Crow Killer back to his people." Bow Legs smiled as he looked over at Jed.

"It is good to be home, my Chief."

"It is good you are back, my son." The older man embraced Jed. "You have been missed."

"I have missed the people."

"Your lodge is there." Slow Wolf pointed. "All of you, go rest your bodies. Tonight, we will eat and talk in my lodge."

As they turned, Bow Legs took the rein from Jed's hand and nodded with his chin. "When our chief finishes talking with you, there is one who waits for you."

Jed looked over under a large oak. "Little Antelope."

"Yes, Little Antelope." Bow Legs smiled. "She has not forgotten. I have not seen her smile since you left many moons ago."

"She worries about Walking Horse."

"Perhaps, Walking Horse, or perhaps someone else."

"My friend, she is a married woman."

"Yes, maybe Crow Killer should tell her that."

"Tell her I will speak with Slow Wolf, and then I will join her."

Slow Wolf raised his hand, sensing Jed wanted to speak with Little Antelope. "Tonight, we will gather at my lodge to feast and talk of what is to be done. Now, you should talk with Walking Horse and his woman, then rest.

Walking quickly to where the young woman stood waiting, Jed smiled down at the small frame, embracing her for a second. In the months that had passed, she had not changed. Maybe a little thinner, but the smile and the twinkle in her eyes were still the same Little

Antelope he remembered. Awkwardly, he looked down into her upturned face and became tongue tied, not knowing what to say or how to begin. Sensing his nervousness and seeing the blush of redness come into his face, she smiled, showing the beautiful row of straight white teeth.

"You have come home?"

"Yes."

"We thought you had forgotten us." The dark eyes searched his face. "Did you?"

"How could I forget a face of such beauty?"

"You have been missed by the people and Walking Horse, my husband." The voice hesitated.

"And Little Antelope, has she missed me?"

This time, she turned red in the face. "Yes, I have missed you greatly."

"How is Walking Horse?"

"He has waited on you."

"He knew I was coming?"

Nodding her head slowly, she looked away. "He knew."

"Take me to him."

"My husband is weak." Little Antelope dropped her eyes. "Like a newborn baby."

"I have heard."

"Come." She turned slightly. "Try to not let your face show sadness when you see him."

"Is he that sick?"

"Yes."

"I will try." Jed took her arm softly. "I missed you, little one."

Only the soft, warm glow of her eyes spoke as she looked up at the tall warrior, then quickly turned toward the lodge of Walking Horse.

Seth watched as Adam Beale jogged slowly down the road from Baxter Springs. Beale's body slumped in the saddle, and Seth could tell the way the man rode, he was a reluctant participant in the coming days. Not wanting Beale with him, he had no choice and needed Beale's help, if they wanted to get out of this mess alive. Beale was a coward, and if he stayed in Baxter Springs he could be made to talk, causing both of them to be hanged. It really didn't matter; soon people would learn that they both had a part in killing Sally Ann Duncan.

"I see you made it."

Beale shook his head. "I still don't like it."

"You like hanging better?"

"They don't know anything." Beale shook his head. "Our pa's won't tell."

"Jedidiah knows, and I'd rather hang than suffer what he'll do to us." Seth exhaled disgustedly.

"You sure are scared of your own brother." Beale looked over at Seth. "What would he do?"

"He's lived with the Indians. You remember on the train, hearing of the tortures an Indian can put you through."

"Your own brother would do that to you?"

"That's just it, he ain't my brother." Seth shook his head. "Yes, I am scared of him. You should be too."

"Well, stepbrother then."

"Don't think our pa's won't tell, mine will." Seth spit. "They'll hang us both for sure."

"He always acted like he thought so much of you." Beale stammered.

"Reckon I've killed that." Seth looked ahead at Carter's cabin. "Let's go talk to Carter."

"You do the talking."

The farmer stood in his yard as the riders approached. He was watching closely as the two young men sat on their horses, talking suspiciously. Carter knew the boys and never liked or trusted either of them. Already, a neighbor had spread the word about the shooting of the Duncan girl, but so far, none knew who the shooter was.

"Morning, Mister Carter."

"Morning, gentlemen." The tall farmer nodded. "Y'all are riding early this morning."

"Yes, sir. We're trying to catch up with my brother, Jedidiah." Seth spoke up. "Did you happen to see him ride by two, three weeks ago?"

"I seen him, but he didn't stop." Carter rubbed his chin. "He didn't even wave, seemed mighty torn up about something, and now I know why."

"Yes, sir. He probably was." Seth nodded sadly. "The killing of his woman and all."

"Yeah, I heard about Sally Ann." Carter looked over at Beale. "What y'all needing here?"

"Like I said, we need to find Jed badly, Mister Carter." Seth couldn't meet the man's eyes with his own. "Would you happen to know which trail he rode over the mountain?"

"Nope, can't say I do, boys." Carter shook his head. "Those mountains out there are no place for a Pennsylvania farmer, and that's a fact."

"Well, would you happen to know the whereabouts of Lem Roden?"

"What do you boys want with that no-account drunk?"

Seth smiled slightly. "Well, sir, he may be a no-account, but he knows these mountains."

"If'n I was you boys, I'd go home and forget about Roden and your brother."

"We need him, and you ain't us." Beale suddenly spoke up sarcastically. "Do you know where he is?"

Carter pointed down the road. "Last I heard, he was holed up in a cave about ten miles down the road where it crosses Little Pine Creek."

"That's a far piece." Beale made a face.

"Yep, it is."

"That all you know?" Seth looked down at the tall farmer.

"Yep, it is. Now, you two get off my land quick." Carter pulled a shotgun from behind the woodpile. "Don't bother coming back. You ain't welcome here anymore. Now, get!"

"We're going." Seth turned his horse. "What's got your hackles up all of a sudden?"

"If you're lying, we'll be back." Beale added kicking his horse.

"Get!" Carter pointed the gun. "Don't come back here."

Hearing his name called several times, Lem Roden staggered slowly out into the brightness of the midday sun. A rat of a man, with torn, dirty clothes, stood before them with beady blue eyes, squinting from the bright sun, as he stared up at the two young men. Beale swallowed hard, he could smell the man from thirty paces. A filthy, matted, grey-brown beard hung from the gaunt, thin looking face. Seth shook his head as he stared at the scarecrow before them. He hadn't seen Roden in a year, and even back then he was dirty, but never this bad.

The rummy blue eyes looked up at the staring men. "What you fellers be wanting?"

"We're needing us a scout."

"I ain't in that business no more." Roden slurred his words. "You boys got anything to drink?"

"Depends."

"On what?"

"We need a scout."

"Done told you, I ain't interested."

"You heard the man, Adam." Seth pulled out a jug of rum from his saddlebag. "Well, Lem, we'll be seeing you."

The scaly tongue flicked out unchecked as beady bloodshot eyes riveted on the jug Seth held. "Now, hold up a minute. You fellers don't need to be in no hurry."

"Like we said, Lem." Seth uncorked the jug and smelled of the contents. "We need a scout who knows the mountains."

"West or east?"

"That away." Seth pointed.

"That's rough country, dangerous." Roden couldn't take his eyes off the sloshing jug as Seth shook it craftily. "What you want a scout for?"

"We need to find a feller."

"Who?" Roden asked, his thoughts centered on the jug. "White or red?"

"A little of both, I expect." Beale piped in, much to Seth's consternation.

"What's that supposed to mean?"

"He's white, Lem." Seth shook the jug. "You'll be paid fairly."

Roden looked up at the mountains, and back at the jug. Turning, he started back to the cave, then stopped and turned. "I'm down on my luck and y'all are out of luck. Shucks, I ain't even got a rifle or horse."

"What did you do with them?"

"Whiskey, rum, tonic spirits." Roden shrugged. "You might say they all went down my gullet."

"You show us over the mountains and we'll keep you in spirits." Seth knew he had the scout hooked. "Long as you get us where we want to go."

"You're a hard man. What's your name?"

"Seth Wilson."

"You any kin to that killer, Billy Wilson?"

"No, but I heard he was killed by a bear last year."

"Poor bear." Saliva dribbled down the filthy beard as Roden eyed the jug. "Probably caught lockjaw."

Seth held his temper, he needed the man. No matter what the man looked like now, once he had been a great mountain man and scout, equal to Lige Hatcher or Bridger. Seth studied the poor wretch and swore he would never become a drunk. Ballads had been written and were still sung around the towns and saloons about Lem Roden, the great scout, hunter, and Indian fighter.

"You ride with us, and we'll keep you well supplied."

"I'll be needing an outfit."

Seth smiled to himself. He had his man. "We'll outfit you."

Roden looked at the jug. "Starting now?"

"A little bit now, some more later." Seth swung the jug in front of the thin man.

"Alright, I'll lead you, but I only scout, nothing more." The slender scout seemed to read their minds.

"That's all we expect, Lem. Just lead us." Beale spoke up.

"Adam, hand me a bottle." Seth held out his hand as Beale handed over a small bottle of watered-down spirits."

Handing the bottle over to Roden, Seth smiled broadly. "We'll ride in and get your outfit. You stay put."

"We got your word on the deal?" Beale didn't trust the scout.

Eyeing the bottle, Roden grinned, then staggered back to the cave. "Yeah, my good word is about all I have left. I'll be here."

Beale shook his head sadly as the horses turned back to Baxter Springs. "We're really gonna follow that into the mountains?"

"Yep. At one time, he was the best there was."

"Maybe at one time."

"He'll do just fine. Let's ride."

"We ain't got any money." Beale shook his head hard. "How we gonna buy him a horse and outfit."

"Who said anything about buying?" Seth slowed his horse to a walk. "We better pass Carter's place in the dark and far off the main road."

"Why?"

"We sure wouldn't want him telling he saw us riding to town, would we?" Seth shrugged. "That is if a horse and supplies come up missing in the morning."

"No, don't reckon that would be good." Beale shook his head. "We sure are getting in deeper all the time."

Seth looked at Beale. "I just as soon they didn't see us in town tonight."

"Don't see how it matters, you said we were riding east after this is over."

"You never know, we might want to come back some day."

Arriving in town, the two found Baxter Springs had folded up and most folks had turned in for the night. A few men still occupied the small building that was used as a saloon, but for the most part, the inhabitants had gone home to their beds. Seth studied the saloon and the few horses tied to the hitching posts out front.

"You get Roden a horse and make sure he's sound." Seth nodded toward the saloon.

"Where you gonna be?"

"I'm gonna get supplies and an outfit for our new scout." Seth looked over at the general store. "Don't mess this up, Adam."

"Make sure to get him some clean clothes." Beale added. "And plenty of lye soap. You hear, several cakes of the stuff."

"Why?" Seth shook his head, laughing at his own question. "He smell or something?"

"Probably take five just to get down to the skin." Beale mumbled to himself.

Seth studied the upstairs windows of the store as he slipped down the alleyway and felt for the side door. He knew the store well. The owner, Elmer Woods and his wife, had their sleeping quarters above the mercantile. Only the kitchen was on the lower floor behind where the merchandise was lined up behind the counters. Using his heavy-bladed hunting knife, he pried open the lock on the door quietly. Inside, the interior was pitch black except for the small glow of the moon as it shined through the front window. The small settlement was still too young to have added street poles with the coal oil lamps at each corner. As a result, the streets were in total darkness after sundown.

Working his way along the counter, Seth felt for the weapon's rack, where the powder and shot lay under the counter. Many times, he had been in the store and knew the layout by heart, but still he had to feel his way along the counters in the dark. Being careful not to bump into anything or make noise, Seth quickly opened two sacks he had found and filled both with supplies. Hearing footsteps overhead, the redhead ducked down behind the counter and eased out his long knife. Barely breathing, he waited until only silence came once again from above. Toting the heavy bags loaded with powder and shot for the rifles, hardtack, salt, coffee, flour, clothes, and a few jugs of rum to keep Roden in check, Seth retraced his steps from the store to where his horse was tied. Securely tying the heavy bags and rifle onto the saddle horn, Seth led the horse back to where Beale was waiting.

"Did you get everything?"

"Yeah, everything we'll be needing." Seth looked at the shadow behind Beale. "Did you get a good horse?"

"Ha, I took Sam McBride's prize sorrel." Beale nodded smugly in the gloom. "Serves him right for making a fool out of me in front of Sara Fletcher at the church social last month."

Tying the two heavy bags on the stolen horse, Seth mounted. "Let's ride."

Daylight found the two back at Little Pine Creek. Dismounting and checking the cave, Seth found the thin scout passed out with the empty bottle lying beside him, but at least he was still there. As disgusting as the drunken man was, they needed him. He was their only hope of finding Jed back in the mountains, a wilderness they knew nothing about. Seth knew they had to find Jed before he found them. Why he hasn't come for them already was a mystery, but his stepbrother had always done things his own way and in his own time. Seth knew no matter how far they ran or where they went, sooner or later Jed would come. He never thought on it much, never wanted to admit his cowardice, but one thing he did know, he was afraid of Jedidiah Bracket.

Backing out of the cave, Seth shook his head as he tried to clear his nose. "He's in there passed out."

"I didn't think we gave him that much."

"Don't matter, we'll be resting up here for a couple days." Seth looked back at the cave entrance. "Man, he smells."

"We can't stay here, Seth. Old McBride will come looking for his horse that I took, not to mention all those supplies you stole."

"That's why we did all that backtracking and riding where he can't track his horse." Seth shook his head at the whining Beale. "You think I was just having fun?"

"To tell you the truth, I didn't know what you were doing."

"First, we'll get Roden sobered up and a bath." The redhead looked over at the hard-ridden horses. "We've got to rest our horses. They've traveled as far as they can without grass and rest."

"Let's put him in the creek while he's passed out." Beale grinned. "I'd hate to ride behind him all day, smelling that filth."

"I'll get the lye, you drag him out."

"Me!"

"You." Seth pointed at the cave. "Get him."

Bare-naked Roden woke up cussing and gasping as he was tossed waist deep in the cold stream. Too small and weak from his drinking bouts to put up much of a fight, he was scrubbed with the stiff brush and lye soap. The scout finally gave up resisting and stood still as the two men scrapped him almost raw.

"That'll be good." Seth waded from the creek. "Rinse off, Lem, and get those clean clothes on."

"You done scrubbed me raw." Roden shook from the chill of the water. "I've probably caught the ague. Give me a drink."

"Get dressed and you'll get a drink."

"Stay out of that flea ridden cave, or you'll get another good going over." Beale warned, bringing a glare of hate from the thin man. "Can't stand those pesky things."

"Your gear and possibles are stacked over there." Seth pointed out a pile of blankets, saddle, and a rifle.

Pulling on his pants and a pair of leather moccasins, Roden walked to the pile, everything he would need. "You boys spent a load on me."

"Yeah, and you're gonna earn it, Mister Roden." Beale warned.

"What about the drink you promised?"

"After you eat."

Roden made a face. "I don't want food, boy. I want the drink you promised."

"Get some sleep, Adam. We're pulling out early." Seth handed Roden a plate full of food and a cup of rum. Watching the trembling hands shake as Roden downed the spirits, Seth only shook his head.

"More." The scout held out the cup. "I've got me a beehive in my stomach."

"Tomorrow, you'll get more. Now, you finish eating and get some rest." Seth leaned back against a tree.

"You're a cruel man, Seth Wilson."

Seth thought of Sally Ann. "Yeah."

Stepping into the lodge behind Little Antelope, Jed let his eyes adjust before moving forward to where Walking Horse normally sat against his backrest. Many had told him about his friend's illness, but still he was not prepared for the drawn, thin face that peered back at him from lifeless sunken eyes.

"You have come back to us, my friend." The voice wavered slightly, but it was still the voice of Walking Horse. "That is good."

"I am here, Walking Horse." Jed took a seat in front of the warrior.

"Just in time, Crow Killer. The Lance Bearers are in need of a strong leader to lead them against the Pawnee."

"You are that leader."

"No, not anymore." Walking Horse shifted position weakly. "It is time for me to meet the ones above."

Jed shook his head. "No, you will grow strong again and you will lead us."

"I have thought this too, but it will not come to pass." Walking Horse shook his head. "The evil ones will not leave my body."

"There are others who can lead the Lance Bearers."

Walking Horse shook his head weakly. "You know better. They are great warriors, but they are not strong leaders."

"Bow Legs or Big Owl?"

"Bow Legs thinks more about women, than fighting." Walking Horse laughed weakly. "Big Owl is too hotheaded."

"White Swan has not been able to restore your strength?"

"No, but you being here, gives me hope for our people, and Little Antelope."

"You will not die." Jed shook his head. "You cannot."

"I wish your words were so, but it is not to be, my friend."

Jed could see how thin the once-powerful warrior had become, but still Bow Legs and the others said he had been leading the warriors, even in his condition. Perhaps, Walking Horse has given up, knowing Crow Killer returned, now he could join his ancestors.

"You will not die, I won't let you."

"Are your powers stronger than White Swan's?"

"No."

For an hour, Jed talked with the weakened one. Finally, becoming fatigued, Walking Horse nodded slightly, and fell into a deep sleep. Motioning for Little Antelope to follow, he exited the lodge and walked outside.

"How long has he been this way?"

"Many days now. At first, I thought he would grow strong again, but now…" She could only shake her head.

"White Swan can't help him?"

"No, he has tried everything, every herb, every medicine, everything."

"He will not die, I won't let him." Jed swore. "He won't die."

"You are a great fighter, Jed, but you are not a medicine man."

"I will return." Jed touched her small shoulder as he turned. "Do not worry, little one, he will not die."

Seeking Bow Legs out, Jed motioned for the warrior to leave the group of warriors he was talking with and follow him. Studying the bustling village, Jed nodded his head, as the lodges were placed in a well defended place, deep within a heavy timbered valley. Slow Wolf's Arapaho had camped there before. Jed remembered the many times he and Walking Horse had ridden out on a hunt from this very place. With proper placed guards, it would be impossible for raiders to attack the village without giving out an alarm as they crossed the deep gulley that lay on each end of the valley.

"You were right, Walking Horse is gravely ill."

Nodding, Bow Legs looked over at Jed. "I have spoken with the old medicine man. He says there is nothing more he can do for him. He says the evil ones will not leave our friend's body."

Tossing a pebble far out into one of the gulches, Jed shook his head. "He will not die."

"What can we do, Crow Killer?"

"I will take him to a white medicine man."

"That is a far place." Bow Legs shook his head. "First, he would not let a white man perform their medicine on him. Second, he is too weak to travel to your white village."

"We will rig a litter between two horses."

"You will leave the village and let the Pawnee attack our people?" Bow Legs looked over at Jed. "I don't believe you would let many die to save one."

"I will not let him die." Jed clenched his fist. "He is my brother, as you are."

"Perhaps, there is another reason."

"Walking Horse has lived many moons since he was wounded." Jed ignored the insinuation about the girl. "Still, he will live longer yet."

"And what of the Pawnee?"

"We will take care of the Pawnee, then we will take Walking Horse to the white doctor."

"You have such a medicine man in your village to the west?"

"Yes." Jed nodded, remembering when Doctor Zeke had come to help Sally Ann. "We have such a man."

"We haven't much time, Walking Horse is very weak."

"Meet me here with horses and food before the night leaves the sky." Jed looked across the village. "Now, I must speak with Slow Wolf."

"Just the two of us go on this trail?"

"Has it not always been so?" Jed nodded at the small warrior. "I will return quickly."

Slow Wolf watched from his place beside the lodge as Jed walked proudly across the village. He was relieved the warrior known as Crow Killer the Lance Bearer had returned to his people. This warrior was needed, a natural leader respected by the other tribes. Crow Killer was known by many tribes as a terrible warrior in battle, some even thought of him as a demon. Perhaps, once the Pawnee found out he had returned and lived once again with the Arapaho, they would return to their villages and forget about seeking revenge.

"Welcome, my son, sit." Slow Wolf motioned to the buffalo hide beside him.

"It is good to be home, my Chief."

"We are glad to have you back." Slow Wolf nodded. "You are needed."

"You fear the Pawnee will attack?"

"Yes, they will attack." The chief nodded. "White Swan sees them in the smoke."

Jed nodded. "Then, I must have your blessing on what I wish to do."

"Tell me, my son."

After explaining his plan, Jed turned his thoughts back to Walking Horse. "I must take him to the white doctor."

"Can the white man medicine cure what is wrong with Walking Horse?"

"I do not know this thing, my Chief. If I do not try, my friend will surely die." Jed shrugged. "He weakens with every passing day."

"My nephew will not let a white treat him." Slow Wolf shook his head sadly. "He hates all whites."

"With your permission, my Chief, I will take him to the white doctor."

"Would you take him against his will?"

"Walking Horse is a great Arapaho; he will wish to live."

"If you succeed with the Pawnee and the village is no longer in danger, you have my permission."

"Thank you, my Chief."

The broad Yellowstone River flowed smoothly as it passed the age-old crossing that had been used by buffalo and the tribes for generations. Jed and Bow Legs sat their horses at the edge of the beautiful river. Finally, kicking their horses forward, the two warriors slipped quietly into the water and started across. Wading beside their wet horses as they emerged from the river, Jed spotted several Crow warriors watching their movements from higher up on the riverbank.

Waving, Jed wanted the Crow to know they were spotted. Mounting the piebald, he and Bow Legs started up toward the high bluff.

Several Crow warriors surrounded the two Arapaho as they topped out on the high bank of the river. Yelling and brandishing their bows, the warriors pushed against the piebald, screaming their taunts. Raising the amulet Plenty Coups had given him for safe passage through Crow lands, Jed nodded as the warriors quieted.

"Take me to Chief Plenty Coups." Jed nodded. "Bow Legs, you will return to the village and wait my word."

"No, Crow Killer, this time I will ride with you." The thin jaw stuck out. "I will not turn back from this trail."

"It could be a dangerous trail, my friend."

"I am an Arapaho Lance Bearer, not a squaw or child to leave behind, hiding in the village."

"Come, both of you." The lead warrior did not like it, but the necklace around Jed's neck had to be honored. None dared to dishonor their chief until they heard different from him.

The warriors proudly led Jed and Bow Legs into the huge Crow Village pushing their horses through the throng of curious people as they made their way to the larger hide lodges. Bow Legs could only shake his head as squaws and kids pushed against their horses.

"They look like they would like to cook us."

"You wanted to come." Jed laughed. "Is the great Bow Legs afraid of a few Crow squaws?"

"Yes." Bow Legs shook his head. "I fear there is not enough of me to go around."

Seeing Plenty Coups and Red Hawk exit the large lodge, Jed smiled and dismounted in front of the two warriors. "It is good to see my friends."

"You are welcome to the Crow Village." Plenty Coups raised his hands, quieting the gathered villagers. "This warrior called Crow Killer is as a son to me. You will treat him as a Crow warrior."

"We caught them crossing the great river into our lands without permission." A warrior spoke up.

"So you led them into our village like captives?" Red Hawk was infuriated. "You see my father's amulet around Crow Killer's neck?"

Confusion spread through the village as complete silence engulfed the assembled people. All knew the Arapaho was the enemy of the Crow and thought these two Arapaho warriors had been captured and brought to their chief. Many, almost all, had heard of the great warrior, Crow Killer, but few knew his face. All listened, as Red Hawk rebuked the warriors, then embraced Jed warmly.

Ushering the two warriors inside his lodge, Plenty Coups motioned Jed to a place of honor and had the squaws bring food. Many older warriors slowly gathered inside the great lodge, curious to find out what had brought the great Crow Killer to the village.

"It is good to see you, Great Chief." Jed nodded at the chief. "And you, my brother."

Red Hawk looked over at Bow Legs. "You have brought a Lance Bearer with you."

"Yes, this is my friend, Bow Legs." Jed shook his head. "He refused to stay behind with the women."

"Then, Bow Legs is welcome here." Red Hawk laughed. "I would have stayed with the squaws."

After finishing eating, Jed placed his bowl in front of him and thanked the women of the lodge. "You have very good cooks, my Chief."

Plenty Coups smiled. "Too good, look at my fat body."

"Your body shows you have been in battle since we saw you last." Red Hawk could see the fresh scars that ran across Jed's body as his sleeveless shirt opened when he moved his arms.

"Yes, I have been in battle many times." Jed nodded. "Too many."

Plenty Coups nodded. "The wind has carried word of your battles with the Blackfoot warriors."

Jed was always amazed the way word traveled between the tribes. Nothing was kept secret over the vast mountains and valleys. "Yes, but they were battles I did not want."

"Why are you here, my son?"

"I wish to avoid more battles." Jed looked across at Red Hawk. "I have come here to ask for your help."

"You speak of the Pawnee."

"Yes."

"The Pawnee say your people attacked them in the pass of the Bighorns and killed many of their warriors."

"This is true." Jed nodded. "But, many Pawnee attacked a few Arapaho that day."

"This one was with them?"

"I was there, my Chief." Bow Legs spoke up.

"Now, you do not want the Pawnee to attack your village?"

"That is true." Bow Legs nodded. "For me, I would fight, but Crow Killer will talk for the Arapaho and Chief Slow Wolf."

Red Hawk looked over at Jed. "What do you wish from the Crow, my brother?"

"The evil ones have entered the body of the one you wounded." Jed tried to speak in words Red Hawk would understand. "He will die if I cannot get him to a white medicine man quickly."

Red Hawk leaned forward. "Does Crow Killer blame me for your friend's sickness?"

"No, you know I do not. Red Hawk is my friend too." Jed shook his head. "When Red Hawk was wounded, I healed your wounds, and it is the same with Walking Horse."

"What do you wish, my son?" Plenty Coups raised his huge hand.

"I need time to take Walking Horse west to a white healer." Jed stared hard at the chief. "I do not have time to wait for the Pawnee to attack our village. If Walking Horse is to live, he must go now."

"We have a medicine man, a good healer. He will go with you to your village to try to help this warrior."

"We have a great medicine man." Jed thanked the chief. "No, my Chief, these evil ones need the white man's medicine to run them from his body."

"You wish the Crow to ride west with you?"

"No, my Chief. I wish for you to send a warrior to the Pawnee to speak for Crow Killer."

Plenty Coups nodded curiously. "What will we say? The Crow are not brothers to the Pawnee."

"No, but you are not the hated enemies of these people, as the Arapaho are."

"Tell us, my brother." Red Hawk spoke.

"Tell the Pawnee the fight was not wanted and that the Arapaho want peace." Jed looked at Red Hawk. "If there cannot be peace and they come against us, the Pawnee will face the mighty Lance Bearers who will kill many."

"There is more?"

"Tell the Pawnee if they wish to fight, I, Crow Killer will meet their best warrior in combat, and no others need to die for this foolishness."

"You do not look healed up from your last fight."

"I grow stronger every day, my Chief."

Red Hawk nodded. "If this is what you want, my brother."

"Want?" Jed shook his head. "I have fought enough for two life-times, but I must take Walking Horse to the north. With the Pawnee wanting revenge, I cannot leave my people unprotected to face them alone."

"There is no other to lead the Arapaho in battle?"

"There are fighters and there are leaders." Jed shook his head. "Walking Horse is weak and that only leaves me."

"You are a good friend to this wounded one."

"As I am to Red Hawk, and his father, Plenty Coups."

"If this is your wish, Crow Killer. I will send a council party to the Pawnee with your words."

"These are my words, my Chief." Jed nodded. "I wish they weren't."

"I will carry your words." Red Hawk spoke up. "I will leave now."

"You and this one will wait here for their answer."

"It will be so."

Blue Darter, Crowfoot, and Little Horse sat across from Chief Deep Water and the council of elders. They listened as the older warriors discussed the tale they had brought back from the east and the Arapaho's valley. Already, the bones of Small Mountain, Standing Bull, and the other dead warriors Crow Killer had killed were placed on scaffolds in the burial grounds of the Blackfoot.

Deep Water had been solemn after seeing the bodies and bones, not saying a word after hearing the account of his son and brother's death. Perhaps the Blackfoot Chief's silence was because his grief was too strong or his rage too great against the warriors for not helping Standing Bull. Now, the council of elders would decide what was to be done, and if they should punish the warriors.

"Tell us, Blue Darter." An elder called Sakooch spoke up. "You have seen this warrior? Do you believe he is a demon or just a man?"

Blue Darter looked into the eyes of the chief and shook his head. "I told Standing Bull, I would ride forward to speak with the Arapaho. The one called Crow Killer told me of killing Small Mountain and the others who had come to his lands to fight, and he did not lie. He said we could take their bones and leave in peace. Against my wishes, Standing Bull rode forth and challenged the Arapaho to single combat."

"Blue Darter did not answer." Another elder spoke up. "Is this one a demon?"

"I answered." Blue Darter looked at the elder. "Small Mountain and Standing Bull both wanted to count coup on this Arapaho. They were foolish."

Deep Water growled. "One does not speak badly of the dead."

"Listen to me, my Chief, this warrior is no demon. He is a mortal just like us, but if attacked, he is a terrible enemy." Blue Darter looked to where Crowfoot and Little Horse were nodding their heads. "Our people do not need this warrior to come against them and become their enemy."

"Does Crowfoot and Little Horse believe the same?" Another elder spoke up. "Speak."

"I have seen this one kill the greatest fighting warrior of any tribe." Crowfoot dropped his eyes. "If we had challenged him as Standing Bull did, we would all be dead."

"You were scared of one man?"

"No, I was scared of a demon, one who walks upright like a man."

"And you, Little Horse, does this one scare you also?" The elder spoke again.

"He does, Bull Man, but not because I think him to be a demon." Little Horse looked at the wise old one.

"Why? You are a Blackfoot warrior, the greatest fighters of any tribe."

"No, the Blackfoot have no warrior who can stand against this Arapaho." Little Horse shook his head. "I tell you this, he is terrible in battle."

"Tell us, all of you have seen this one?" Deep Water raised his hand for silence. "I have seen you in battle against our enemies many times. No Blackfoot can call you cowards. What would you have me do?"

Blue Darter looked at the other two warriors, then back at the elders. "Twice, he has spoken to me of peace, and twice, our warriors have attacked his lodge. I say, stay away from his valley and the demon that resides in him."

"Do you all agree?"

Both warriors nodded. "We do."

"Then he is a demon?"

"He is a man of peace, but he will kill like a demon if he must." Crowfoot spoke up. "If we leave him in peace, he will leave our village and people in peace."

"I must sleep on this thing, to lose a son and a brother in battle and do nothing." Deep Water shook his head. "I must think on this."

Blue Darter looked over at the troubled face. "Think on it hard. We may kill this one, but is it worth losing many warriors to do so?"

Nodding the Blackfoot Chief waved them from the tepee. "I will decide soon."

"Tell us, Bull Man." Crowfoot stopped the elder outside the lodge. "What will our chief do?"

"This I cannot say, but others will say he is a coward if he does not avenge his son and brother."

"Who would be so foolish to do this?"

"There will be some."

"Then let them go alone and face the Arapaho, or challenge me if they want to fight so badly." Blue Darter raised his voice for all to hear.

"You like this demon warrior?"

"I respect him for a brave warrior, nothing else." Blue Darter turned and walked away to his lodge.

"Will you fight this warrior if your chief orders this?" The old one questioned Little Horse.

"I am still Blackfoot, old one. Yes, I will do as my chief wishes."

CHAPTER 7

Early morning found Seth leading Beale and Roden back toward Carter's homestead, then they stopped at one of the small mountain trails leading east. The tracks of four horses, turning south, were still visible in the soft dirt where they sat their horses and surveyed the trail.

"Here's where you take over, Lem." Seth looked over at the scout. "Think you're up to it?"

"I reckon I am." Roden's appearance had completely changed, as well as his smell. The new duds were a bit large for the small-framed man, but back in the dark store, Seth hadn't done too bad picking the clothes. Only the bloodshot eyes were the same as they studied the sign of horses passing. "I need a drink."

"Tonight."

"No, my insides are tied in knots." Roden pleaded. "I need one now."

"Just one jolt, no more, Lem." Beale handed Roden the bottle of drinking sauce.

Pushing the cork back into the bottle, the man smacked his lips. "I'm a thanking you for that and these duds."

"You find my brother and there'll be plenty more of this stuff, plus money."

Looking over at the two, Roden nodded. "That's fine, real fine, but I'm telling you this now; last time Lige Hatcher was in Baxter Springs, he spoke of this feller you're a wanting me to track."

"What'd he say?"

"He didn't mince words. Lige said this was one terrible, dangerous

Injun." Roden eyed the bottle hungrily. "He also said he was a good man that minded his own business, if let alone."

"So?" Beale shrugged. "What you getting at, Roden?"

"So just this, I'll find Jedidiah Bracket, but you'll do your own killing. You boys understand? I'll do no killing for you."

Laughing lightly, Seth shook his head. "Now, Lem old hoss, who said anything about killing?"

"I may be a drunk, a fool, and anything else you care to name, but I'm not stupid." Roden looked up the trail. "I'm riding McBride's favorite saddle horse, an animal he sets store by and wouldn't sell. I'm carrying a new Hawken rifle and wearing new clothes. No sir, this smells kinda fishy to me."

"You saying you're backing out on us, Lem?" Seth's face hardened.

"Nope, nothing of the kind." Roden kicked the sorrel. "I gave my word so let's ride. Sooner we find your brother, sooner I can get off this horse."

"Can you track him over these mountains?" Beale was doubtful.

"Reckon so, he's leaving marks on the ground, ain't he?"

All day, Jed and Bow Legs either sat in the lodge provided by Plenty Coups or spent their time soaking in the stream that meandered through the village. Young women walking by with their baskets flashed their pretty white teeth as they passed, flirting with the two newcomers.

Bow Legs waved and smiled, grumbling as Jed ignored them. "You could at least wave instead of lying there soaking your body."

"And have one of their suitors get jealous and scalp us?"

"Bah." The warrior pouted. "Tell me, my friend, what has happened? You no longer smile as you once did."

"Did you not ask Silent One the same question?"

"He would not speak of it."

"Good."

On the third day, Red Hawk and two others rode their tired horses into the village at sundown. Dismounting stiffly, Red Hawk thanked the two tired warriors. Turning his sweat soaked horse loose in the village, he sat down beside Jed and Bow Legs. Thanking one of the women for bringing him food and water, he leaned back on a backrest and ate.

Jed was eager to hear what the warrior had said, but good manners dictated that a guest be allowed to eat before any talks begin. Squirming beside Jed, Bow Legs was beside himself with curiosity. Finally finished, Red Hawk declined another bowl of food and thanked the old squaw.

"We will wait for my father and the pipe before speaking." Red Hawk spoke to a young boy nearby. "Go ask Plenty Coups to come to this place."

"Your pony says it was a long hard trail."

Red Hawk nodded. "You asked me to hurry and I did."

For several minutes, the four warriors smoked and made only small talk until they were finished, then returned the pipe to the chief.

"I have done as you wished." Red Hawk looked at Jed. "The Crow and Pawnee are not allies, but we do not war on each other if we can help it."

"Tell us, my son." Plenty Coups was as curious as Bow Legs. "What did the Pawnee dogs say?"

"They want to avenge the ones they lost." Red Hawk continued. "They do not want to lose more of their young men. They are willing to let a warrior from each tribe settle this."

"Good." Jed nodded. "When?"

"They will meet us on the forks of the grass plains beside the Blue River in two days."

Plenty Coups smiled. "Good, that is halfway between our hunting grounds and theirs."

"Only five warriors from each tribe will ride to the Blue."

Plenty Coups nodded. "This is a good thing because too many warriors watching, they could become hot-blooded and want to fight."

Mentally calculating, Jed figured the ride would take at least two weeks to get Walking Horse to a doctor in Baxter Springs.

Red Hawk looked over at Jed and dropped his eyes, unable to look Jed in the eye.

"Tell me, Red Hawk." Jed saw the look and the downcast eyes. "What is wrong?"

"I am sorry, my friend, but they insist and will only fight a warrior from the Arapaho, who had been in the fight, one who had killed their warriors." Red Hawk looked over at Bow Legs. "Their warriors, spying out your village, followed as you rode here. They know this one was one of the ones in the fight, and he did kill."

"No." Jed looked across at his friend. "I asked for this fight; it is I who will fight."

"The Pawnee know you, Crow Killer." Red Hawk warned Jed. "They know you were not in the fight that killed their warriors."

"No matter, I am Arapaho."

"It matters to them, my friend. They are afraid of you." Red Hawk looked at Bow Legs. "If this one does not fight one of theirs, they have warned their warriors to wait and raid your village when it is unguarded."

Plenty Coups could feel the strong bond between Jed and Bow Legs. "Is that their final word?"

"The Pawnee said no matter how the fight ends, there will be no more revenge taken against the Arapaho People of Slow Wolf."

"And you believe them?"

Red Hawk nodded. "The Pawnee are great liars, but this time I believe them."

"I will fight this Pawnee." Bow Legs stood up. "He is just a man, nothing more."

Red Hawk watched the slender warrior as he disappeared among the lodges. "He is a Lance Bearer and brave, but he is small."

"You have seen the Pawnee he is to fight?"

"Yes." Red Hawk nodded slowly. "He is a Pawnee dog, but he is twice the size of Bow Legs."

"I can't let him fight."

"Either let him fight and maybe live, or let Walking Horse die."

Jed shook his head. "Walking Horse would not want this."

"Would you shame your friend in front of the Crow and Pawnee?" Plenty Coups asked. "He is a Lance Bearer and a warrior. He has pride and you must not dishonor him."

"My father is right, my friend." Red Hawk shook his head. "To shame one with his pride would be worse than death."

"I know." Jed nodded. "He's small, but he has a brave heart."

The small creek, the tribes called the Blue because of its bluish color, drifted slowly in front of five warriors as they watched the Pawnee warriors ride down to the shallow creek and splash across. The flat, grassy spot on the Crow side had been chosen as the place for the fight. Jed watched as one of the Pawnee warriors gestured at a war lance, sticking up plainly in the center of the flats. Another Pawnee, much larger than the first, rode to the lance and whirled his horse. The rider was big, not heavily muscled like Standing Bull, but he was much taller, with gangly long arms and legs. The warrior's tall body made the horse he was astride seem small as his long legs dangled down, almost touching the ground.

Jed shook his head. Would Bow Legs stand a chance against such a giant as this? He knew the Arapaho was brave, but would bravery be enough against an opponent as this. Smiling, Bow Legs handed Jed his bow and quiver of arrows, then took up his war axe and shield.

"I want you to ride the piebald. He is bigger and more powerful than that little thing the Pawnee rides. He will give you a better chance as the fight goes on." Jed started to dismount.

"No, my friend, this fight will not be won by a horse, but by a good thrust of the knife." Bow Legs declined the horse. "But, I thank you."

Red Hawk looked at the warrior. "You are a Lance Bearer; no lone enemy can stand against you."

"Did you tell him that, Red Hawk?" Bow Legs grinned at the Crow.

"If he gets after you, run between his legs." Plenty Coups added. "I had a Sioux warrior do that to me once."

"You must tell me the story when this is finished." Bow Legs looked to where the Pawnee warriors let out with a yell.

As they watched the Pawnee advance to the edge of the flat, Jed had to hold his position. He wanted to ride forward to fight the warrior, but he knew he could not shame his friend and deny him his right to fight for the Arapaho. A Lance Bearer without pride and respect was no warrior at all.

"Good luck, my friend." Jed nodded.

Kicking his sorrel horse, Bow Legs rode out to the edge of the flats and faced the Pawnee. The warrior was huge; bigger than any man he had ever fought or seen before. For several minutes, the two warriors sat and studied each other before screaming their war shout, then whirled their horses before charging forward. Jed watched helpless, bound by his word to Red Hawk to let the fight play out, no matter who won. All he could do was watch as his friend and the Pawnee clashed together. Bow Legs was faster as he swung the mighty war axe with all his might. However, even with his speed, Bow Legs was no match for the superior strength of the Pawnee, whose longer arms gave him the advantage. Reaching out powerfully, the Pawnee slammed his war axe against the shield of Bow Legs, each blow driving the smaller man back. Slashing and pushing forward, the two warriors fought back and forth across the flats like two enraged mountain goats. Bow Legs was courageous, trying his best, not giving up, but courage against such a large opponent was not enough.

The small Arapaho was tiring, and Jed could see the tattered shield, of his fellow Lance Bearer, lowering as the blows continued. Even with the pride and strength of the Arapaho beating in his chest, Jed knew Bow Legs would lose this fight, as he was no match for the giant Pawnee. Shaking his head, Jed watched as the smaller warrior suddenly flung himself under the outstretched arms of the Pawnee as their horses clashed together. Both knife blades flashed in the morning sun, then slowly both warriors slid to the ground unmoving. Riding forward, both the Pawnee and Crow looked down at the two dead fighters. With his last bit of strength, Bow Legs had given his life to get in close to the Pawnee for a deadly, killing thrust with his knife.

"Is this the end of it or does one or two Pawnee wish to challenge Crow Killer today?" Jed glared across at the Pawnee.

Red Hawk kicked his horse forward, as he could feel the rage in Jed. Bow Legs had already given his life today for his people. He didn't want to see Bow Legs sacrifice come to nothing if the Pawnee were shamed into fighting Crow Killer.

"We have also lost a warrior who we thought of as a brother." An older Pawnee rode forward two steps. "Let the fighting end here now."

Lust for battle emitted from Jed's face as he sat the piebald and looked down at the small body of one who had been a close and dear friend. He wanted to fight, to kill these warriors, but he knew to do so could cost Walking Horse his life. Slashing his hand at the Pawnee, he nodded. "As you say, it is finished for now."

"I can see your thoughts, Crow Killer. You wish to kill. You wish our blood." An aristocratic looking warrior spoke. "Let there be no more spilling of blood this day."

"I said it is finished." Jed's blood ran hot, wanting nothing more than to kill these warriors, but he had to think of Walking Horse. Bow

Legs had given his life so Walking Horse might live, and he would not let his friend die for nothing.

"Then, it is finished." The Pawnee looked at his warriors. "We have lost two brave men here today. Let us leave this place with honor."

Jed watched as the body of Bow Legs was placed on a travois and covered with a fine blanket. Shaking his head, he mounted the piebald and took the lead line of the horse pulling the drag. A friend he had cared for, enjoyed the hunt with, and been in battle with now was dead. Why had he brought Bow Legs with him to this place?

"You did not know the Pawnee would choose this, my friend." Red Hawk could read Jed's face. "You did not know."

"It was my fight, he should not have died."

"He died a warrior's death for his people, Crow Killer." Red Hawk shook his head. "Honor him, my friend. Be proud he was your friend."

"I honor Bow Legs, he was brave. I do not honor myself."

"You must move on and save Walking Horse if it is possible."

"It is hard to do. I have lost so much."

"And you have given much for your people."

"Have I, Red Hawk?"

Smiling, the Crow looked at Jed. "You only have to look at your body, Lance Bearer. Yes, you have sacrificed much and I am proud to call you brother."

Jed built a small raft to float Bow Legs' body across the wide Yellowstone. After swimming both horses across the river, he dried off and put his buckskins and moccasins back on. Noticing movement, high on the ridge across the river, Jed watched as Red Hawk appeared at the edge of the tree line and rode down to the river. Waving, Jed waited as the Crow swam his great spotted stallion across the river.

"What are you doing here, my friend?" Jed was shocked as the Crow waded from the river.

"If you can keep me from being skinned alive by the Arapaho, I will ride with you to the west and help with Walking Horse." Red Hawk replaced his moccasins as he spoke. "You must promise to keep the Arapaho maidens from attacking such a handsome warrior as me."

"Handsome hah, you are the ugliest warrior in your village."

"My friend, everyone knows the ugliest Crow is still better looking than an Arapaho." Red Hawk laughed. "Just to be safe, I will stay behind you."

"Thank you for coming, Red Hawk."

"Just remember, keep Little Antelope from scalping me." The warrior laughed.

"If you keep quiet and do not make her mad, you may be safe."

"Keeping quiet is hard for one like me to do."

The mourning cries and wailing went up across the village as Jed and Red Hawk led the travois carrying Bow Legs through the lodges. Women screamed, and Bow Legs' wife, recognizing her husband's horse pulling the travois, chopped at her hair, and sliced two fingers from her hand. The village was in total mourning as Jed dismounted before Slow Wolf's lodge. Red hawk, seeing the threatening looks of several warriors, sat his spotted horse where he could watch their movements.

Slow Wolf and White Swan stood before the great lodge, watching as Jed dropped the travois and turned it over to the screeching women. Looking to where Red Hawk sat his horse, Slow Wolf waited for Jed to speak first.

Feeling the hatred from his people and seeing the looks Red Hawk was being given, Jed raised his hand to silence the throng of warriors. "This is my friend and brother, Red Hawk." Jed looked at each warrior, then over at Slow Wolf. "He has stopped the Pawnee from raiding our people, and has helped me bring Bow Legs home to his people. I want every Arapaho to respect this one as an Arapaho."

"No, this is Red Hawk, our sworn enemy!"

"He is my brother, not an enemy."

"Bow Legs was a great warrior." Slow Wolf raised his hand quieting the warriors.

"He died a great warrior, my Chief." Red Hawk spoke. "It is an honor to have known a warrior as proud and brave. One who now has given his life for his people."

"This is the great Red Hawk we have heard so much about?" Big Owl looked up at the mounted Crow.

"This is Red Hawk." Jed motioned the Crow down from his horse. "He is my brother and I want every Arapaho to treat him as such. If you try to do him harm or dishonor him, you dishonor me."

"He saved me from the Nez Perce." All eyes turned as Little Antelope walked to where Red Hawk stood, and smiled up at him. "Treat this warrior as one of your own, Arapaho. He is a great warrior and friend of our great warrior, Crow Killer."

Extending his arm, Slow Wolf motioned for Jed and Red Hawk to sit with him and White Swan before his lodge and the whole village."

"You are welcome here." Slow Wolf turned his attention to the gathered villagers. "No one will disrespect our friend and brother, Red Hawk."

"Thank you, Uncle." Red Hawk nodded at the chief.

"Crow Killer, tell us of Bow Legs and how he died."

Quickly, Jed told of the fight and how Bow Legs had given his life for his people. Tomorrow, the small warrior would be placed on a scaffold in the burial grounds of the Arapaho. Dead but never forgotten, and they will sing his praises for many years to come.

"He was not a Crow, but he was a brave man, a great Lance Bearer." Red Hawk looked quietly into the fire. "I was honored to know him."

"Red Hawk treats the Arapaho with great respect and we thank you."

"I wish to see Walking Horse. We will return, my Chief." Jed and Red Hawk walked to where Little Antelope was comforting the wife of Bow Legs.

"I am surprised to see the mighty Red Hawk here in the lowly village of the Arapaho." Little Antelope looked up into the Crow's eyes.

"I see our little woman has not lost her sharp tongue." Red Hawk smiled. "Thank you for speaking for me."

"Now, we are even, Crow."

Red Hawk laughed, and whispered to Jed. "I see why you are taken with this one, she has fire in her."

"She is also married."

Jed placed the bow and lance of Bow Legs in his squaw's bloody hand and spoke his condolences for his friend's death. The woman placed her head against Jed's chest and wept softly. Pulling back with dignity, she thanked Jed and turned into her lodge.

Turning to Little Antelope, the warriors, one Arapaho and one Crow, followed the small woman to the lodge of Walking Horse. Stooping as they entered the silent lodge, both warriors sat across from the frail warrior. Surprised, his eyes focused on the warrior dressed as a Crow. Walking Horse looked first at Little Antelope and Jed, then recognized the warrior.

"Red Hawk, your appearance here surprises me." Walking Horse's voice was low, weak. "A friend of Crow Killer is welcome in my lodge."

"Thank you, Walking Horse." Red Hawk nodded. "I am sorry you are not strong."

"It is not your fault." Walking Horse coughed slightly. "I would have done the same if it was the other way around."

"Still, I hate to see a great warrior as yourself, feeling as you do."

"I thank you." The voice became weaker. "Also, I thank you for saving Little Antelope at the river."

Jed looked over at Little Antelope and motioned for her to follow him outside. "You will feed our guest."

"Where do you go, Jed?"

"I must speak with Slow Wolf."

The small face looked up at him. "Do you speak with him about Walking Horse?"

"Yes." Jed took the small woman's arm. "I want to take my friend to a white doctor who maybe can heal him."

"He will not go." She shook her head. "You know my husband and his feelings toward the whites."

"Talk with him, Little Antelope. He must not die."

"He hates all whites, except you, Jed." Little Antelope shook her head. "You are Arapaho."

"Talk with him and tell him he will be strong again soon." Jed held her small hand. "Tell him he must see the white doctor to get well so he can protect his people."

"Do you believe this?" She looked up at him. "I mean, do you think your white medicine man can heal my husband?"

"The white man has powerful medicine, and yes, I believe this."

"Jed." The dark eyes looked up at him seeming to beg.

"What?"

"Nothing." She turned quickly, rushing back into the lodge. "I will feed the Crow."

Jed smiled. "If you were Crow, would you have eyes for this warrior?"

"He is a Crow, so I could not."

Jed nodded. "You think he is ugly?"

Little Antelope teasingly smiled. "No, actually the Crow is handsome."

"For a Crow?"

"I have eyes for only one warrior." She looked up at him. "My husband, Walking Horse."

"That is good. Now, I don't have to worry about Red Hawk."

"Would you be jealous, my warrior?"

Looking across at her, he smiled again. "Yes, little one, I would."

Jed sat before Slow Wolf's fire and looked across at the chief and White Swan the medicine man. "I have no wish to insult our great Medicine Man, White Swan, who I consider my grandfather."

"You say the white medicine man can heal Walking Horse?"

"Yes, the whites have strong medicine to cure the evil spirits Walking Horse has inside his body."

"You do not trust my medicine, Crow Killer?"

"It is not that, Grandfather, but Walking Horse has been sick many months."

"Will he go with you?" Slow Wolf interrupted. "You know he hates all whites."

"Walking Horse is the proud leader of the Lance Bearers." Jed looked at the two elders he admired above all men. "He will come with me, if he wishes to live."

"Will the Pawnee keep their word? They are the mortal enemies of the Sioux and Cheyenne." Slow Wolf asked quietly. "We have no war leader if you and Walking Horse are gone from the village."

"I do not trust the Pawnee, but I trust Plenty Coups." Jed nodded. "He has given his word to defend the Arapaho if attacked, and you still have Big Owl."

"Yes, Big Owl is a Lance Bearer and a brave warrior, but he is not a leader of men."

"You only have to send a rider for me if I am needed."

"You have given our village safety from the Pawnee and the Crow." The chief looked over at White Swan. "If he will go, you have our permission to take him to this white doctor."

"Thank you, my Chief." Jed looked over at White Swan. "It is for the respect I carry for my brother that I do this, Grandfather."

"I understand, my son. Go with my blessings."

"Plenty Coups is a great chief, and I trust him to guard his side of the river against Pawnee raiders."

Busy splitting wood beside his house, Ed Wilson didn't see the lone rider approaching his farm. Reining in his tired horse, Lige Hatcher dismounted stiffly and approached the farmer.

"Hello, Ed."

Stopping his axe in mid-swing, Wilson looked behind him where Hatcher stood leaning against a fencepost. "Lige Hatcher, what are you doing here?"

"Didn't you send for me?"

"I told Bate Baker to get word to you, sure enough." Wilson shook his head. "I thought you were trailing for Chalk Briggs out of Fort Bridger."

"A rider came in, said you needed me badly." Hatcher shrugged. "The train had an easy pull this year. We had good weather, not much trouble, and we were ahead of schedule. Chalk let me ride on ahead to Baxter Springs, so here I am."

"Oh, how I was praying you'd come in, and here you are." Wilson shook his head sadly. "Thank you."

"What's wrong, Ed? What's so important?"

"It's Jedidiah." Wilson laid down the axe. "He could be in real danger, and I don't know where he is."

"What kind of trouble?"

"You didn't stop in the settlement?"

"No."

"Sally Ann was killed a month ago, but you wouldn't have any way of knowing."

"Sally Ann's dead?" Hatcher shook his head in dismay. "What happened?"

Wilson dropped his head. "In a way it was an accident, but still it was murder."

"Who killed her and how?"

"My son Seth and Adam Beale were responsible. They were trying to scare Jedidiah off, but they accidentally shot through Elmer's storefront and killed her."

"Where is Jedidiah?"

"Don't know. He buried his wife and rode off to the east."

Hatcher studied the farmer. "Why did you send for me, Ed?"

"I'm afraid Seth is hunting Jed to kill him." Wilson took Hatcher's horse. "He and the Beale boy rode out a week ago, heading east."

"What else? Those two sure don't know the mountains well enough to find Jed." Hatcher shook his head. "Even if they did, they sure ain't no match for him."

"No, they don't, but Lem Roden does."

"Lem Roden, how does he play into this?" Hatcher cocked his head curiously. "He's been on a roaring drunk now for a year or better."

"A farmer named Carter, who lives east of Baxter Springs, told me in town that Seth and the Beale boy took Roden with them into the mountains." Wilson watched Hatcher unsaddle. "Also, a farmer named McBride had his horse stolen and the mercantile reported some of its merchandise was stolen."

"Did Carter see them with Roden?"

"Sure did. He said they turned south just past his place a mile or so."

"And Roden was leading them?"

"He was, and Carter said he was riding McBride's sorrel horse." Wilson nodded. "Plus, he had a brand-new set of duds on."

"A week ago, you say?"

"Yep, Carter was out hunting and the three of them didn't see him as they turned into the mountains."

"You sure?"

"Yep, he'd know Roden and that horse of McBride's anywhere." Wilson swore. "Carter said last time he passed where he was holed up, Roden was afoot and stunk worse than a loco skunk. The other day, Carter said he was dressed in new clothes and looked like he just had a bath."

"Why would Seth want to kill Jed?"

"He's scared of Jed." Wilson shook his head. "He knows if he doesn't kill him, one day Jed will come for him."

"He's that scared?"

"Yes, he's that scared. They took Roden to track Jed down and they intend to kill him."

"Roden is good. He'll track Jed to his valley, there's no doubt of that." Hatcher rubbed his whiskered chin. "Jed won't figure on anyone following him."

"They'll kill him for sure."

"I've known and rode with Lem Roden for many a year, and he'd have no part of a killing." Hatcher shook his head. "He'll kill warring Indians, but not a white man."

"If he leads them to Jedidiah, they'll ambush the boy."

"Not if we can get there in time."

"When do we leave?"

"At daylight."

"I'll ride over and get my neighbor, Sam Franks, to take care of things here after I fix you some grub." Wilson sank his axe in the chopping block.

"I could use a bite and a night's shuteye sure wouldn't hurt none either." Hatcher nodded, following the farmer to the house.

Blue Darter looked up from his seat in front of his lodge where he had been talking with Little Horse. A young boy brought word he had been summoned by Deep Water and the elders.

"I will go with you, my friend." Little Horse stood up.

"No, I will go alone and see what Deep Water and the old ones want."

Waving his hand, Blue Darter stopped Little Horse from following, then started for the large lodge sitting in the middle of the Blackfoot village. Being summoned so late was not a good thing and the warrior feared what he knew was coming. Deep Water was mad about his son, Small Mountain, and his brother, Standing Bull, and would not listen when Blue Darter had explained how and why both warriors died. He had not been disloyal or afraid to die defending them. Both warriors and the ones that had followed Small Mountain had been warned to leave the Arapaho in peace. The warrior did not want to kill, but the warriors would not listen, as they only wanted to count coup, win glory, and it wound up costing both of them their lives, plus the lives of others.

Without hesitating, Blue Darter ducked through the open flap and entered the chief's lodge, finding the elders and Deep Water sitting around a small fire. Taking the place Deep Water pointed to, Blue Darter sat down, normally a place of honor, but not tonight. The mood in the lodge was solemn as the older men stared somberly at him. Every eye was focused on him as the withered faces waited for the chief to speak first.

"We thank Blue Darter for coming." The chief opened the council.

"I was summoned here." Blue Darter didn't back down or show emotion. "It is late."

"My son and brother were killed by this Arapaho who you think is honorable." Deep Water glared across the fire. "You and your warriors did nothing."

"I was not there when Small Mountain was killed." Blue Darter looked into the dark eyes. "As I said, Standing Bull was a fool to challenge the Arapaho."

The dark face of the Blackfoot Chief turned redder as he tried to control his temper. Glaring across at Blue Darter, the chief turned his eyes toward the elders. "You have shown cowardice on the war trail. Now, we banish Blue Darter from our village."

"For how long?" One of the elders asked.

"He will take his women, children, and horses, and they shall never return." Deep Water growled.

"This is harsh punishment." Another elder spoke up. "He has not been judged by the warriors of the village, my Chief."

"I have judged him. I have spoken."

"You would punish and endanger my woman, children, and me for the stupid thing your son and brother had done?"

"Go, Blue Darter, before I kill you here and now."

"You think me a coward, Deep Water? You are wrong." Blue Darter stood and looked down at the faces. "You are our hereditary chief and we are bound by tribal custom to obey your words, but do not make threats you cannot back up."

Walking from the lodge, Blue Darter ignored the gesturing of the elders trying to speak with him. Entering his lodge, he sat heavily against his backrest as Little Horse and Crowfoot entered.

"Is it true?" Little Horse shook his head in disbelief. "Has Deep Water banished you from the village?"

"It is true."

"The elders did not object?"

"No, they are old and fear Deep Water."

"What will you do, Blue Darter?" Crowfoot was shocked. Never had a warrior been banished for life or called a coward without being judged by the warriors of the village.

"I will sleep." Blue Darter relaxed against his backrest. "The new sun will come soon."

"We will go into banishment with you." Little Horse started for the flap of the lodge. "Do we leave with the coming of the sun?"

"We will see what the new day brings."

The sun peeked slowly over the tall mountains, shining its brightness over the Blackfoot lodges as the village came to life. On the flats, past the smoke of the early morning cooking fires, squaws looked over to find Blue Darter already mounted, sitting his grey gelding boldly at the edge of the wide plain that ran the length of the village. The warrior's face was painted for battle with blue and yellow paint streaked across his face and his horse in bright colors. Stripped to his breechcloth, Blue Darter sat stoically, holding only his hide war shield and battle axe. The grey horse pawed the ground, wanting to move. As the village came to life with the squaw's warnings, several warriors raced to the lodge of Deep Water.

An elder who had been present at the council walked across to where Blue Darter waited and looked up at the warrior. "What do you wish?"

"Tell your Chief Deep Water; I, Blue Darter challenge him to battle."

"Why do you do this?" The elder asked. "He is our chief and has the right to banish."

"No." Blue Darter kicked his horse forward, pushing the elder backward. "He called me a coward and banished me and my woman to death."

"And if we could change his mind?"

"He will not." Blue Darter shoved the horse into the elder. "He will fight, or I say he is a coward."

The elder shrugged. "You would fight your hereditary chief?"

"I have challenged Deep Water and he must answer, or he no longer deserves to be chief!" Blue Darter yelled so loud the whole village could hear. "Go, send him out or tell the coward to leave this village and go into banishment himself."

"You will not leave this village, as our chief has ordered?"

"No, you can carry me from this place if I am killed."

Several minutes passed before Deep Water rode his horse out onto the plain, facing Blue Darter. Villagers separated and spread out on the sides of the field. No warrior rode forth to stop the fight. Deep Water had been challenged, and never in their tribe's history had they seen any hereditary chief challenged to fight. Little Horse and Crowfoot were shocked, but still they were mounted on their war horses, ready to side with Blue Darter if any warrior tried to interfere.

Deep Water looked across at the younger warrior and at the war paint covering his face and horse. "You challenge your chief to fight and you wear war paint?"

"You are no longer my chief." Blue Darter shook the war axe at Deep Water. "You have spoken words that dishonor me. Now, you will see if I am a coward."

"One of us will die."

"You, Deep Water, can leave this village and live."

"Banishment?" The chief shook his head. "I am the hereditary chief of the Piegan Blackfoot, I will never be banished."

"Then, we will bury you with your chief's war bonnet on." Blue Darter was furious, and red with rage. "This I promise."

With a growl, Deep Water slapped his bay horse with the flat of his war axe and charged forward in a hard run. Blue Darter's eyes were red from the rage he felt. Kicking the grey horse hard, he raced toward the oncoming bay in a headlong rush. To be called a coward was the worst insult a warrior could endure, leaving him no choice but to fight. Living or dying was not considered in this battle. A warrior could not live without honor. If he allowed anyone to call him a coward, then he was the same as dead.

The hard blows of the axes slamming against heavy, buffalo hide-covered shields drummed across the village. Every inhabitant of the village watched in fear as the two warriors fought. No warrior has ever challenged a chief, as it was not heard of. Now, there was one of their favorite sons, fighting to kill his chief.

"Blue Darter is younger than Deep Water." Crowfoot looked over at Little Horse. "What will happen if Blue Darter kills Deep Water?"

"I do not know." Little Horse shook his head. "Deep Water is older, but he is still a mighty warrior."

"No longer." Crowfoot shook his head. "Deep Water is soft and has not been on the war trail in many suns."

Everyone watching could see the fury in the younger warrior's actions. Blue Darter fought with a vengeance, the heavy war axe viciously slamming against the chief's war shield. The grey horse pressed forward, pushing the smaller bay horse slowly backward as Blue Darter leaned forward, swinging wicked blows at Deep Water without fear of getting hit.

"Am I a coward, great Chief?" Blue Darter jeered. "Your son and brother were not cowards. They were brave, but now, both are dead because of their foolishness."

"Soon, you will join them."

"I would rather die than be called a coward, oh great Chief."

The fight continued, both fighters striking killing blows when they landed. Adrenaline flowed through Blue Darter's veins as he pushed forward as hard as he could, swinging with all his might. Again and again, the heavy war axe crashed heavily into Deep Water's shield. Finally, the exhausted bay horse fell heavily on his side pinning the leg of the equally exhausted Deep Water underneath him.

Leaping from his horse, Blue Darter grabbed the chief's long hair, yanking the head backward. "Now, Deep Water, great Chief." Blue Darter glared down into the defenseless face. "Do you see a coward in front of you?"

"No."

Screams and wailing went up from the squaws of the village as Blue Darter drew back his war axe. Hearing the cry of terror coming from the women, Blue Darter studied the villagers as they pushed forward begging. Releasing the downed man, Blue Darter mounted the heaving grey horse and turned his back on the defeated chief. Raising his arm in victory, Blue Darter never looked back at the chief as he rode to where his woman had their belongings already packed for travel.

"Now, I will leave this place." Blue Darter turned and looked about at the gathered warriors, daring any to step forward to challenge him. "Does any warrior here wish to challenge me? Have them step forward."

"We will ride with you, Blue Darter." Little Horse, Crowfoot, and a warrior named Flying Bat rode up.

"Quickly, gather your women, lodges, and horses. We go!"

CHAPTER 8

Jed entered the lodge of Walking Horse and accepted the bowl of meat, Little Antelope handed him. Looking to where Red Hawk sat smoking his pipe, he nodded.

"Your woman is a good cook, Walking Horse." Red Hawk exhaled smoke into the air.

Smiling, the warrior nodded weakly. "Yes, she is a good woman."

"But, she talks too much for a Crow."

Little Antelope glared at the Crow. "Perhaps my sharp tongue would not be tempted so much if Red Hawk would keep quiet."

Walking Horse shook his head and looked at Jed. "I think they could be brother and sister. All they have done since you left is fight."

Jed knew Little Antelope truly liked Red Hawk, if she didn't there would be no light banter between them. "Perhaps she is a Crow woman." Jed laughed. "Maybe she was taken captive when she was little."

"I need to ask her brother."

"Men." Little Antelope stormed from the lodge. She really wasn't mad, as she knew Jed and Red Hawk were merely teasing her, plus she knew they needed to speak with Walking Horse.

Putting his bowl down, Jed looked closely at Walking Horse. "My friend, you grow weaker with each passing day. White Swan, our great medicine man, cannot help you."

"What does the old one say, Crow Killer?"

"White Swan says there is nothing more he can do."

"Am I to die?" Walking Horse took in a deep breath. "Is this what the old one spoke of?"

"I wish to talk with you, my friend." Jed didn't quite know how to start. "No, you will not die if you will listen."

Walking Horse nodded. "In my condition, I am at your mercy. What would you have me listen to?"

"Perhaps, I should go?" Red Hawk started to rise.

"No, Red Hawk, stay." The weak one raised his hand. "This is going to get interesting, I think."

Jed shook his head. "My friend, you don't have much time."

"I know this. Tell me what you wish me to hear."

"It was me and Bow Legs that found you and gave you back your life." Jed looked across at the warrior. "Now, we have lost our friend, but you still owe me a life."

"Are you saying Bow Legs gave his life for me?"

"Partly, and partly for his people."

"He died a brave death, worthy of a Crow." Red Hawk added. "He did give his life for you, Walking Horse."

Nodding slowly, the warrior studied the fire for several minutes, then finally looked up. "I did not know this. What do you want of me that he should do this thing?"

"He loved you, my friend. He wanted for you to live and be strong again."

"He was a good friend and he will be missed." Walking Horse looked at Jed. "Speak."

"I wish to take you to the west, to a white medicine man."

Jed expected the warrior to explode in rage but was shocked when the wounded one only blinked and shook his head. "That is a long journey, my friend. I do not have the strength."

"Walking Horse will ride there in comfort." Jed promised. "I have watched the white soldiers carry their sick ones on a litter."

"I do not wish to live like a cripple." The warrior nodded, admitting the truth. "Can this white medicine man drive the evil ones from me?"

"I think so, but I won't lie, you are very sick."

"Go, Walking Horse." Red Hawk spoke. "If you are not strong, I will have nobody to fight."

"I owe my brother, my life." Walking Horse looked at Jed. "If he wishes this, I will go."

Relieved, Jed smiled and nodded. "We will leave with the sun."

"Our village will be safe?"

"It will be safe."

Two gentle, old broodmares were caught by the young boys of the village while others brought in long poles and hides. Red Hawk watched curiously as Jed scratched his head, trying to remember how the soldiers had rigged the harness on their horses. The poles had to be mounted between the horses tight enough to hold Walking Horse's weight and stay balanced as they climbed and descended the mountain passes. Several times, Jed flung himself into the mobile hammock only to be tossed out the other side. To the laughter of the village children, Jed adjusted the makeshift harness, finally getting the rawhide binding tight enough to hold.

The mares were broke to ride and used by the elderly squaws of the village to pull a travois, but they weren't too comfortable with the contraption Jed lashed to them. Two extra gentle horses were caught in case one of the mares came up crippled or sore footed on the rough mountain trails. Finally, satisfied with the litter, Jed had the women cover the pole and rope framework with soft hides. Nodding as they finished, Jed swung up on the piebald as Red Hawk mounted his spotted stallion.

"Let's take a turn around the village." Jed nodded at Red Hawk. "Hang on to her for a few steps."

"You have some weird ideas, my friend." The Crow smiled. "If this works, maybe Little Antelope will fix me one to ride."

Hearing the warrior, Little Antelope scoffed. "If I had my way, you would walk, Crow."

Laughing, Red Hawk grasped the lead halter and held the mare tight as she made her first tentative steps with the litter. The front mare tried to hump up and kick at the poles, but a hard jerk from Jed brought her into line. After a few trips around the village, Jed announced the horses were ready and had Walking Horse brought from the lodge. Slow Wolf, White Swan, and the entire village gathered to watch as the party prepared to depart the village. Wishing them the best of luck, Slow Wolf had several warriors help the weak Walking Horse onto the litter.

The warrior protested to Jed. "I feel like an old woman being carried like this, but I know I am too weak to ride a horse down the rough mountains."

Motioning forward, Jed started west toward the Yellowstone with Little Antelope leading the extra horses and supplies. Two Kills, one of the Arapaho warriors who had ridden to the valley to find Jed, handed Red Hawk his Hawken rifle, shot pouch, and powder horn.

"You may need this more than I do, Crow."

Thanking the warrior, Red Hawk looked at the weapon curiously, as he had no idea how to use it. "I don't know the use of this weapon."

"In the days to come, you will learn, my friend." Jed thanked Two Kills, then turned the horses to the west. "I will teach you."

Roden was an experienced tracker, following the tracks Jed left on the narrow trail was second nature to him. The horse tracks were several weeks old, but since there had been little rain, the tracks were still visible in many places even though the wind erased some of them. Wild horses, deer, antelope, and elk left their tracks atop Jed's tracks, but to a scout and tracker with Roden's capabilities, it was still an easy trail to follow. The man was a drunk, but even though his eyes showed a rummy look from consuming a year of rum and whiskey, they were still sharp, like the eyes of a hawk.

"You boys took your time getting me on this trail." Roden looked back over his shoulder. "We're lucky there hasn't been much rain."

"I don't see how you know which tracks are which." Beale chewed absently on a piece of dried elk meat. "They all look the same to me."

"It's simple enough, sonny, if you had been observing the tracks closer when we first found them."

"Don't call me, sonny."

"We've been traveling south for three days now." Seth absently pulled at the coarse mane of his horse. "How much longer, you figure, to the valley he spoke of?"

"He turned a little to the west, back a ways. Maybe we're getting close." Roden looked contemptuously at the two. "Course, you city boys wouldn't have noticed."

Not used to riding, Beale shook his head. "I hope so, my backside is hollering."

Roden shook his head, these two were both farm boys, soft and spoiled. Maybe he should stick around and watch the fun. These two will probably wet their pants when they actually come face to face with Jedidiah. He knew nothing of the girl's death so he couldn't understand why they were so impatient to catch up to the man. He knew they were up to something, and what it was, he did not know.

Late in the afternoon as the three topped out on the tall mountain pass, Roden looked down onto a huge valley and knew he found Jedidiah's valley. Far out across the flat valley, Roden could make out smoke back in a grove of trees, and it had to be a campsite. Somewhere below, they should find the man they sought, providing he didn't find them first.

"This is it, and down there's his stomping grounds." Roden nodded. "He'll defend it, and you can bet on it."

Both Seth and Beale stared unbelieving and in awe at the beautiful, large valley. Somewhere below, they knew Jed would be waiting and maybe even watching them. Beale was spooked, as the words of the Nez Perce about a demon still echoed in his ears. Even as a child, the tales of hobgoblins and witches at Halloween spooked him.

"What you boys aiming to do, now that you're here?" Roden smiled to himself.

"We're gonna ride down there and find Jed." Seth leaned forward as if to get a better view. "Lead out."

"Nope." Roden shook his head. "You wanted him found, I found him."

"You'll ride down there with us. We don't even know if this is his valley."

"Yeah, Roden, we've just got your word." Beale chimed in.

"You see them trees across the valley?"

"We see them, what of it?"

"Look closer, that smoke down there is from his camp, I bet."

"Lead out." Seth looked down at his saddlebags. "You thirsty? Find him and there will be a jug in it for you."

"I'll lead you on in, but I don't want your spirits." Roden shook his head.

Beale laughed. "You telling us, you're quitting the jug?"

"I'm through with a lot of things."

Seth tightened his finger on the Hawken. "Meaning?"

Roden could see the wild look in Wilson's face. Kicking his horse, he started down the trail leading to the valley floor. Both youngsters were scared, and why they were doing this, he didn't know. One thing he did know, they were spooked and capable of doing anything.

Through the doorway of the cabin, Silent One noticed the black mule's ears perk up from where she was tied. Grabbing his rifle, he stepped outside and looked across the valley, surveying everything in sight. Across the creek, the rest of the mules and horses stood looking toward the north trail, leading up and out of the valley. Carefully scanning the valley floor, he searched along the tree line and to the open valley floor. Nothing appeared on the grassy flats, nothing stirred, not even a rabbit. Shrugging, the youngster turned back inside the cabin where he was busy working on a new buffalo-hide coat. Jed had told him how much value the fur buyer in the white settlement had put on them, and he wanted the coat to be a surprise when Jed returned from the south.

"It's him." Seth slipped back to where Roden and Beale stood, holding their horses. "It's him."

"Did you see him?"

"I seen him plain as day, standing in the doorway of his cabin." Seth shook his head. "He looks more like an Indian than an Indian would."

"In the morning, he'll come out to feed, and then we'll kill him." Beale looked at Roden.

"So you boys do plan on killing him?" Roden shook his head. "Why? I thought he was your brother."

"Brother?" Seth scoffed. "He's a stinking breed, like you're a stinking drunk."

Turning to his horse, Roden mounted while their attention was focused on the cabin. This time, he had the advantage with his Hawken pointed in their general direction and cocked. Turning, their faces paled as they looked at the huge rifle bore staring down at them.

"I'm riding out." Roden started backing the sorrel. "I want no part of what you're aiming to do."

"You're yeller." Beale spit. "Plumb yeller."

Both of the young men disgusted the old scout, and he detested them both. "It's gonna be interesting to see what Jedidiah does to you two, so I'll overlook them words."

"When we get through with him, we'll come for you, Lem Roden." Beale warned.

"You ain't out of here alive yet, sonny." Roden spit. "You forgot one thing, boys."

"Yeah, what's that, Lem?"

"Lige Hatcher, he's kinda partial to that boy." Roden waved his Hawken. "Now, you boys set them rifles down, real easy like against that tree, and walk down the mountain a ways, while I ride out."

Several paces down the mountain, Seth looked back to find Roden had disappeared. "Now, ain't that something."

"What Seth?"

"Old Lem Roden giving up the spirits." The redhead shook his head and laughed. "Seems kinda weird to me."

"What started him on the skids, you reckon?"

"Don't rightly know for sure, but I heard it was a woman back at Fort Bridger."

"A woman can do that to a man."

Seth thought of Sally Ann as he heard the words. "I reckon they can at that."

Silent One set his coffee cup on the rock fireplace and turned to the table. Holding up the finished coat, he smiled with satisfaction, as both sides of the buffalo coat matched perfectly in hair texture and color. The young Assiniboine had remembered the old squaws of his village, sorting through hide after hide until they had found two hides that matched. Buffalo coats were valuable to the white fur traders who would give many trade blankets and trinkets for them, more so if they matched perfectly as the coat the youngster held up. The coats were too heavy and burdensome for a warrior to wear on the war trail or out hunting, but horseback on a cold blustery day, they were snug and warm.

Picking up his coffee, Silent One poured himself another cup, then walked to the door. He had become partial to his early morning coffee, enjoying at least one cup before putting the horses out to pasture. Looking at the cup of steaming liquid, he smiled. Jed always warned him of becoming addicted to the hot brew. Opening the heavy door, the youngster stepped out into the bright light of the early morning. His eyes not yet accustomed to the full light so he did not notice the ears of the animals pointing toward the creek.

Enjoying his coffee, Silent One couldn't hear the roar of two Hawken rifles, and only felt the searing lead as it entered his chest. Flung backward by the heavy caliber slugs, he leaned against the heavy door several seconds, watching as his coffee cup rolled across the ground. Slowly his eyes closed as he slid down the bloody door.

"It's not Jedidiah." Seth rushed forward to the cabin, then turned in confusion after examining the prone body. "I would have sworn."

"Is he dead?"

"With two fifty caliber slugs in his chest?" Seth shook his head at the stupid question. "What do you think?"

"Who was it?" Beale looked away from the dead body.

"I don't know, but this isn't Jed." Seth shrugged. "Just some Injun, a good one now."

"Is this Jed's cabin?" Beale looked about the room.

"It's his alright." Seth fingered one of the traps hanging beside the door. "Some of those traps have my brother's mark on them."

"We need to ride and get away fast."

"No, we're staying." Seth tossed a rawhide rope at Beale. "Drag that carcass out of here."

"Are you serious?" Beale was scared. "No, we've got to head east as far and as fast as we can."

Shaking his head, the redhead glared at Beale. "We're waiting right here until he shows."

"You're serious." Beale was terrified. "He's bound to have heard those shots."

"You cross me on this, Adam, and I'll kill you." The Hawken stared into Beale's eyes.

"Listen to me, Seth." Beale looked into the crazed eyes of the redhead. "We gotta get out of here before he comes back."

"There's no hurry, besides I kinda like this place. Maybe, we'll make it our new home." Seth seemed to giggle as if he was in a trance of some kind. Pointing at Silent One's body, he grinned crazily. "Now, drag that out of here."

Beale shook his head doubtfully. "What about Hatcher? You heard what Roden said."

"He's just a man like any other. We'll kill him, soon as we tend to Jedidiah."

"I don't like it, Seth." Beale shook his head. "I'm getting out, now."

Shaking his head in disgust when Beale fell over Silent One's body, the redhead swore. "Then git your sniveling hide from here and ride, you coward."

Beale quickly ran to his horse and mounted, kicking the horse and racing back to the north trail in a dead run. Terror rode with him as he climbed the pass out of the valley. Behind him, Seth was holding his Hawken and he knew the redhead had gone mad, loco enough to shoot. Somewhere in these broad mountain ranges rode Jedidiah Bracket also known as Crow Killer. Now, they had killed an Indian in Jed's cabin. Beale was scared and wanted to go home. He hoped he could find his way back out of the deep mountains. In Baxter Springs, he could face a trial and maybe hanging, but his chances for survival was better there than staying in the mountains with Wilson. Seth Wilson had gone mad, and now he was as bloodthirsty as his brother Billy, thinking he could kill both Jed and Lige Hatcher was pure craziness.

Roden doubled back and returned to the high trail, overlooking the valley, where he had last seen Beale and Wilson. All night, he sat against a rock outcropping, waiting and watching over the dark valley until the break of dawn. As the fog slowly lifted, bringing the valley into view, the scout took in its real beauty. The land and mountains were breathtaking, and Roden had seen many a mountain and valley in his travels.

Suddenly breaking the quiet of the morning, the report of two heavy caliber gunshots reverberated across the flats. Rising to his feet, Roden swore, the two skunks had actually ambushed and probably killed Jedidiah. He didn't know Jedidiah personally, only what Hatcher had told him of the man, the Arapaho called Crow Killer. Cussing himself for not riding down to warn him, Roden sat back down against a rock. He knew it wasn't his fight and he could kill the two men easily, but it would only bring him trouble if he was found out. Neither was worth the bullet it would take to kill them. Still, he remembered with bitterness, the vile way Beale had spoken to him back at the cave and on their way there.

Wiping his lips, Roden thought of the bottle in Seth's saddlebag. His tongue was sour, and right now, he was in need of a drink. Looking down across the valley, he watched as several horses and a couple of mules raced out onto the valley floor. He didn't see Beale or Seth, but he could feel Jedidiah was dead by their hands. Rising, he walked to where his horse stood tied. Cinching up the sorrel gelding, Roden mounted and turned back north. A drink would sure taste good and Baxter Springs was the nearest settlement. He knew he would have to explain to McBride why he was riding his favorite animal, hopefully before the Swede's temper and great strength killed him.

Beale was fleeing in a panic, not stopping to look back as he passed the high ridge they had looked down and spied out Jed's cabin only yesterday. Goose bumps raced up his back as he knew, any minute now, he would feel Seth's bullet in his back. Terror drove him as he pushed his blowing horse hard, back to the north and home.

McBride's sorrel horse was a powerful animal, but this morning Roden needed to feel the beauty and serenity of the mountains so he kept the sorrel in a slow walk. He had lived his whole life with pride as a scout and trapper, and couldn't understand how he allowed himself to sink into the depths of a jug of whiskey. Was his drinking over a woman or just weakness? Now, he had even let the likes of two worthless boys destroy a good man. Reining in the horse, Roden looked out across the beautiful mountains. He had to take McBride's horse home, and repay someone for the clothes and rifle he carried. Perhaps, he would turn his back on civilization and return to the mountains where he belonged. Roden at one time was a great and respected hunter, but now, after the death of Jedidiah, he was ashamed.

Beale kept his tiring horse moving without rest until midmorning. Reining in at a small water hole, he dismounted and let the horse drink his fill. Pacing nervously as he watered his horse, his back still crawled and his nerves were shot.

"Well, Adam Beale, did you kill him?" The voice came from behind a tree. "You look kinda scared."

Whirling, Beale searched for the voice. "Where are you?"

"Right over here, boy." Roden spoke again. "I asked you, did you kill Jedidiah?"

"No, no we shot an Injun, is what we did." Beale swallowed hard. "The wrong Injun."

"You best drop that rifle, boy." Roden stepped from behind a tree and raised his rifle. "Drop it."

"What are you gonna do to me?"

"Nothing." Roden shook his head in disgust. "Peers to me, you're doing it to yourself."

Dropping the rifle, Beale retreated as Roden advanced on him. Before, with Seth siding him, he had looked down on the man as a drunk. Now, alone with the small man advancing on him, the drunk loomed as a giant. Terrified, Beale whirled to run, not realizing he backed too close to a nearby drop off from the trail and couldn't stop himself as he plunged from the high pass.

Looking down the hundred-foot drop to the lower trail, Roden shook his head, studying the broken body of Beale. "Well, young feller, looks like you found your peace."

Blue Darter, leading Crowfoot, Little Horse, Flying Bat, and their women and children, followed the well-used game trail that would take them close to Jed's valley. For two weeks, riding slowly, they had crossed the treacherous trails covering these mountains. Pushing their many horses across the trails, along with watching over the women and small children as they swam across fast flowing rivers, the four warriors were kept busy.

"Are you leading us to the valley of the demon?" Crowfoot rode up beside Blue Darter.

"No, it is not in this valley, but we will ride near it on our way to Chief Lone Bull's village."

Little Horse shrugged. "Do you think Lone Bull will permit us to live in his village after being banished from our village?"

Blue Darter looked over at Crowfoot. "You are from Lone Bull's village, what do you think?"

"Until I took Little Flower as my woman and came to Deep Water's village, I was a warrior and a friend of Lone Bull's son." Crowfoot shook his head. "My friend, you must remember, Lone Bull is the brother of Deep Water."

"I remember." Blue Darter nodded.

"My friendship with Lone Bull's son means nothing when the chief finds out you dishonored and almost killed his brother, your hereditary chief." Crowfoot shrugged. "He may fear you, Blue Darter, and may not want you in his village."

"We will see."

Once again, the Yellowstone River lay before them as Jed floated Walking Horse across the mighty river on a small raft while Little Antelope and Red Hawk swam the horses across. With only the weight of Walking Horse and the litter, the cedar raft was easy to handle and beached safely on the opposite bank. Ahead, lay only the long, steep trail over the mountains to Jed's cabin. Walking Horse so far had not weakened further, but at their camps, he ate very little to keep up his strength. Jed kept the small caravan moving as he looked at the sick man, knowing the urgency of reaching a doctor as quick as they could. They were down to only three litter horses, as one of the older mares had become stone bruised, the second day on the trail, and had to be left behind.

"We have only one more day before we reach my valley." Jed pointed out the landmarks along the steep trail. "From the next pass, we will be able to breathe the air from the mountains that stand guard over the valley."

Little Antelope nodded tiredly, exhausted from the tiring journey. "That is good, I fear Walking Horse weakens now."

"He hasn't said anything."

"No, he is too proud to complain."

"We will be home soon."

"Home, that is a nice word." She looked over at Jed.

Early afternoon found the party at the pass that Jed had spoken of with Little Antelope earlier in the morning. Raising his arm as the far mountains loomed before them, Jed smiled at Walking Horse. Less than a day ahead was the valley where his cabin stood.

"How do you feel, my friend?" Jed turned on the piebald, and looked back at Walking Horse. "We're almost there."

"She is tired." The warrior looked over at Little Antelope. "I do not want her harmed just to help me."

Jed looked at the woman. "She is strong and she can rest when we reach my lodge."

Nodding, Walking Horse tried to smile. "Push on then, my friend."

"Can you go further?"

"All I have to do is lie here and watch the mountains pass by."

Suddenly, Red Hawk pointed, bringing Jed's attention back to the trail. "Warriors on the trail below."

"Quick, Little Antelope, hold this horse." Jed dismounted from the piebald and helped Walking Horse from the litter.

"There are four warriors with women and children." Red Hawk raced back to where Jed was waiting. "They do not know we are here."

"What tribe?"

"Blackfoot."

"We cannot retreat from this narrow place." Jed looked around the narrow pass. "I will go forward and speak with these warriors."

Red Hawk stepped forward. "I hope this white man weapon works for an Indian."

Jed smiled. "It will, old friend, just remember to pull the trigger."

Several times, when they had made night camp, Jed showed Red Hawk the working of the rifle, but at times he forgot to pull the trigger. Finally, after he had fired the rifle successfully, Red Hawk nodded his head in satisfaction.

"I will remember."

"Stay here and protect them." Jed looked over to where Walking Horse sat with Little Antelope.

Riding the piebald down the trail, Jed reined in where the trail narrowed and after checking the priming on his rifle, he waited for the oncoming warriors. The hoofbeats of plodding horses climbing the rocky trail came to Jed's ears as the tension mounted. Finally, the lead horse, rounding a bend in the trail, came into view. Jed's face tightened as he recognized the warrior, Blue Darter, on the horse. Repositioning the rifle across his arm, he watched the warrior rein his horse in hard as he discovered and recognized Jed in front of him.

Blue Darter raised his hand and ordered his people to wait. He kicked his horse forward to within a few feet of where Jed sat the piebald. Several minutes passed as the two warriors took time to study each other.

The warrior was shocked and could not understand how the Arapaho knew his people were on this trail. "Crow Killer, we did not know you were on this trail."

"It is good to see you, Blue Darter, if you come in peace."

"My followers pass over this trail on our way to another village to the north."

"Are you on a hunt?" Jed could see the small party and many horses waiting back down the trail. "Why do you leave your village?"

Blue Darter dropped his eyes. "It shames me to say this."

"Tell me." Jed ordered. "A warrior should never be ashamed to tell of his deeds."

"Chief Deep Water banished me and my squaw from our village." Blue Darter looked up. "In my rage, I challenged my chief to fight."

"Did you do battle?"

"Yes, we fought." Blue Darter nodded sadly. "I fought my hereditary chief."

"Did you kill him?"

"No, I could not." Blue Darter shook his head. "I took the ones you see and we are on our way to join the people of Lone Bull's village."

Jed studied the sad face before him. "Tell me, was this fight because of me?"

"I would not say you were a demon, and I did not help Standing Bull when he fought with you."

"For this I thank you. I am sorry it caused you trouble."

"I do not lie for any man, not even my chief." Blue Darter shook his head. "So, we were banished from our village."

"Will you be welcome at this other village?"

Blue Darter nodded at the lead warrior behind him. "Crowfoot is from that village, but we do not know if we will be welcome. Lone Bull is the brother of Deep Water."

"When you challenged your chief, was it against your people's law?"

"Yes."

"You have not attacked me." Jed spoke. "You have helped me twice. Now, you are in trouble because of me."

"It was not your fault." Blue Darter smiled. "It was a matter of honor, Crow Killer."

"These lands are big, if you wish you are welcome to bring your people here." Jed nodded. "Your enemies will be mine."

"You are generous." Blue Darter smiled. "It's funny, you have Assiniboine, Arapaho, and now Blackfoot; all enemies living in one land."

"Also a Crow."

"Crow?"

"Yes, Red Hawk the Crow is just over that ridge guarding an Arapaho woman and her husband."

"But, the Crow are enemies of the Arapaho."

"Like you said, this is a strange bunch of folks."

"I will speak with my people." Blue Darter shook his head. "When they decide, we may come to your lodge."

"Bring your people, Blue Darter, you will be welcome."

"I tell you this, Crow Killer; my chief Deep Water may raid your lands." Blue Darter spoke. "I do not know if this will happen, but he might come to avenge his son and brother."

"Thank you for speaking."

"I give you my word, if he comes to your lands, your battles will be ours."

"Then you are welcome."

Both parties passed each other in the narrow confines of the mountain trail. None spoke as they passed, but age-old enemies passed each other looking straight ahead without fighting. The litter with the sick warrior did take their attention, as they had never seen such a travois. Jed pushed on, never slowing his pace, wanting to reach his cabin so Walking Horse could rest, and then he would ride ahead for the doctor.

Lige Hatcher and Ed Wilson crossed the Snake, then rode south as fast as their horses could travel without laming them on the rough rocky trails. Wilson wasn't sure how much lead Seth and Beale had on them, but they had to push hard and try to reach Jed's cabin ahead of them. One advantage was theirs, Hatcher knew exactly where the cabin was located. The farmer, Carter, told Wilson, about a week or so back, when he had last seen Lem Roden leading the boys south into the mountains. The farmer had no idea where they were now, or if they had continued into the mountains.

Holding up his hand, Hatcher motioned for Wilson to follow him into a stand of trees to hide their horses. Something was coming along the south trail heading their way. Their horses sensed someone or maybe another horse ahead of them. The ears of both horses perked forward causing Hatcher to move deeper into the dense trees bordering the mountain trail.

"What is it?" Wilson was a farmer, lacking the knowledge of the mountains and mountain ways. "Why are we hiding?"

"Stay still." Shaking his head, Hatcher quieted the farmer with his hand. "Someone or something is heading our way, up the trail."

Both men dismounted and held the muzzles of their horses, keeping them from nickering or making any sound. After several minutes, they finally heard the soft sound of two horses sounding on the rocky mountain trail ahead. Less than fifty yards separated them from the oncoming rider. Only a sharp bend in the trail kept whoever was coming up the path out of sight.

"He's stopped." Hatcher strained his eyes and ears. "He's smart, his horse probably has us located, same as ours have him."

"Indian or white?" Wilson looked over at Hatcher.

"Your guess is as good as mine, Ed."

"What are we gonna do?"

"You hold the horses. I'll go take a look." Hatcher handed Wilson the reins of his roan horse. "If things don't work out well, you're on your own, old hoss."

As Hatcher started to step forward, a voice rang out from down the trail. "Who you be out there, pilgrim?"

Hatcher grinned. "If I ain't missed my guess or gone deaf that's Lem Roden's caterwauling."

"Lem Roden?" Wilson was dumbstruck. "What in blue blazes is he doing back here?"

"How about we ask him." Hatcher stepped out into the open. "Come outta there, you little varmint."

"Well, I'll be horn swaggled." The smiling face of the thin scout grinned as he stepped from behind a tree and raised his hands in greeting. "If it ain't Lige Hatcher in the flesh."

Walking forward, the men laughed and shook hands as they reached one another. "As Ed Wilson put it, what in the blue blazes are you doing here?"

"Well, Lige, I was headed for Baxter Springs to get me a drink." Roden swallowed, thinking of the drink he sorely needed. "Now, let me ask you two the same question."

"Lem, we're following your tracks I reckon, hoping to catch up with your ornery old hide."

"Well, you've found it, what's left of it anyway."

Wilson studied the thin scout before him. The man had changed since the last time they met in Baxter Springs. "You're looking good, Lem."

"I'm feeling good, Ed. I've dried out some." Slightly embarrassed, Roden nodded at the farmer. "So you boys are looking for me?"

"I'm looking for my boy Seth, and Adam Beale."

"We were told you were seen leading them into the mountains looking for Jedidiah Bracket." Hatcher wanted Roden to know he had been spotted with the boys.

"Don't know who seen us." Roden nodded. "Yep, I did lead them there."

"Where are they, Lem?" Wilson piped in.

"Last time I seen them they were on a high pass looking down on Jedidiah's cabin. I can't rightly say where Seth is right now."

"When was that?" Hatcher studied the scout.

"Yesterday, almost at sundown."

"Anything else?"

"Yep, I backtracked them two just to see what they would do." Roden rubbed his face. "Early this morning, right at daybreak, I heard the report of two rifles going off down near the cabin, at least near the place where the smoke came from across the creek."

"You figure Jed's done for?"

"No, from what I found out, he wasn't home when the boys did the shooting." Roden shook his head. "Beale said they killed a young Indian, thinking he was Jed."

"Well, we're fixing to ride down and find out for ourselves." Hatcher turned for his horse. "You coming ain't you?"

"I need to get McBride's horse back to him." Roden was thinking of the saloon in town, needing a drink bad. "Maybe, I best ride on."

"It'll wait. I'll speak to McBride when we get back." Hatcher's voice was hard.

Figuring Hatcher wasn't asking but telling, Roden shrugged and mounted his horse. "There's one other thing, Lige."

Hatcher looked over at Roden. "What is it?"

"A mile back down the trail, you'll find the remains of Beale." Roden nodded at the other horse he led. "This is his horse and possibles."

"You do for him?"

"Nah." Roden shook his head. "Dang fool was so scared when he spotted me, that he stumbled and fell off the trail, and landed about seventy feet down. Sure didn't do him any good, that's a fact."

"What about Seth?" Wilson asked.

"Can't say for sure of his whereabouts. He wasn't with Beale when the polecat rode up on me earlier." Roden shrugged.

"Let's ride."

"Beale said something funny though just before he met his demise." Roden stared as Hatcher and Wilson looked over at him curiously. "He said something about Seth Wilson being plumb loco."

"He could be." Hatcher nodded. "Sometimes a man can be so scared, out of his mind, that it can drive him to act crazy."

CHAPTER 9

Finally, after traversing the rough mountain passes, the piebald stepped out onto the lush, flat ground of Jed's valley. Kicking the horses into a fast walk, Jed hurried to reach the cabin to check on Silent One. He had hardly been away two weeks now, but the time spent away felt like a lifetime. He had been worrying about the youngster since riding to the Arapaho village. He knew the boy could take care of himself, but he was still just a youngster.

"One more hour, my friend, we will be at my lodge, and then you can rest." Jed looked back at Walking Horse reclining on the litter. "How do you feel?"

"I will be happy when you get me out of this thing." Walking Horse patted the litter. "I am tired and I know she is."

Jed turned to where Little Antelope was nodding. "You will rest soon, little one."

"How much further is it to the white medicine man's lodge, from your lodge?"

"Four more sleeps."

"Walking Horse will not survive the trail four more suns." Little Antelope shook her head. "He is far too weak to travel on."

Jed nodded, knowing she spoke the truth. "Then, he will remain at my lodge, and I will ride alone for the medicine man."

Looking down at Walking Horse and his sunken face, she shook her head again. "You must hurry, Jed."

"I will hurry; my friend will live."

Reining in the piebald, Jed looked toward the north end of the valley, in the direction where his cabin set back in the trees, across the small creek. Nothing stirred, something was wrong. By now, Silent One would have spotted them crossing the valley. Jed knew the young Assiniboine was always alert, careful so an unseen enemy wouldn't slip up on him. Doubt grew in his mind. Holding up his hand, Jed stopped the small caravan from advancing further toward his cabin. Scanning the far tree line for several minutes, he looked for any sign of the youngster. Out on the valley floor, he could see the loose herd of horses and the two mules. All his horses and mules were out grazing, and the way they stepped out as they moved, he could tell none were hobbled.

Motioning Red Hawk forward, Jed waited until the Crow stopped beside him. "Something is wrong."

"How do you know this?" Red Hawk studied the valley. "What do you see?"

"It's what I don't see that worries me." Jed nodded. "The Assiniboine youth that lives with me is nowhere to be seen, and my horses aren't hobbled."

"Maybe, he sleeps in your lodge."

Jed shook his head, as he knew Silent One would not be asleep this time of day. "No, not this one."

"What will we do?"

"I will ride ahead. You wait here with Walking Horse and Little Antelope until you see my signal."

As Jed rode forward, Red Hawk led the horses carrying Walking Horse's litter back into the cover of a grove of trees. Slipping to the ground, he motioned for Little Antelope to dismount, then turned his full attention to watching Jed as he crossed the flat valley.

Concealed in the trees, lining the creek, Seth watched as the riders stopped far out on the valley floor, conversing about something. Looking over at the cabin, he looked at the dead body of Silent One, still in the same place where he had fallen. Beale in his fright and headlong rush to get away, had fled back to the north, not waiting long enough to help Seth with the body. Seth could have drug the body away with his horse, but he didn't want to take his attention from the surrounding valley for a minute. The body wasn't going anywhere, and when this was finished, he would drag it away. The redhead had no way of knowing when Jedidiah would come. He was terrified of Jed, and for two days, he hadn't slept because he wasn't about to let his stepbrother ride in and surprise him.

Checking the priming on his rifle, Seth made himself as comfortable as possible on an upturned chunk of wood. Eventually, Jed would come, this was his cabin, the place he had told Sally Ann about, and he wouldn't stay away for long. Seth had turned his own horse into the corral in case he was needed quickly. Preparing for a long vigil, beside him lay a skin full of water, a sack of dough biscuits, and crackers. Seth was ready, he would wait no matter how long it took, and sooner or later, Jed would come. Seth absentmindedly fingered the rifle. Soon the valley and cabin would be his, but not until Jedidiah Bracket was dead.

His desperate mind knew he could never return to Baxter Springs and he didn't have money to go east. No, his only future was to take over this valley and make it his home until he could make enough money to leave. That meant, Jed had to die, and Seth had no qualms about killing his half-brother, not one.

Hatcher led as Wilson and Roden followed him, bottoming out into the broad valley, but instead of crossing the valley, Hatcher kept to the tree line, keeping out of sight in the trees. He wanted to get as close to the cabin as possible without being discovered. Seth Wilson was down there somewhere and Hatcher knew the young man would be nervous, ready to shoot at anything that moved. The scout knew Seth Wilson from the wagon train and knew he was an expert shot. Killing the young Indian at the cabin had proved his skill. Hatcher was curious who the dead Indian was that Beale said they killed, because Jed was alone when he left last fall.

Riding in as close to the cabin as they dared, without being heard or alerting Seth, Hatcher dismounted the others and had them check their rifles. The herd of horses and two mules already detected their presence, but Hatcher hoped Seth didn't see their ears prick up. The valley was quiet, and only the gurgling of the creek water running over the rocky bottom made the slightest noise. Even the wind was calm, not a sound was heard, no rustling of leaves, no chatter from squirrels or birds, nothing. It was too quiet and Hatcher didn't like the silence as they started forward on foot, moving slowly toward the cabin. Stopping suddenly at the edge of the tree line, Hatcher knelt behind a mountain pine and pointed to where several riders sat their horses out on the valley floor. Even at a far distance, Hatcher and Wilson recognized Jed and the big piebald horse. Shifting their attention back to the cabin, the three men knelt silently, studying the dead body beside the doorway.

Touching Hatcher's arm, Roden nodded toward the larger trees near the creek. "You know, it looks like he could have at least taken the Indian's body away from the cabin." Roden swore. "It ain't decent, just leaving him there."

Hatcher nodded. "Yeah, I figure he's so scared, he ain't thinking straight."

Seth Wilson with his attention fully focused on the riders out on the valley floor lay hidden, waiting for the riders to approach the cabin. The redhead was scared, almost petrified, never once looking Hatcher's way and never knowing they were anywhere near him. Several times, he raised the rifle and sighted down the barrel, waiting and ready to fire. Finally, seeing the riders weren't moving forward toward the cabin, he lowered the weapon back to the ground in disgust.

Roden touched Hatcher's arm as he noticed a lone rider moving across the valley floor toward the cabin. "Somebody's coming in."

"It's Jed, coming in." Wilson whispered as he watched the piebald move closer. "It'll be a turkey shoot at this range, Seth will kill him."

Seth was tired, his eyes burned from lack of sleep, but still he didn't miss the piebald as Jed moved toward the cabin. Taking up the Hawken, he rested it over a small log and waited. Even from a distance, Hatcher could see the younger Wilson smiling cruelly as he waited on Jed to come in closer. Hatcher had been wrong about the redhead; he wasn't scared he was completely crazy. The old scout knew Seth didn't aim for his shot to miss so he would wait until the piebald brought Jedidiah into very close range.

The suspense of death played out as the three men watched and waited. The piebald brought his rider ever closer to the cabin and death as Jed closely studied the creek bank and the horse herd. Scrutinizing everything as he moved nearer the creek, it was impossible for Jed to see the hidden form of Seth waiting, cloaked by the shadows of the trees. Hatcher watched as Seth squinted down the barrel, preparing to fire. He knew the redhead was only waiting for the piebald to take a few more steps forward as he brought his rider in close enough, making it impossible for Wilson to miss his target.

Hatcher couldn't wait any longer, Jed was moving closer, too close. Stepping out into plain sight, he yelled at Jed to get down, causing Seth to whirl in his direction. Shocked at Hatcher's yell and sudden appearance, the redhead stood still, paralyzed with fear. Suddenly, as he stood with his mouth open in surprise, he was knocked back as the roar of the Hawken went off behind Hatcher. Dodging sideways out of habit and self-preservation, Hatcher blinked as the smoke from the flash of the rifle cleared.

Ed Wilson slowly dropped his rifle and moved forward to where Seth lay crumpled on his back. The blue eyes already started to go blank as Wilson knelt beside his son. "Seth, my son."

"Pa, is that you? Can I come home?" The words were barely audible. "I can't see you, Pa, where are..."

The words trailed off as the final breath of air rushed from the dying young man. Looking at his son, Wilson slowly stood and shook his head. "Oh Seth, what have I done?" Wilson wiped his face. "It's finished. Now, I'll take you home, son."

Jed sat the piebald and looked down at Seth's dead body, then back at Wilson. Noticing the still form of a body near the cabin, he crossed the clearing and dismounted beside Silent One. Picking up the dropped coffee cup, Jed shook his head. Noticing the two large bullet wounds in the youth's chest, Jed touched Silent One's still face.

"I shouldn't have left you alone." Jed shook his head slowly. "You were truly a great warrior and my friend. You were much too young to die."

Walking up beside Jed and looking down at the body, Roden shook his head. "If it's any consolation to you, young feller, the two that did for him are both dead."

Once again, White Swan's words came back to Jed. "A warrior's walk through life can be short, my son, but it is filled with pride and love for his people."

"His people didn't even want him."

"What?" Roden didn't understand the words.

"Nothing." Jed looked up at Roden. "Who are you?"

"He's a friend of mine, and a great hunter and scout." Hatcher walked up and stared down at the dead body. "Your friends are coming across the creek."

Nodding, Jed stood slowly and turned, watching as Red Hawk brought in Walking Horse and Little Antelope. Jed walked over to where his stepdad was waiting, standing over Seth. "I'm sorry, Pa."

"Don't be Jed, he brought it on himself." Wilson shook his head. "It must have been my weakness."

"No, Pa, it wasn't anything you've done." Jed touched Wilson on the arm. "Let me get my friend Walking Horse inside, then we have burying to do."

"I want to take him home." Wilson shook his head. "He wanted to go home."

"Alright, Pa."

"Someday, I want to bring Billy's remains home too."

"Alright." Jed nodded solemnly. "Whenever you decide, we will do that."

Walking Horse lay on Jed's bed that had been moved closer to the small fire in the hearth for warmth. Little Antelope fussed over the sick warrior as she looked around the cabin, letting her eyes take in everything. She had never been in a white man's lodge before and didn't know what to think. A meal had to be prepared, but the little woman wasn't sure how to cook in such a place. Jed could see her dilemma. Moving to the wall, he started removing pots and pans plus the battered coffeepot, placing them on the rock hearth. Nodding, she watched as he rotated the metal rack suspended over the small cooking fire. Pushing him aside, Little Antelope stoked the fire, bringing it back to life, and turned to the cooking.

Silent One was placed on a high scaffold as his tribal custom dictated. Seth was wrapped in hides, preparing him for his journey back to the Wilson farm in Baxter Springs for burial.

Jed watched as Red Hawk chanted and danced the Crow burial rites, then abruptly stopped. Looking up at the feathers fluttering in the breeze attached to the pole platform holding the remains of the Assiniboine, Red Hawk shook his head. "It is not Assiniboine, but it is the best I can do."

"It honors Silent One." Jed nodded. "I thank you for him."

"He should have a horse to ride on into the afterworld."

"No, he came here on foot, and he will leave the same way."

Jed needed to ride, but the trails out of the valley were too treacherous to ride at night. With Walking Horse badly needing a doctor, he didn't want to take a chance and cripple a horse which could slow him down. He would rest tonight and ride out before dawn. Wilson had to get his son's body back as quick as he could, before it started decomposing, so he and Roden opted to ride with Jed west to Baxter Springs. It would be a hard fast ride. Walking Horse was weakening and he had to get a doctor. Jed already warned them, he couldn't slow down or wait on them to catch up.

Jed looked to where Little Antelope and Hatcher fussed over Walking Horse, trying to make him comfortable. The warrior's labored breathing and thin emaciated body tempted him to grab the horses and ride, but the trails were just too dangerous at night for hard riding. Standing as Red Hawk started for the door, Jed followed him outside.

"Your friend Walking Horse is a great warrior, but he weakens with every day."

Jed nodded. "I know."

"How long will it take to get this white medicine man back here?"

"If I ride hard, maybe five or six days." Jed's face showed worry as he thought of the doctor.

"What is wrong?"

"The doctor of the whites is old." Jed remembered the elderly man that had come to help Sally Ann. "The ride will be hard, and he might not want to come here with me."

"To cure a savage Indian?"

Jed could only nod, Red Hawk was right. "He'll come, even if I have to drag him back kicking."

"I will protect them for you." Red Hawk looked to where Little Antelope sat.

"You are a good friend."

"I know your heart, Crow Killer." Red Hawk looked back across the darkening valley. "It is a hurtful thing to have a friend such as he, and the woman."

Jed stood as Hatcher called them for supper. "Come, my friend, let's eat."

Hatcher sipped slowly on a cup of coffee as Jed filled his shot and powder horns, getting ready for the long ride come daylight. Looking over at the fevered Walking Horse, he shook his head.

"I'm afraid it'll all be for naught, Jed."

"I've got to try, Lige."

"You know old Doctor Zeke may be too old for such a long pull over the mountains, even if he consents to come." Hatcher studied the cup he was holding. "Which I doubt he will."

"I've thought of that."

"You gonna kidnap old Doc?'

"I'm gonna do what I've gotta do, Lige." Jed looked over at the scout. "I won't let Walking Horse die, not without trying my best."

Hatcher nodded. "Been giving it some thought, Jed. I figure Chalk's train of pilgrims just might be a day or better closer, maybe even two days closer than Baxter Springs."

"So, what are you getting at?"

"Just this, boy, I know a doctor who's with the train and owes me a favor."

"You're kidding me, a real doctor?" Jed looked over at the scout curiously.

"I don't know about being a real doctor, but I've seen this doctor heal folks with everything from fever to arrow wounds." Hatcher nodded absently. "Were I you, I'd take the gamble and head for the train, it's your best chance."

Jed looked over at Walking Horse. "Where do you think Chalk will be about now?"

"I'd cut east along the bank of the Snake, then turn north at Blackhorse Pass, pick up the wagon road, and they shouldn't be far."

Calculating in his head, Jed nodded. "That would make the train two days closer, if'n I don't miss it."

"Jed, even a blind man could find that train." Hatcher laughed. "A train that big is bound to leave some sort of tracks, even on solid rock."

"I know, Lige, but there's a lot riding on me finding a doctor." Jed thought on the train. "I can't afford to lose the time, if I were to miss it."

"You can't miss it, boy. You'll cut sign of the train soon as you reach the wagon road."

"Reckon you're right, they'll leave tracks for sure."

"It's your choice, but this doctor is young and like I said owes me a favor." Hatcher handed Jed a small beaded pouch. "Take this with you. Tell the doctor that it's me asking and hand this little bag over."

Examining the small pouch, Jed slipped it inside his hunting shirt. "Never seen anything like that, what is it?"

"Oh, just a do-dad I was given." Hatcher seemed to smile. "A keepsake from the good doctor."

"Looks like something a woman would carry."

"Yeah, it's kinda strange, ain't it though?"

"I'll ride with Pa and Roden to the crossing on the Snake, then I'll do as you say and head east for the train."

"Your piebald's been ridden hard, Jed." Lige looked to where the horses were grazing. "He needs rest, would be a shame to ruin a good horse like him."

"We've been a long ways, alright." Jed nodded. "I'll take two of the Blackfoot horses."

"When you find the train, have Chalk give you two fresh horses." Hatcher pulled out his pipe. "My boy's life depends on you making good time."

"He ain't gonna take too kindly to that idea, Lige." Jed nodded. "You know Mister Briggs sets quite a store by his horses."

"They're mine. You just tell him."

Jed sat leaning against the cabin wall as the sun dipped below the mountaintop, disappearing slowly behind the western skyline. He knew he needed to rest, but he needed to be on the trail and was too eager to sleep. He wanted to ride now because Walking Horse needed a doctor.

Jed promised him one and he would have one. The warrior suffered on the long ride from Arapaho Lands with no complaints, and now, it was up to Jed to get a doctor.

Little Antelope touched his shoulder lightly as she looked down at him. "You should sleep."

"I want to ride." Jed took her small hand. "I fear for him, little one."

"He grows weak, but he will wait for you, Crow Killer. He has faith in you." Little Antelope let her hand linger on his shoulder.

"I only hope I have done right." Jed stared into her downcast eyes. "To have brought him all this way."

She smiled. "You have always done what is right, Jed. You have never dishonored him."

"I have wanted to."

"I know, but we must not, it would shame us both." Her smile was sad. "You have pride and honor, and nothing is worth losing them."

"Hatcher and Red Hawk will guard over you while I am gone."

Letting her hand slip slowly across his face, she lightly touched his cheek with her lips. "Ride fast and be safe, my warrior."

Red Hawk sat down beside Jed as Little Antelope went back inside. The dark eyes studied Jed in the gloom of the evening for several seconds. "Perhaps, my friend, it would be better if Walking Horse died."

"You know better than that, Red Hawk." Jed shook his head. "Don't speak those words."

"I know, just a Crow's way of thinking."

"If the Blackfoot we met back in the pass come here, let them stay in peace."

"You would have a Blackfoot for an ally?" Red Hawk shook his head. "I thought a Crow was bad enough."

"I would, I trust him." Jed nodded. "Be on the alert for any other Blackfoot, though."

"I heard him speak of his chief, and the challenge."

"That chief's name is Deep Water and he might just come here to avenge his son and brother."

"It is wrong to challenge your tribal leaders." Red Hawk nodded thoughtfully. "Even the mighty Crow do not do such a thing."

"You might, if you were provoked."

Red Hawk nodded. "It would take a very deep insult to cause such a thing."

"Blue Darter was insulted, and his woman and children were put in danger by this chief."

"We will be vigilant." Red Hawk, noticing Little Antelope coming back to the doorway, moved away into the darkness.

"This wood lodge is much better than a skin lodge." Little Antelope moved again to where Jed sat against the log wall. "It will be much warmer in the cold times."

"Sometimes, I reckon it is."

"It needs a woman's touch."

Jed thought of Sally Ann and shook his head. "Yes."

"You will ride for the white medicine man with the coming of the new sun?"

"Yes."

"I came back out so they could speak." Nodding, she looked to where Hatcher and Walking Horse talked. "It is good Rolling Thunder is here. Walking Horse now has another reason to live."

"Having you, little one, is enough reason for anyone to live." Jed smiled at her. "Walking Horse is a lucky man."

"Do you feel this way, Jed?"

Looking through the door where Walking Horse talked with Hatcher, Jed turned his face. "This is not for me to say, Little Antelope, he is my friend."

"And if he wasn't."

"Then I would say yes, I feel this way." Jed smiled. "I would steal you away and keep you always."

The dark eyes staring up at him seemed to melt for only a moment, then in a flash she turned back inside the cabin to her husband.

Red Hawk moved back beside Jed and leaned against the wall. "She is a beautiful woman, my friend." The warrior looked up at the stars. "She cares much for you."

"Yes." Jed nodded. "And I for her."

"She is torn between you and Walking Horse."

"Walking Horse is her husband and my friend." Jed shook his head. "There is nothing more to say."

"You do not have to ride to the west."

"No, I don't have to, but you know there is no other way for me."

"You are a good friend."

"Tell me, Red Hawk, if I didn't ride for the white medicine man, wouldn't you think badly of me?"

Looking over where Little Antelope wiped Walking Horse's forehead, Red Hawk nodded. "She is an amazing woman, beautiful, and loyal. As a man, I would not think badly of you, but as a friend, I must."

Jed nodded. "The two of you are my best friends. I would trust both of you with my life as I already have. I would never betray that trust for any reason, no matter how beautiful."

"I know, I was just wondering what your answer would be."

"Now, you know, and tomorrow I will ride west." Jed spoke softly, not wanting to be heard. "Hatcher will stay behind with you."

"Do you expect trouble?"

"I hope not, I have already lost two good friends, I do not want to lose anymore." Jed shook his head. "The Blackfoot warrior we met was Blue Darter. He warned that his chief might ride against us here."

"Do you think they will come?"

"I don't know, but if they do this cabin is strong." Jed looked around. "With Hatcher here to help, you will be safe. Just stay inside and don't let them catch you outside as they did Silent One."

"I will look after them, as I would my own."

"I know." Jed smiled slowly. "I will return as fast as I can."

Red Hawk looked through the doorway again. "She is a beautiful woman, but she has a sharp tongue."

Jed laughed. "And a sharp knife, be careful, my Crow friend."

An hour before sunup, the three men were mounted and ready to head north. As he swung agilely upon the bare back of the smaller Blackfoot gelding, Jed felt a hand touch his leg. Looking down as Little Antelope handed him the rawhide lead rope of the second horse and laid her small head against his leg. Jed touched her dark hair softly, then looked to where his pa and Roden were waiting.

"I'm counting on you and Red Hawk to keep them safe, Lige."

"You just keep your powder dry, young'un. We'll handle things around here." Hatcher saw the emotion that passed between Jed and the woman. "On that you can depend. You just watch your topknot."

Nodding at his friends, Jed turned the horse toward the north end of the valley, kicking him into a hard trot. Stripped to his buckskins and the essentials to survive, Jed was traveling light. With every passing day, Walking Horse was growing weaker so he had to hurry. Roden and Ed Wilson followed behind him leading the horse carrying Seth Wilson's body. Halfway up the pass, all the horses snorted and tried to shy away when they smelled Adam Beale's body.

"We should have afforded him a decent burial." Roden looked up the steep mountain where the body remained. "At least put him under where the varmints couldn't get to him."

"Why? He sure didn't bury Silent One." Jed spit. "He got what he deserved. Let 'em have him."

"It would have been the Christian thing to do."

"Maybe you're right, but they say I'm a demon."

"Don't say that, you're no demon, boy." Wilson spoke up. "Let it go, Lem."

Topping out on the tall mountain pass, Jed dismounted at a small stream and let the horses have a breather. Looking out over the beautiful mountains and valleys, Jed took the fresh air and the smell of the colorful flowers into his lungs. Today, he was preoccupied and had no time to enjoy the scenery or fragrances that blew on the air. His mind was both on the trail ahead and the ones he left behind in the cabin, as their lives depended on him. He felt responsible for them and he couldn't let them down, nor could he let Walking Horse down. Speed was of the essence, and he had to bring the doctor back quickly.

All day, Jed kept the horses in a fast walk or a ground-eating trot. He didn't know what was happening back at the cabin, and the unknown worried him, making him push the horses harder. At sundown, Jed reluctantly pulled into a small stand of trees and dismounted. Leading his two horses over to water, he hobbled both animals with rawhide and turned them onto the green grass along the trail.

"I can read your thoughts, Jed." Wilson pushed a few small branches together for a fire. "I know what you're thinking."

"Yeah, Pa."

"We're slowing you down, and with Seth's body, we can't keep up."

"It'll be alright."

"No, boy, it won't." Wilson shook his head. "You need to ride on without us. Walking Horse's life depends on you making speed."

"I can't just leave you out here, Pa."

"Yes, you can." Wilson looked at Roden. "Lem here knows these mountains better than anyone. He'll get me and Seth home, sure enough."

Jed nodded slowly. He wanted to ride on, but didn't know how to leave Wilson behind. "I'll be riding as soon as the moon shows itself."

"You're not going to rest?"

"I'll push on and I should reach the Snake by morning easily." Jed looked at Roden. "What do you think, Lem?"

"With no unforeseen problems, I figure you'll be there by daybreak alright."

"I'll see you two in the spring." Jed shook hands with both men.

The darkness and gloom of the half-moon lit the mountain trails, leading north and west, with an eerie light. Only the steady hoofbeats of the traveling horses made a sound on the sandy paths as Jed pushed the animals throughout the night. The fog filtered in low, making the darkened trail difficult to follow. Only the sharp eyes and keen senses of the horses allowed Jed to keep to the trail without stopping. Several times, they pulled up short and walked slowly over the rocky trail where heavy rains had washed away the top soil leaving the steep trail slippery and barely passable.

Jed knew the smart thing to do was stop for the night and wait for daybreak, but caution was thrown to the wind, as he had to travel and ride through the night. Finally, as the horses stopped suddenly, detecting where the trail sharply dropped off, he dismounted and led them slowly forward, feeling his way along the dangerous track. In the dark, murky fog, he recognized the steep part of the trail he was on. At the bottom, the trail would level off into a small valley where the Snake River flowed through. Hatcher told him to turn east along the riverbank and not to cross there, but cross further along at Blackhorse Crossing where the waterway made a curve north.

As the fog thinned, Jed slipped back on the horse and hit a hard trot through the early morning hours until he reached the river. Sliding to the ground, Jed led the horses down to the river's edge for a much-needed drink. Lower in the valley along the riverbank, the darkness was far worse. The fog covering the water was so thick, it could be cut with a knife. Jed had no choice, as he didn't know the terrain upriver so he had to wait until daylight to follow the trail. He cursed the heavy fog, wanting desperately to keep going, but the trail was far too dangerous, and he couldn't afford for one of the horses to fall or break a leg.

Daylight came to life, peeking slowly through the gloom from the east, but the heavy fog still lay on the ground. Leading the horses, Jed started east following the riverbank as Hatcher had instructed him. Finally, an hour after daylight with the heavy fog lifting, Jed mounted the horses and started forward. Hitting a slow lope, he knew he had to make up the time he had lost during the long night. His stomach growled, awakening his hunger. In his worry about Walking Horse, he had forgotten all about the small parcel of dried meat he carried inside his leather shirt.

Two hours before high noon, Jed reined in and studied the broad river. Across the water, he could discern the trail Hatcher called Blackhorse Pass. Hatcher explained the reason for the trail's name. Years ago, in the shining times, a trapper had lost his favorite horse while crossing the Snake in flood times and the trail had been called Blackhorse Trail since then. If anyone doubted they were on the right trail, all they had to do was look up and find the horse's head looming overhead in a tall oak. The gleaming head was eerie, looking down from its perch as if it was grinning at any passerby. How long it had been there was unknown, but Hatcher said he recalled seeing it many a year. Jed figured the tale was the imagination of some long ago mountain man, but it existed and the head was there in the tree.

Kicking the horses forward, Jed rode into the water and started across. Midstream, he slid into the warm water and paddled alongside the swimming animals. Wading, dripping wet from the river, Jed lost no time mounting and starting the horses along the trail. According to Hatcher, Blackhorse Pass Trail should intersect the immigrant trail only a few miles to the north. Jed knew the trail he had ridden to Baxter

Springs was only a short distance across the mountains from the Snake River. Further along the mountain trail he followed, the land quickly tailed off into miles of flatlands.

Midafternoon found Jed sitting in the middle of a wide trail of wagon ruts running east and west across the grasslands. Studying the road carefully, Jed could see no fresh tracks coming from the east; the direction Chalk Briggs' immigrant train would come from. A few tracks did show on the sandy trace, but not the deep rutted tracks of heavy wagons of a train. Pointing his horses back to the east, Jed kicked the tired horses into a slow, ground-eating lope. He had been on the trail almost two days, pushing the horses hard, hoping the train would be close.

Jed didn't see the train yet, but he heard the sounds of bullwhips cracking, rattling trace chains, and squeaking wagons as they rolled across the rough road. Also, the coarse, heavy language of the teamsters as they yelled at their teams, alerted Jed to the presence of the wagon train. The road had several swells and tall grass inhibiting him from seeing the wagons. Finally, topping out on a swell on the trail, Jed spotted the first of the train's outriders as he watched them throw up their arms, stopping the wagons. Knowing he had been spotted, Jed held up his free arm and waved at the watching men. He remembered well when he was with Chalk Briggs, the fear of an Indian, any Indian, always put terror in the minds of the people on the train. He also remembered the immigrants were prone to shoot first and ask questions later.

Jed's sharp eyes detected heavily-armed outriders with large caliber rifles resting in the crook of their arms. As the train rolled to a halt, a large man loped his horse up beside the two outriders and reined in. Even from a far distance, Jed recognized the big rider, as the wagon master, Chalk Briggs.

"An Injun ahead, Captain." One of the men pointed at Jed.

"He alone?"

"So far, we only spotted one, quite a ways out there in that tall grass." The rider nodded.

"I'll ride out and see what he wants." Briggs scanned the tall grass closely. "You boys keep a close watch, but keep your fingers off them triggers, unless you need them."

"You keep a keen eye out there, Chalk." One of the riders looked around suspiciously. "They're sneaky, could be a heathen hiding out there behind every blade of grass."

"Just stay easy on them triggers." Briggs warned. "Don't shoot me by accident."

"Why, Cap'n, we surely couldn't miss you." The outrider laughed.

"Funny, Wade, very funny."

Jed dropped his hand as the big rider rode toward him in a slow walk. Not wanting to do anything that would arouse the watching riders, Jed kept his free hand well away from the rifle resting across his arm. As the man came near, Jed remembered the strong, heavy-jawed face, and the wide set eyes and forehead. He liked Chalk Briggs; the man had always treated him kindly. He was a good wagon master, but he meant for people to jump when he said frog. Out there to hesitate might mean to die.

Jed watched as the big man reined in only feet from him. "You speak English? What can I do for you, Indian?"

Jed rubbed his stomach in the universal sign of hunger. "Me hungry."

Briggs studied the dark, scarred face across from him. "Alright, we'll feed you. You got any friends out there?"

Jed smiled. "Sure, Mister Briggs, I've even got friends here."

"You white?" Briggs looked Jed up and down. "You look familiar."

"I'm Crow Killer of the Arapaho people, but you know me as Jedidiah Bracket."

Shock showed on the big man's face, then he smiled. "I'll be horn-swaggled, it is you, Jedidiah."

"Yep, it's me, Mister Briggs."

Briggs looked Jed up and down again. "A feller could mistake you for an Indian."

"I am an Indian."

"Hatcher told me he'd seen you, and said you hadn't gone under like we thought."

"Lige is at my cabin right now, waiting on me to get back."

"You've grown considerably, Jed." Briggs could see the bulk of muscle under the doeskin shirt.

"I try to eat regularly."

"Why are you here?" Briggs raised his hand. "Never mind that question, I'll bet your hungry."

"You'd win that bet, but I haven't got time to eat."

"Let's ride back to the train." Briggs turned his horse. "Surely, you can't be in that big of a hurry?"

"I am." Jed nodded. "I've got a sick man dying behind me."

"You come here for medicine. Is that it?"

"Partly."

The train immigrants gathered as word passed from wagon to wagon that a real live Indian was coming in. Men, women, and children stood around in groups gawking at the warrior riding in among them beside Chalk Briggs. Men fingered their weapons nervously as women paled and children pulled back in fright as Jed passed them. Jed looked down as one youngster hit him in the back with a rock.

"That'll be enough of that." Briggs dismounted quickly confronting the people. "This man is a white man. He is my friend, Jedidiah Bracket."

"If he's white, I'm an elephant." A huge teamster growled.

"You look like one, Sam Long."

"And smell like one." Another immigrant spoke up, making the people laugh, breaking the mood fear had brought on.

Whirling, the big teamster pretended rage. "Who said that? I'll wring his neck like a chicken."

"That'll be enough." Briggs held up his hand. "He is white, and I don't want to hear anyone say different."

Dismounting, Jed led his horses and followed Briggs to the supply wagon. He could feel and see the fear in these people's faces as he passed near them. Years pass by and time changes, but he knew people who hate and fear a redskin, never change.

"What's wrong here, Mister Briggs?" Jed was curious. "When I was on the train we were cautious, but I see hate in these people's eyes."

"We had a rough time crossing the green after Lige left us a while back." Briggs shook his head. "We thought we were safe, but then out of nowhere the Sioux hit us hard, real sudden like."

"Kill many?"

"A few and they got away with some horses."

"That's why they're so sweet acting?"

"That's it." The big man nodded, and motioned to the wagon driver. "Dig out some biscuits and a few of those cookies you baked last night."

"Yes, sir, Captain."

"Alright, spit it out, Jedidiah. What's on your mind and why are you here?"

"Lige said you have a doctor on the train." Jed thanked the driver for the food. "I've come for him."

"Him?"

"Yes, like I said, I need a doctor real bad." Jed bit into a biscuit. "We got a man close to dying."

"What if the doctor doesn't want to go with you?"

Jed stopped his hand in midair as he was about to take another bite. "I ain't leaving here without him."

"There's almost two hundred rifles here." Briggs looked around. "They just might have something to say about where the good doctor goes."

"I'm taking the doctor, one way or the other."

Briggs looked into the dark eyes that suddenly turned hard. He remembered Hatcher saying Jed had become a dangerous man to cross. "I reckon we'll have to ask the good doctor. Here she comes now."

Jed's jaw, filled with hard biscuit, dropped as he turned to see a tall, dark-skinned, young woman approaching the wagon. "The doctor, he's a her?"

"Never said different, did I?"

"No, but I thought all doctors were men." Jed was shocked. "Hatcher said a doctor was here."

The woman heard the last remark, and Jed's face turned red as she smiled. "Well, sir, this doctor is a woman, but at least I'm a healer."

"Yes, ma'am. I can see you are a woman." Jed eyed the woman. "Yes, ma'am."

"Well, Ellie, I was just a fixing to come looking for you." Briggs smiled and turned to Jed. "Jedidiah meet Elizabeth."

"Ma'am."

"So tell me, I heard my name mentioned as I walked up, Mister Briggs." The woman asked curiously. "You're looking for me, why?"

The voice was soft, but firm belonging to a strong character and someone used to being in charge of every situation. When her dark eyes settled on him they seemed to look deep inside his thoughts. Long dark hair, not quite black, but still dark, hung almost to her waist as she stood before them.

"Miss Ellie, this gentleman came here looking for a doctor." Briggs cleared his throat. "Says he needs one badly."

"What's wrong with your sick person, mister?" She hesitated. "I didn't catch your last name."

"Bracket, ma'am." Jed looked across at her. "I don't know what's wrong with him."

"What are his symptoms?"

"He was wounded by an arrow. Now, he's losing weight, weak, and sweats a lot with fever." Jed shrugged. "Frankly, ma'am, he seems to be dying slowly."

"How long has he been this way?"

Jed shrugged. "Several moons."

"Moons?"

"Months, ma'am."

"I see, and I doubt I can help him at this point, Mister Bracket." The woman studied the dark figure before her. "Why hasn't he seen a doctor sooner?"

"He's seen a doctor." Jed thought of White Swan. "They haven't been able to help him."

"Then I probably can't either."

"You can try." Jed studied her face. "I've come a long way after you."

"There are people here that might need me." The woman appeared to smirk. "Sir, I'm not a horse to be loaned out to anybody."

"They might one day, but Walking Horse needs you now." Jed's voice grew hard. "Ma'am, I'm not borrowing you."

"An Indian?"

"Ellie if you want to try to help Jedidiah, it'll be okay." Briggs interrupted what could turn into a disagreement. "We'll be in Baxter Springs in two days, and we'll be fine until then."

"I don't know, Mister Briggs."

"You don't like Indians or don't you trust me?"

"It's not that, Mister Bracket. Well, I might be needed here."

"You already mentioned that." Jed reached inside his shirt and pulled out the small bag. "My friend needs you badly. He is my blood brother and stepson of Lige Hatcher. Lige said to give you this."

The dark face paled slightly as she took the bag and looked over at Jed. "I will go with you."

The answer coming so fast, made Briggs curious. "You sure, Miss Elizabeth?"

"I'm sure, Mister Briggs."

"We need to leave, now." Jed nodded. "We haven't got any time to lose."

"I'll get my things." The woman disappeared behind a wagon where a tall man grabbed her roughly by the arm. "Turn me loose, Taylor Reese."

"I heard." The man's grip tightened. "You ain't going off with that heathen alone."

"I'm going."

"I'll ride with you."

"No, you're needed here." The woman jerked her arm. "I don't need you."

"I'll protect you, from that heathen, Ellie." The tall man glared over at Jed.

Ellie jerked back from the enraged man. "I don't know what right you think you have to tell me what to do, but you're mistaken in your intentions, sir."

"You can't leave me, Ellie."

"I can and I am, Mister Reese." She stepped on the wagon rung. "Don't make me scream for Mister Briggs."

"You'd do that, wouldn't you?"

"You remember what he did to you last time, don't you?" Once before, the man had stopped her as she was getting water, insisting he carry her buckets.

"I'm your only protector." Whirling, the tall man stalked off. "You'll see."

"I figure I'll be well protected."

"By that Injun?"

"No, Mister Reese, by that white man."

Jed and Chalk stood talking as they waited for the doctor. "Whatever that little bag is, it sure did the trick."

"It sure did, but maybe it was Lige's name." Briggs shook his head. "They got real close when he found her on the train at Bridger's."

"She's half his age."

"I didn't say romantically inclined, Jedidiah." Briggs laughed. "I said close."

"Well, at least it got her to come with me, that's all that matters."

Briggs had a wrangler bring Hatcher's spare horses up so Jed could take his pick of the animals. A sorrel and a long legged bay were picked and a saddle was put on the bay. Both horses have seen little work other than following the wagon train mixed in with the large herd of extra work animals. They were in good flesh, with good strong hooves, but both were soft. Jed figured they would be strong enough to last for the two day long, tortuous trail over the mountain passes back to his valley.

"Thank you, Mister Briggs." Jed extended his hand as the girl reappeared. "I promise I'll take good care of Miss Elizabeth."

"I know you will, Jedidiah." Briggs shook hands. "We'll see you in Baxter Springs, Miss Ellie. Jed, I'll leave your horses with your pa."

"We've got a long way to ride." Jed lifted the woman bodily onto her horse, making the girl shake her head in awe of his strength. "We best be riding."

"He'll take good care of you, Miss Ellie." Briggs smiled up at her. "Tell Lige we'll rest up for a few days in the settlement, but I'll need him when we head west out of Baxter Springs."

"I'll be fine, Mister Briggs, and I'll tell him." The woman looked over at the figure of Reese standing alone behind the wagon. "When you get to Baxter Springs, tell my grandfather I'm safe and I'll see him soon."

Putting the horses into a hard lope Jed was relieved, at least the girl could ride. Actually, as he watched her, he found she was a good rider. Worried about Walking Horse and in a hurry to return, Jed kept the horses in a lope until they reached the Blackhorse Pass cut off. Pulling in at the trail, Jed slowed them to a slow trot as they turned and started across the flats leading up into the mountains. The horses were sweating, but holding up well. Jed was relieved and thankful Hatcher had an eye for good horseflesh. Slowing to a walk as they started up the first of the rough passes, Jed looked over at the woman.

"You need to rest, ma'am?'

"You can call me, Ellie." The woman smiled slightly. "I'll rest when you do."

"Yes, ma'am, Ellie." Jed nodded. "My name is Jed."

After dark, the moon came up full, illuminating the landscape, making the trail and passes easy to follow. The fog and dark gloom on the mountain trail the previous night did not return. The trail leading down to the crossing on the Snake River was lit up, almost like daylight. Sliding to the soft sand on the riverbank in the darkness, Jed helped the woman to the ground.

"We'll water them, rest a couple hours, and then ride on if you're up to it."

"Your friend, Walking Horse, that is his name?"

"Yes."

"We must reach him as soon as possible." Ellie spoke softly. "It sounds like an infection to me."

"Is that bad?"

"It can be, and can cause death."

"Tell me, doctor, are you doing this for a sick patient or for Lige Hatcher?"

"I'm doing it. Does it matter why?"

"It matters to me." Jed frowned.

"Are you afraid I won't be a good doctor for him?"

"It's not that at all."

"You're curious about my relationship to Lige?"

"That's none of my business."

"No, it isn't."

"You should rest." Jed gave up and changed the subject. "We've got a long ride ahead of us."

"No, you answer my question."

"Walking Horse is my friend." Jed looked across the river. "I want the best for him."

"I have heard the name Walking Horse, and I know who you are Crow Killer."

Jed was shocked. "Well, now, you must have been talking to Lige about me."

"You were discussed. You were the reason he left the train, some kind of trouble, I figured."

"You're right, now tell me." Jed nodded. "Are you a good doctor, Miss Ellie?"

"From the time I could reach an operating table, I have been at my grandfather's side helping him."

"Your grandfather?"

"Doctor Zeke in Baxter Springs happens to be my grandfather."

Jed was shocked as he wasn't listening to Chalk Briggs when he was introduced to her. "I'll bet he's proud of you."

"I hope he is."

After a quick meal and a drink of river water, Jed helped her back on her horse and swung up on his. Once again, the Snake River had to be forded. The moon lit up the slow moving water as Jed eased the horses forward into the river, then he took the reins from Ellie.

"Can you swim?" Jed reined in the horses. "Are you scared?"

"Yes, sir, I can swim and no, I am not afraid." Ellie smiled.

Stopping the horses again short of swimming water, Jed removed his moccasins. "I'd do the same if I were you."

As she pulled off her heavy shoes, Jed kicked the horses forward. Slipping from his animal, Jed pulled Ellie slowly from the saddle and showed her how to hold onto a stirrup to let the bay horse pull her across the river.

Splashing onto the far bank, she laughed as she wrung out her dress. "That was fun, Jed."

"Don't reckon I ever thought of it as being fun."

She smiled. "Why, don't you like fun?"

"Same as most, I reckon." Jed shook his head. "Let's ride."

The fog remained high in the clouds, not engulfing the river as it had on his way east. Unwrapping his trade blanket, he leaned over and wrapped it around her shoulders. The night was warm, but her dress was still wet from the crossing and he didn't want her to catch a chill.

"Thank you, I was getting cold."

"It might smell like an Indian."

"Really? Tell me, what does an Indian smell like?"

Reining in suddenly, Jed grabbed her reins and led her from the trail. "Get down, quick."

"What is it?" She could sense his urgency.

"Someone is behind us, maybe following us."

"How do you know?" She looked down their back trail, straining her eyes. "It's too dark to see very far."

"I'm an Indian, remember?" Jed dismounted. "Us heathens are like animals, we can see at night."

"That's not funny."

Handing over the reins of both animals, Jed also gave her a rifle. "You scared?"

"Well, yes, this time I am scared." Ellie looked at him in the gloom. "The way you are acting, I don't know what's fixing to come out of the dark."

"Stay here, don't let the horses move about and don't you move one foot."

"You're scaring me even more."

"Good, being scared will keep you quiet and still."

Ellie blinked, one moment he was talking to her, and the next, he vanished. Looking about, she strained her ears, trying to hear anything coming out of the darkness. Standing stock still, she listened several minutes before a scream of stark terror and the thud of something falling came from the trail. Only the sounds of scuffling and begging sounded as Jed was dragging Taylor Reese into what moonlight there was.

Ellie recognized the whimpering voice of Reese through the gloom, even though she couldn't get a good look at him yet. "Taylor Reese, what are you doing here?"

"Don't let this heathen cut me, Ellie." The tall man pleaded. "I just came to protect you, like I said."

"Some protection you are." Ellie shook her head. "Quit your whining, he isn't going to use his knife."

Jed shook his head as he released his iron grip on the shaking man. "Who is this critter?"

"You heard him, Mister Bracket." Ellie smiled slightly. "He's my bodyguard."

"Like you said, some bodyguard."

"His name is Taylor Reese. He's with the wagon train."

"He dang near crippled me, pulling me off that horse, and slamming me to the ground like he did." Reese whined.

"I normally scalp my prisoners." Jed touched the man's forehead with the knife. "Tell him if he's still in my sight after I blink, I will do exactly that."

"You best get back to the train, Taylor." Ellie warned. "Now!"

"My horse, I can't find him in the dark."

"He's probably back at the train by now." Jed waved the knife at the spooked man. "Git!"

Both watched as the shaking man backed away, then turned and broke into a run, out of their sight. Jed only shook his head as he sheathed his skinning knife. He couldn't believe any man as scared as Reese would dare follow them all the way from the train, cross the river, and in the dark of night.

"Let's ride." Jed lifted the woman back on her horse.

"Were you serious?"

"About what?"

"Scalping him." Ellie looked at Jed curiously. "You scared him out of ten years of growth."

Shaking his head, Jed kicked the horses on down the trail slowly traversing the moonlit path. Did she really think he was going to scalp the man alive? Maybe she did think of him as a heathen.

CHAPTER 10

Early morning found the two riders reining in at a small stream and another trail leading back to the Snake River. Jed could still see the tracks Roden and his pa had made as they headed to the river. Slipping to the ground, Jed studied the trail for several minutes, then helped Ellie down.

"We'll eat and rest here one hour, and then we'll ride hard." Jed led the horses to water.

Ellie studied the tall, dark man as he led the horses to the stream. Lige Hatcher had told her he was a loner, a strange one, and now she knew why. She actually believed, he was going to scalp poor Taylor, and she was sure he was capable of it. On the trail, few words had been spoken between them, but for most of the ride, he kept his thoughts to himself. Yes, she sensed he was indeed a strange and dangerous man. The scar on his face and the ones across his arms were scary, and his incredible strength was unbelievable.

Many miles later, reaching the high pass overlooking the valley where his cabin stood, Jed reined in and looked out across the wide valley with its grass, flowers, and abundance of trees. Ellie could only nod her head and admire the majestic beauty of the high mountains and the wondrous valley. Never, even in her travels to the west, has she seen anything that could compare with this wonderland.

"It's beautiful, Jed, so beautiful."

"Yeah, it hit me the same way when I first saw it." Jed nodded. "It still does."

"I can see now what Lige was telling me about."

"He described it to you?"

"Partly, but it would be impossible for words to describe all the splendor stretching as far as the eye could see."

"We're almost there. The smoke in the distance is my lodge."

Ellie smiled, his use of Indian words seemed natural to him. "I hope your friend is still alive."

"Walking Horse is weak, but he promised me to stay alive and he will."

"You think a lot of this man."

"He is one of the bravest warriors I know." Jed nodded. "You will meet another one, a warrior called Red Hawk when we get there."

"Is he your brother too?"

"No, but he is as close a friend as a man could ever want." Jed kicked his horse. "And he has an eye for pretty squaws."

"Then Jed, you are blessed to have two men for friends." Ellie looked across at him. "Most men are lucky if they have even one reliable friend in a lifetime."

"You're missing one."

"Who?"

"Lige Hatcher."

Red Hawk and Hatcher stood up and walked toward the creek when they spotted the two horses crossing the valley. Rifles rested lightly across their arms as they waited beside the creek for the oncoming riders.

"It's them." Hatcher stepped closer to the edge of the creek and waited. "I told you he'd be back quick."

"He pushed his horses hard to return this fast."

"My horses, Red Hawk, but I'm glad he did."

"It is a squaw who comes with him." Red Hawk shook his head in shock. "Is she the medicine man?"

"She is that, and much more." Hatcher smiled.

"Walking Horse will not permit a squaw to perform her medicine on him." Red Hawk looked over at Hatcher. "You know that, Rolling Thunder. The spirit people would frown on a woman."

"He will let her if he wants to live."

"We will see." Red Hawk raised his hand in greeting as Jed and Ellie splashed across the creek. "This could get interesting."

"We made it, my friends." Jed looked over at the cabin. "Walking Horse?"

"He still lives, my arrows were weak."

Jed frowned at the Crow. "They weren't that weak."

With Red Hawk and Hatcher following, Jed led Ellie to the cabin and slid to the ground.

Hearing the horses, Little Antelope hurried to the door. Startled, she looked up at the mounted woman, then back at Jed.

"How is he?"

"He lives. Where is the white medicine man?" Her eyes looked about the clearing, then returned to Ellie as Jed helped her dismount. "He would not come?"

"This is Ellie, she is the medicine man." Hatcher laughed, pulling the woman to him in a crushing hug. "Or medicine woman."

"No, my husband will never allow a squaw to help him."

"Told you." Red Hawk piped up. "It is against a warrior's medicine."

Ellie looked at the handsome Crow then over at Jed. "Is this the friend that likes pretty squaws?"

Jed nodded. "It is."

Red Hawk looked questioningly at Jed as the woman laughed. He knew the words were about him. "What does she ask, Crow Killer?"

Hatcher pushed Little Antelope ahead of him into the cabin. "Let me speak with Walking Horse, then bring the good doctor in."

Minutes later, beckoning from the cabin door, Hatcher had Jed bring Ellie inside, over to where Walking Horse lay watching from his bed. Greeting Jed, the warrior looked closely at the tall woman before him as Hatcher whispered something in her ear.

"This is my friend and brother, Walking Horse." Jed turned to Ellie.

Setting her medical bag on the table, Ellie sat beside him on the bed. "Tell him, I am his white medicine man."

Jed nodded. "She is here to help you, my friend."

"No." Walking Horse shook his head. "She is a squaw."

"Red Hawk said you would not permit her to save your life." Jed looked down at the warrior. "He said you would be too weak and afraid."

Ellie took Jed by the arm and led him to the door. "Let me be alone with him."

"You don't even speak his language."

"We'll be fine." Ellie had heard Little Antelope when she spoke to him in broken English. "His wife and I will handle this."

"Her name is Little Antelope." Jed started away. "She doesn't speak very good English."

"We'll figure it out." Ellie pointed at the doorway where Red Hawk and Hatcher were waiting. "Now, go and let us squaws get to work."

As the heavy, log door closed behind them, Jed walked away with Hatcher and Red Hawk following. Finding seats away from the cabin, the three sat where they could keep watch over the valley flats. Jed was curious about her last remark about squaws as she pushed him from the cabin.

"You picked my best two horses and rode them hard." Hatcher nodded, eyeing the horses that were turned out on the tall grass in the valley.

"That's what horses are for, or to eat." Red Hawk added.

"They're good animals." Jed agreed. "You seen anything of the Blackfoot?"

"Them, there across the mountain." Red Hawk pointed his finger to the south.

"The Blackfoot came here." Hatcher lit up his well-worn pipe. "We took Blue Darter and his people into the small valley southwest of here."

"They couldn't have had time to ride to the village of Lone Bull." Jed leaned back against the wall. "Reckon what happened?"

"They didn't get that far. Blue Darter told us he decided to come here instead of going to Lone Bull's village."

"He would not be welcome in the village of Lone Bull." Red Hawk nodded. "To challenge a village chief is bad. A warrior does not do this."

"Blue Darter said he figured old Lone Bull would be afraid he might challenge him as well." Hatcher laughed. "He sure didn't want any part of that."

"When Walking Horse is out of danger, I will ride to Blue Darter and speak with him."

"It is good they are there." Hatcher blew smoke into the air. "Blue Darter and his warriors have promised to watch the high pass for any raiders coming into the valley."

Jed looked up as Ellie walked from the cabin and called to him. Standing, he walked back to where she stood. "How is he?" Jed questioned her. "Did he let you examine him?"

"Finally, after he found out who I was."

"Is it bad?"

"It is very bad. He has an infection from an arrowhead in his back." Ellie looked to where Hatcher and Red Hawk sat. "Do you know what the arrowhead was made of?"

"Red Hawk will know." Jed motioned for Hatcher and Red Hawk to join them.

"How is he?" Hatcher asked as he neared them.

"He is very weak." Ellie shook her head. "We have to operate now, right now."

"Red Hawk, the medicine woman needs to know what the arrowhead you used on Walking Horse was made from."

"The grey rock."

"Not iron or metal of any kind?" Ellie questioned as Hatcher interpreted the warrior's words.

"Grey rock." Red Hawk repeated.

"Red Hawk means flint stone." Jed added.

Ellie nodded. "How was the head attached to the arrow?"

At Jed's request Red Hawk handed Ellie one of his arrows. "This is some kind of animal sinew."

"It's the tendon from a buffalo, very fine and strong." Jed nodded.

"That's probably why he is so sick with infection, but not dead."

"What does the white squaw mean?" Red Hawk looked at Jed as her words were interpreted.

"If the arrow was the white man's metal, Walking Horse would be dead from blood poisoning many sleeps ago."

"Walking Horse is weak, but we have no choice." Ellie looked at the cabin door. "The splinters of the arrow must be removed from his body, so the poison can be drained out."

"What does squaw mean poison?"

"The evil ones." Jed explained. "The arrow's poison keeps them in the warrior's body."

"What will she do?"

"I will operate." Sensing Red Hawk did not understand the word, she added. "Cut it out."

"There will be much blood."

"I've explained the procedure to Walking Horse." Ellie looked at the faces around her. "He is ready."

"Hard to believe he'd let you cut on him." Jed shook his head. "How did you get him to agree?"

Ellie looked over at Hatcher and smiled. "We talked, he agreed."

"Simple as that, nothing more?" Jed shook his head.

"Yes, simple as that, Mister Bracket."

"Tell him, Elizabeth." Hatcher spoke up.

"I'll need your help, all of you to hold him down."

"Tell me what?"

"We will not be needed." Red Hawk spoke up, shaking his head. "Walking Horse is a great warrior, he will not move."

"He's right, Ellie, but we'll go in with you, just in case we are needed." Hatcher stepped forward. "Let's get this job done."

As Ellie ordered, Little Antelope had hot water boiling and clean cloths folded near the bed. She rolled Walking Horse on his back where a large, purple bulge surrounded where the arrowhead had penetrated. Staring in fascination, Little Antelope watched Ellie pull out the operating instruments and arrange them in a tin pan full of steaming water.

The little woman's eyes widened, then looked at Jed frantically as Ellie picked up the scalpel and moved toward the wound. In her short years, Little Antelope had skinned hundreds of buffalo and other animals, but this was Walking Horse, her husband, who she thought was about to be skinned alive. "Is she going to skin my husband?" Little Antelope looked at Jed.

"It is the white medicine man's way to cure their patients." Jed smiled. "She will not skin him, she will heal Walking Horse."

Looking at Jed, the small, frightened woman asked. "Are you sure?"

Ellie listened as the small Arapaho woman spoke with Jed. She couldn't understand the words, but she could feel the closeness of the two as they looked at each other.

"I am sure, little one." Jed reassured her.

With the first pass of the razor, sharp scalpel, pus and blood gushed forth from the opening. Jed waited and watched anxiously, prepared to help if Walking Horse moved. The gritting of teeth and a low groan came from the warrior, but only his arm muscles flexed, twitching with the pain. Little Antelope watched in fascination as Ellie opened the wound, and inserted probes searching for pieces of the arrow that was causing the infection. Pieces of flint and sinew that had remained in the wound were pulled out slowly with tweezers and deposited in the metal basin. Satisfied the wound was clean, Ellie quickly rinsed out the bloody wound and stitched it closed after tincture was placed in the opening. Bandaging and wrapping the wound tightly, Ellie pulled the trade blanket across Walking Horse.

"Tell her not to let him move." Ellie nodded at Little Antelope. "Make sure to keep him warm."

"What do you think, Doc?" Jed translated Ellie's words. "Will he live? Do you want some bear grease to smear on the wound?"

"You want to kill him?" Ellie shook her head. "I'm hungry and very tired."

"I imagine you are. I'll fix you something to eat." Jed thought of the long ride from the train. "Silent One always used bear grease on me and it seemed to help."

"Answering your question, Mister Bracket." Ellie sat down tiredly at the table. "The fever will come, but hopefully the infection will leave his body now that the problem has been removed."

Red Hawk nodded and spoke quietly to Jed. "She is a strong squaw."

"Yes, she is." Jed agreed thankful Ellie couldn't understand his words. "Very strong."

"She would give a man many strong sons."

"Well, maybe for enough horses, her grandfather will sell her to you."

Laughing, Red Hawk walked to the open door. "How many horses would Crow Killer give?"

A deep frown came from Little Antelope as she heard the words. "Go outside with your words, Crow."

Clearing his throat, Hatcher took out his pipe and started for the door. Jed started to fix Ellie something to eat when Little Antelope touched his arm, motioning for him to go with the men.

"Thank you, little one."

"Will my husband live?"

"The doctor said we will know soon. For now, we must wait."

"I will bring you food."

Jed looked over to where Ellie sat watching their gestures as they spoke, not understanding their words, but she still understood the closeness between the two. Nodding, Jed walked outside where Hatcher and Red Hawk had resumed their seats beside the cabin.

It had been a long four days, and Jed was dog tired. He was worried about Walking Horse so he knew sleep would be fleeting. Looking over at Hatcher, Jed leaned back against the log wall. "Tell me, Lige, what did you want her to tell me?"

"Nothing, Jed, I was just anxious over Walking Horse."

Jed looked over at the old scout. "Tell me, Lige."

Hatcher pulled out his pipe and placed it in his mouth absently. "Alright, Jed, it's bound to come out sooner or later. Elizabeth is my daughter and Walking Horse's half sister."

Hatcher and Jed spoke in Crow and sign language so Red Hawk could understand their words. "Your daughter, then she is an Indian?"

"Yes." Hatcher nodded. "Her mother was Walking Horse's mother. She had Elizabeth after I went back east, but later she was killed by the Pawnee. I didn't know anything about Ellie until I came back to the Arapaho when she was about three years old. The old woman of White Swan had taken her into their lodge and cared for her. When I returned to the tribe and found out about her, I took Ellie to Doctor Zeke back in St. Louis. I visited with her every time I came back to civilization."

"What about Walking Horse?"

Hatcher shook his head. "I left him with his people, that's where he belonged."

"He had hard feelings against you for leaving him."

"He's my stepson, but he's Arapaho and I knew he wouldn't be welcomed in a white town." Hatcher tapped his pipe. "That's why I left him behind to live with his own people."

Jed shook his head. "So that's why Walking Horse let her operate on him."

"That's why."

"How did he know she was his sister? She can't speak Arapaho."

"You know they say, blood is thicker than water." Hatcher nodded. "Have you noticed the scar on her right cheek?"

"No."

"Elizabeth was in her mother's arms when the Pawnee attacked the village." Hatcher dropped his head. "The arrow that killed my wife, Pretty Moon, hit her face, leaving a bad scar that she would carry for life."

"Walking Horse recognized the scar?" Jed couldn't believe it, he hadn't even noticed the scar.

"Elizabeth is the spitting image of Pretty Moon, her mother; taller, but that is what Walking Horse saw when she entered the cabin."

Red Hawk looked at Hatcher. "The spirit people brought the medicine woman here to meet her brother, so she could save him."

"Doctor Zeke left Elizabeth in St. Louis to further her education when he came west to Baxter Springs." Hatcher smiled. "She's quite a lady, like her mother. We got reacquainted on the train this spring."

Jed could only shake his head in disbelief. He noticed Ellie had dark complexion, but the woman being the daughter of Hatcher and sister to Walking Horse was still hard to believe.

"She didn't know he was her brother on the trail here?"

"She knew she had a brother and that I was her father." Hatcher shook his head. "No, she didn't know Walking Horse by name. I told her who he was before she went inside."

"She is really your daughter, Rolling Thunder?" Red Hawk smiled. "She is far too pretty."

"She is, and she is half Arapaho." Hatcher frowned at the grinning Crow. "Don't you get any ideas."

"She is a beautiful squaw."

"Who would have ever thought?" Jed shook his head. "He couldn't believe he had used the word squaw in front of her."

"I've tried to keep her identity hidden from the whites and didn't want them finding out about her."

"Is Rolling Thunder ashamed of his Indian daughter?"

"No, my friend, I am not." Hatcher shook his head. "You know how whites feel about Indians."

Red Hawk shook his head. "Yes, Rolling Thunder, I know very well what whites think of us."

"That is exactly why I have kept her secret." Hatcher filled his pipe with tobacco. "I didn't want her mistreated."

"She will never be mistreated." Jed promised. "I promise you that."

Little Antelope stepped outside and handed Jed a plate full of deer meat and greens. "I have fed the white medicine woman."

"Thank you, little one." Jed accepted the food. "You do know she is Walking Horse's sister?"

Little Antelope nodded as she looked down at Jed, then over at Hatcher. "My husband spoke of this."

"You have a white medicine woman for a sister now." Red Hawk laughed. "I wonder what your old one White Swan, will think of his replacement?"

"Your mouth is still running, Crow." Little Antelope turned to the cabin. "It could be worse."

"What does Little Antelope speak of, worse?"

"I could have a Crow for a brother-in-law." The little woman straightened her back as she walked away from the laughter of Hatcher.

Red Hawk chuckled as she went into the cabin. "For a small one, she has a huge bite."

"You should have learned that by now, my friend." Jed shook his head. "You two have been fighting ever since you met."

"You know a Crow is hardheaded."

Hatcher stood up and put away his pipe. "I'll go in and sit with Walking Horse and let the women sleep."

"Crow Killer should sleep." Red Hawk stood up. "I will guard the lodge."

Warmth from the rising morning sun awoke Jed from a sound sleep, bringing him quickly to his feet. Quickly rolling up his sleeping blanket, he noticed Red Hawk walking from the creek where he had released the horses out onto the valley. He knew he was really tired, because he has never let the early sun catch him still asleep in his blankets as it did this morning.

"Crow Killer was tired." Red Hawk walked up. "You slept like a papoose."

"You should have awakened me to stand guard."

"No, you were tired." Red Hawk shrugged. "We are in no danger. Blue Darter and his people guard the south trail."

"So you trust the Blackfoot, now?"

"I have looked into Blue Darter's heart, and yes, I trust them." Red Hawk nodded. "He is a strong warrior."

"How is Walking Horse doing?"

"Little Antelope looks at me with knives, but she says he is talking this morning." Red Hawk nodded. "You know, Crow Killer, I think she would like to take my scalp."

Jed laughed. "You are probably right about that, my friend."

"Come, I smell the white man's bread cooking." Red Hawk acted like he smelled the aroma. "The squaws have been cooking."

"Were I you, I wouldn't call Ellie a squaw in front of Hatcher."

"Well, she is a squaw." Red Hawk shrugged. "She is at least half squaw."

"My friend, I swear." Jed shrugged. "You've been warned."

"Come, I'm hungry."

"You've learned to like biscuits I see."

"Whites do have some things that are good." Red Hawk shrugged. "Very few."

Walking Horse was awake, propped up against the cabin wall in his bed. His eyes focused on the two warriors as they entered the doorway. Nodding weakly, he waved them closer.

"Should you be sitting up so soon, my brother?" Jed stood over the warrior.

"It is what the white medicine woman wishes." Walking Horse shrugged, then looked over at Ellie. "She says it will make it easier for the evil ones to leave my body."

Little Antelope glared at Red Hawk, and placed the plates on the table where Hatcher sat. Seeing the hard look from her, the Crow kept his mouth shut and sat down. Jed patted Walking Horse on the shoulder, and took his seat at the table.

"You have done a splendid job, Doctor."

"It is still too early to celebrate." The woman took a plate from Little Antelope and walked to where Walking Horse sat. "However, his fever has broken."

"How long will you be needed here, Ellie?" Hatcher asked.

Looking over at Walking Horse, the tall woman shrugged. "It is hard to say, but I must stay for a short while yet."

"He's still in danger?"

"Yes, the infection could return."

"Okay, daughter, we will stay here until your brother is stronger." Hatcher looked at Jed. "Jed says Chalk sent word he needs me in Baxter Springs before long."

Jed nodded and looked over at Hatcher. "If you will watch over the women, Lige, tomorrow I will take Red Hawk and ride to Blue Darter's lodge to speak with him."

"I can do that."

"We won't be long."

Leaving the cabin, Jed and Red Hawk spent the remainder of the day searching out the valley, looking for any signs of intruders. Raised in the dangerous surroundings of tribal warfare and raids, Red Hawk watched the valley suspiciously as they crossed through the tall grassland. He had been taught by his father Plenty Coups, always trust no one and leave nothing to chance. Always alert and watchful of everything and everybody, the warrior trusted only his own instincts. Today, they had found nothing, returning to the cabin in time for supper, the two turned the horses into the corral and walked to the cabin. With the coming of day, they would ride over the mountain and visit the camp of Blue Darter and the Blackfoot.

Midmorning found Jed and Red Hawk crossing the rough pass leading to the valley where Blue Darter had settled his people. Topping out on the tallest peak of the mountain, the two warriors could plainly see the smoke from the skin lodges set up across the valley. Kicking their horses forward, almost halfway down the mountain trail leading to the valley, Blue Darter rode out onto the trail from his place of concealment. Raising his arm in peace, the warrior waited until the two warriors rode up close.

"Crow Killer has returned from the north." Blue Darter nodded. "This is good."

"Or maybe the demon has returned." Red Hawk spoke up.

"A friend has returned, Blue Darter." Jed frowned over at the Crow. "It is good to see you and your people."

"Thanks to you and the Crow giving us a place to live, they are safe."

"What about the Blackfoot, Deep Water, tell me of him?"

"Ride with me to my village, and there we will talk." Blue Darter turned his horse without waiting.

Four white lodges sat along a small stream that held plenty of freshwater for the Blackfoot and their horses. Squaws and a few small children watched as the three warriors rode past the lodges. Jed noticed one lone warrior watching from a nearby ridge overlooking the lodges. Dismounting, the three men found seats in front of Blue Darter's lodge.

"Where are your other warriors?" Jed studied the women.

Blue Darter followed Jed's gaze. "Two of my warriors are watching the passes from the west and Crowfoot watches over the village."

"Only four?" Red Hawk scoffed.

"Four Blackfoot warriors are worth a hundred Crows."

Jed coughed slightly, trying to hold back a laugh as the two warriors bickered with each other. "I thank, Blue Darter, for helping guard our valleys."

"Again, I thank, Crow Killer, for letting my people live here."

"This is your valley, Blue Darter. Now, tell me about Deep Water and Lone Bull." Jed refused the food a squaw brought him. "Tell me what you think, tell me."

"Two suns ago, we watched as many riders passed from the east heading west to the low country."

"Blackfoot?"

"Little Horse, one of my warriors says it was warriors from Lone Bull's village. They probably rode to Deep Water's village."

"What does this mean?" Red Hawk spoke up.

"I think there may be a council of war." Blue Darter swiped his hand. "I fear Lone Bull will join with his brother, Deep Water, and attack us here."

"For revenge?" Jed asked.

"Revenge against you, Blue Darter, or against Crow Killer?" Red Hawk bit into the elk meat the squaw had handed him. "Which one does he hate worse?"

"Deep Water must kill me to regain his respect, but he must kill Crow Killer to avenge the deaths of his brother and son." Blue Darter flattened his hands. "He wishes us both dead. We will be greatly outnumbered if they come together to attack us here."

"Lone Bull, even the Crow have heard of this great warrior." Red Hawk shook his head. "He is a bloody warrior, even for a Blackfoot."

"This is true, his brother, Standing Bull, was another." Blue Darter nodded. "Both were born fighters, the strongest and fiercest of all the Blackfoot warriors."

"Now, Standing Bull has joined his ancestors and Blue Darter thinks Deep Water will come here to avenge his dead." Red Hawk stared at the warrior.

"I believe, he will come here." Blue Darter nodded. "When he comes, we will join Crow Killer and fight."

"You have four warriors, counting yourself." Jed nodded. "With me and Red Hawk that makes six."

"You do not count Rolling Thunder?"

"When Walking Horse grows stronger, Rolling Thunder will take his daughter, Elizabeth, to Baxter Springs."

"Do you worry about the white medicine woman, my friend?" Red Hawk queried Jed.

Jed looked closely at the Crow. He could see the half smile under the dark face. "Yes, I am worried."

"You do not worry about the woman of Walking Horse?"

"Yes, I do." Jed nodded. "You could take her and Walking Horse back to their village for me."

"This I cannot do, even for you, Crow Killer." Red Hawk shook his head. "I will stay here and see these mighty Blackfoot warriors."

"Thank you, my friend."

"What should we do, Crow Killer?" Blue Darter asked. "Do not be fooled, the Blackfoot warriors are mighty fighters."

"Deep Water and Lone Bull will not challenge us alone?" Jed looked over at Blue Darter. "In a fight strictly between you and me, and him and his brother?"

"Deep Water fought me alone once, and he won't be so foolish again. Every warrior he brings with him to this valley will attack us as one."

"What is your plan, Crow Killer?" Red Hawk repeated.

"For now, I need Blue Darter to watch the trails closely." Jed looked up at the mountains. "We must know quickly if and when Deep Water rides here with his warriors."

"Will we run and hide?"

"I won't run or hide. I will fight for this valley."

"I, Blue Darter, and my warriors will fight with Crow Killer." The warrior swore. "We will watch the high passes coming here."

"I will think on what we will do." Jed mused. "We must discover Deep Water and his warriors before they cross the High Rock Trail."

"We will attack him there?" Red Hawk questioned. "With only six warriors?"

"Six warriors, six rifles, and a very narrow passageway will help us."

"Deep Water will lose many warriors." Blue Darter spoke. "The pass is very narrow there and they will be forced close together."

"Locate our enemy, Blue Darter." Jed stood up. "Send a warrior for me, then we will see how much Deep Water wants revenge."

"It will be as you say, Crow Killer."

Red Hawk swelled his chest. "We will destroy these warriors."

"They are still my people and some are my friends." Blue Darter looked at the Crow.

"Maybe they will not come here." Jed could sense the sadness in Blue Darter's words. "Perhaps, none will have to die."

Blue Darter shook his head. "Deep Water will come here, his pride is too strong."

Red Hawk looked over at the lodges. "Would Blue Darter rather lose his Blackfoot friends coming here to kill, or his women and children?"

"I will fight, but some are still my friends." Blue Darter frowned.

Later in the day after finishing their talks, Blue Darter watched as Jed and Red Hawk rode back across the valley, disappearing back along the mountain trail. Nodding, he knew his people would be safe in this valley. He felt complete trust in the Arapaho Lance Bearer, the warrior, known as a demon among the Nez Perce. Crow Killer would lead them against Deep Water, Lone Bull, and their warriors no matter how many come against them. Waving Crowfoot down from his lookout place, Blue Darter caught up his horse.

"I ride after Little Horse and Flying Bat." Blue Darter looked down at Crowfoot as he mounted the horse. "Keep a sharp watch until I return."

"I will guard the village."

Waving at Hatcher and Little Antelope as they stepped from the cabin, Jed turned the piebald into the corral and tossed him some dried grass. As always, when he rode into the cabin yard it was good to be home, but still he was worried, knowing a big fight was coming. Hopefully, Deep Water and Lone Bull would not come to the valley with their warriors.

"How is my brother, Walking Horse?"

"My husband is very weak, but the medicine one says the evil ones have left his body." Little Antelope stepped close to Jed. "She says his body cools. Now, he will grow strong again."

Hugging her around the shoulders, Jed smiled down at the little woman. "That is the best news I have heard today."

Nodding, she started to the cabin. "I will fix you and the Crow something to eat."

"She loves you, Red Hawk." Hatcher laughed. "I think."

"She has a very strange way of showing it."

"What did you find out, Jed?"

"There seems to be trouble coming, Lige." Jed sat down heavily against the cabin. "As soon as Walking Horse is out of danger, I want you to take Ellie over the mountain to Baxter Springs."

"Bad trouble?"

"It could be if Blue Darter is right."

"Then you will need me here to help."

"Thank you, Lige, but I don't believe one more rifle will matter." Jed shook his head. "I want her safe. She came here to help, not get hurt."

"Am I to leave one child, to save another?"

"Yes."

"It would be better, Rolling Thunder, if you left with your daughter, then we wouldn't have her to worry about." Red Hawk spoke up, eyeing Jed.

"What if Walking Horse still needs her?" Hatcher argued. "What then?"

"Ok, Lige, we'll wait and see."

Entering the cabin, Jed was surprised as he neared the bed where Walking Horse rested. Already, the color started returning to the warrior's face and he was in better spirits. Sitting down on the small bed, Jed smiled and greeted his friend.

"You, my brother, are back among the living again." Jed smiled. "I am happy to see you are regaining strength."

"Thanks to you, and my sister." Walking Horse nodded over to where Ellie stood. "She is a great medicine woman."

"This is true." Jed looked at Ellie. "Yes, she is a good doctor."

"You have been riding hard. I can see the sweat from your horse on your leggings."

"We crossed over the mountain to Blue Darter's village." Jed changed the subject. "You seem much stronger."

"Already, I feel stronger." Walking Horse smiled slightly. "Not ready to run a footrace, but yes, I am stronger."

"Is there anything you want?" Red Hawk looked down at the warrior.

The dark eyes settled on the Crow. "You gave me an arrow that got me here. Now, if you could give me a nice fresh buffalo tongue, it would bring life back into these bones."

"A buffalo tongue?" Jed shook his head. "That's a big order, right now."

"The buffalo are a long way from here, my friend." Red Hawk laughed. "What about a fresh elk steak?"

Walking Horse smiled. "That sounds good, not as good as a tasty buffalo tongue, cooked by my woman, but good."

"Tomorrow, the great Walking Horse will have his wish." Red

Hawk shook the arm of his age-old enemy. "Providing, you can get your woman to cook it."

Only the rattling of tin plates sounded as Little Antelope frowned, glaring over at Red Hawk. Walking Horse smiled, as he knew she was mostly playing and did not dislike the Crow as she let on. Her brother, Yellow Dog, had told him of how she saved Red Hawk back at the Yellowstone, the day Bow Legs wanted to kill him.

"Tomorrow, I will hunt with you." Hatcher stretched his arms. "I am bored sitting here watching Walking Horse grow fat, while I baby-sit the women."

Looking down at his bony ribs, the warrior laughed. "This is true, my father, but even skinny, I am still fatter than you, Rolling Thunder."

Hatcher smiled, this was the first time Walking Horse called him father in many years. The old scout remembered when the warrior was young, once they had been close with a father son relationship. Perhaps, when Walking Horse's health returned, they would hunt the woolies, the elk, and be close once again.

All three men finished their supper and retreated outside to smoke and discuss the coming problem with the Blackfoot. Jed laid out his plans to deal with the coming warriors, if indeed they rode into his valley. Jed knew their chances against the mighty Blackfoot depended on how many Deep Water brought against them. He would fight for his valley and the people there, still he knew the odds against fighting so many were bad.

"I have asked Blue Darter to send his warriors to the west to watch the passes leading here. He will warn us, giving us plenty of time to prepare for an attack." Jed looked over at Hatcher. "So until we hear from him, I will hunt and prepare for the cold times ahead."

Red Hawk nodded. "This is good, perhaps I will get to fight these Blackfoot warriors."

"They're a rough bunch." Hatcher lit up his pipe. "I've seen them in action against the northern tribes."

"Fine." Red Hawk threw out his chest. "The mightier an enemy is, the greater the one that takes his scalp will become."

"I believe you're already known far and wide across these mountains as a great warrior and great Crow." Hatcher smiled. "Why push your luck?"

"Because, Rolling Thunder, one can never be too great." Red Hawk was amused by the question.

"Tonight, I'll take the first watch." Jed stood up and started for the corral. "Let's switch the horses out."

There were too many horses and mules to keep them all corralled together, so only half the herd was let out to graze at a time. The piebald and the more valuable animals were kept up at night, while the others and the mules were let out at night. Jed liked the mules being out on the big pasture at night where their loud braying could be heard easily. Also, the mules were natural sentinels, sounding off if any intruders came into the valley. Several times, Jed or Red Hawk had ridden out after dark to investigate whatever they were braying at just to find a strange band of the wild ones harmlessly crossing the valley. So far, the system worked well as the domesticated, broken horses hadn't drifted from the valley or followed their wilder mustang cousins. Hatcher laughingly accused Jed of being half mule himself as his ability to discern what the mules were braying about came easy to him.

Picking up his rifle, Jed slipped silently from the cabin almost running into Little Antelope as he started toward the creek. Seeing her dripping wet hair, he figured the little woman had been downstream taking a bath where a deep hole of water lay.

Stopping in front of her, he smiled, as she flashed her pearly white smile. "Is the water warm?"

Looking at his sweat-stained leggings, she looked down the stream. "You should go find out."

"Why, do I smell?"

"No, but you should look good for the sister of my husband."

"Now, why would I want to do that?" Jed frowned.

"Don't you find her pretty?"

"She's pretty enough." Jed blushed. "Why do you ask?"

"I think." Little Antelope smiled mischievously, as she could see the color coming up in his face. "She would make Crow Killer a good squaw."

"I've got to go." Jed shook his head. "Goodnight, Little Antelope."

She smiled again as she watched his broad back stalk silently away. "The cold times are coming, Jed."

Turning, Jed swiped his finger across his throat in warning. "The dark hours are coming so go inside, little one, where it is safe."

"If my strong warrior is out here watching, I will always be safe." Little Antelope flipped her head and turned as she laughed, continuing toward the cabin where Red Hawk stood listening.

"Are you listening again, Crow?"

"I didn't hear a word."

"Get!" Little Antelope shook her finger at the warrior.

CHAPTER 11

True to their promise to hunt for fresh meat for Walking Horse, Red Hawk, and Hatcher rode out before daylight, heading to the higher end of the valley in their quest for game. Hatcher carried his Hawken's rifle while Red Hawk carried only his strong bow. Two hours later, a young bull elk was killed while following a harem of does from where they had bedded down for the night. Red Hawk dropped the elk with an arrow through its chest cavity, killing him almost in his tracks. Quickly, the elk was quartered, cut up, and tied to the packsaddle on the black mule.

"A young bull will be tender and juicy." Hatcher wiped his bloody hands on his horse's tail. "Walking Horse will grow strong again."

Red Hawk nodded. "I hope so. He is a good man, even for an Arapaho."

"Yes, he is." Hatcher agreed.

"Rolling Thunder, look!" Red Hawk pointed out across the valley. "A grizzly and her cubs."

"She's a big girl, and those cubs are big, probably coming into their second year."

"I have heard the story of Crow Killer and the bear that killed the redhead." Red Hawk watched as the bear and her cubs moved slowly to the south. "He said there were two cubs with her. Could this be the same bear?"

"It's hard to say about a grizzly, at a distance, they all look about the same." Hatcher scratched his beard. "A grizzly travels many miles in their lifetime."

"This is a bad sign."

"It's just a bear, Red Hawk, just a bear." Hatcher could see the uncertainty in the Crow's demeanor. "Don't let it spook you."

"Nothing spooks me, Rolling Thunder." The warrior's eyes were glued on the bear. "It does spook my horse a little."

"Let's get this meat home."

The warrior watched the bears as they disappeared into the thick foliage. "It is a bad sign, I feel it."

"Superstitious poppycock." Hatcher laughed. "It's just three bears."

After eating heartily of the fresh elk liver, Walking Horse patted his bulging stomach and smiled contentedly. "Red Hawk has kept his promise."

"And your woman has done her job." Red Hawk smiled. "She is a good cook."

"And Ellie stirred up a tasty gravy." Jed added, not wanting to leave the girl out as the compliments were passed around. "Thank you, Ellie."

"You're welcome."

"I will trade you four of my best buffalo runners for your woman." Red Hawk grinned over at Walking Horse. "Maybe five."

Walking Horse smiled, as he knew the Crow was just having fun with Little Antelope who was glaring at him from where she sat eating her supper. Never letting on, she actually has grown to like Red Hawk, even with his continual teasing.

Little Antelope looked over at Jed, then at Ellie, and noticed something passed between them, as she could almost feel the feelings in their words. Taking Walking Horse a cup of coffee, she sat down beside him and leaned back against the wall. Turning her attention, she listened as Red Hawk was telling Jed about the bear and cubs they had seen in the valley.

"She was a huge silver tip." Red Hawk explained.

"How old were her cubs?" Jed thought back on the she bear that killed Billy Wilson.

"Maybe, coming two years old." Hatcher reached for a stick of burning wood to light his pipe. "They were quite a ways off, couldn't really tell."

"If it was the same bear, she's a man killer and dangerous. Watch out for her." Jed thought about Billy Wilson and the attack on him and Bow Legs.

"Well, at least she was heading south and not coming this way." Hatcher puffed on his pipe.

Red Hawk repeated Hatcher's words. "A bear changes direction many times in its life."

"I just as soon go in a different direction myself." Hatcher laughed. "Them things scare the by Jiminy out of me."

Jed could remember the bear's roar and the brush thrashing about as she broke through the thicket. Mostly though, he remembered the fiery, red eyes glaring with rage as she charged after them as they ran to their horses. He knew, no matter how long he lived, he would never forget the savagery of the bear on that mountain trail.

"Keep a sharp eye out for her." Jed looked over at Little Antelope. "We'll have to kill her if she comes back into this valley."

"I doubt she'll come back this way." Hatcher puffed contentedly. "She was heading back to the south."

"She will return here." Red Hawk predicted.

"Why does Red Hawk think she will come here?"

"She has Crow Killer's scent in her nose." Red Hawk shrugged. "He touched her kill, and a bear never forgets the smell of her enemy."

"You may be right, my friend." Jed nodded.

"I never heard of a bear or any animal killing humans unless they were disabled in some way." Hatcher shrugged. "Now, you're saying we may have three man-killers in our backyard?"

Red Hawk shook his head. "In my lifetime, I have seen a bear kill a warrior two times while hunting, but never have I seen a bear eat a man."

"I've never heard of any animal coming so far to look for a man." Hatcher shook his head. "I just don't believe it is the same bear, this far from her home range."

"Well, let's keep a sharp lookout. You women stay close to the cabin and be alert when you go out." Jed looked at Ellie and Little Antelope.

"You're scaring me, Jed." Ellie shook her head.

"I mean to." Jed nodded. "This bear, if it is the same animal, is dangerous."

"How would the bear know we are here?" Ellie asked.

"Tell her, Walking Horse." Jed spoke to the warrior.

"Little sister, a bear can smell its prey for many miles." The warrior looked over at Ellie. "We have bloody pelts here, horses, and humans."

Red Hawk repeated. "I think this bear has Crow Killer's scent."

"What do you mean?" Ellie looked over at the Crow.

"I think this bear seeks out a warrior who touched her kill." Red Hawk insisted. "I think she remembers his scent and comes here for Crow Killer."

"But you said she was heading south."

"I've heard of a bear stalking their prey for months." Hatcher added. "It's been said by Bridger and Carson that once a bear gets your scent, they never forget it."

"Enough." Jed raised his hand. "You girls got the idea, be careful outside."

Everything at the cabin remained quiet as Walking Horse slowly regained his strength. Jed spent the better part of a week cutting grass to put up for the cold months ahead. It would take many more days to put up enough dry hay to fill the barn, but already he had a good start. In the high country, the cold came earlier, lasted longer, and the snow was much deeper than in the lower lands below. The barn would have to be completely full, clear to the pole rafters, to feed all the horses and mules. As he swung the sickle, Jed thought of Silent One and the few months he had shared with the young Assiniboine. He missed the humorous young man. His death was such a waste and his loss saddened him.

"You do squaw's work, Crow Killer." Red Hawk stood silently watching Jed swing the sickle.

"I don't have a squaw." Jed smiled. "The horses like to eat in the cold times, as we do."

"Is this a white man thing?"

"Yes, it keeps their war ponies strong during the heavy snows." Jed leaned on the blade handle. "You should have your warriors do this."

"Why should we do this thing?"

"The white warriors keep their horses strong so they can attack their enemies in the worst of times."

"I have seen this myself." Red Hawk nodded in thought. "If our ponies were strong during the cold times, we could raid our enemies when the snow is deep on the ground."

"True, but more important your people would be safer if your ponies were stronger during the cold times." Jed took up his sickle. "If your village is attacked, you could get your people to safety."

"We're at peace with the white warriors."

"Now, you are, but a wise chief should prepare for the worst." Jed looked off across the valley. "Times change, my friend. The future is uncertain."

"Could you get me many of those long knives?"

Jed smiled, he knew there was no way Red Hawk was serious. "I could."

"I will think on it." Turning, the warrior started back to the creek. "Already our squaws are overworked."

"Let your men work for once."

"They would not do this." Red Hawk looked aghast at Jed. "They work hard enough already."

Jed was curious, as he had never seen a warrior doing anything in the villages, only lying around eating, gambling, or just talking. "Working hard at what?"

"They protect our people, fight our enemies, and hunt for food."

"That's work?" Jed laughed. "Among whites that is play when there is no work to do."

"You come with me to my village and tell the Crow warriors what you want them to do with that thing." Red Hawk shook his head as he turned toward the cabin. "I would like to see this."

The cabin smelled of cooking elk steaks, onions, and greens the women had gathered during the afternoon. The threat of the bears still worried Jed so he had Red Hawk and Hatcher guarding the women while they gathered the greens. Across the table, Red Hawk sat honing his hunting knife on a whet rock Hatcher had given Jed on his first visit to the valley.

Little Antelope watched him closely as he touched his finger to the blade. "Test it on your tongue, Crow."

"I would test it on yours, squaw, but your tongue is sharp enough already." Red Hawk did not look up, but just kept working on his knife.

"You two quit fighting." Jed shook his head as he poured Walking Horse a cup of coffee. The warrior had become almost addicted to the hot liquid. "If you want to fight, go outside and fight the bear."

"Enough." Ellie spoke up. She knew they were all becoming cabin sour, cramped together in the small cabin. "After we eat, we'll all go out into the yard."

"What for?" Hatcher was curious. "The place need airing out?"

"No, but we all need to get outside."

Red Hawk shrugged. "I just came into the lodge."

"We're going out, and so is Walking Horse." Ellie helped Little Antelope hand out the plates. "Now eat."

Jed shrugged. "I reckon a doctor knows best."

"I do." Ellie frowned slightly.

The afternoon sun was slowly sinking as Jed and Hatcher helped Walking Horse to a seat outside the cabin. This was the first time the warrior went outside since arriving at the cabin. Ellie knew the sunlight was good for sickness and would help strengthen the weak man. Time spent out of the confines of the cabin would give everyone the opportunity to relax and take in some fresh air. Walking Horse was naturally a superb specimen of manhood, and at one time his frame was layered with solid muscle. Now, with his appetite returning, hopefully he would quickly regain his weight and strength, but it would take many months for him to get back to normal.

The sweet air coming off the valley was refreshing as everyone found seats and sat around enjoying the evening as they talked. Hatcher had his ever-present pipe lit, sending small smoke rings skyward. The scout leaned back against the cabin and started spinning yarns of his deeds. Several times, his listeners laughed and waved their hands at the speaker as his tales became unbelievable. Still, the stories were mesmerizing, as the old scout's tales were entertaining, enjoyable, and had the desired effect Ellie wanted. By the time daylight faded, it was time to take Walking Horse back inside the cabin, out of the evening dampness. Everyone seemed to be in better spirits, as they laughed and talked.

Red Hawk and Jed led the two mules and spare horses out onto the valley and turned them loose. Catching the piebald and the others, Jed quickly removed the hobbled animal's bindings and returned them to the corral.

"We will enlarge and strengthen the corral soon." Jed looked at the bunched up horses with their ears laid back as the dominate ones upheld their pecking order, inside the enclosure.

"Why? Soon, many will leave when we return to our villages." Red Hawk shrugged. "The Crow do not use these wooden enclosures."

"The Crow have many young ones to ride and watch their horses." Jed shook his head. "If the Crow did have these corrals, their enemies couldn't raid their herds and steal their horses so easily."

"We steal more than we lose." Red Hawk could not understand the corrals. "If our enemies could not steal our horses, we would not be able to fight with them."

"A game, is that what it is?"

"Perhaps, a dangerous game sometimes." Red Hawk laughed. "It is better than swinging the long knife you use on the grass."

"Um-huh." Jed shook his head and turned toward the valley. "It's time for someone to stand watch."

"At least, watching over our lodge is the work of warriors, my friend."

Jed had lived with the Arapaho and became friends with Red Hawk the Crow, but he still couldn't understand the Indian way of thinking. They seldom let much worry them unless they were starving or an enemy was raiding their village. To try to convince Red Hawk about the value of dried grass or corrals was useless. He knew without asking, his words had fallen on deaf ears, the Crow would never do what they considered women's work. There was no use wasting his words on Walking Horse either, the warrior would feel the same way. They were steeped in years of hereditary beliefs, living the life of nomads, and Jed knew it would take a disaster to change their minds.

Midmorning found Jed back at his backbreaking work of swinging the sickle, laying the tall grass flat. Hatcher volunteered his help, pulling the drag from the valley floor, and stacking many loads of dried grass into the barn. Red Hawk stood watch over the valley, but steadfastly refused to take a hand with what he called squaw's work.

Walking to where Jed swung the sickle, Red Hawk squatted and casually looked out across the valley. "Did you see the ponies looking across the tall places?"

Nodding his head, Jed studied the horses. "Let's catch our horses and go have a look-see."

"I will get our bridles."

Whistling a shrill whistle, Jed got Hatcher's attention and gave him the cut throat signal to stay at the cabin. Grabbing his rifle as Red Hawk trotted up with the bridles, Jed laid the sickle aside and caught the piebald. Kicking the horses into a hard lope, the two men headed to the south, plowing through the belly deep grass that blanketed the valley.

Reining in hard, as they topped over a swell in the grass, both men watched as a lone rider raced his laboring horse hard toward them. Much too far away to tell the identity of the rider, but they could plainly see his arm waving, trying to get their attention.

"It is the Blackfoot warrior, Crowfoot." Red Hawk's sharp eyes focused on the rider. "There is trouble. He runs his pony hard."

Kicking their horses forward, Jed and Red Hawk rode slowly toward the racing warrior, pulling in as the man reached them. The horse was heaving. He had been ridden hard and lathered sweat foamed on the horse's sides and chest.

"Blue Darter has sent me." The warrior looked across at the two warriors. "Deep Water, Lone Bull, and their warriors come."

"How many?"

The warrior shrugged. "I do not know this thing, but I think there will be many who ride this way."

"Follow us to my lodge."

"I must return to my people, they are in need of me."

Red Hawk pointed at the rider's horse. "Your horse will not make it back across the mountain."

"Then I must walk."

"How close are they?"

"I do not know." Crowfoot looked over his shoulder. "I must go."

"No." Jed shook his head. "We will get you a fresh horse and return with you."

"We must hurry, Arapaho." The warrior looked off to the south. "They come."

"Come, Crowfoot."

Hatcher watched from the cabin door as the three riders crossed the creek and rode up to the cabin. He recognized Crowfoot as one of the Blackfoot warriors that rode to the cabin with Blue Darter, the day he asked permission to settle his small village of followers in the valley to the southwest. Hatcher studied the horses as they approached. The Blackfoot's horse had been ridden hard, and the scout knew trouble was not far behind.

Sliding from their horses, Jed quickly had Red Hawk catch a fresh horse for Crowfoot, then had Little Antelope bring the warrior food. Jed knew they must hurry, as time was against them. Somewhere across the tall mountains, many Blackfoot warriors were in route to this valley. Where they were, he didn't know, but there was no time to lose. They needed to prepare their defense of the valley. The raiders must be stopped. Quickly explaining to Hatcher what was happening, Jed looked over to where Little Antelope and Ellie stood waiting.

"I'll ride with you Jed."

"No." Jed shook his head. "I want you to take Ellie out of here."

"What about Little Antelope and Walking Horse?" Ellie stepped forward. "My father will ride with you. They have to be stopped before they reach here. Walking Horse cannot ride a horse."

"Take Ellie and go! Crow Killer and Red Hawk will protect us." Little Antelope spoke up. "Go, Rolling Thunder!"

Hatcher looked at Little Antelope in shock that a squaw would dare speak up. "We're staying."

"I don't have time to argue with you." Jed started to say more, then was cut off.

"Then don't, we have faith in you." Ellie smiled. "All of you."

Jed motioned Little Antelope outside, and spoke to her quietly. "I don't know how this will turn out, little one, but be alert. If we can't stop the Blackfoot, do not let them catch you inside in the cabin."

"Walking Horse is weak but he can walk a little." Little Antelope took his arm. "We will hide, but I worry for you."

"It seems I'm always leaving you behind to hide." Jed remembered the river, when Little Antelope and Red Hawk had to hide in a small cave.

"You have always protected me and my husband."

"Be safe, little one. I'll see you soon."

Little Antelope smiled. "You be careful, my warrior. I will take care of the medicine woman for you."

"One of these days, I'm gonna paddle you good." Jed threatened.

Laughing, Little Antelope turned to the cabin. "Is that a promise?"

Red Hawk and Hatcher filled their shot pouches while Jed retrieved Silent One's smaller rifle plus his own and the strong bow Walking Horse had given him. Inside the cabin, Jed approached the chair where Walking Horse was watching the proceedings.

"Again, you are in danger, my friend." Walking Horse nodded his head weakly. "Here I sit, like a buffalo calf, too weak to help."

"You would be in the fight, if you could."

"You are Crow Killer and you will overcome your enemies." The warrior shook his head. "Since you came to the Arapaho, you have been in one battle after another."

Jed remembered White Swan's words. "It was prophesied by White Swan."

"Good luck, Crow Killer." Walking Horse smiled weakly. "My friend and brother."

"I will do my best." Jed nodded. "If things go bad, Little Antelope will hide you until you are strong enough to ride back to our people."

"You have come far, Crow Killer." Walking Horse nodded. "Remember, you are a Lance Bearer of the great Arapaho People."

"I will remember, I was trained by the great Walking Horse." Jed nodded. "I must ride."

Walking Horse stood up shakily. "Help me to the door, my friend. I will watch you ride away on this war trail."

Jed waved one last time as he crossed a ridge and rode out of sight of the cabin. His last thoughts as he rode were the pleading eyes of Little Antelope as he looked down on her from the piebald. He had no way of knowing her thoughts, but her eyes were sad. Ellie hugged Hatcher and wished them all well with the promise she would help look out for Walking Horse.

Jed pushed the horses hard, but still conserved their strength for the final climb up and over the steep mountain. No words had been spoken between the four riders as they rode, as none were needed. Each man had been involved in many battles between the tribes, and each man was a well-honored warrior. Still, no matter how brave or good of fighters they were, the odds were against them.

Topping the pass that led down into the valley, Jed only let the horses breathe a few minutes before starting the descent down into the valley. Somewhere ahead, Blue Darter would be waiting if he hasn't already engaged the invaders. Passing the Blackfoot lodges, Jed could see no activity. Apparently the women and children were already in hiding.

Kicking the tired animals into a lope, Jed crossed the smaller valley and reined in. "Where will we find Blue Darter?"

Crowfoot shrugged. "I do not know, Crow Killer, but he probably watches us as we speak."

"Let's go."

Topping the rough, western pass and starting their descent, Jed reined in as one of the Blackfoot squaws moved from a grove of trees and blocked their path. Nodding, she pointed across the valley.

"Blue Darter, there." The woman held a strong bow in her hand and a quiver of arrows hung from her back.

"Lead us." Jed turned to where Crowfoot rode behind him. "Can she use that bow?'

The warrior laughed. "She is Elk Woman, the wife of Little Horse and a Crazy Buffalo."

Red Hawk was stunned at the words. "What is a crazy buffalo?"

"A woman warrior."

"You allow that?"

"Crow, you tell her she can't fight with us and see what happens next." Crowfoot laughed.

"She is not my woman. I will let her fight." Red Hawk shrugged.

"A very good idea."

The riders trailed the woman across the valley, then up into the pass that followed the mountain trails into the next smaller valley. Almost halfway down the trail, Blue Darter, Flying Bat, and three more women waited, hiding behind mountain boulders.

The Blackfoot nodded as Jed and the riders with him pulled up. Crowfoot had made good time. The sun was low in the afternoon sky and the day was almost over. Looking up at the sun, Jed knew it was late, and there would be no fight today. For most tribes, they believed dying at night was taboo and if killed, their spirits would wander forever in darkness.

"Deep Water and his brother are just across the next valley ahead." Blue Darter pointed. "Little Horse has been watching them since the sun was high above."

"Do they know we are here?"

"No, they have no idea they were spotted." Blue Darter shrugged. "If they knew we were here, they would attack before darkness comes."

"What are they doing?"

"Little Horse says they are resting their horses." The warrior nodded. "They will come here with the coming of the new sun. They want their horses fresh for battle."

Jed studied the terrain of the trail, then dismounted to let the piebald graze on the sparse mountain grass. The trail was narrow where they sat, still it was wide enough to allow several mounted warriors to come at them side by side. Jed needed a smaller place to defend, a place where only three or four of the Blackfoot could ride forward at one time.

"Is there another trail out of this valley?" Jed looked down on the valley.

"No, Crow Killer, this is the only trail out of this valley to the north" Blue Darter shook his head. "There is another trail that leads south, then west."

"Is there a narrower place along the trail further down?"

"There is one a short distance ahead."

Picking up the piebald's rein, Jed swung up on the big horse and looked over his small group of men and women. "Lead out, Blue Darter, and move us down to the narrow place."

"Will we make our fight there?" The warrior asked as he mounted his horse. "There are high boulders, but also there is a clear view of the valley so we can see them crossing."

Jed nodded. "Our only chance against so many is to fight them a few at a time in a confined space."

Kicking his horse forward, Blue Darter led the small party of fighters along the trail as night started to fall. Only the muffled horse's feet, plodding along the sandy trail, sounded as they made their way slowly down the trail. Arriving at the place, Blue Darter spoke of, Jed nodded his head in satisfaction as he studied the high boulders. A party of mounted attackers could only send three or four riders against them through the rocky passage, giving the smaller party a slight advantage. Jed didn't know how many Blackfoot would be coming against them up the trail, but any advantage would help.

"When the light comes again, they will ride this way." Blue Darter spoke in the darkness. "We will be able to see them when they cross the flatland."

"Where is your warrior, Little Horse?"

"He will come, before the new day starts."

Jed passed the food out that Little Antelope had hastily put together for them, before they started across the mountain. Sitting with his back against a hard boulder, Jed studied the pass and the darkness that engulfed it. In the morning, many warriors would be coming. For the sake of Walking Horse, Little Antelope, Ellie, the ones waiting with him, and the children back in the valley, he knew they had to stop the Blackfoot warriors there on the pass. If the raiders managed to overpower him and his fighters, Jed knew the Blackfoot would kill the men and take the women and children captive. They had to be stopped there.

During the long hours, Jed tried to teach one of the women how to reload the rifles, as he knew the thunder guns would be their best chance of stopping the Blackfoot warriors. All the Indian people had seen the white man's weapons that produced the fire and thunder, killing from afar, but few had faced the deadly firepower of rifles in battle. Jed knew the Hawken's rifle would be their lone chance of defeating the mighty Blackfoot. Hatcher had spent many hours telling of the fighting prowess of the northern tribe. Now, these warriors' courage would be tested with the first deadly volley of the rifles.

Leaning back against the hard rock, sleep was at best fitful, as Jed could not close his eyes for long. Touching the scar on his cheek, Jed thought back to the raging Platte River and the log that carried him racing downstream. The vivid face of Slow Wolf standing over him on the water drenched bank of the Platte, and the following years he had spent with the Arapaho. White Swan's prophetic words came back to him, "You will be an Arapaho Lance Bearer, and your trail will be hard, but will lead to honor, pride, and maybe death." Jed wondered if the old medicine man's words would be fulfilled in this place. In his few years as an Arapaho Lance Bearer, Jed's young body had become covered in scars from combat, and now, in this remote pass, he faced death once again.

"Does Crow Killer worry?" Red Hawk could sense Jed's uneasiness in the dark.

"We will face many, tomorrow." Jed looked off into the darkness of the pass. "We cannot let them pass this place."

"You worry about the women back at your lodge?"

"I just said we can't let the Blackfoot get past us."

Red Hawk nodded. "Which do you worry about the most?"

"Go to sleep, Crow. Tomorrow, we will fight, and you will need all your strength." Jed ignored the probing question.

Despite his worries, somehow during the night, Jed had fallen into a deep sleep, waking only to the beckoning of Hatcher's moccasin. Seeing Jed open his eyes, the old scout backed away and looked out across the awakening valley.

"They're coming, Jed." Hatcher pointed. "I watched as one lone warrior came across the valley in a hurry. Now, there's a whole passel of them varmints crossing."

Standing to his feet, Jed looked out across the small valley, following Hatcher's gaze. "The first rider must be Little Horse."

"Looks like we're gonna have our hands full pretty quick." Hatcher watched the approaching warriors closely. "Yep, we're a fixing to be busy."

Jed nodded. "Looks like plenty of them to go around."

"Ain't they a sight to behold, with all their feathers and proud bearing?"

Jed nodded. "Yes, sir, that they are."

CHAPTER 12

Little Horse rode his blowing horse into the small pass and anxiously looked down as his people surrounded him. Jed could tell the warrior was visibly shaken about something, more than the Blackfoot. The warrior was nervous and kept looking behind him as if the Blackfoot were already closing in.

Blue Darter sensed the same thing. "What is wrong, Little Horse?"

The warrior studied Jed for several minutes, then looked out across the valley. "They come, Deep Water and Lone Bull, with their warriors."

"How many?"

Little Horse shrugged. "Many, but there is more."

"What else, Little Horse?" Blue Darter studied the nervous warrior. "Tell us quickly, there is little time before they come to this place."

"Something is out there." Little Horse pointed down the trail where tall grass and heavy brush lay thickly along the valley floor. "My horse spooked as we passed that place."

"What?"

Little Horse looked over at Jed. "I do not know, but something lurks there."

"Deep Water comes." Crowfoot warned from his place higher on the ledge.

"We will wait for them to reach the small gulley." Jed pointed to a natural run off for the heavy rains that crossed the mountains and eroded the trail. "Then, the thunder guns will fire, and your bows will protect us as we reload."

"It will be as you say, Crow Killer." Blue Darter gave the orders so all understood. "We may lose this day, but we will kill many and they will never forget us."

Red Hawk was curious. "Are they not your brothers?"

"They were, but no longer." The warrior frowned. "They come here to fight and kill, so we must kill them."

Catching Blue Darter's attention, Little Horse motioned him away. "Has the Arapaho been here, in your sight, all night?"

Blue Darter looked over at Jed. "He has been here with us. Why?"

Shaking his head, Little Horse looked away. "Nothing, I just saw something back down the trail as I rode here."

"We will speak of this later, Deep Water will come to this place soon."

Jed watched as the Blackfoot warriors rode bunched up, in a trot, across the valley. The valley was small, less than half the size of the valley where the cabin stood. Jed knew the raiders would be on the trail, out of the flatland, in only minutes. The valley was grazed on lightly so the summer grass stood belly high on a horse, almost obscuring the legs of the riders. Jed shook his head worrying as he counted almost fifty enemy warriors on the valley floor. Looking at his few defenders, including the women, Jed knew they were fixing to be in the fight of their lives.

"They'll be coming up the trail quickly now." Jed spoke to Hatcher and Red Hawk. "Make every shot count."

"I like the bow better." Red Hawk touched the bow and quiver of arrows hanging across his shoulder. "It is much faster."

"We'll use the rifle as long as we can, then we'll use the bow." Jed looked over at the Crow. "Just shoot straight."

"They'll respect a weapon that can kill them at three or four times the range of a bow." Hatcher checked the priming of his rifle. "If they don't now, believe me they will soon enough."

Red Hawk nodded. "I will use the rifle, but I still like my bow."

Jed blinked, as pandemonium broke out below among the Blackfoot warriors. Straining their eyes and ears, the defenders high on the trail tried to understand what was going on in the valley below them. Every Blackfoot rider was retreating from the narrow trail, racing in terror, back onto the valley floor. Gesturing with their arms and screaming at the top of their lungs, the warriors rode their frightened horses in circles, searching the tall grass around them.

Suddenly, everything grew quiet as the warriors stopped their horses and looked about the area. From closer to the trail, where a few warriors had reined in and waited, a horrific scream sounded. The loud screaming and roaring of some kind of animal sent the terrified warriors into a frenzied state. Then, the unmistakable roar of a bear sounded again, blocking out the awful cries and screams of a warrior. From the tall grass, the form of a huge bear stood up above the grass holding in its mouth the limp form of a bloodied, torn warrior. The bloodshot eyes of the grizzly showed red as its arms waved in front of him, tearing at the warrior, as the dead body hung lifeless in its teeth.

Jed could hear the terrified screams of several warriors hollering and retreating further out onto the valley floor. Out of the tall grass, Jed watched in shock as another large bear charged the riders that sat their horses watching the first bear. Screaming in terror, many of the warriors raced to the west, abandoning Deep Water and Lone Bull in their fright. From his position higher on the ridge, Jed could see the rustling of the tall grass and the huge shape of the first bear, dragging the unlucky warrior into the heavy brush.

As sudden as the attack had started, it was over, and complete quiet covered the valley. Less than half of the Blackfoot warriors remained sitting their horses far out in the valley with their two chiefs. Jed couldn't tell what the big warrior was saying, but he could tell one chief was urging the frightened warriors to follow him. After the frightful attack by the bear, Jed could not believe Deep Water was still trying to compel his warriors to ride forward. Several times, he heard the chief yelling out at the warriors.

Red Hawk laughed, then looked over at Jed. "They are afraid of you, Crow Killer."

"I'm not a bear."

"Maybe not, but what is important, they think you are." Hatcher watched the frightened warriors in the valley. "Here they come, not near as many as there were before, but they're coming."

"Do your demon thing, Crow Killer." Red Hawk laughed making Jed frown. "Maybe, they will all run away."

"After what I just witnessed." Jed shook his head in amazement. "If I were them, I would run myself."

Never would he have thought the Blackfoot below would ride directly into the path of grizzlies without warning. He couldn't understand how their horses failed to smell or detect the bears waiting in the small valley. Jed only had a fleeting glimpse of the huge bear's back as it pulled the screaming warrior from his horse and killed him. There was no way at this distance he could tell if it was the same man-killing bear that had killed Billy Wilson. He knew, even if he was face-to-face with the killer bear, he wouldn't be able to say it was the same animal. Little did it matter, somehow miraculously the bear had appeared, attacking one warrior and sending more than half the raiding warriors fleeing in terror back to the west.

Watching the retreating warriors, Hatcher laughed. "Those boys won't stop this side of the Pacific Ocean."

Red Hawk looked over at Jed curiously. "How did the bear know to come here and attack the Blackfoot?"

"I couldn't say." Jed shook his head at the question. "Bears move about, you know that."

"But, to be here, now." The warrior shook his head. "I believe it is the spirit people speaking."

"No, my friend, it's just a man-killing bear speaking." Jed smiled. "It's not a spirit of some kind."

Finally, after calming their warriors, the chiefs convinced them it was just a bear that had attacked them, not a demon. Deep Water and Lone Bull led the remaining warriors up the narrow trail to the small pass where Jed and Blue Darter's people waited. Hearing the hoofbeats of the horses plodding up the trail, Jed had his fighters get ready. Picking their places behind boulders, rifles rested easily in the men's hands, while bows notched with deadly arrows were ready. As the Blackfoot passed the last turn of the trail before coming into plain sight of the defenders, Jed stepped out into the trail and stood waiting.

"Tell them you are a demon, Crow Killer." Red Hawk laughed. "Maybe, they will all run away."

"It would be okay by me."

"Not me, my friend." Red Hawk shook his head. "I wish to fight and count coup on these great Blackfoot warriors."

"Fighting could get you killed, Crow." Hatcher puffed casually on his pipe. "Dead."

"Yes, then my people and squaw would mourn me."

"I'd rather be full of life, not mourned in death."

"How does Rolling Thunder wish to die, in your lodge under a buffalo robe?"

"That'd be okay by me, old hoss." Hatcher laughed. "Long as I'm warm, I'd be happy."

Deep Water reined his horse in hard as he spotted Jed standing alone in the middle of the narrow pass. Looking about the rocky terrain, he spotted Hatcher and Red Hawk, but not the warriors and squaws of Blue Darter. Holding up his hand, halting his warriors, the chief advanced alone several feet toward Jed.

"You Arapaho, you are the one called Crow Killer." The Blackfoot Chief didn't ask, he stated.

"Some call me a demon, Blackfoot."

"Superstitious fools call you that, not a Blackfoot Warrior and Chief."

"Did you not see me below as I attacked your warriors?"

"We saw a grizzly bear kill one of our warriors." Deep Water scoffed. "Not a lowly Arapaho."

"Go back to your lands, Blackfoot. There is nothing for you here." Jed pointed his chin. "Leave this place or many of your people will die here today."

"We do not fear you, Arapaho." Deep Water studied the warrior before him. "You have killed my son, brother, my people, and now, you tell me to leave this place without tasting your blood."

"My blood may be bitter to swallow."

Deep Water glared across at Jed. "I will tear out your heart and eat it."

Jed nodded. "Leave, or your bones will join theirs."

"Enough of this foolish talk, we fight."

Jed watched as the chief returned to his warriors and spoke with Lone Bull. Looking back to where Hatcher was motioning him back behind the rocks, Jed nodded and rejoined Red Hawk. Several minutes passed before a roar of wild war cries went up from the Blackfoot warriors. Every warrior started toward the small pass where Jed and the others were waiting.

Red Hawk frowned. "I guess they didn't believe the part about you being a demon?"

"No, reckon not." Jed watched the warriors spread out with what little room they had in the narrow confines of the trail. "Too bad, now some of us will die."

"More important, Crow Killer, many of them will decorate my scalp pole." Red Hawk leaped out in front of the boulder, then raised his breechcloth and laughed.

"I reckon that'll bring them, alright." Hatcher knew the Crow had just given the oncoming warriors the worst insult he could. "Yep, someone is gonna die now, for sure."

Jed could only shake his head. He did not want this. "Pick your targets well."

Watching the antics of the Crow, Deep Water and Lone Bull led the screaming Blackfoot warriors forward in a hard run, right down the narrow trail and straight into the sights of the Hawken rifles. Three warriors, including Deep Water fell with the first volley causing the others to pile up as their horses tried to avoid the fallen bodies. Again, the rifles spoke, spilling more riders, then the strong bows of Blue Darter and his people started lofting arrows down the trail into the warriors. Seeing their warriors falling without getting off a shot, Lone Bull shouted and led a full retreat out of range of the rifles. This was not the way the Blackfoot fought, losing men without closing in on an enemy. The warriors sat their horses, looking across the space that divided the two forces. Deep Water and many others along with horses were lying dead. Lone Bull wanted to fight, but how could he get past the thunder guns of the whites?

The big Blackfoot Chief rode into plain view on the trail and stopped. "Come out and fight like men, do not hide like squaws."

"You are many, Blackfoot." Jed stepped from behind the boulder. "We are few."

"Now, Arapaho, you have killed my brother and the Crow dog has insulted us while hiding like a woman!" Lone Bull screamed.

"You are next, Lone Bull, if you do not leave this place."

"Will you meet me in single combat?" The Blackfoot Chief raised his war club. "Can you fight without your thunder gun?"

"I can, if you wish to die."

"It will not be me that dies." Lone Bull pointed to where Red Hawk stood listening. "I challenge that one. He likes to insult us while he hides behind rocks. I will fight him if he has the courage to come out and face me."

"No." Jed thought of Bow Legs, not this time. He wouldn't lose another friend in single combat. "You will fight me, Blackfoot."

"I will fight him." Red Hawk stepped forward. "It was I that insulted them."

"No, it is my fight, Red Hawk."

"Does Crow Killer wish to have all the fun?" Red Hawk laughed. "I will fight this one and count coup on his dead body."

Blue Darter slipped forward but remained out of sight of Lone Bull. "Be careful, Red Hawk. This one is a mighty warrior."

"So am I." The Crow looked over at Jed. "This is my fight, Crow Killer. Let me have this day."

Nodding slowly, Jed shrugged. "If this is what you want."

"It is exactly what I want."

The trail was too narrow to fight on horses so the two warriors approached each other on foot. Meeting halfway between the two groups of fighters, the men circled slowly, then rushed forward, swinging the heavy war clubs with all their might. Jed studied Lone Bull and the Blackfoot was powerful, but the heavy muscles encumbered him, slowing him down. Red Hawk was faster and the Crow loved a good fight, and now, he had one. Blood ran down their arms from a few minor wounds each warrior received as they fought back and forth across the trail. Slowly, it dawned on Jed that Red Hawk was merely playing with Lone Bull. The bulky muscles were useless in this type of fighting and the Blackfoot grew weary fast.

Faster than the eye could see, the Crow ducked under Lone Bull and plunged his knife to the hilt into the man's chest. As Lone Bull sunk slowly to the ground, Red Hawk looked the warrior in the eye.

"You said you would eat my heart, Blackfoot." Red Hawk plunged the blade deep, cutting out the heart of the dying warrior. Standing upright, he waved the heart, still dripping blood, high for the other warriors to see, then took a bite out of it and screamed.

They had seen enough. First the bear, then the thunder guns of the whites, now their great Chief Lone Bull easily defeated, and his heart eaten by the crazed one before them. Turning as one, the once-proud Blackfoot warriors retreated down the trail into the valley. Today, in this place, they had lost both their chiefs, their warriors, and their pride. No longer could they brag they were the greatest warriors of the north.

Jed watched as the retreating warriors crossed the valley without slowing down or looking back, disappearing quickly from sight. Walking forward among the dead and wounded men, he shook his head as the rifles had done their deadly work. Jed doubted there would be any more trouble from the Blackfoot tribe, at least not from one, as Chief Deep Water lay dead on the trail.

Blue Darter looked down on the faces of the dead brothers. "The Blackfoot have lost much this day."

"They came here for a fight, well they got one." Hatcher showed no sympathy as the women hovered over the wounded warriors of the Blackfoot, trying to help them.

"We do not fault you, Crow Killer." Blue Darter shook his head.

"What will you do with the wounded?"

"Deep Water is dead, Lone Bull is dead." The warrior looked about the trail. "I will take my people and the wounded back to our village when they are well enough to travel."

"Will you be welcome?"

"He will be welcome." Crowfoot stepped forward. "He will become head Chief of the Piegan Blackfoot People."

Little Horse nodded. "No one will dare challenge Blue Darter."

Jed was in a hurry to return to the cabin, but he didn't want to leave Blue Darter and his few warriors alone, in case the Blackfoot returned. Sending Hatcher and Red Hawk to follow the retreating warriors out of the valley, Jed caught the piebald and rode down the trail.

"Where do you go, Crow Killer?" Blue Darter watched as Jed checked his rifle priming.

"I will seek the trail of the grizzly, and then I will bring in food for your people." Jed looked around the makeshift camp at the wounded warriors.

"I am sorry, but I will not ride with you." Blue Darter dropped his face in shame. "I fear the demon bear because it is a spirit bear and cannot be killed."

"We'll see." Jed nudged the piebald.

After picking up the trail of three grizzlies, where the bigger bear had killed the first warrior, Jed followed them west until finally losing their trail in the rough rocky terrain of the mountain ridges. The bear and her cubs were nowhere in sight along the valley or the mountain slopes. Apparently, the killer bears were scared away by the sound of the rifles during the battle. Jed knew she would return someday, until then, he could only be watchful of her. Turning the piebald back into the far reaches of the valley, Jed stalked a nice doe and brought her down with a neck shot.

Leading the piebald out onto the trail, Jed spotted Hatcher and Red Hawk coming toward him down the trail. Neither rider was in a hurry, so he figured the warriors he had sent them to follow, had left the valley.

"We'll eat handsomely tonight, Jed." Hatcher smiled as he looked over the carcass of the doe.

"Let's ride." Red Hawk took the deer carcass behind him and kicked the shying horse. "I'm hungry and I have scalps to take."

"No, my friend, do not insult Blue Darter and his people by scalping their chief." Jed mounted the piebald. "I ask this thing as a friend."

Returning to the camp, Jed watched as the squaws quickly cut up the deer and spitted it across the hot fire. The wounded warriors watched from where they lay, their eyes fearfully studying the man known as a demon.

Sitting down beside Blue Darter, as the women brought the hot meat to them on fresh cut bark, Jed smiled and looked around the camp. "Red Hawk and Rolling Thunder say the Blackfoot have left, departing for their own lands."

"That is good, Crow Killer." Blue Darter nodded. "Will you return to your lodge soon?"

"When will these warriors be able to go?"

"We will break camp, build travois for the wounded, and start for our village with the coming of the new sun."

"We will leave tomorrow as well." Jed bit into the meat. "If you should run into the ones that just left, will you be safe?"

"They will not attack us." Crowfoot spoke up. "They know Blue Darter will be our new chief."

Red Hawk looked at the warrior, Crowfoot. "How will they know this?"

"Who defeated Deep Water in personal combat?" Crowfoot questioned. "None would dare question Blue Darter, he will be our chief."

"We will go back to our lodge with the new sun."

"I fear the demon bear more than the Blackfoot." Blue Darter looked around the darkened pass and then over at Jed. "The Nez Perce, Squirrel Tooth, spoke the truth about the bear."

Jed only nodded. If the northern tribes thought him a demon, so be it. His valley would be safer from attack and raids.

Jed, Hatcher, and Red Hawk sat their horses and watched as the small column started across the lower valley, dragging several travois, transporting the injured warriors. Deep Water, Lone Bull, and the ones who died with them were raised on pole scaffolds, buried in their traditional ways. Jed looked about the pass and down into the valley, knowing out there somewhere was a killer bear, a bear according to Red Hawk had his scent. Why the bear was there to help them with the Blackfoot, he couldn't understand. Hatcher said it followed his scent and would until one of them was dead. Jed knew of Arapaho superstitions, but it wasn't an Arapaho, it was Red Hawk, who told him about the bear stalking him. Perhaps it was true, but he didn't know. One thing he did know was the bear came into his valley and showed up in the smaller valley before the fight. What he didn't know was how it happened, by chance, luck, or was the bear really a devil bear?

Walking Horse was the first to spot the three riders as they crossed the last rise in the valley, blocking their view from the cabin. Calling for the women to come out, the warrior limped slowly down toward the creek bank.

"They have returned." Walking Horse announced as Ellie and Little Antelope rushed from the doorway to support him.

As soon as Hatcher crossed the creek, he dismounted and grabbed Ellie and hugged her. He looked over at Walking Horse. "My son walks."

"Slowly, very slowly." Walking Horse took Hatcher's outstretched hand.

"It is good to see you healing, my brother, and you, Little Antelope." Jed smiled as he slid from the piebald.

Walking Horse looked to where Red Hawk dismounted slowly. "Red Hawk has been in a battle."

Hatcher laughed. "He fought the Blackfoot Chief, Lone Bull."

"Who won?"

"It is good to see you again, Walking Horse." Red Hawk nodded.

"I am glad you won over the Blackfoot."

Red Hawk looked over to where Little Antelope stood. "You're thinking we may do battle another day?"

"No, we are friends now." Walking Horse shook his head. "There will be no more fighting between us, Red Hawk."

"So, you defeated the enemy?" Little Antelope spoke up.

"A mighty Crow cannot be defeated by a mere Blackfoot."

"Bah!" Little Antelope quipped. "Come, sister, let us prepare food for the great Red Hawk."

Watching as the women disappeared inside the cabin, Red Hawk laughed. "I see she still loves me."

"You'll grow on her one day." Jed smiled.

"I will not forget you would not let me have the scalps of my enemies."

"He didn't?" Walking Horse looked over at Jed.

"No, and it is the second time he stole scalps from me."

Walking Horse was curious. "Second time?"

"Yes." Red Hawk laughed and looked at the warrior. "Your scalp should be on my lodge pole. I think it would look good there."

"Red Hawk." Jed could only shake his head at the laughing warriors.

Three days later, Jed stood beside Hatcher as the old scout helped Ellie onto her horse, then mounted his. Looking up at the girl, he felt awkward, not knowing exactly what to say. Walking Horse, Red Hawk, and Little Antelope stood by the horses as Hatcher and Ellie said their good-byes.

Walking Horse smiled up at Ellie. "Thank you, Sister, for saving me from the spirit people."

"The next time I see you, you'll be as good as new."

"These are for you, Sister." Little Antelope handed Ellie a beautiful pair of beaded moccasins. "Wear them and remember us."

"I will wear them with pride, they are beautiful. Thank you, Little Antelope."

"You'll be coming into Baxter Springs, Jed?" Hatcher looked over at Ellie and smiled.

"When the cold times are over and the passes clear, I'll bring in my pelts." Jed looked up at Ellie.

"You mean in the spring?" Ellie laughed.

"Yes, in the spring." Jed smiled. "Will you be there?"

"You can bet on it." Ellie seemed to wink. "If you're coming in."

Flipping his rawhide whip, Hatcher touched his hat and kicked the horses. "You boys keep your powder dry."

As the horses crossed the creek, Little Antelope stepped close to Jed. "You should leave this place, Jed. Go with her to your white village and make your life there."

"No, this valley is my home and I will make my life here."

"Alone?" The dark eyes looked softly up at him. "You are a great warrior and you should have a woman to give you many sons."

"I had a woman."

"I'm sorry, my warrior." Little Antelope looked to where Walking Horse had returned inside the cabin. "I wish things could have been different."

Two days later, Jed rode with Walking Horse, Little Antelope, and Red Hawk to the bank of the big river and watched as they crossed. Walking Horse was still weak, swimming beside the horse could be too much for the warrior, but Red Hawk swam beside him, supporting him. Jed waited and watched, wanting to be sure Walking Horse made the crossing safely. Their parting was sad, but Red Hawk had to return to his village as the big hunt for the shaggies would begin soon.

Their conversation on their last night's camp had been solemn. Jed had remembered his words to Red Hawk only the day before. The last day before heading east, Red Hawk and Jed hunted for deer to cook the meat for the long journey back to Arapaho Lands.

Slipping to the soft ground, the warrior traced the outline of a huge grizzly with his forefinger. Looking up at Jed, he shook his head. "She still looks for you, my friend." The warrior shook his head. "She has again returned to your valley."

Jed slid from the piebald and studied the huge paw print. "One day, one of us will kill the other."

"Even the rifle cannot stop this one." Red Hawk shook his head sadly. "She is truly one of the evil ones."

"The rifle will stop her."

Red Hawk shook his head again. "No, my friend, do not fool yourself. The bullet must be placed in her brain to kill her, and it is a very small brain."

"I'll kill her." Jed touched the print again. "It looks like I'll have to."

"I will stay here and help you kill this spirit."

"We don't know where the bear walks." Jed shook his head. "No, you must get them home safely."

"This bear is a silver tipped grizzly and a killer." Red Hawk looked out across the valley. "She will come for you, Crow Killer."

Jed knew the Indian Tribes believed in spirit people entering an animal's body. "Why does she follow me, Red Hawk?"

"I do not know this thing, my friend, but she does."

"Say nothing to Walking Horse and Little Antelope."

Red Hawk nodded slowly. "I will take them to their village."

"I'll see you in the summer, my friend."

"Be watchful, Crow Killer, always." The warrior looked again at the tracks. "This one is very dangerous and she will come for you."

"No, I will go after her." Jed nodded. "You be careful on your return journey."

"Do not forget, my friend." Red Hawk shook his head. "She has her cubs to help her."

"I won't forget."

Waving as they crossed over the high ridge, Jed smiled as Little Antelope turned her horse and waved back. Again, as his friends rode out of sight, he was alone. Well, maybe not too alone, there was a huge grizzly that would keep him company for a few more days. He knew one of them must die, but which one? Reining the piebald, Jed turned back to his valley, the valley of the beckoning light, the light that had been so fleeting, so elusive. Someday, he would find it, but for now, he would return to his cabin. Before the cold times come, he had to gather wood, cut and store tall grass, and he had traps and stretch boards to get ready for the pelts he would bring in. Come spring, he would head for Baxter Springs with his winter catch. Jed looked up, searching the heavy timbered passes, somewhere up high a lone wolf howled his lonely call. Jed's spine tingled, somewhere roaming these huge mountains, the demon grizzly walked, waiting for their paths and destiny to cross. Kicking the piebald, Crow Killer headed for his valley and home.

As the miles passed, Jed's mind sadly wandered to Sally Ann, as she would have loved this valley. Now, she was gone forever. His thoughts turned to Ellie, and perhaps in the spring after the winter thaw, he would again meet the medicine woman who had saved the life of Walking Horse. No, he shook his head, she would not come here to the high meadows. Elizabeth's place was in the settlements, helping the sick, not in these remote mountains. Jed knew he would live and die alone in his beautiful valley, and could never be happy anywhere else. Absently, his face formed a smile as he thought of Little Antelope, the beautiful woman that had taught him so much and had been so close, so very close.

Daydreaming of his friends, as the piebald plodded along slowly to the cabin, Jed was unaware of the giant figure of the grizzly as it stood on its haunches at the edge of the timberline. The sharp nose sniffed the air as its bloodshot eyes with their poor eyesight tried to follow him across the broad valley. High on a mountain ridge, the moaning howl of the great grey wolf sounded again.

The End